MARRIAGE AND MURDER

THE CASEBOOK OF BARNABY ADAIR: VOLUME 10

STEPHANIE LAURENS

ABOUT MARRIAGE AND MURDER

THE TENTH VOLUME IN THE CASEBOOK OF BARNABY ADAIR NOVELS

#1 NYT-bestselling author Stephanie Laurens returns with a puzzling case in which her favorite sleuths must untangle a slew of secrets to expose a coldblooded murderer.

When a middle-aged spinster is found strangled in her country cottage and scurrilous gossip implicates Henry, Lord Glossup, he appeals to Barnaby and Penelope Adair along with Inspector Stokes to unravel the mystery of who killed Viola Huntingdon.

Henry, Lord Glossup, arrives on Barnaby and Penelope Adairs' doorstep and begs their aid—and that of Stokes—in identifying the murderer of Viola Huntingdon, a middle-aged spinster who lived a largely blameless life in a country cottage in a tiny village close to Henry's home. As Stokes has already been tapped to take the case, the investigators travel to Salisbury and thence to Ashmore village and throw themselves into the case.

While initially Henry was touted as a suspect, he is quickly eliminated, and with the help of the victim's sister, Madeline, the investigators set out to discover all they can about the victim and who might have wished her ill. In such a small village, with a commensurately small population, the list of possible suspects is short, but the existence of Viola's 'secret admirer, H' has everyone stumped. First, how could Viola, living in such a small community, have had a secret visitor, a man no one saw except at a distance? And who on earth is he, this H?

As the investigators piece together the clues of missing jewelry and sightings of H and follow the leads generated by opportunistic thieves, dodgy jewelers, and local moneylenders, a picture emerges that points to only one conclusion. But in small villages, things are rarely as they seem. Have the investigators got the right man in their sights, or have they been led astray?

A historical novel of 82,000 words weaving mystery and murder with a touch of romance.

PRAISE FOR THE WORKS OF STEPHANIE LAURENS

"Stephanie Laurens' heroines are marvelous tributes to Georgette Heyer: feisty and strong." *Cathy Kelly*

"Stephanie Laurens never fails to entertain and charm her readers with vibrant plots, snappy dialogue, and unforgettable characters." *Historical Romance Reviews*

"Stephanie Laurens plays into readers' fantasies like a master and claims their hearts time and again." *Romantic Times Magazine*

Praise for Marriage and Murder

"When Charlie Hastings becomes a suspect in the murder of Viscount Sedbury, he turns to high-society investigators Penelope and Barnaby Adair to clear his name. Navigating the haut ton alongside Inspector Stokes, the sleuths peek at the darker side of some noble families, where greed, jealousy, and depravity weave a tangled web among supposedly proper gentlefolk." *Kim H., Copyeditor, Red Adept Editing*

"When Viscount Sedbury, one of the most loathed men in London, is found murdered next to the Thames, it's up to husband-and-wife team Barnaby and Penelope Adair to help the police find the killer. The clever duo uses their social connections to track down a murderer in this suspenseful mystery where no one is free from suspicion." *Brittany M., Proofreader, Red Adept Editing*

"Readers will love the engaging characters and unexpected twists of this mystery set in the deceptive elegance of London's haut ton." *Irene S., Proofreader, Red Adept Editing*

OTHER TITLES BY STEPHANIE LAURENS

Marriage and Murder

The Murder of Thomas Cardwell (July 17, 2025)

Bastion Club Novels

Captain Jack's Woman (Prequel)

The Lady Chosen

A Gentleman's Honor

A Lady of His Own

A Fine Passion

To Distraction

Beyond Seduction

The Edge of Desire

Mastered by Love

Black Cobra Quartet

The Untamed Bride

The Elusive Bride

The Brazen Bride

The Reckless Bride

The Adventurers Quartet

The Lady's Command

A Buccaneer at Heart

The Daredevil Snared

Lord of the Privateers

The Cavanaughs

The Designs of Lord Randolph Cavanaugh

The Pursuits of Lord Kit Cavanaugh

The Beguilement of Lady Eustacia Cavanaugh

The Obsessions of Lord Godfrey Cavanaugh

Other Novels

The Lady Risks All

The Legend of Nimway Hall – 1750: Jacqueline

Medieval (As M.S.Laurens)
Desire's Prize

Novellas
Melting Ice – from the anthologies *Rough Around the Edges* and *Scandalous Brides*

Rose in Bloom – from the anthology *Scottish Brides*

Scandalous Lord Dere – from the anthology *Secrets of a Perfect Night*

Lost and Found – from the anthology *Hero, Come Back*

The Fall of Rogue Gerrard – from the anthology *It Happened One Night*

The Seduction of Sebastian Trantor – from the anthology *It Happened One Season*

Short Stories
The Wedding Planner – from the anthology *Royal Weddings*

A Return Engagement – from the anthology *Royal Bridesmaids*

UK-Style Regency Romances
Tangled Reins

Four in Hand

Impetuous Innocent

Fair Juno

The Reasons for Marriage

A Lady of Expectations An Unwilling Conquest

A Comfortable Wife

MARRIAGE AND MURDER

MARRIAGE AND MURDER

Copyright © 2025 by Savdek Management Proprietary Limited

ISBN: 978-1-925559-74-3

Cover design by Savdek Management Pty. Ltd.

First print publication: March, 2025

Savdek Management Proprietary Limited, Melbourne, Australia.

www.stephanielaurens.com

Email: admin@stephanielaurens.com

The names Stephanie Laurens and the Cynsters and the SL Logo are registered trademarks of Savdek Management Proprietary Ltd.

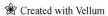 Created with Vellum

CHAPTER 1

OCTOBER 19, 1840. ALBERMARLE STREET, MAYFAIR.

"*F*lutter-by, Mama! See?"

Through the thick lenses of her spectacles, Penelope Adair duly studied the black-and-white-and-red butterfly that had captured her elder son's attention. The insect had perched on a late rose and was flexing its wings. "Butterfly, darling."

Penelope, Barnaby, and their two sons were indulging in a morning amble in the rear garden of their Albemarle Street home. Hettie, the boys' principal nursemaid, stood nearby, ready to assist if required, and the family's black-and-white spaniel, Roger, sniffed and snuffled about the garden beds, thrusting his nose into drifts of brightly colored autumn leaves.

Ferociously focused on the butterfly, Oliver frowned. "No," he insisted. *"Flutter-by."*

Roger came along and jumped up to investigate, and the butterfly obligingly fluttered on to the next bloom.

Observing the insect's movements, Penelope decided not to argue further; in this case, logic seemed on Oliver's side. Just then, Pip, doggedly crawling across the thick grass, reached Penelope's legs, and he clutched her skirts and started hauling himself to his feet, then lost his grip and fell and rolled onto his back, chortling delightedly.

Penelope grinned at her younger son. He was the happiest child she'd ever come across; every little thing was a source of wonder and happiness to Pip. "There you are, my little man." She swooped and scooped him up and hoisted him so that his face was level with hers. She blew gently at him, and he shut his eyes and shrieked and wriggled.

With his coat unbuttoned, his hands sunk in his trouser pockets, and a fondly besotted smile on his face, Barnaby watched his wife and sons, the sources of true joy in his life, play in the weak October sunshine. Such moments of quiet domesticity were precious. He caught Penelope's dark gaze. "I'll admit I'm amazed that we've been able to make your notion of spending an hour or so with the boys every morning into a commitment verging on a habit."

She readily nodded. "I'm rather astonished, too." She glanced at the boys, maternal love shining in her eyes. "Then again, the incentive is significant."

Barnaby grinned. "Nevertheless, your notion was inspired."

"Luckily, since deciding to put my idea into practice, other than the time we spent on the Sedbury case, we've really only had social events to juggle," Penelope pointed out. "And we can always cancel those if we feel so inclined."

"Except for our visits to Cothelstone and Haverstone," he said, referring to their annual summer pilgrimages to catch up with their respective families.

"But that was all time spent with this absorbing pair"—Penelope tickled Pip's tummy, making him shriek anew—"so those were all extra hours on the right side of our family ledger." She paused, then added, "And of course, we had Charlie and Claudia's wedding, but that was just a few days of excitement, although we must make a point of catching up with them when they return from their wedding trip."

Barnaby nodded. "An unexpected but highly beneficial outcome of the Sedbury case."

"Indeed." Penelope settled Pip on her hip, and they turned to watch Oliver playing tug with Roger, who had found a suitable piece of wood. "Yes, well," she went on, "it's back to work for me, now."

Barnaby glanced at her. "I thought you finished your translation for the university."

"I did! But the History Department have begged—literally *begged*—me to assist with two scrolls they're having no luck deciphering." She wrinkled her nose. "I have to say, I think it's going to require more than my expertise to solve their riddle. I might have to call in Jeremy Carling to help."

The sound of rapid footsteps approaching through the garden parlor had Barnaby turning to see Mostyn, their majordomo, come hurrying out through the open terrace doors.

Penelope saw, too. "What is it, Mostyn?"

Mostyn halted and reported, "Lord Glossup has called, asking to speak with you both. I feel I should mention he seems in something of an agitated state."

Penelope blinked and shot a faintly incredulous glance at Barnaby. "Henry agitated?"

Barnaby returned an equally surprised look. Henry Glossup was a rather staid, solid sort not given to histrionics much less drama. As Henry had dined at the house on several occasions over the past years, Mostyn was acquainted with the man, and Mostyn's observation was likely to have some foundation.

"Apparently so." Barnaby nodded to Hettie, and Penelope handed Pip over.

Hettie secured Pip on her hip, then held out her hand to Oliver. "Come along, Oliver. Let's see what Cook has for our morning tea."

Oliver hesitated for only a second before reaching for the offered hand. "Shortbread?"

"I'm not sure," Hettie replied. Already wise in the ways of little boys, she added, "It might be jam tarts today."

Unsurprisingly, there were no further questions or resistance from the boys.

Barnaby and Penelope followed Mostyn, Hettie, and the boys inside, with the puppy trotting hopefully at Oliver's heels.

In the front hall, Hettie and the boys turned for the kitchen, and Barnaby arched a brow at Mostyn. "The drawing room?"

"Indeed, sir." Mostyn hurried to open the door.

Penelope glided in, and Barnaby followed.

Henry Glossup—Lord Glossup—was sitting on one of the pair of long sofas, staring at his tightly clasped hands, which hung between his spread knees. At the sound of their footsteps, Henry looked up, and from the frantic expression in his eyes and the set of his features, Barnaby knew Mostyn had read the man aright. Henry Glossup was in a state.

Exactly what sort of state and in relation to what subject were intriguing questions.

"Henry!" Penelope swept forward, offering her hands, and Henry rose and grasped them.

He half bowed over Penelope's fingers, then, raising his head, nodded to Barnaby. "Barnaby. Penelope." He returned his gaze to Penelope's face, then glanced at Barnaby. "I'm here because I need your help."

A little over forty years old, Henry was tallish and solid, yet overall, rather lean, with broad shoulders and long rider's legs. In character, he was reserved, a trifle reticent, not one to put himself forward, yet for all that, in his own domain, he was a man of quiet command. With straightish dark-brown hair and pale, chiseled features, Henry possessed a certain gravitas, a cloak of trenchant respectability and adherence to the country gentleman's views of the way things ought to be that hung about him, as inescapably a part of him as his well-cut, expensive, but well-worn conservative attire.

Henry was the sort of landowner who spent most of his days on his land, overseeing and caring for his acres in a way not all landholders did. His tenant farmers loved him for it, but in many ways, it kept him out of society. Barnaby had always felt that, in Henry's case, that was largely by choice and design rather than any accidental outcome.

Her expression one of open concern, Penelope waved Henry back to the sofa, drew in her skirts, and sat beside him, angling so she could keep his face in view. "Tell us what's happened."

Barnaby moved to sit on the sofa opposite. "And of course, we'll be happy to help in any way we can."

Henry was the older brother of James Glossup, who was a longtime close friend of Barnaby's and now married to Henrietta Cynster, a connection of Penelope's. Barnaby had known Henry for many years, having spent school holidays at Glossup Hall with James. Penelope's acquaintance with Henry was more recent, yet Barnaby felt confident she shared his view that whatever was troubling Henry, the man's honesty and integrity could be relied on absolutely.

Henry Glossup was simply that sort of man.

Barnaby and Penelope's welcome and willingness to help plainly reassured Henry. He drew a deep breath, then said, "I've been accused of murder—again!"

Penelope blinked and glanced at Barnaby. Both knew the story surrounding the murder of Henry's late wife, Kitty. Her lover, Ambrose Calvin, had strangled her, but of course, as the cuckolded husband, Henry had come under suspicion at the time. Neither Barnaby nor Penelope had been present at the house party during which the murder occurred, but their knowledge of the crime stemmed from Penelope's sister, Portia, who had been there, along with her now-husband, Simon Cynster, as well as

Charlie Hastings and James Glossup, all three of whom were close friends of Barnaby's.

Indeed, Barnaby and Penelope's understanding of the facts of that case was as detailed as if they had been there, and to cap it all, the lead investigator had been a then-recently-promoted Inspector Basil Stokes. The Glossup Hall murder had been one of Stokes's first cases as a Scotland Yard inspector.

Seeing the surprise in their faces, Henry went on, "It happened on the lawn after church yesterday morning. I was accused—to my face and in front of the entire congregation—of strangling a village spinster, essentially because Kitty had been strangled five years ago, and of course, village gossip being what it is, the current whispers are that I must have been guilty of Kitty's murder all along and somehow got away with it, and"—his expression one of frustrated agitation, he flung up his hands—"apparently, I've now murdered another woman in the same fashion!"

His brown gaze haunted, clearly rattled, Henry stated, "I didn't know what to do. It's as if Kitty and that damned Ambrose have come back to haunt me—to taunt me. It's been five years, and I'd thought it was finally all in the past, but this murder has brought the whole business back into people's minds." He looked at Barnaby. "I didn't know who else to appeal to—who else might be able to help. So after lunch yesterday, I drove to Salisbury, took the train to town, stayed at White's overnight, and came here first thing this morning." He glanced at Penelope. "I hope you don't mind."

"Of course not," Penelope trenchantly assured him.

"We don't mind in the least," Barnaby added. "We're always available to help friends, and of course, we'll assist in whatever way we can to sort out this matter—whatever it is."

"Exactly!" Penelope's expression was calming and supportive. "Now, for us to properly grasp the situation, you need to start at the beginning, Henry, and tell us everything you know."

Henry glanced at Barnaby, read his encouraging look, then blew out a breath and paused to order his thoughts. After several seconds, he began, "I suppose it all started last week. There's...there was a woman who lived in the village—a gentry lady, a spinster—at Lavender Cottage."

"Ashmore village?" Barnaby asked.

"Yes. Lavender Cottage is one of those on Green Lane, north of the pond. Next door to the Penroses, who are more or less opposite the pond."

Barnaby nodded his understanding. He knew the village reasonably well and could vaguely recall the cottages mentioned.

Henry went on, "Miss Huntingdon—Viola Huntingdon—bought the cottage nearly five years ago. I know it was a bit after Kitty died. Anyway, Viola is—was—a fusspot, a stickler for this and that, always harping on about this person or that doing something of which she disapproved. All minor matters—nothing meaningful. You know the type. Usually, I give Viola a wide berth, but last Thursday morning, I was riding past her cottage, heading out on Green Lane for a ride eastward over the weald, when Humphrey, my hound, who was with me, decided to…well, cock a leg against the hedge bordering the lane.

"Unfortunately, he chose Viola's lavender hedge, and she happened to be walking up from the pond, and she saw him and set up a screech! She came running up, and of course, she couldn't catch Humphrey, but I'd paused and circled back, and she ranted and railed at me about how people should control their animals and not allow them to damage other people's property. She went on and on and threatened to have me up before the magistrate if her hedge withered and died." Henry shook his head. "As I'm the local magistrate—which she was well aware of—I'm not sure how she thought that would work. However, there were others about, and they were listening, and I made a few comments back, like dogs being dogs, after all. But when Viola threatened to take a gun to Humphrey—and I know she has a shotgun and can and does use it—I saw red." Henry grimaced and rather glumly confessed, "I told her that if she pointed a gun at one of my animals, I would ensure she never did so again."

Bleakly, Henry looked at Barnaby and Penelope. "I never said anything about killing her! I meant having the magistrate—me—order her gun to be taken away from her. That's what I was threatening her with—not death!"

Penelope grimaced. "But the local rumor mill isn't that discriminating, I assume?"

"No." Henry deflated, shoulders drooping. "They're taking it to mean something I never intended." He paused, then, voice lowering, went on, "But worse, later in the afternoon, I'd calmed down, and I decided I should apologize. Offer to replace the bit of hedge if it died—something like that."

Barnaby had no difficulty believing that was what Henry would have done. At base, he was a kind and gentle soul who valued peace and harmony.

"So," Henry continued, "on my way home, I stopped at Lavender Cottage, dismounted, went up the path, and knocked on her door. I knocked twice and waited, but she didn't answer. I thought she must have gone out, so I left." He drew in a long breath, then exhaled and said, "Now, it seems she was probably lying dead in her parlor at that time."

Barnaby gently inquired, "I take it you were seen walking away from her door?"

Henry nodded. "By two of the village's biggest gossips. Iris Perkins and Gladys Hooper had just left Penrose Cottage, and they both saw me walk out of the Lavender Cottage gate. I nodded to them, then mounted my horse, called Humphrey, and rode on home."

By her expression, Penelope was cataloguing every fact, moment by moment. "What," she asked, "do you know of this woman who was killed? What was her name again?"

"Miss Viola Huntingdon. She was strangled, apparently sometime on Thursday afternoon, but her body wasn't found until the next morning, when her housekeeper—Mrs. Gilroy, who lives elsewhere in the village— arrived to start her day."

"So that was Friday morning," Penelope stated.

Henry nodded. "Thursday afternoon is one of Mrs. Gilroy's half days off. She's said that Miss Huntingdon was bothered about something and rather distracted, but hale and whole and well when she—Mrs. Gilroy— left the cottage at noon on Thursday. But when Mrs. Gilroy came in on Friday morning, Miss Huntingdon was dead and cold, lying in her parlor."

Penelope shifted to directly face Henry. "Let me see if I have this correctly. You had an argument with the victim on Thursday morning, and she was found dead, strangled"—*exactly as Kitty was; small wonder the situation is haunting poor Henry*—"early on Friday morning."

Glumly, Henry nodded. "That's right."

"So what was this accusation?" Penelope asked.

"And," Barnaby added, "who made it?"

Henry sighed. "It happened after church yesterday. As usual, the congregation gathered to chat on the church lawn, and yesterday morning, the talk was all about the murder. Miss Huntingdon's sister—another Miss Huntingdon—had come down from London, and she was there, standing with Mrs. Foswell, the minister's wife, with the rest of the village scattered about, and I thought I should offer my condolences. Miss Huntingdon hadn't expected to find her sister dead, and so she wasn't in mourning clothes but had one of those gauzy veils over her hat, so as I approached, I couldn't see her face. Perhaps if I had…" Henry grimaced. "Anyway, I walked up and stated my name and said how sorry I was for her loss and held out my hand, and this Miss Huntingdon looked down at my hand, and veil or no veil, I swear she looked at my hand as if it was diseased. Then she said—" Henry broke off and closed his eyes. He was obviously reciting from memory as he went on, "My sister wrote to me about you. She called you 'her secret admirer, H.' And I've heard you had an argument with her on Thursday morning, and you were seen leaving her cottage on Thursday afternoon, and after that, she was found dead, strangled, just like your late wife." Henry paused and, his eyes still closed, reported, "Her voice was low and husky as if she'd been crying, and she hauled in a breath that was shaky and sobby and went on"—he opened his eyes and continued—"'I can only hope that the police get the right man this time!'"

He looked at Penelope and Barnaby, a species of hopelessness in his eyes. "She thinks I killed her sister."

In a matter-of-fact tone, Barnaby asked, "What did you do?"

"What could I do?" Henry shook his head. "I froze. I was so stunned, I didn't—couldn't—say anything. Then I lowered my hand, turned on my heel, and walked away. I could hear the whispers start up behind me, like a swarm of wasps." He shuddered. "I was so shaken, I drove straight home, then after luncheon, I drove to Salisbury, got on the train, and came here."

His expression baffled and pleading, Henry looked from Penelope to Barnaby. "I have no idea why anyone would think Miss Huntingdon would label me 'her secret admirer.' I barely knew the woman—well, just to nod to, given she'd lived in the village for the past five years." Henry's shoulders sagged. "But the whispers have started up again and…" He shrugged and said nothing more.

Penelope was frowning. "Is there any other man in the village or around about whose name starts with *H*?"

Henry grimaced. "No. That's just it. For my sins, I'm the only *H* around."

Barnaby snorted. "Being accused of murder because your name begins with a particular letter is absurd."

"I know, but…" Henry shrugged again. "It's a small country village, and you know what such places are like. Something like that connects in people's minds with Kitty being strangled, and they talk, and the more they talk, the more their conjecture starts to sound like fact." He straightened and looked at Barnaby, then at Penelope. "I've heard you work with that Scotland Yard inspector, Stokes. He's the one who came down to Glossup Hall five years ago and unraveled the truth of Kitty's murder. He knows all about that, and so I thought, if you could see your way to contacting him…"

Penelope leaned forward and patted Henry's clasped hands. "Of course! As it happens, we work closely with Stokes on any matter that involves members of the ton, and recently, that remit has been broadened to include whatever cases we think we can help with, and on both counts, this is unquestionably one."

"Indeed." With a decisive nod, Barnaby rose and crossed to the bellpull beside the fireplace. "The first thing we need to do is summon Stokes. With any luck, he'll be tapped on the shoulder for this case, assuming, of course, that the local police force requests Scotland Yard's assistance."

"Regardless," Penelope firmly stated, "I'm sure Stokes will agree that we three should go down to Ashmore and take a good look around."

Relief suffused Henry's expression. "Thank you." To Penelope, he said, "I apologize for pulling you away from the social round."

"Pfft!" She waved aside the notion. "Now that the majority of the ton have retreated to the country, there's nothing—absolutely nothing—going on in town that can possibly compete with murder."

Having tugged the bellpull, smiling reassuringly, Barnaby resumed his seat. "In truth, I rather fancy a nice little jaunt into the country."

Penelope grinned at Henry. "Don't worry. We'll come down and sort this out and discover who really strangled Miss Viola Huntingdon."

In Ashmore village, wrapped in the peace and quiet of the nave in the church of St. Nicholas, Madeline Huntingdon kept her eyes closed and prayed for fortitude and also courage.

The atmosphere within the thick stone walls was cool, and the chill of the flagstones, even felt through the thin kneeling pad, permeated to her bones.

She was a minister's daughter, and praying was in large part second nature. In her current emotionally troubled state, she'd come to the church to find the solace necessary to commune with the Almighty and, hopefully, find some degree of calm and reclaim at least a small measure of her customary rationality.

Since the moment she'd arrived in the village and discovered her sister had been cruelly slain, she'd been surrounded by well-meaning people whose smothering sympathy had only intensified her geysering emotions. Worse, those sympathizers' frequently misguided albeit well-intentioned advice had left her adrift on a turbulent sea of impulse and compulsion, driven by a host of feelings of which she'd previously had little experience—vengeance, a thirst for justice, and an overwhelming desire to see the villain responsible pay.

Part of that drive came from a sense of guilt, misplaced though that assuredly was. Viola wouldn't have welcomed Madeline interfering in her life decisions, any more than Madeline would have welcomed Viola meddling in hers. Despite being sisters and, in general terms, quite close, they had always been different people, and they'd had the sense to honor the other's life choices.

But now, Viola was dead, murdered, and Madeline needed to dry her tears, get her feet on firm ground, and proceed in her usual calm, sensible, logical fashion.

In her heart, she'd vowed to Viola that she would see her killer brought to justice, and in the peace of the church, that sentiment grew more solid in her mind.

That was her way forward.

Ever since their father had died five years ago and she and Viola had gone their separate ways, Madeline had always stood ready to help and defend her less wise and definitely less worldly older sister, even though, being the older sister, Viola had always felt that shoe ought to have been on the other foot.

Their father had been something of a closet investor with a particular fascination with the burgeoning railways, and despite having no other income beyond what he received as a cleric, he had built a significant nest egg he'd bequeathed to his daughters.

On leaving the vicarage in Salisbury, Viola had chosen to use her half of their inheritance to buy Lavender Cottage in the village of Ashmore, located just over the border in Dorset, twenty or so miles from Salisbury. Madeline had always thought that the tiny village—with its commensurately tiny community—suited Viola in the sense that it afforded her the opportunity to be a big fish in a small pond.

Being of a different, far more adventurous bent, Madeline had taken her portion and bought a small house in a respectable part of London. She lived on the upper floor and rented the two lower floors to academics and otherwise spent her time following—quite successfully, as it had transpired—in their father's footsteps.

Over the past nearly five years, Madeline's life and Viola's life had been poles apart, yet they'd remained close. Madeline had visited Viola at least three times each year, remaining for several weeks on each occasion. In return, Viola had visited Madeline in London—rather trepidatiously, it had to be said—once every year.

Their lives had settled into comfortable patterns. The very last thing Madeline had expected was to have to bury Viola.

Anger at Viola's murderer surged anew. Viola might have been a trifle annoying at times, but she'd always tried to do the right, proper, and Christian thing, and she'd harbored not a single malicious bone in her body.

Viola had been harmless, supremely so, and none of her very human failings could possibly have justified her murder. Yet someone had placed their hands about Viola's throat and squeezed the life from her.

For Madeline, being able to think that thought without more than an emotional wobble was reassuring. Yesterday, when she'd sat through the service in the church and, afterward, been offered so many condolences from various villagers, some of whom she knew were not entirely sincere, she'd been in such an emotionally overwrought state that she'd barely recognized herself. Level-headed was her normal condition, and being so far removed from that had been thoroughly disconcerting.

That was her only excuse for what had occurred when Lord Glossup —owner of nearby Glossup Hall—had approached to offer his condolences. Her grief—and yes, her anger at whoever had killed her really quite helpless sister—had surged and drowned what had remained of her good sense, and she'd lashed out.

She'd accused his lordship of being Viola's "secret admirer, *H*"—the gentleman Viola had recently written about in such glowing terms to Madeline. She'd heard about the argument his lordship had had with Viola on the morning of her death and had proceeded to connect that with him being seen leaving her cottage later that day at a time at which she was now believed to have been dead. Madeline had then gone one step further and drawn a direct line between the murder of his lordship's late wife, who had also been strangled, and Viola's murder and had capped her implied accusation with the hope that, this time, the police would arrest the right man for the crime.

The memory of her outburst sent shame coursing through Madeline. The accusation had been fueled by the whispers poured into her ears since she'd arrived on Saturday to find Viola's body being taken from the cottage, yet as soon as the words had left her lips, she'd started to doubt their accuracy.

What she could not doubt was the emotion she'd seen—as plain as day and impossible to mistake—in his lordship's brown eyes and in the lines of his face. There'd been real sympathy—honest and sincere—in his gaze as he'd approached, and that emotion had resonated in the simple, gently spoken words of condolence he'd uttered. But then she'd coldly flung his words back at him, and the look in his face, in his eyes, as her rejection had struck him...

Hurt. A wounded look. The sense of a cut that had struck deep, far deeper than she'd expected.

With her eyes still closed, Madeline shifted on the cold, hard floor. She couldn't get the image of his lordship's stunned face out of her mind. In and of itself, his expression was a powerful counteraccusation that in uttering the words she had, she'd been wildly wrong.

Later, troubled by the incident, she'd sought counsel of Reverend Foswell, the minister of St. Nicholas' Church, the village church Viola had attended and where Madeline was currently praying. From the reverend and his wife, who had been Viola's closest village friend, Madeline had learned the truth of his lordship's wife's murder. Yes, Catherine Glossup had been strangled, but by her lover. The case had been investigated by Scotland Yard, and while in small country villages, there were always rumors and questions as to whether the distant police force in London hadn't simply covered up matters for the local lordly landowner, Madeline had lived in London for years and was not so quick to condemn all police as corrupt or fools.

What truly weighed on Madeline now was the likely reality that by uttering her accusation as she had—in full view and hearing of the majority of the villagers—she'd cruelly stoked the fires of village gossip in a way that would result in a repeat of a horrendous period in his lordship's life.

Her words had been unwise. She hadn't meant to hurt anyone, much less to cause harm to one who was—she suspected—still emotionally vulnerable over the matter of his wife's death. That must have been a terrible time in his life, and her unjust words would have brought it all back.

She'd been wrong. She'd falsely accused an innocent bystander, and she would have to apologize.

Immediately she formed that intention, the turbulence inside her settled and calmed.

The fog that had clouded her brain since she'd seen Viola's body taken away thinned and lifted, and Madeline was suddenly perfectly certain that in apologizing to Lord Glossup, she would be taking her first definite step toward claiming control of this unprecedented situation rather than being a victim of its vicissitudes.

That's what I need to do. Take charge.

She drew in what felt like her first clear breath since that dreadful moment on Saturday, then she opened her eyes and looked at the altar, at the stained glass window behind it. After a moment, she smiled softly and whispered a last prayer for their late father, then she rose, stepped out of the pew, and turned up the nave toward the church's open door.

She raised her head, looked toward the door, and paused. There was a man standing just inside the doorway, patently waiting for her. Because of the brightness outside and the dimness within the church, she couldn't yet see well enough to determine who he was, but he was tallish and had dark hair, and for an instant, she wondered if she would be able to make her apology immediately and ease the weight from her soul. But as she walked forward in hope, she realized that the man's stance, his posture, wasn't that of Lord Glossup.

In dawning surprise, she realized that the gentleman by the church door was the very last man she would have expected to encounter, especially then and there.

Years before, when she'd been an innocent twenty-year-old, sheltered, motherless, and living the constrained life of a Salisbury minister's daughter, she'd set her cap at handsome Montgomery Pincer, and for several months, he'd led her on, only to cruelly dash her girlish matrimonial hopes. That said, at least he'd been ruthlessly honest in telling her that although she had a decent portion and, given her father's successful investing, would ultimately inherit more, she was far too independently minded for Monty to consider taking to wife.

Now, nearly seventeen years later and knowing a great deal more about men, Madeline could appreciate that not only had Monty's assessment of her been accurate, he'd also done her a great service in allowing her to escape.

Not that he'd intended to do her any service, yet nevertheless.

As she approached the doorway, Madeline swiftly studied him and had to admit that, physically, he hadn't changed much with the years. He was still a tall, decidedly handsome gentleman, with wavy dark-brown hair—perhaps a little less wavy and glossy than previously—falling rakishly over his forehead. His long-lashed blue eyes were just as engaging and attractive as before despite the fine wrinkles radiating from their corners. He was more than two years older than she, so had to be nearing forty, yet he still possessed an excellent figure—about six feet tall, lean, long boned with broad shoulders—and an athletic build, and she felt sure he would move as gracefully as he always had.

As ever, he was dressed well, this time in a tailored coat with a fashionable waistcoat over simple breeches and top boots. At first glance, he appeared the epitome of the successful country gentleman, but this wasn't Madeline's first glance. Regardless, she had to admit that Monty looked more the part of lord of the manor than Lord Glossup, in his plainer countryman's attire, had.

She halted a yard away and inclined her head. "Monty."

"Madeline." Smiling with just the right blend of charm and sympathy, Monty stepped forward and reached for her hand.

She allowed him to take her gloved fingers, and he bowed—as gracefully as she'd expected—over her hand, then straightened. Before he could direct the conversation, she asked, "What brings you to Ashmore?" She assumed he was still living in Salisbury.

Monty's smile didn't dim. "I was passing and saw you walk in here. I'd just heard the grave news of your sister's death and thought to offer my condolences." His tone subtly implied that the answer should have been obvious, but his effortless charm smoothed everything over. "I am, indeed, deeply sorry for your loss."

Cynically, Madeline acknowledged that he hadn't lost his touch. She reached for graciousness and replied, "Thank you. It came as quite a shock."

"I imagine so."

As she withdrew her hand from his clasp, he ran his gaze appreciatively over her quietly expensive gown.

She stepped past him, and he turned and fell in beside her as she walked out of the cool dimness of the church. She expected him to ask about Viola, whom he'd known, albeit not as well as he'd known her, but instead, he said, "I confess I'm quite curious. What have you been doing with yourself? I heard that you had come down from London."

The last statement was uttered as a question. Not wishing to encourage him, she replied, "I live there now."

She took the path toward the rectory and ignored Monty's quizzing gaze.

After a moment, he looked ahead. "I must admit I've rather lost touch with all those I knew before."

His pensive tone had her glancing his way. "Did you move elsewhere, too?" From experience, she knew that keeping the focus on him would effectively distract him from her.

He smiled rather mischievously. "Yes, indeed. I've been in America for some years and only just got back yesterday, so you might say I'm fresh off the boat from New York."

"What were you doing in America?" Madeline returned her gaze to the rectory gate.

"This and that. I became involved in various businesses located throughout the northeast of the country, and in all truth, I did rather well. Ultimately, however, I felt I needed to come home again. There's just something about England that lives in your bones."

They'd reached the rectory gate, and she halted and faced him. "That's wonderful. But I must go in—luncheon will be served soon."

Monty eyed the rectory with a frown in his eyes. "You're living here?"

"For the moment. The Foswells insisted that I stay with them. No one thought I should be alone at the cottage at this time." She was planning to move back to the cottage later that afternoon, but she wasn't about to tell him that.

"Ah. I see." Monty looked at her, then with apparent sincerity, asked, "Are you all right?"

She summoned a weak smile. "I'm managing well enough."

His charming mien returned. "If there's anything I can do to help, know you have only to ask." His expression turned faintly rueful. "For old times' sake, if nothing else."

She responded with a nod of polite civility. "Thank you. I'll bear that in mind."

It struck her that she now viewed him through a strictly objective lens.

He and their shared past exerted no lingering hold on her heart, even at this time when all her emotions seemed so much closer to her surface. The observation was reassuring. Given their past, Montgomery Pincer wasn't a man she would ever trust again.

She held his gaze and inclined her head. "Goodbye, Monty."

He reached for her hand, and she watched him bow over it.

Straightening and releasing her, he caught her eye. "I meant what I said. If you need anything, I'll be happy to help."

With a distant smile, she dipped her head and turned away. She opened the gate and went through, pushed it closed behind her, then walked the few steps to the rectory door. As she turned the knob and crossed the threshold, she knew beyond question that no matter what help she needed, she wouldn't be appealing to Monty. There was no circumstance that would induce her to invite a man like him into her now well-ordered and successful life.

Gently, she closed the door, then peeked through the lace screening the glass side panel. Monty hovered on the other side of the gate, apparently staring at the closed door.

He remained there, seemingly indecisive, for nearly a minute, then turned and walked toward the lane.

Madeline straightened and realized she was relieved he'd gone. She couldn't quite understand why, yet she found it strange that after nearly seventeen years, Monty had chosen that moment to reappear in her life.

CHAPTER 2

*P*enelope had just sent away the tea tray, and she, Barnaby, and Henry were exchanging news of their various relatives' children when sounds of arrival in the front hall were followed by Stokes walking determinedly into the room.

Barnaby and Henry rose, while Penelope remained seated.

Stokes half bowed in her direction, then held out his hand to Barnaby.

After shaking hands, Stokes, whose gray gaze had fixed on Henry, nodded in greeting and offered his hand. "Lord Glossup." With a faint smile teasing his lips, Stokes added, "I would say that it's a pleasure to see you again, but given the circumstances, you might not feel the same. Be that as it may, I'm actually glad to find you here."

"Oh?" Henry shook hands, then he and Barnaby resumed their seats on the pair of long sofas, and Stokes moved to the place opposite Penelope.

"Indeed." Stokes sat. "I left the commissioner's office to find Adair's summons waiting. As it happened, courtesy of the commissioner's direction, I was already heading this way. The Salisbury City Police, who are in charge of investigating the suspicious death of"—Stokes drew out his notebook and consulted a page—"one Viola Huntingdon, spinster, have requested Scotland Yard's assistance in the matter of apprehending the man they believe to be the guilty party." Stokes looked at Henry. "Given that you're here, I assume you're aware that you are the Salisbury police's prime suspect."

Henry briefly closed his eyes, then sighed, opened them, and admitted, "I was worried it would come to that."

Penelope leapt to say, "We've already heard the basis of the case against Henry, and it seems entirely circumstantial and altogether weak."

Stokes's expression was as close as it ever got to reassuring. "I suspected as much. That's why the Salisbury Superintending Constable has passed the hot potato to us. He might wish to say it's an open-and-shut case and they have their man, yet even he isn't entirely convinced."

Stokes focused on Henry. "You'll be pleased to know that we at the Yard"—grinning, he tipped his head to Barnaby and Penelope—"and especially our two consultants here are not so inclined to leap to conclusions."

"Thank God for that," Henry muttered, and it was plain he was greatly relieved.

Stokes continued, "Needless to say, especially in light of my previous visit to that part of the country, the case has officially landed in my lap, along with the recommendation to inquire whether you two"—again, he nodded to Barnaby and Penelope—"are available to assist."

Penelope promptly replied, "We are, indeed, available and keen to help."

Barnaby was faintly frowning. "Ashmore's in Dorset, isn't it? Why is it Salisbury City's case?"

It was Henry who replied, "Because Ashmore is close to the county border, and although Wiltshire has a countywide police force, Dorset is yet to appoint one, so in the Ashmore area, Salisbury City Police are the responsible police force."

"In addition," Stokes said with a questioning look at Henry, "there are, I'm told, local constables."

Henry nodded. "They're stationed in various villages and report to Salisbury. In Ashmore, Constable Price is our local man. He lives on the family farm nearby and watches over several villages, not just Ashmore."

"Right, then." Stokes flipped to a fresh page in his notebook, then looked at Henry. "I would be obliged if you would tell me all you know of the victim, Viola Huntingdon, and anything pertinent regarding her death."

Henry blinked, then ventured, "I'm not sure I can tell you much of Viola—I didn't know her all that well."

Penelope took pity on him and asked, "Had she lived in the village for long?"

"Oh. I see. About five years." Henry paused, then added, "She bought Lavender Cottage a little after that business with Kitty."

Busily scribbling, Stokes caught Penelope's eye and nodded encouragingly.

She continued, "Was Viola well-liked in the village?"

"Ah, well, not entirely."

"My memory of the village is that it's quite tiny," Barnaby put in. "Who else lives there?"

"It is very small," Henry agreed, "and as for those who live there, those who had more to do with Viola are Reverend and Mrs. Foswell in the rectory of St. Nicholas' Church, and Mrs. Iris Perkins and her family, and Gladys Hooper and the Hoopers, and Arthur and Ida Penrose." He paused then added, "Penrose Cottage is more or less opposite the village pond, and Lavender Cottage is the next house along Green Lane."

"Did Viola have any staff?" Penelope asked.

"Not live-in," Henry said. "Mrs. Gilroy—she lives in a cottage along Halfpenny Lane, which is opposite the church—was Viola's housekeeper. And Jim Swinson, who lives nearby and works several days for Arthur Penrose, did Viola's garden on his days off from the Penroses."

"Did Viola have a particular friend in the village?" Penelope asked.

"That," Henry stated, "would be Mrs. Foswell—they were as thick as thieves—and I believe Viola was also on friendly terms with Iris Perkins and Gladys Hooper. I've never heard of any difficulty between Viola and Mrs. Gilroy, either."

"What about the neighbors?" Stokes asked. "The Penroses."

"Ah," Henry replied. "Relationships there were a trifle strained—something to do with a boundary dispute. But other than arguing back and forth, I haven't heard that either party has been moved to any more definite action. There haven't been any threats uttered, as far as I know." Henry paused, then sighed and went on, "One doesn't like to speak ill of the dead, and this isn't really all that ill, but amongst the villagers, Viola had a reputation of being a stickler. It might have had something to do with being a minister's daughter—I did mention that, didn't I? That her father had been the minister at St. Edmund's Church in Salisbury until his death about five years ago?"

"No," Stokes said, busily jotting, "but you have now, so please continue."

"Yes, well, Viola had standards, and she expected everyone else to live up to them. I've heard that she could be quite…insistent. And stubborn with it. Yet all that could simply have been an entrenched belief that she knew best. I never heard any malicious word or deed attributed to her."

Barnaby offered, "Could she be described as an inveterate do-gooder? One who was determined to do good even if the party involved didn't want her advice, much less to follow it?"

"Yes!" Henry nodded. "That's Viola to a T. And as you can imagine, such an attitude didn't always endear her to others."

"So there might well be other sources of tension between the victim and various villagers," Stokes said.

"I suppose so," Henry replied, "but I'm afraid I know little of such matters."

"All right." Stokes looked at Henry. "Now, tell me what interactions you've had recently with the victim."

Henry grimaced. "Generally speaking, until this past Thursday, we haven't had any particular interactions at all. Just nodding politely when we pass in the lane and at church—that sort of thing."

"But on Thursday…" Penelope prompted.

Henry drew in a breath and, with his hands pressed together, described to Stokes the Thursday-morning exchange in Green Lane, more or less exactly as he had to Penelope and Barnaby.

"So you remained mounted the entire time and rode on to where?" Stokes asked.

"I often ride toward Tollard Royal. It's a pleasant run, and I own several farms that way. I stopped and chatted with two of my tenant farmers, then fetched up at the King John Inn in Tollard Royal for lunch—the food's excellent and the ale quite palatable."

Stokes nodded. "I remember it. That's the inn you recommended I stay at when I was last down that way."

"Yes, well, the innkeeper and staff know me well, so they can vouch for me being there," Henry said. "I was a bit late and left about three and rode directly south to visit the last of my farms. It must have been about four when I left there and rode west to Green Lane. I rode along it until I came to Lavender Cottage. By then, I'd calmed down and felt I should apologize and perhaps offer to replace any of the lavenders in the hedge if they died. So I stopped at the cottage."

"What time was that?" Stokes asked.

"About four-thirty. The light was waning, but there was still enough to see by."

"Where did you leave your horse?" Barnaby asked.

"And the dog?" Penelope put in.

"I left Stiller, my horse, tied to the hedge by the gate," Henry replied. "And I told Humphrey, my hound, to wait with him, which he did."

Stokes looked at Barnaby and faintly grinned. "That's hardly the actions of a man trying to hide his presence while he murders the occupant." Stokes looked at Henry. "I take it the villagers would recognize your horse and dog?"

Henry nodded. "I ride Stiller every day, and I often take Humphrey along as well, so I'd be surprised if they didn't."

"What happened when you called at the cottage?" Stokes asked.

"Nothing. I knocked and waited, then knocked again, but no one came to the door." Henry shrugged. "So I left. Iris Perkins and Gladys Hooper were leaving Penrose Cottage at that time, and both saw me coming out of the Lavender Cottage gate. I tipped my hat to them, then mounted up and rode home. My staff can vouch for when I got in."

"Hmm." Stokes flicked back through his notes. "The information from Salisbury is patchy to say the least. What have you—and I assume the villagers—heard about how and when Viola Huntingdon died?"

Accustomed to hearing testimonies in court, Henry paused to order his thoughts before relating, "Thursday afternoon is one of Mrs. Gilroy's half days off, so she left the cottage at noon, and she says Miss Huntingdon was hale and whole, if a bit distracted, at that time. Other than that, we haven't heard much, but I gather that the consensus of opinion is that Miss Huntingdon was strangled and already dead by the time I knocked on her door."

"I understand," Stokes said, "that the Salisbury medical examiner believes the death occurred between twelve and four, and for some reason, the police believe the critical time is three-thirty." He glanced at Barnaby. "If Henry left the King John Inn at three and called on his tenant farmer between then and four, he can't have been at the cottage at three-thirty."

Barnaby smiled. "No, indeed." He looked at Henry. "I believe you're off the hook."

Henry exhaled gustily. "I can't tell you how relieved that makes me— that there's some actual evidence that proves I couldn't have committed the crime."

"Ask Henry to tell you about the accusation leveled his way," Penelope said. "There's a clue or two buried in the words, I would say."

Stokes looked at Henry, and after pulling a resigned face, Henry recounted the charge he'd faced on the church lawn the day before.

At the end of his recitation, Stokes grimaced with distaste. "My sympathies. That must have been difficult. I had heard there's a sister who lives in London and that she'd traveled down to Ashmore just in time to see the victim's body being carted out of the cottage." He looked at Henry. "I find that timing curious. Can you tell me anything about her?"

"I believe her first name is Madeline. She's visited the village several times before—I recall seeing her with Viola on multiple occasions over the years—but until Sunday, I had never spoken with her. Apparently, she received a letter from Viola that Mrs. Gilroy had posted on Thursday in which Viola had begged Madeline to come down and assist her in dealing with this 'secret admirer, H.'" Somewhat diffidently, Henry added, "Arriving at the cottage at the moment she did must have been a terrible shock."

"Indeed," Penelope said. "And I suppose being overcome with grief might go some way to excusing her ridiculous accusation." She studied Henry. "What does she look like?"

To Penelope's surprise, Henry faintly blushed. "Well," he temporized, "I couldn't actually see her face—her features or her hair. She was wearing one of those black veils over her hat." He paused, but when Penelope simply watched him and waited, he added, "She's of about average height, I would say, perhaps a touch taller, with a good figure, and I did notice that she was very well dressed but in a quiet, unobtrusive way."

That was significantly greater detail than Penelope had expected Henry to have observed. She was suddenly much more curious about Miss Madeline Huntingdon.

Stokes had been jotting. "Right." He looked up. "So what can you tell me about this secret admirer? Are there any other gentlemen with names beginning with H in the vicinity?"

Henry shook his head. "Not that anyone's aware of. I'm the only H around. As you know, Ashmore is a very small village, the sort where everyone usually knows everyone else's business. Yet it seems that Viola had a secret admirer whose name begins with H, but other than that, no one has the faintest idea who he is."

Stokes frowned. "I remember Ashmore village. I assume it hasn't changed much with the years, so how on earth did Viola Huntingdon manage to meet with a secret admirer without anyone seeing him?"

Henry replied, "We all now think he must have gone back and forth via the rear garden of Lavender Cottage. The rear of the block is bordered by a thick stand of trees—an old windbreak that's become an established strip of woodland. Beyond the trees, the fields run all the way to the Tollard Royal-Ashmore lane, which is lined with trees and bushes with open fields on both sides. It's possible that someone could have left a horse by the lane—or even on the other side of it—and walked to the cottage across the fields. There's an old right-of-way that leads into the windbreak, more or less at the back of Lavender Cottage."

Stokes grunted. "Of course. And, I assume, no neighbors look out over the rear garden."

"No. The Penroses are the only near neighbors, and there are trees and bushes along their boundary wall that block their view of Lavender Cottage."

"What about the housekeeper?" Penelope asked. "Mrs. Gilroy. Had she seen or noticed anything?"

"She says not. Indeed," Henry said, "she seems as shocked as anyone that Viola had a secret admirer and she didn't know of it. It seems he only visited on Mrs. Gilroy's half days off—on Thursdays and Sundays."

"And Miss Huntingdon had no other live-in staff." Stokes sighed and shut his notebook. He looked at the others. "I believe our next move is to visit the scene of the crime, although we'll need to call on the Salisbury City Police first to inform them that I'm taking over the case."

Looking even more relieved, Henry said, "I can put you all up at Glossup Hall, if that suits?"

Penelope exchanged a look with Barnaby and Stokes, then turned to Henry. "Actually, we've found it's best not to stay with anyone involved, however tangentially, in the crime we're investigating. That way, we aren't seen as taking sides."

Henry nodded in understanding. "In this case, that's probably wise." He grimaced. "Tongues would wag even more than they are already."

Stokes uncrossed his ankles and sat up. "As it seems the King John Inn is still the best place to stay, we'll make that our base." To Barnaby and Penelope, he explained, "It's only a short drive from Ashmore."

Barnaby nodded. "Having our own carriage down there will help, so I suggest we drive down tomorrow morning."

"Early," Stokes said. "We'll need to leave before dawn if we're to reach Salisbury, speak with the police there, then get to Ashmore in time to start interviewing the locals." He looked at Penelope hopefully. "I'll come in time to join you for breakfast."

She laughed. "I'll let Mostyn know that we'll require breakfast before setting out. Shall we plan to leave at six?"

When all agreed six would be early enough, Penelope turned to Henry. "Please do stay overnight, Henry. Then we can all breakfast together and leave at first light."

Barnaby rose and headed for the bellpull. "I'll get Mostyn to send one of the footmen for your bag. White's, I think you said?"

Henry looked from Barnaby to Penelope, then back again. "Thank you. Staying here would be most welcome."

Barnaby smiled and tugged the bellpull.

When Barnaby finished giving Mostyn the required orders, Stokes rose. "I'll send O'Donnell and Morgan down with the police coach. That way, we'll have two conveyances at our disposal."

Everyone agreed that was a wise idea, and while Penelope, Barnaby, and Henry accompanied Stokes into the front hall, they finalized their plan to drive directly to Salisbury, where Henry had left his curricle in a stable near the railway station. Before parting from them, Henry would direct them to the police station, then collect his curricle and drive home to Glossup Hall.

Stokes nodded. "So"—he looked at Barnaby and Penelope—"from Salisbury, I'll send O'Donnell and Morgan on in the police coach to secure rooms for us all at the inn. Meanwhile, we'll make ourselves known to the Superintending Constable, extract all the evidence we can from him, then follow the others to Tollard Royal."

"If we leave at six," Barnaby said, "we should be able to reach Salisbury by noon—at least, our carriage should."

"That will work." Stokes accepted his hat from Mostyn and set it on his head. "The murder was committed last Thursday afternoon, and it's already Monday. I'd like to get to Ashmore in time to inspect the cottage and get some idea of its surrounds before the light fails."

"We might even get a chance to conduct a few interviews," Penelope put in.

"We can certainly hope." Stokes nodded in farewell to them all. "And now, I'm off to break the news to my dear wife that I'll be going out of town."

"Indeed." Penelope caught his eye. "And please tell her that even though I'll be going with you, I hope her planned visit with your little ones on Wednesday will still go ahead. Our two are so looking forward to it, and I'm sure Megan will be, too."

Stokes tapped his hat. "I'll convey that message." Mostyn opened the door, and Stokes walked out, calling over his shoulder, "And I'll see you all bright and early tomorrow morning."

Barnaby and Penelope laughed, and even Henry chuckled.

Then Mostyn closed the door, and they turned back toward the drawing room.

Penelope looped her arm in Henry's. "Now, Henry dear, I've never been to Ashmore village. I need you to describe it to me. In detail."

Barnaby smiled and followed the other two into the drawing room.

By the time the Adairs' coach drew up to the curb in Salisbury, Penelope was more than ready to get out and stretch her legs. As planned, they'd set out from Albemarle Street at six o'clock and had caught up with the police wagon, which must have left Scotland Yard in the middle of the night, just outside Salisbury.

Stokes descended from the carriage first, followed by Barnaby, who reached back and offered Penelope his hand. She took it and climbed down the steps, then moved aside to allow Henry to join them.

As curious as ever, Penelope looked around. She'd never visited Salisbury before. From what she'd seen on their way into the town's center, the layout was typical of larger provincial towns that had grown up around a central market square, with a castle in one direction and, in this case, the famous cathedral some way to the south. She could just spot the spire in the distance, rising above the city's rooftops against a hazy blue-gray sky.

The street they were in was called Endless Street, and despite the name, a short way away, the southern end gave onto one corner of the market square. According to Henry, the solid, squat redbrick building before which they stood was the main office of the Salisbury City Police.

The police coach from Scotland Yard, with Sergeant O'Donnell on the box seat and Constable Morgan beside him, drew up behind the carriage. With the conveyances one behind the other, the contrast between the sleek, well-sprung modern traveling carriage and the much older, smaller, cramped, and dumpy black coach was stark. It was entirely unsurprising that Stokes had elected to join Barnaby, Penelope, and Henry in the traveling carriage.

"Let me get my bag." Henry suited action to the words and, half a minute later, returned to where Stokes, Barnaby, and Penelope were waiting. "I'll leave you here, then." Henry nodded at the police station. "As I mentioned, the man in charge is Superintending Constable Mallard." Henry paused, then added, "I've always found him to be a decent sort, but he can be stubborn."

"We'll speak with him," Stokes said, "and see what he can tell us, then head down to Ashmore." He looked up at O'Donnell and Morgan, who'd remained on the box of the police coach. "You two can drive directly to Tollard Royal and hire rooms for all of us at the King John Inn."

"One moment." Barnaby turned to look up at their coachman, Phelps, and the groom-cum-guard, Connor, who was seated alongside. "Connor, you might as well go with O'Donnell and Morgan. You know what Mrs. Adair and I require by way of rooms, and you can also arrange for a private parlor for our party."

"Yes, sir." Connor readily climbed down from the carriage, walked back to the coach, and swung up to the bench at the coach's rear.

"Right, then." O'Donnell saluted them all with his whip, then shook the reins, and the coach slowly lumbered off down the street, continuing toward the market square.

Henry hefted his bag. "I'll be off." He tipped his head in the opposite direction. "The stable I use is nearer the station."

"One last thing." Stokes focused on Henry. "I realize you have to drive through Ashmore village to reach Glossup Hall, but for the moment, it would be helpful if you would avoid spending time in the village and not speak to anyone about the case until we've had a chance to get there and assess the situation firsthand."

Penelope put it more bluntly. "In other words, until we've learned what people can tell us without them being reminded of your involvement or, indeed, of the past."

Barnaby added, "We don't want them speculating or inventing things to be interesting."

"We would infinitely prefer them to tell us facts rather than what they think might have happened," Penelope said.

"Of course," Henry replied. "I have more than enough to get on with managing the estate. I'll avoid the village for now." He shook hands with Barnaby and Stokes and tipped his hat to Penelope, then strode off.

Penelope, Barnaby, and Stokes watched him go, then as one, they turned and looked at the police station.

"Right," Stokes said. "Let's get to it."

There was a certain relish in his tone that made Penelope smile as he led the way into the building, and she and Barnaby followed.

Stokes strode directly for the front counter, currently manned by a fresh-faced constable. Stokes introduced himself and added that Barnaby and Penelope were consultants working for Scotland Yard. "We're here to speak with Superintending Constable Mallard."

The young constable's eyes couldn't have got any wider. "Yes, sir! At once, sir!" He glanced around, plainly wondering what to do next, then piped, "I won't be more than a minute, sirs. Ma'am." With that, he rushed to a door along the wall behind the counter and disappeared through it.

Significantly less than a minute later, a large, heavily built man of about fifty summers, with graying-brown hair and a heavyset figure garbed in a neat but well-worn police uniform, came out through the same door, moving with a slow yet deliberate flat-footed gait. In keeping with his size, his features were large in his round face and, overall, unremarkable and tending toward the fleshy. The only element about him that was smallish was his gray-blue eyes, and the expression in them was shrewd and calculating as he rapidly took stock of his visitors.

Unruffled and urbane, Stokes nodded in greeting. "Mallard."

Mallard's answering nod was respectful. "Inspector Stokes." Shifting his gaze to Penelope and Barnaby, standing at Stokes's shoulder, Mallard blinked several times, clearly not knowing what to make of them.

Stokes took pity on him and gestured in their direction. "This is Mr. Barnaby Adair and Mrs. Adair. They act as consultants to Scotland Yard, especially when a case touches the aristocracy, as I believe this case does." Stokes paused a beat, evaluating Mallard, then added, "They're here at the express request of the commissioner."

Mallard nodded heavily. "I see."

Barnaby took that to mean that Mallard now recognized the futility of any move to limit Barnaby and Penelope's involvement in the investigation. That didn't mean that Mallard was, as yet, entirely happy over their presence.

"In that case, if you'll come through to my office"—Mallard waved at the door through which he'd come—"we can discuss the details thus far known regarding the murder of Miss Viola Huntingdon."

They followed him through the door, which gave access to a narrow corridor, then turned left and went through a door on the opposite side of the passageway. The room beyond was a decent-sized office, the central focus of which was a large desk half covered by a collection of messy papers and file folders. One large chair sat behind the desk, and wooden filing cabinets lined the walls. While Mallard drew forward two more chairs to join the single chair already facing the desk, Barnaby saw Penelope to that chair, then accepted another straight-backed chair from Mallard, placed it beside her, and sat.

Stokes set his chair on Penelope's other side and made himself comfortable while Mallard rounded the desk and sank into his customary chair.

"Right, then." Mallard clearly wished to keep control of the exchange. "Now you're here, we can get on with closing this case. It's as open-and-shut as they come." He clasped his hands on his blotter and regarded them steadily. "As I mentioned, the victim was a Miss Viola Huntingdon, a forty-two-year-old spinster lady, and she was strangled to death in the parlor of her cottage. That's Lavender Cottage, in the village of Ashmore."

Mallard focused on Barnaby and Penelope. "I take it you're here because of Lord Glossup's involvement, and indeed, him being involved is why I sent for Scotland Yard." He switched his gaze to Stokes. "I didn't feel I have the standing to arrest a lord."

Stokes studied Mallard, then replied, "Before we discuss any arrest, perhaps you should outline your case against Lord Glossup."

Mallard nodded, leaned forward slightly, and obliged. "First, on the morning of the murder, we have two witnesses to an argument—apparently quite a heated one—between the victim, Miss Huntingdon, and his lordship. At the conclusion of the exchange, his lordship issued a threat to the victim, along the lines that if she did a certain thing he disapproved of, he would make sure she didn't live to do it again."

Grimly, Mallard nodded and went on, "Then, later in the day, we have two other witnesses who saw his lordship leaving the victim's house at a time when we now know she was dead." Mallard paused, then continued, "And if that weren't enough to put Lord Glossup in the dock, there's the fact that his late wife was murdered in exactly the same way just five years back. She was strangled, too." Mallard studied their faces, but

Barnaby knew he would read absolutely nothing in any of their expressions. A trifle uncertainly, Mallard pressed on, "It's hard to overlook the similarities in the two deaths, both associated with the one person. I wasn't here then, but in light of this new murder, the locals are all whispering about how his lordship must have killed his wife, too, but he got away with it that time."

Barnaby glanced at Stokes to see how he would react, but his friend was looking down at his notebook.

Without looking up, Stokes asked, "I understand the medical examiner has given an estimate of the time of death?"

Mallard looked pleased. "He has, indeed. To the minute. I took Doc Carter down with me as soon as we were told of the death. That was at noon on the day after the murder. By examining the body, Carter put the time of death as between twelve and four o'clock, but there was a carriage clock that plainly got broken in the struggle, and it had stopped at three-thirty-three. The housekeeper said the victim was very fond and proud of the clock and wound and set it every morning. The sister of the victim, who arrived the next day, confirmed that, so it seems we're on sound ground in declaring the murder was committed at three-thirty-three."

"I see." Stokes was assiduously taking notes. "So at present, it appears that the murder was committed at three-thirty-three or close to that." He finally looked up and pinned Mallard with his gaze. "You said his lordship returned to the cottage sometime in the afternoon. When, exactly?"

Mallard frowned. "As to that, we don't actually know when he got there, but we have two witnesses who saw him leaving, and that was at about four-thirty."

Stokes nodded. "We'll get to those witnesses in a moment, but first, do you know how his lordship arrived at the cottage?"

"Apparently, he rode," Mallard replied. "Seems he rides everywhere."

"Indeed. Where did he leave his horse?" Stokes asked.

"According to our witnesses," Mallard replied, "it was tied up in the lane by the gate."

"I see," Stokes said. "And what, exactly, did the two witnesses see?"

Mallard paused, then slowly supplied, "They saw his lordship walking down the path from the cottage's door and out of the gate."

Stokes considered his notes, then said, "So if I understand your argument correctly, you're saying that his lordship rode to the cottage, tied his horse to the hedge by the gate, and went inside, and at or about three-thirty-three, he strangled Viola Huntingdon. Then he waited inside the cottage for an hour before walking out to his horse, which had remained in the lane throughout, mounting up, and riding home." Stokes caught Mallard's gaze. "Is that an accurate summation of your case?"

When Mallard pressed his lips tightly together and didn't immediately respond, Stokes leaned back and said, "Quite aside from the issue of the horse in the lane virtually announcing his lordship's presence for all to see, why do you think he waited an hour beside a dead body? I have to say that's rather unusual behavior for a murderer."

"Ah, but"—eagerly, Mallard leapt for the straw Stokes had waved— "that was because he was searching the house. Turned the place over thoroughly, he did."

"What was he searching for?" Penelope asked.

Barnaby had wondered for how much longer she would remain silent. For his part, he was content to allow Stokes to deal with the delicate task of opening Mallard's eyes to the flaws in the case against Henry without antagonizing the man. While investigating in his territory, they would need Mallard's assistance, not his enmity.

"Jewelry," Mallard replied with considerable relish. "The victim's sister, Miss Madeline Huntingdon, says that the victim's favorite pieces— a necklace and matching bracelet, both set with aquamarines—are missing. The housekeeper confirmed that the victim valued both highly."

"I see," Stokes said. "And how do the necklace and bracelet connect with his lordship?"

Mallard blinked.

Stokes glanced at Penelope. "You're our expert in jewelry. Aquamarines. They're not especially valuable, are they?"

"Not really," Penelope said. "They go in and out of fashion somewhat, as all semiprecious stones do. Very large, perfect, high-quality aquamarines will be worth something, but at present, they would rank less highly than, say, garnets, and all such stones will never approach the value of diamonds, rubies, emeralds, and sapphires."

Stokes returned his gaze to Mallard. "It's difficult to see what Lord Glossup would want with what to him would be little more than baubles, yet you're suggesting his lordship killed Miss Huntingdon for the jewelry."

Put on the spot and faintly irritated and frustrated with it, Mallard returned, "Well, regardless, he must have taken them. Who else could have?"

The murderer, perhaps? Barnaby exchanged a look with Penelope and knew exactly what she was thinking as, figuratively, they bit their tongues.

Returning his gaze to Stokes, Barnaby felt his friend was demonstrating extraordinary patience.

"Perhaps," Stokes said, "if we return to the argument earlier in the day between his lordship and the victim, we might find some clue. Have the witnesses given you any idea what the argument was about?"

Somewhat reluctantly, Mallard described the altercation more or less exactly as Henry had. "Miss Huntingdon took strong exception to the actions of his lordship's hound. She was, by all accounts, very proud of her hedge."

"Was any mention made of the jewelry?" Stokes asked.

Mallard faintly frowned. "No."

Stokes raised his brows. "No mention of the jewelry at all?"

Starting to look decidedly uncertain, Mallard shook his head.

Stokes glanced at his notebook, then looked at Mallard. "You mentioned a threat made during this exchange. What was the nature of the threat his lordship made in relation to the victim?"

Mallard visibly perked up. "His lordship was heard by our two witnesses to declare that if she—the victim, Miss Huntingdon—pointed a gun at one of his animals, he'd make sure she never did so again."

His expression unreadable, Stokes studied Mallard as if waiting for more, then when nothing more was forthcoming, sighed and asked, "Was anything said about killing her?"

"Well, no," Mallard conceded. "Not in so many words, but what else could he have meant?"

Stokes regarded Mallard steadily. "Lord Glossup is the local magistrate and has been for many years. Did it not occur to you that he might well have meant to use the law to remove Miss Huntingdon's gun from her, something he could easily have done?"

Mallard's expression stated that, until that moment, the answer had been no. But from the frown forming in his eyes, he was finally starting to set aside his preconceived notions and think about the facts and evidence.

"At present, Mallard," Stokes went on, "you allege that Lord Glossup had an argument with the victim over a dog's behavior and was subsequently seen riding off, but that later, unseen by anyone, he returned to the cottage, left his horse tied up in the lane, and strangled the victim, ransacked her cottage, and stole a bracelet and necklace that were set with aquamarines, and for some reason, attaining the jewelry was his true if entirely unexplained motive."

Mallard grimaced, and his frown deepened.

"And," Stokes continued, "returning to the witnesses who saw his lordship leave the cottage at about four-thirty, did they see him leave the cottage? As in, come out of the door and close it behind him?"

Mallard was not just seeing the light but, albeit reluctantly, finally accepting the reality. "No. They saw him walking down the path to the gate and stepping into the lane."

Stokes nodded. "Do you have any evidence at all that places Lord Glossup inside Lavender Cottage on that afternoon?"

Mallard's lips turned down. "No."

"And when the medical examiner assessed the scene, did he find anything to suggest that the murder took place anywhere other than in the cottage parlor?"

"No." Mallard sighed, then muttered, "Quite the opposite."

Penelope sensed that Mallard was at the point of accepting that his case against Henry simply wouldn't hold water, but to make certain of it, she shifted on the chair, and when Mallard and Stokes glanced her way, pointed out, "We shouldn't forget his lordship's horse. He tied it up in the lane where everyone in the village could see it, and everyone in Ashmore would know whose horse it was."

Mallard wrinkled his nose. "He made no effort to hide the fact he was there."

"Indeed." Stokes shut his notebook. "As matters stand, Mallard, there are no evidentiary grounds upon which to charge Lord Glossup with the murder of Viola Huntingdon."

Mallard's expression resembled that of a bulldog whose bone had been taken away. "But his lordship's late wife—"

"Was murdered by someone else," Stokes calmly cut in. "His lordship just happened to be in the house—his home—at the time."

Mallard frowned darkly at his blotter, then glanced at Stokes. "I know Scotland Yard sent down an inspector at the time, but I heard it was his first big case, and perhaps he got it wrong, and it was his lordship as killed his wife the whole time." Almost challengingly, Mallard went on,

"He killed then, and he's killed now. First his late wife and now, Viola Huntingdon."

His expression impassive, Stokes regarded Mallard levelly. "Superintending Constable Mallard, I would advise you to be very careful about making such wild accusations. As it happens, I was the investigating officer Scotland Yard sent to Glossup Hall five years ago, and I made no mistake in charging Ambrose Calvin with the murder of Catherine Glossup. Aside from all else, he confessed before a small army of witnesses, including"—Stokes glanced at Penelope and Barnaby—"Mrs. Adair's sister and brother-in-law and three of Mr. Adair's close friends, all of whom attended the same house party."

Barnaby thought Mallard looked like he'd swallowed a frog and didn't know if he was allowed to cough.

Smoothly, Stokes went on, "Now, where can I find the medical examiner—Mr. Carter, was it?"

Apparently struck dumb, Mallard nodded, then rather uncertainly pushed to his feet. He cleared his throat and gruffly said, "I'll show you to Carter's office."

They all rose and followed Mallard into the corridor. He led them up a flight of stairs and along a corridor to a door close to the corridor's end. He tapped perfunctorily on the panel, opened the door, glanced inside, then announced, "Inspector Stokes of Scotland Yard and his two consultants would like a word about the Huntingdon case."

With that, Mallard stepped back, and Penelope led the way into the office. Barnaby followed, and Stokes walked in behind him. As Stokes passed Mallard, Barnaby heard Stokes say, "That will be all for the moment, Mallard."

A cool dismissal, and while Mallard's features pinched, he accepted the unstated rebuke with a dip of his head and, reaching into the office, drew the door closed.

In Barnaby's eyes, Mallard definitely deserved the reprimand for his investigative blindness. While the case against Henry would never have prospered in court, being charged with murder would have been Henry's worst nightmare.

Penelope bustled eagerly into the medical examiner's office. She was keen to hear what facts he had to impart. After listening to Mallard's conjecturing for the past half hour, she was looking forward to getting her teeth into cold, hard evidence.

The man who rose from behind the desk to greet them was a surprisingly chipper individual. Carter was short, neat, and round, with a round cheery face and rotund torso. He had pale-brown hair and twinkling hazel eyes and appeared to be every bit as curious about them as Penelope was about his findings.

He smiled at her and Barnaby and half bowed, then held out his hand to Stokes. "Inspector. I'm Carter, medical examiner for the district."

Stokes introduced Barnaby and Penelope, and with a "Very pleased to meet you," Carter waved them to three chairs lined up before the desk. "I'd heard you were with Mallard and hoped you would stop by. It's quite a case, evidence wise." Carter resumed his seat and confided, "Mallard's generally a sound man, but in this instance, I fear he's picked the wrong bone to chew on."

Penelope pounced. "You don't think his lordship strangled Miss Huntingdon?"

"Well," Carter temporized, "based on what we know to this point, strictly speaking, it's possible he might have, but given the evidence I have to hand, it's difficult to see why he would have."

Stokes settled his notebook on his knee. "So what can you tell us?"

"Right, well, I went with Mallard to the scene—he's good like that, taking us along if we're here when he's called." Carter paused to marshal his facts. "The deceased was lying on her back in the parlor, a yard or so away from the hearth, the fire in which had burned to ash some considerable time before. The hearth was cold, as was the parlor, which allowed me to narrow the time of death despite the lengthy period between death and my examination of the corpse." Carter broke off and directed an apologetic look at Penelope. "I do hope my use of such terms won't offend you, Mrs. Adair."

Penelope smiled reassuringly. "I've attended several murder scenes in my time, Mr. Carter. Trust me when I say it would take a great deal more than properly used words to upset me."

Barnaby hid a grin. *Im*properly used words were forever a source of considerable offence to his wife.

"Good-oh. Well, as I was about to say," Carter went on, "based on my examination of the body, Miss Huntingdon was killed—strangled—sometime between noon and four o'clock on Thursday afternoon."

Stokes prompted, "Mallard mentioned a broken clock."

Carter nodded. "The carriage clock, which had fallen from the mantelpiece and broken and, apparently, stopped, showing the time as three-thirty-three. By all accounts, the clock should have been correct as to the time it displayed, so the implication is that the murder was committed at three-thirty-three that afternoon, which falls within the window defined by physiological criteria."

"Was Miss Huntingdon strangled by someone facing her?" Barnaby asked.

"Indeed, she was." Carter held up his hands, fingers splayed to either side and thumbs touching. "Like this."

"So," Stokes said, "it's likely she knew her murderer."

Carter agreed. "I would say so. There was nothing to suggest that she'd fled the clutches of a stranger, and I suspect that, with a lady of her age and type, there would have been signs of flight and struggle if she hadn't known the person. She allowed her murderer to get close, face to face, and there was very little by way of her fighting back."

"Would you say the murderer was taller than she was?" Penelope asked.

"Most definitely," Carter replied. "The deceased was of average height." Carter looked at Penelope. "Several inches taller than you, Mrs. Adair, and the angle of the pressure exerted by the murderer's thumbs strongly suggests that the murderer was at least a few inches taller than that."

Carter continued, "I would say you're looking for a man of at least average height, possibly taller. One reasonably strong, but a man with decent, average strength would, I believe, in this case, have been able to do the deed. Miss Huntingdon was a well-fleshed woman, but she was one of those very soft creatures, if you know what I mean. Very little muscle to speak of."

"Could the murderer be a woman?" Barnaby asked.

Carter waggled his head. "Hard to say, and I certainly can't say with absolute certainty, but in my view, a female as murderer is less likely. Not many women would be sufficiently tall and also sufficiently strong to exert the necessary pressure at that elevated angle." He paused, then added, "Based on what I saw at the scene, the attack was swift and over very quickly, again, in my opinion, arguing against a female. Whoever killed our victim did so in such a quick and forceful fashion that there was little resistance. For instance, the deceased had frizzy hair that she wore up in a neat bun. Despite the ordeal, very few strands of her hair had come loose. Also, I found no other wounds or even bruises on the body. And sadly, she was a nail-biter with nails bitten down to the quick, so even if she'd scratched at her attacker, I doubt she would have left any mark on him."

They were silent for a moment, digesting all that, then Penelope asked, "Was there anything else about the body or clothing that struck you as unexpected or odd?"

"Well, not about the clothing itself, but there was a very light dusting of white powder on the upper bodice of her gown. It's difficult to be certain with such a small amount, but I believe the powder is flour. Much as if the victim had eaten a floury bun and hadn't noticed that some flour had fallen down her front."

Stokes was deep in his note taking. "Who found the body?"

"The housekeeper, a Mrs. Gilroy. That was on the morning after the death. She doesn't live in and comes in most mornings from her cottage in the village."

When they didn't ask anything else, Carter straightened in his chair and said, "Something that might help you with your investigation—the constable who was summoned is a local lad, Constable William Price." Carter smiled self-deprecatingly. "He's my sister's boy and, if I do say so myself, observant and keen to be of help. You'll find him waiting at the cottage. I asked him to remain there and make sure that nothing was moved until you arrived and had a chance to examine the scene."

"Thank you!" Stokes uttered in sincerely heartfelt tones. He nodded to Carter. "For that alone, I'll keep an eye out for your nephew. He sounds like just the observant sort we'll need to pave our way."

Carter beamed. "It's a very small village—not even a village shop. Just a few cottages gathered around the village pond."

Stokes glanced inquiringly at Barnaby and Penelope, but there was nothing more they could think of to ask, and when appealed to, Carter confessed he had nothing more to tell them, and so, more cordially than with Mallard, they took their leave of the man and, with their brains now churning with assorted facts, headed outside.

CHAPTER 3

$\mathcal{I}$f Penelope had been ready to stretch her legs when they reached Salisbury, she was even more eager to quit the carriage when, some twenty miles farther on, it rolled into the tiny village—barely more than a hamlet—of Ashmore.

They'd elected not to stop at Tollard Royal on their way through in order to have as much time as possible before sunset to view Lavender Cottage and, they hoped, conduct their first interviews.

The carriage slowed to negotiate a left turn, and as it swung around, Penelope looked out to see a shallow pond in the center of a small expanse of green. "Henry said the Penroses' cottage, the one next to Lavender Cottage, was opposite the pond, so we must be close."

Stokes grunted and opened his eyes. "Good." He looked out of the carriage on the opposite side, then said, "There it is. I can see the lavender hedge."

Sure enough, the carriage slowed again, then rocked to a halt.

Stokes leaned forward, opened the door, and climbed out. Barnaby followed, and Penelope gripped the hand he offered and descended the carriage steps to the packed-earth surface of the narrow lane.

She paused to shake out her skirts, then straightened and looked around. The grassy area surrounding the roughly circular pond appeared to be the village green, but in such a small village in the middle of the afternoon, there was no one out strolling. The pond and green filled a triangular space south of the junction where Green Lane, on which

Penrose Cottage and Lavender Cottage stood, met the larger north-south road. The signpost at the junction labeled the road heading north as Noade Street, while south of the junction lay High Street.

With his hand at her waist, Barnaby urged Penelope toward the cottage, and she readily turned and walked to the gate. There, she paused to take in her first view of the victim's home. Behind the chest-high lavender hedge and beyond a bountiful cottage garden currently in autumnal decline sat a neat redbrick cottage typical of the area, with a lead roof and two medium-tall chimneys. The white-painted front door stood squarely in the middle of the front façade, flanked by twin bow windows with leaded panes. The window placements were echoed by dormer windows on the upper floor. Penelope suspected the cottage would prove to be one of the common two-up, two-down variety, yet the overall impact was of a residence of quiet prosperity.

Eager to investigate further, she glanced at Stokes, who had also halted by the gate.

Stokes had been studying the house and obligingly swung the gate wide. At that instant, the cottage's front door opened, and a young man looked out. He saw them, and his expression lightened, and he came quickly down the path. Judging by his crisp blue uniform and his eager expression, Penelope deduced that they were about to meet Constable Price.

By the time he reached them and halted, Constable Price had taken in Penelope and Barnaby's presence, and he was no longer so certain whom he was welcoming. Clearly deciding not to assume, he opened with "Can I help you?"

Stokes smiled approvingly. "We're hoping you will. Constable Price, I take it?"

"Indeed, sir." Price looked hopeful. "And you are?"

"Inspector Stokes from Scotland Yard, and these two are Mr. and Mrs. Adair. They act as consultants to Scotland Yard in certain investigations."

Price nodded respectfully. "Welcome to Ashmore, Inspector, ma'am, sir." He looked at Stokes. "Sir, as instructed, I've kept everyone out of the parlor and away from the area where the body was found and the medical examiner says the murder took place. But I'm afraid I haven't been able to keep the victim's sister, Miss Madeline Huntingdon, out of the house entirely. She stayed at the rectory on Saturday and Sunday nights, but on Monday afternoon, she insisted on moving back here, to the room she customarily uses when she visits. I did get her to agree not to touch anything in her sister's room, which is where most of the searching took place."

"Good work. That was sensible thinking." Stokes was sincere in his approval, and Price relaxed. Stokes waved up the path. "Now, please lead the way and guide us. The parlor first, I think."

"Yes, sir!" Price came to attention, turned smartly, and strode for the front door.

As she, Stokes, and Barnaby followed, Penelope noticed that both men were smiling, as was she.

"Ah," Barnaby murmured to Stokes, "to have the enthusiasm of youth."

Stokes's smile deepened, and he murmured back, "Regardless, I'm sure we're all grateful that he's managed to preserve the scene to the extent he has."

"Indeed," Penelope murmured, engaged in a critical survey of the large garden beds to either side of the path. Despite the season, the plantings offered up a profusion of color and artful displays composed of flowers and foliage. The path from the gate to the door was not quite straight and, as it wended slightly this way, then that, afforded varying perspectives of the garden's vistas.

They reached the front door, and Stokes waved Price ahead, then gestured for Penelope to follow. She did, entering a narrow front hall at the rear of which, to the right, an even narrower staircase ascended to the upper floor. To her immediate left, an open door gave onto what appeared to be the fateful parlor, while farther down the hall, opposite the bottom of the stairs, another door presumably led to the kitchen.

As Penelope paused at the parlor door and Barnaby and Stokes halted behind her, a woman stepped off the bottom stair and turned to face them.

She was tallish, with a stately figure and glossy reddish-brown hair gathered in a loose bun on top of her head. Her heart-shaped face, with its peaches-and-cream complexion, hosted a pair of large hazel eyes, a straight nose, and a determined if rounded chin. The woman moved toward them, and Penelope noted that she had excellent posture, which, combined with her other features, rendered her quite striking.

Her pallor and the lines of grief etched in her face made her identity obvious.

Penelope stepped past Price, who had halted by the parlor door, and extended her gloved hand. "Madeline Huntingdon?"

The lady frowned slightly but nodded and instinctively reached out and lightly grasped Penelope's fingers. "And you are?"

With her other hand, Penelope waved at Stokes. "This is Inspector Stokes of Scotland Yard, who has been called in to take charge of your sister's sad case. I am Mrs. Adair, and my husband and I act as official consultants to Scotland Yard and are often called on to assist in cases such as this."

"I see." Having taken stock of them, Madeline Huntingdon looked faintly overwhelmed.

Penelope offered their condolences on her sister's death, and Barnaby and Stokes echoed the sentiments.

Stokes glanced through the doorway at the disarranged parlor, then refocused on Madeline Huntingdon. "We appreciate that this is a difficult time for you, Miss Huntingdon. Perhaps we might sit in the kitchen, and you can tell us what you know of the circumstances of your sister's death."

Madeline visibly rallied, and a hint of determination entered her gaze, along with a tiny spark of curiosity directed Penelope's way. "Yes." Madeline stepped back and gestured to the kitchen door. "Please, do come through."

Penelope waved Madeline forward and followed, the men at her heels.

The kitchen proved to be a squarish area, with the range built into the inner wall and the back door directly opposite. Counters ran around the wall, with cupboards above and below, and a sink sat beneath a window that overlooked the rear garden.

"We can sit and talk in here." Madeline led them through an archway in the far wall to where a small round dining table circled by four straight-backed chairs sat in a nook at the corner of the ground floor. Windows on two sides shed ample light into the small chamber. As she claimed one of the chairs, Penelope noted that a door in the inner wall connected the dining room with the parlor and was glad it was firmly closed.

As the men claimed seats and Price took up an unobtrusive stance in the archway, Penelope turned her attention to Madeline Huntingdon and saw that Madeline's gaze had fixed on the closed door, and there was a haunted expression in her really very fine eyes.

Thinking to distract Madeline and set the tone for the interview, Penelope asked, "Was anything in the kitchen disturbed by the murderer?"

Madeline's attention immediately refocused, and she looked at Constable Price. "I have to admit I'm not entirely sure." Returning her gaze to Penelope, she explained, "Mrs. Gilroy had come in all unknowing, and she would have immediately tidied anything out of place."

Stokes drew out his notebook. "We'll ask Mrs. Gilroy when we speak with her."

Stokes looked at Penelope, clearly inviting her to lead the questioning.

She focused on Madeline. "If you would, Miss Huntingdon, can you give us a description of your sister, both in terms of physical state and of character? We've learned from experience that the more we know of the victim, the better our chances of understanding why someone might have wanted to kill them."

Madeline digested that, then nodded. "Yes, I see." She paused, clearly ordering her thoughts, then went on, "As far as I know, Viola was in excellent health and suffered from no chronic ailments of any sort. She was forty-two years old, hale and well, and should have lived for many more years. She wasn't a particularly vigorous person—she didn't ride or enjoy long walks. She and I grew up in Salisbury, and walking around the market and along the shops in Castle Street or as far as the cathedral was Viola's idea of a long ramble."

Madeline's lips had lightly curved, but her emerging smile wavered and fell. After a moment, she went on, "Character wise, she was…I suppose you would say a product of our upbringing as daughters of a minister. She was rigidly conservative in her views. It was important to her that everything was always as correct, as in its place, as it could be. As it should be. Society's rules were her framework for living, and much in the manner of a minister's wife, she viewed herself as a guardian of social mores." She glanced at Stokes and Barnaby. "It was no surprise to me that, once Viola moved down here to Ashmore, her closest friend was Mrs. Foswell, the minister's wife."

Stokes, jotting, nodded encouragingly, leaving it to Penelope to ask, "Was there ever any talk of Viola marrying? Either here or back in Salisbury?"

"No." Madeline paused, then amended, "At least, not until very recently. Prior to August, to my certain knowledge, Viola had never been interested in any man, and the subject of marriage had never arisen."

"For how long had your sister lived in the village?" Penelope asked. "We understand your father was a minister in Salisbury."

"Yes, Papa was the minister of St. Edmund's in Salisbury. He died just over five years ago and left us—Viola and me—quite well off." In explanation, Madeline added, "He was an investor of sorts and had done well in the railways, so our inheritance was larger than one might suppose. Viola took her half and bought this property. She'd always dreamed of living in a cottage in a small village." Madeline's voice quavered.

"And what did you do with your half?" Penelope promptly asked, once again hoping to distract Madeline.

Madeline drew in a deeper, calming breath, then replied, "With my half of our inheritance, I went to London and bought a house there, and I've lived there ever since." She looked at Penelope. "I visited Viola every few months and generally stayed for a week or even two. Although we lived apart and had different lives, we weren't estranged. It was simply that we liked different things, enjoyed different activities, and that was reflected in the lives we each chose and built for ourselves."

Penelope nodded understandingly. "I have much the same relationship with my sisters."

"Purely for the record," Stokes said, "what's your address in London?"

"Number twenty, Bedford Place."

Penelope knew the area. "Between Bloomsbury and Russell Squares." The observation wasn't a question. When, surprised, Madeline looked at her, Penelope explained, "I'm often in that area, visiting the university and associated departments."

Even more surprised, Madeline glanced at Barnaby and Stokes, then returned her gaze to Penelope and offered, "My house has three floors, and I live on the upper floor and lease the first-floor and ground-floor rooms to two history professors."

Penelope beamed. "Which ones? I know most of them."

Somewhat warily, Madeline answered, "Professor Atkins and Professor Gardner."

Penelope nodded. "Ancient history and Roman history. There must be many discussions in their rooms."

Madeline faintly smiled. "Indeed. They always seem to find some ruin to argue over."

Feeling that she—and Stokes and Barnaby, too—now had a very much firmer grasp of Madeline and her background as well as Viola's, Penelope glanced at Stokes, wordlessly passing him the questioning baton.

Accepting it, he said, "We were told you've reported that some of your sister's jewelry is missing, presumably the items the murderer searched for and took. Can you describe the pieces?"

"I can tell you about the bracelet," Madeline said. "It was my mother's, and my father passed it on to Viola on her twentieth birthday. She loved that piece and was deeply attached to it. She would rarely go on a visit anywhere without it on her wrist." Madeline went on to describe a simple antique gold setting framing seven decent-sized aquamarines. "I understand the stones were considered rather fine. As for the necklace, I never saw it. Viola said it had been given to her by her 'secret admirer, H,' whom she'd met since I was last here in early August. She wrote to me that the necklace was made to match the bracelet, and she described it as a beautiful and thoughtful gift."

"So this secret admirer definitely gave her the necklace?" Barnaby asked.

Madeline nodded. "He did, sometime in September, and she said it matched the bracelet perfectly. She was over the moon about it and giddily happy with it and him. Until this past week."

"Before we move on to why her opinion of the man changed," Stokes said, "are you certain both necklace and bracelet are gone?"

"Yes." Madeline sounded quite sure. "I know where Viola would have kept them—where she kept the bracelet—and I've checked, and they're definitely not there"—she glanced at Constable Price—"or anywhere else in the areas I've been allowed to search."

"Were any other items taken?" Penelope asked.

"No." Madeline frowned, puzzled. "Viola had some quite nice garnet drops and a silver cuff, and they are still in the box on her dressing table." She glanced at Price. "I had William check."

"So," Penelope mused, "it was only the aquamarine set—the bracelet and necklace—that was taken."

Madeline nodded, and Barnaby put in, "That suggests that this wasn't any random robbery conducted by someone after sellable goods."

"No," Penelope agreed. "Not if they passed up garnet earbobs. They're very much in fashion at the moment."

Barnaby glanced at Stokes, then ventured, "It's difficult to see the theft of jewelry of such lowly worth as sufficient inducement to murder."

A momentary silence fell while they all digested that.

"The only logical way," Penelope eventually said, "for the theft of the jewelry to be the motive for the murder is if the theft was in progress and

Viola walked in on the thief and recognized him. Then the threat of exposure becomes the motive."

"That won't wash," Stokes said. "Viola was killed in the parlor, not anywhere near where we believe she kept the jewelry, and there were no signs of her having fled there or of her fighting off an attacker."

"Huh," Penelope said. "So much for that idea."

Madeline had been nodding. "I, too, have been puzzling over how the missing jewelry links with Viola's murder." She glanced at Barnaby. "As you pointed out, the aquamarines are pretty, but not valuable enough to lure any serious thief." She shifted her gaze to Stokes. "To my mind, it keeps coming back to this 'secret admirer, H.'"

"As to that," Penelope said, "we've heard that you suggested that Lord Glossup was the man involved, as his name is Henry and there are no other gentlemen around whose names begin with *H*, and there is a similarity between the manner of your sister's murder and that of his lordship's late wife. However, the earlier murder was committed by someone else, who, indeed, confessed to the crime, and his lordship was in no way involved."

"As it happens," Stokes said with a faint smile directed at Penelope, "I was the investigating officer in charge of that case, and we unquestionably caught the right man. Consequently, any suggestion his lordship is responsible for your sister's death appears to be pure conjecture. We've checked with the senior man in Salisbury"—Stokes glanced at Price, presumably to make sure he was paying attention, which he was—"and there are no facts to support any case against Lord Glossup."

To their joint surprise, Madeline sighed and admitted, "I realized I'd allowed my grief and ill-judged rumors to sway my judgment. On calmer and more rational reflection, I must accept that an argument about a dog being a dog isn't a motive for murder, no matter the degree of heat involved. And yes, I can readily see Viola getting exceedingly hot under the collar over that. Quite aside from being very proud of her garden, she was something of a prude and tended to overreact to such occurrences."

At that point, Constable Price cleared his throat, and when they all looked his way, he colored slightly, but gamely volunteered, "I've asked around, Inspector, and several people say they've spotted a man, a gentleman by his dress, walking over the fields just north of here." With his head, he indicated the rear of the cottage. "No one saw him close up, not enough to identify. Could have been his lordship, far as anyone could tell, but the thing is, Glossup Hall lies south of the village, and I've never seen his lordship walk anywhere—he rides all about on that great bay hunter of his. Yet it seems this other gentleman was always on foot, and as it's easy to get from the fields to this cottage via the wood, he might have been the one who visited Miss Viola in secret, like." Price looked at Madeline. "Her secret admirer and all."

Stokes nodded. "Good work, constable. We'll need to speak with the villagers who saw this man later, but for now…" He returned his gaze to Madeline. "Do you have any idea who your sister's secret admirer might be?"

Madeline's lips thinned, and she shook her head. "She wouldn't say. I pressed her in my letters, but she clung to the information." She paused, then went on, "Viola hadn't had any suitors previously, and I think, when one came knocking, that she wanted to keep him, well, to herself for a time." Madeline looked at Penelope. "If that makes any sense."

Penelope nodded. "It does. She wanted to glory in the moment, and at the same time, from what you've said of her, she was very likely insecure enough to fear people thinking it was somehow wrong. She was forty-two, I think you said?"

Madeline nodded. "And she felt her age weighing on her—I know it troubled her, that she was alone and growing older. All those sorts of thoughts. But I have to say, she was never so taken with any gentleman as she was with this H, whoever he is. She was inherently suspicious and critical—some might say hypercritical—of others, especially unmarried men, but in her eyes, H could simply do no wrong. She was quite moon-struck, and in all our correspondence—we exchanged letters every week —she referred to him as 'my secret admirer, H.'"

"*Secret* admirer," Barnaby said. "She specifically labeled him that?"

Madeline nodded. "Virtually all the time. She wrote that he was hand-some—very handsome—and utterly charming." She made a faint, deri-sive sound. "He must have been to have won her over so completely."

"How long ago did she first mention him?" Stokes asked.

"About two months ago," Madeline said. "I last came to visit in late July and left in early August, and he didn't feature at that time. I would have known if Viola was trying to hide something from me, and she wasn't—not then." Madeline frowned, clearly thinking back. "I believe she first mentioned meeting some gentleman later in August, and by September, she'd started to refer to him as 'my secret admirer, H.'"

Stokes looked up from his notebook. "I understand you arrived here on Saturday."

Somewhat grimly, Madeline nodded. "Just as Viola's body was being taken from the cottage."

"That must have been a terrible shock," Penelope observed.

"It was." After a moment, Madeline focused on Stokes. "But to answer your unvoiced question, Inspector, Viola and I exchanged letters every week, mid-week. Last Thursday afternoon, I received her letter penned and posted on the morning of the Wednesday before, and all seemed entirely normal." She paused, then added, "Other than—and this is me reading between her lines—she seemed extra excited about H's next visit, and I got the strong impression she was expecting him to ask for her hand, if not at that time, then very soon after. She was, perhaps understandably, excited beyond description, which is more or less how she put it."

Madeline drew a deeper breath and went on, "Then on Friday afternoon, I received another, entirely unexpected letter in a very different tone. In it, Viola railed at Fate and *H* and wrote that she'd been betrayed and that she should have known better than to trust him and that I would understand once she explained, but the long and short of it was that she begged me to come down and support her." Madeline shrugged. "Of course I came. I was on the train first thing Saturday morning and arrived here early that afternoon, only to discover she'd been murdered." She paused, then added, "I nearly fainted when I saw her body. Constable Price was here and helped me inside, then sent for Mrs. Foswell and the Reverend, whom I know quite well."

Penelope was frowning. "This unexpected letter—did you bring it with you?"

Madeline blinked, then reached into her skirt pocket and pulled out a creased sheet of paper. She smoothed it out, looked at it for a moment, then handed it to Penelope. Speaking to Stokes, Madeline said, "I would like to keep the letter." Her gaze shifted to the sheet in Penelope's hands. "Those are the last words Viola wrote to me."

Stokes thought, then nodded. "I'll make a copy, and you can have the original back."

"Thank you," Madeline murmured, her gaze on Penelope.

Having scanned the letter, Penelope opted to read it aloud. "*Dearest — please, I implore you, if you can at all manage it, come down to Ashmore as soon as you can. I have discovered that H is a monster! He has deceived me most dreadfully and betrayed my trust at the deepest level. I should have known better than to place any faith whatsoever in a snake such as he, but I was dazzled. Charmed! You'll understand when I tell you his name! Please come immediately. I'm not sure how to manage the matter, but I am determined*—determined is underlined three times—*to see him pay for his perfidy! I need your wise counsel, my dear, and pray I will see you soon. Your loving sister, Viola."*

Barnaby had been studying Madeline, and in a deliberately matter-of-fact vein, observed, "It appears that your sister shot off the letter to you on Thursday morning and was killed on Thursday afternoon."

Price put in, "Miss Viola gave Mrs. Gilroy the letter to post when she left here at noon, it being her half day off. Mrs. G was surprised there was another letter so soon, and she says that Miss Viola was bothered about something and muttering to herself, which is not something she normally did."

"That's true," Madeline remarked.

Stokes had swiftly copied the letter and now handed it back to Madeline. "Purely for the record, Miss Huntingdon, and for completeness's sake, is there anyone in London who can vouch for you being there on Thursday afternoon?"

Madeline all but glared, but refolding the letter, said, "My live-in maid, of course, and I met with my lodgers on Thursday in the late afternoon. They'd invited me to tea and wanted to hear my opinion on the barrow mound recently found on Salisbury Plain."

Stokes's lips twitched as he jotted down the information. "Thank you." Then he looked up and asked, "Do you know of any local men with whom your sister recently had any disagreement?"

"Other than Lord Glossup and his dog, Viola has a long-running dispute with her neighbors, the Penroses. Over the past few years, Viola maintained that the Penrose orchard encroaches on Lavender Cottage land. Consequently, she felt justified in taking many of the apples from the offending trees. In turn, the Penroses accused her of stealing their apples. And so it went." Madeline shrugged. "I don't know the rights and wrongs of it, so I tried not to get involved. Other than that…" She paused, then rather reluctantly said, "Jim Swinson—he's the Penroses' man-of-all-work, but in his time off, he was Viola's gardener. He worked for her twice a week, I believe, but they didn't really get on. Not that I ever heard of any outright argument or any other reason for it, but there was always an undercurrent of irritation between them, and that went both ways."

Barnaby noticed that Constable Price had been nodding in confirmation of much of what Madeline said. "Anyone else?" Barnaby asked.

Madeline sighed. "I hesitate to mention it, but Viola made…well, not quite accusations, more like hurtful observations about Mrs. Gilroy's son, Billy. I could never fathom why Viola had taken so definitely against the lad, but I think that part of it was that Mrs. Gilroy is such a hard worker, and Billy certainly appears to be a layabout, scrounging off his mother rather than doing anything to help her. And again, the animosity between Viola and Billy was mutual, I would say, but on his part, it might simply have been a reaction to her nagging. I've heard Billy mouth off to Viola when he didn't know I was there to hear, and in turn, she would get on her high horse and lecture him about being such a drain on his poor mother's purse and so on." Madeline paused, then added, "Viola could be quite pointed and hurtful at times, and although I don't think she was actually malicious or intentionally vindictive, others could easily have taken her comments that way."

Barnaby noted that Constable Price was, in general, still nodding along to the bulk of Madeline's revelations.

"What about local friends?" Penelope asked. "You mentioned Mrs. Foswell, the minister's wife."

"Yes. Mrs. Foswell and Viola felt and thought along similar lines about many village matters, although I would say that Mrs. Foswell was generally more charitable. She tended to rein in Viola somewhat. Tact was never Viola's strong suit. I know Viola was on nodding terms with Iris Perkins and Gladys Hooper, but I'm unsure how deep in each other's confidences they were. But Viola and Mrs. Foswell were close, so if anyone can tell you more about recent village happenings in my sister's life, it will be Cynthia Foswell."

Penelope nodded determinedly. "We'll definitely be interviewing Mrs. Foswell."

Stokes tapped his pencil on the open page of his notebook, then looked at Madeline. "That brings us to the matter of finances and the possibility that your sister's wealth was a motive in her death."

Madeline colored faintly but returned Stokes's gaze levelly. "As I'm Viola's only kin, then I assume her portion—what's left of it—will come to me." She glanced around. "Along with this cottage and the attached land, which isn't all that extensive. I'm certain that she made no further will and that inheritance will be governed by our father's will. However, I can assure you that I have no need of Viola's money. I have my own funds and am hardly destitute."

"Well," Penelope prosaically pointed out, "if you own a house in Bedford Place, that's obviously the case."

Madeline's expression as she nodded suggested she was pleased to have that clearly stated.

Stokes caught Madeline's gaze. "Just so you are aware, we may need to confirm that with people in London. Purely by way of dotting our i's and crossing our t's."

Madeline's lips primmed, then she curtly said, "Check all you wish. You'll find all I've said borne out. My man-of-business in London is Mr. Thomas Glendower, and I'm sure he'll vouch for my financial standing."

Penelope grinned, and Barnaby smiled. Even Stokes looked faintly amused.

Seeing their reaction, Madeline looked at them, openly puzzled.

Penelope explained, "We're good friends with Thomas, and if you're one of his clients, then I believe we can take your financial standing as read."

Stokes also nodded. "I, too, am acquainted with Glendower, so yes, I accept that you being his client is sufficient testimony to you not coveting your sister's portion."

"Frankly," Penelope said, "you being a client of Thomas's only makes me more curious…" She broke off when Stokes shot a baleful glance her way, then grinned and concluded, "But perhaps that's a discussion for another day."

"Indeed." Stokes shut his notebook and half bowed over the table to Madeline. "Thank you for your help, Miss Huntingdon. If you don't mind, we would like to take a look at the parlor and the other rooms that were searched, and once we have, I can release them to you to tidy and clean as you wish."

"Thank you, Inspector." Madeline inclined her head. "That would be much appreciated."

Barnaby pushed away from the table, stood, and drew out Penelope's chair.

"Constable Price," Stokes said, making the young constable snap to attention. "If you would show us around?"

"Yes, of course, sir!" With an apologetic look at Madeline, Price moved to the closed door. "The parlor's through here."

Barnaby, Penelope, and Stokes followed Price into the room. The curtains had been left open, as they would have been on the Thursday afternoon, and there was more than enough light streaming inside for them to appreciate the salient points.

Price outlined where the body had been found, on the rug about a yard before the hearth on the side closer to the window. A low table had clearly been nudged farther away from the fireplace, leaving the rug beneath it slightly rucked.

It was Madeline, who had come as far as the doorway and was standing with her arms wrapped about her, who drew their attention to the carriage clock lying broken on the mantelpiece. "I gather that was found on the floor, not far from Viola's body."

Penelope picked up the clock. Standing beside her, Barnaby saw the hands frozen at three-thirty-three, just as Carter had reported.

"The clock was our father's, and Viola was very proud of it," Madeline said. "She always kept it correctly set and wound. She checked it every morning without fail."

Constable Price murmured, "Mrs. Gilroy said the same."

With Penelope and Stokes, Barnaby scanned the room, taking in the bright chintz in a pattern of roses that covered the sofa and was repeated in the curtains. There was little else to see, and with a nod to Price to lead the way, Stokes followed him into the hall and up the stairs.

Rather more slowly, looking about her with her usual eye for detail, Penelope followed, and Barnaby followed her. After dithering for a moment, Madeline came slowly up the stairs in their wake.

Price led them to what was plainly the main bedroom of the cottage, and it was instantly apparent that the room had been thoroughly ransacked. The dresser drawers had been pulled out and upended and the clothes that had been in them flung about. All the items on the dressing table had been disarranged, but the search had been more careful and methodical there.

Viewing the scene, Penelope stated, "He went first to the dressing table, expecting to find the jewelry there, but then he panicked and searched furiously everywhere."

From behind them, Madeline said, "That seems odd." When they turned to look inquiringly at her, she moved forward and past them, going toward the bedside table that stood between the bed and one wall. She stopped before she reached the small table and pointed at a box on the floor. "Viola kept the bracelet in that box."

A small blue-velvet-covered box, entirely empty, lay open and discarded on the rug.

Madeline pointed to the bedside table drawer, hauled out and flung against the wall. "She kept the box in that drawer." Madeline tipped her head, regarding the box. "Surely, he would have searched the bedside drawer before the chest of drawers." She turned to survey the clothes flung about the room. "So why bother with all this"—she flung out her hand—"and the mess elsewhere if he'd already found the jewelry he was after?"

For his part, Barnaby couldn't think of a good answer.

Finally, Stokes said, "Sometimes, murderers are so angry they act irrationally. He might simply have thoroughly lost his temper."

None of them, Barnaby suspected, felt entirely happy with that answer, but as there were no other clues waiting in the disarranged room or in the upended upstairs closet, within a few minutes, they were trooping back down the stairs.

"I wonder," Penelope said as they gathered in the front hall, "whether there's any way to trace the necklace." She looked at Stokes. "The bracelet design sounds sufficiently unique that any jeweler who had been asked to duplicate such a piece would surely remember who had commissioned the work. Especially given that it was only done in September."

Stokes stared at her for a moment, then nodded. "Good point. That might well be why he was so keen to take the necklace—and the bracelet, too." He looked at Madeline, who had followed them downstairs. "Can I trouble you to make a sketch of your sister's missing bracelet?"

"Of course." She appeared heartened to have something she could do that might help. "I'll work on it tonight and have a sketch ready for you in the morning."

"Thank you. We'll leave you now, Miss Huntingdon, but if you don't mind, I would feel considerably happier if you would allow Constable Price to put up here for the next few nights. I'll have need of his knowledge of the locals and the area. He could return with us to the inn at Tollard Royal, where we're staying, or remain with you as a guard, but I'm sincerely hoping you'll agree to the latter. At this point, we can't be sure that the only thing the murderer wanted was the jewelry. I would prefer not to risk him coming back for another look one night while you are the only one here."

Madeline's eyes had widened at Stokes's words. She glanced at Price, then smiled weakly. "If you don't mind staying, Constable, I admit I would feel more comfortable with someone else in the house."

Price's chest rose, and he saluted. "I'll be honored to remain on guard, miss." He looked at Stokes. "Inspector."

"Excellent. But for now, Price," Stokes said, "I would like you to take us to speak with the Penroses next door. Once we're finished there, you can return to Lavender Cottage." He looked at Madeline. "If that will suit?"

"That plan will suit admirably, Inspector." Madeleine seemed to have reclaimed a degree of natural confidence. "I need some air, so will be going out for a short walk, but I'll be back by six if not before."

Stokes nodded, and Barnaby and Penelope took their leave, then the three of them followed Constable Price down the path, out of the gate, and along the lane to the cottage next door.

CHAPTER 4

*P*enelope followed Constable Price up the ruler-straight brick-paved path that led to the front door of the uninventively named Penrose Cottage.

The contrast between the front gardens of the neighboring cottages could not have been more marked. Where Lavender Cottage's garden was whimsical, soft, and fluttery, this garden was bare clipped lawn with a single large beech tree, already mostly leafless, to the right of the path. Despite that, there was not a single leaf to be seen dotting the lawn, and the edges of the path had been recently trimmed with ruthless precision.

No softness, Penelope thought, *and little delight.*

She halted behind Constable Price when he stopped on the narrow porch and beat a crisp *rat-a-tat-tat* on the front door.

As the door opened, the young constable stepped back, and Penelope found herself facing a tallish middle-aged woman in a plain, dark-colored gown. Her graying hair was pulled back so tightly from her angular face that it almost made Penelope wince in sympathy. The woman's dark eyes and sharp features set in a long face presently wearing a dour expression reminded Penelope of the garden—no softness, little delight. Indeed, everything about the woman screamed neat, no-frills practicality.

The woman's dark gaze swept over their party, and before any of them could speak, she stated, "I'm Ida Penrose. Who are you?"

Stokes stepped up beside Penelope. "I'm Inspector Stokes of Scotland Yard." He proceeded to introduce Penelope and Barnaby, then said, "We would like a word with you, Mrs. Penrose, and also your husband, Arthur, and Jim Swinson, if he's about."

"Arthur and Jim are busy in the orchard out back," Ida flatly stated.

Undeterred, Stokes replied, "In that case, perhaps we can have a word with you first. Inside would be preferable."

Ida's gaze went to the lane behind them, then returned to Stokes. "Of course." She stepped back and waved them in. "I assume this is about that dreadful business with Viola Huntingdon."

"Indeed," Stokes replied.

Penelope urged Stokes to lead the way, and after throwing her a curious glance, he obliged, following Mrs. Penrose deeper into the hall. Penelope followed more slowly, using the moment to look about her. Somewhat to her surprise, she found the atmosphere in the cottage oddly stifling, as if the house had been closed up or the owners didn't appreciate fresh air. As they followed Ida Penrose, with her determined stride and no-nonsense countrywoman's attitude, into the cottage's scrupulously neat parlor, Penelope judged the latter cause more likely.

Mrs. Penrose halted before one of the armchairs to one side of the fireplace and waved her visitors to the sofa and matching chair. Penelope claimed a place on the rather hard sofa, and with his customary elegance, Barnaby sat beside her. Stokes took the spare armchair, and Constable Price again elected to stand unobtrusively by the door.

After seeing her guests seated, Ida Penrose subsided onto her chair and bluntly stated, "I can't see how I can help you. We never heard anything from next door on Thursday afternoon." She eyed them intently. "That's when she was done for, wasn't it?"

"We believe so," Stokes replied, setting his notebook on his knee. "However, we're here to ask you for your opinion of Miss Huntingdon. Did you get along with her?"

Ida Penrose glanced at Constable Price, then returned her gaze to Stokes. "One doesn't wish to speak ill of the dead."

"Naturally not," Penelope said. "But in this case, we need to learn about the victim in order to understand who might have murdered her, and I'm sure everyone in the village will be keen to see the murderer caught."

Ida's dark gaze had settled on Penelope, and Ida appeared to consider her words, then slowly, she inclined her head. "That's true enough. So, it's common knowledge that Viola Huntingdon was not an easy woman to like. She always insisted things had to be done the way she thought they ought, and her way was the only way, and she was the judge of it all. As if she was better than most of us villagers." Ida's face clouded. "For instance, she liked all those fussy flowers, and we don't. My Arthur would have a conniption if we had an untidy garden like that. He doesn't like untidiness."

Well, Penelope thought, *that was the front garden explained.*

"But," Ida went on, "Viola was forever sniping about people who had no pride in their property and how it just showed." Ida paused, then added, "Mind you, she never said what it showed. She just used the issue to make a point."

"I see." Stokes was jotting in his book. "So in the main, your difficulties with Viola Huntingdon were over relatively minor matters—the usual sort of neighborly tensions."

Ida thought, then allowed, "I suppose they were. Nothing I'd think to murder her for, if that's what you're asking."

Stokes inclined his head in acceptance of the statement. "Purely for our records, where were you on Thursday afternoon?"

Ida paused as if thinking, then replied, "Thursday afternoon, I was here. I was in the kitchen baking scones, then I had Iris Perkins and Gladys Hooper around for afternoon tea." She focused on Stokes. "It was when they were leaving that they saw his lordship coming out from Lavender Cottage."

His gaze on his writing, Stokes nodded. "Thank you."

"Returning to the matter of gardens," Penelope said, "we understand that your man-of-all-work, Jim Swinson, tended Miss Huntingdon's garden. Did that cause any ructions?"

"Not really." Ida had the sort of face on which expressions were muted and therefore hard to read. "Jim said it gave him flowers and such to work with. He's one as likes to work outside, and he helps Arthur in the orchard and fields, so I can understand that it was a bit of something different for him, and he was only over there on his days off from us."

"Did Jim and Viola Huntingdon get on?" Barnaby asked.

"Not especially," Ida admitted. "They weren't what you would call friendly to each other, but you'll need to speak with Jim about that."

Stokes asked, "Are you aware of any specific incident between Jim and Viola?"

Ida shook her head. "Not that I ever heard of, but Jim's not one to say much about others, and Viola would never have said anything about any disagreement to me."

"Very well. Now"—Stokes raised his head and fixed his gaze on Ida—"was there any specific cause of disagreement between your husband and Viola Huntingdon?"

Ida's expression hardened, and she glanced, narrow-eyed, at Constable Price. "No doubt you've heard"—she swung her gaze back to Stokes—"that there was a disagreement between my Arthur and Viola Huntingdon about the boundary of the orchard. These are old parcels of land, and I don't know how anyone can know the rights of such things, but Viola insisted that the boundary lay more over our way, which meant that the three most easterly rows of Arthur's prize apple trees were on her land, not ours."

Ida shook her head. "They've been on about it for months now, and no one knows who has the right of it, but with the season's apples just in, there was such an argy-bargy outside the church Sunday before last that Reverend Foswell had to step between them and tell them both to go home and cool off. He told them once they'd calmed, they should sit down and sort it out once and for all. Not that they did." Ida sighed heavily. "All the village is as sick of the to-do as I am."

Stokes sent a questioning look at Barnaby and Penelope, one Penelope interpreted as wondering if Arthur Penrose or even some other irritated villager had thought to put an end to the dispute in a more direct and permanent fashion.

That was certainly something to ponder.

Stokes glanced at his notebook, then looked at Ida. "One last question, Mrs. Penrose. Did you see anyone acting suspiciously around Lavender Cottage in the days or even weeks prior to Miss Huntingdon's death?"

Ida primmed her lips, then volunteered, "Depends on what you call suspicious. Over the past few weeks, I've seen some man—gentleman, he looked like—walking over the fields toward Viola's cottage. He was never close enough that I could see who he was. There's a gap in the trees, and when I'm standing at my sink, I can see across the fields a fair way. I couldn't imagine why a gentleman would be taking the path through the fields, but I saw him clear as day at least three times." She paused, then added, "I did note that it was always on the afternoons that Pat Gilroy had off."

Ida focused on Stokes. "I mentioned seeing the bloke one day, and Jim said as he'd seen him, too. No surprise as Jim's out in the fields more often than not. He might be able to tell you more."

Stokes nodded. "Thank you. That might be relevant." He looked up and faintly arched his brows at Barnaby and Penelope, but both shook their heads. They had no further questions for Ida Penrose.

Stokes returned his gaze to Ida. "Thank you for your time, Mrs. Penrose. Now, if we go down to the orchard, I take it we'll find your husband and Jim Swinson there."

"Like as not," Ida said, pushing to her feet. "But with the light waning, they'll be packing up their tools and coming in soon."

Stokes, Barnaby, and Penelope rose.

With a smile, Stokes promised, "We won't keep them long."

They left Penrose Cottage via the back door and, with Constable Price assisting, followed Mrs. Penrose's directions to a large, well-established, and healthy-looking orchard. The trees were old, their trunks gnarly, but they were plainly well cared for, pruned, shaped, and nurtured. Although by now all the fruit had been picked and carted away, the scents of ripe plums, apples, and pears still hung in the air.

Walking beside Penelope along the path between the rows of trees, Barnaby noted that their footsteps were deadened by the thick layer of fallen leaves. Consequently, they saw Jim Swinson and Arthur Penrose before the pair, who were busy gathering various tools and placing them in canvas slings, noticed them.

Eventually hearing their approach, the men glanced up, then put down their tools, straightened, and faced them.

Arthur Penrose was a short, slight, wiry man somewhere in his late forties, while Jim Swinson was much younger, perhaps twenty-two or -three, and was taller by a head and more. As broad as he was tall and solid with it, he was a strong, young working countryman. Both men were dressed in typical country worker's garb of thick canvas trousers, warm shirt, and worn jacket, with heavy well-scuffed boots on their feet.

Constable Price hailed the pair, and when their group halted before the men, Price introduced Stokes, then Stokes introduced Barnaby and Penelope.

Although plainly curious, the men bobbed their heads respectfully and mumbled greetings.

Stokes calmly stated, "As I'm sure you've guessed, we're here to investigate Miss Huntingdon's death, and we're currently gathering whatever information people have to share about the victim. As you know, she was murdered in her parlor last Thursday afternoon, at some point between twelve and four o'clock."

Arthur Penrose's rather shaggy brows rose. "That early, was it?"

"It seems likely," Stokes said, "that Miss Huntingdon was dead at the time Lord Glossup called at her cottage at four-thirty, and she failed to come to the door."

"Ah." Jim Swinson nodded. "You know about his lordship calling, then, and his argument with Miss Huntingdon that morning."

"Yes. We have heard about that," Stokes replied. "What we've come here to ask is for confirmation, Mr. Penrose, of your ongoing disagreement with Miss Huntingdon over the boundary of your property."

That was enough to get Arthur Penrose to share his angst in exhaustive detail. "She had no right, I tell you, but she took those apples before we got to them. It had to have been her, because who else could it have been, and smug as a goose, she was, when I asked her about it."

He carried on at some length, arguing the minutiae of the competing claims, but although the matter plainly exercised his temper and was, to him, a deeply serious issue, Barnaby caught no hint of the sort of deep-seated fury that might prompt a man like Arthur Penrose to murder.

He was irritated and annoyed by Viola and her claim, but moved to murder?

Indeed, as short and slight as Arthur was, it was difficult to see how he could have strangled Viola Huntingdon. Arthur was only slightly taller than Penelope, who was distinctly petite. According to Carter, Viola Huntingdon had been of average height and her murderer taller still.

To strangle Viola, Arthur would have had to stand on a stool, and such a scenario really wouldn't fly.

While Arthur continued with his plaint, Barnaby shifted his gaze to Jim Swinson. Jim could have committed the crime without the slightest difficulty. Just looking at him was enough to assure the observer that he was strong and able. He was also the type of quiet countryman of few words, stoic in the face of whatever life threw his way, and therefore very difficult to read.

Finally, Arthur wound down, and Stokes asked, "Where were you on Thursday afternoon, Mr. Penrose? We're asking everyone in the village so that we know who was around about."

Arthur looked at them, then shifted his gaze beyond them. Then he pointed farther along the row of trees, deeper into the orchard. "I was over thereabouts. Jim and I had got that far with the neatening and pruning."

Barnaby swung around and surveyed the area, then turned back to Arthur. "So you and Jim were here all that afternoon?"

Arthur and Jim nodded, and Arthur confirmed, "Aye, until about now. We don't waste daylight when we have a clear day, and Thursday last was clear."

Stokes regarded the pair. "Were you always within sight of each other? Neither of you left at any time, even for just a few minutes?"

Arthur and Jim looked at each other, then both looked at Stokes and shook their heads.

"We were here together," Jim said. "We were pruning those trees down there, and they're old and the branches big enough that it's easier to do with four hands. We'd've noticed if one of us wasn't there."

Arthur nodded. "We'd've had to stop, and that would've slowed us down. A lot."

"Thank you." Stokes turned his attention to Jim. "Given you were here, we can strike you out as a potential suspect as well. However, we understand that you worked for Miss Huntingdon for two days a week and that you weren't entirely happy in her employ."

Jim frowned, then offered, "It wasn't the work—I was happy doing that. Her garden is different from here or from fields or orchards. It was always interesting, and I liked that. But she...well, she wasn't what you would call nice. She was always finding fault, not with me and my work so much as with everyone around. She was forever complaining and carping about this or that as if she was better than all those hereabouts. I learned to switch off me ears, most of the time. Had to if I wanted to work in her garden, and I did. I had the time, and she paid well and promptly. She never tried to chouse me out of my coin, I will say that for her."

"I see." Stokes was furiously scribbling. "So it was her personality that was the issue—she grated on your nerves, so to speak."

Jim nodded. "Aye, that's it. But that's not the sort of thing one kills over, is it?"

Stokes managed not to sigh. "No, and as I said, neither you nor Mr. Penrose are suspects. But we also wanted to ask you both if you'd noticed anyone lurking around Lavender Cottage in the weeks before Miss Huntingdon's murder."

Barnaby knew that Stokes and Penelope were as eager to hear what Jim would say as he was.

Jim didn't disappoint. "There was this one bloke—a gentleman, I'd say, given how he was dressed and the way he walked. I've seen him over the past weeks, mayhap for over a month now, walking back and forth along the right-of-way at the back of Lavender Cottage. I never saw him close enough to say who he was, and I never actually saw him going into the cottage nor even into the rear garden—that's screened by the woodland. But he was always headed that way or coming from that direction, so I don't know where else he might have been going if it wasn't to see Miss Viola."

Arthur was nodding. "I was with Jim once when he saw the fellow. I caught just a glimpse, but like Jim said, he looked to be a gentleman heading for Lavender Cottage." Arthur paused, then added, "If Viola had been a different sort of lady, I would've called around sometime and just asked about him—just checking in a neighborly way. But if I'd've asked her, she would likely have taken on about us spying on her or some such, so I didn't say anything." Arthur grimaced. "Now she's been killed in such a way, no matter how obstreperous she was, I kind of wish I had."

Stokes inclined his head. "Thank you both. That's all very clear."

Penelope finally spoke. "Do you remember what days you saw this man? Can you recall whether those were the days Mrs. Gilroy had off?"

"Well," Jim said, "it was only four times that I saw him, and it was mostly afternoons, but I'm sure once was a Friday morning, and Mrs. Gilroy's half days are on Thursday and Sunday afternoons."

Arthur shifted and said, "But Pat Gilroy goes to the market on Friday mornings, so she's not at the cottage then, either."

"Oh, aye." Jim nodded. "I'd forgotten about that." He looked at Penelope. "I guess you could say that I only saw him when Mrs. G wasn't at the cottage."

"Thank you." Stokes had written the information down. "Now, is there anything you know about Miss Huntingdon's movements on the days before her death that was any different to what she normally might do?"

Jim frowned. "I'm not sure if this is what you want to know, but I drove her into Salisbury that Wednesday."

"The day before she was killed?" Barnaby clarified.

Jim nodded. "I drove her into town about once a month, sometimes more often. Wednesday is one of my days off, and I have a gig, and she used to ask me to drive her in whenever she needed to go there. She didn't have any other way to get to town unless she went with Mrs. Foswell in the Foswells' carriage, and she sometimes did that, too. But last Tuesday, she asked me to drive her in on the Wednesday. As I've said, that wasn't unusual, and she was in her usual mood on the way there. If anything, I'd've said she was eager and looking forward to doing something in town. I dropped her off where I always do, at the nearest corner of the market. I've a mate who works at the Hare and Hounds, and I always go there for a pint and a bite and a chinwag while I wait for Miss Viola to do whatever she was there to do."

"Last Wednesday"—Stokes was scribbling furiously—"was she there for long?"

"Well, she said she'd be just an hour, and I was to pick her up at the same spot I left her—by the market cross. I got there at the right time, and she's usually waiting ready to go, but not that time. I waited, and eventually she rushed up, more than half an hour late. That was odd. And she was out of breath, too—I could see she'd been hurrying—and that wasn't normal for her, either. Very cool and correct, she was. Never flustered, yet she was that time."

"Did she say anything about what had happened?" Penelope asked.

"Or about what she'd done or where she'd gone in Salisbury?" Barnaby added.

But Jim shook his head. "She never did speak to me much. That was just her way. She didn't talk to staff unless she wanted to, and in general, I suppose, she didn't believe we was worth sharing things with." He paused, clearly thinking back, then added, "Mind you, this time—last Wednesday—the way she sat there, all bottled up, I thought that at any moment, she was going to burst into tears or start raving at something. And the farther we drove, the more she grew…I think it was angry? Angry and upset with it. But by the time we rolled into the village, she'd swallowed it all back down, I'd say. Just pushed whatever she was feeling down inside and locked it away, but it still seemed like, inside, she was a powder keg ready to blow, yet she was determined to behave normally on the outside."

Jim suddenly looked faintly embarrassed. "That's just me talking, mind. She didn't say anything about her feelings to me. And that was the last I saw of her. She paid me as usual, then she turned and hurried up the path—and she didn't normally hurry, especially not like that, with her shoulders all hunched up and looking down but not seeming to see."

Barnaby was quietly amazed by just how observant and insightful Jim Swinson had been. It just went to show one shouldn't assume those who were quiet didn't pay attention.

Stokes had been jotting madly. Finally, he looked up and shut his notebook. "Thank you. Your information is likely to be very helpful. Aside from all else, we now know that Miss Huntingdon went to Salisbury on the day before she died, and there, she learned something that overset her."

"Aye." Jim nodded. "She did that."

Stokes thanked both men again, and Barnaby and Penelope echoed his words, then they left Arthur and Jim to finish gathering their tools and, with Constable Price, headed out of the orchard.

As they rounded the house and crossed the front lawn, passing under the leafless beech, Penelope juggled the new facts into some semblance of order in her mind. The shadows were lengthening as they passed through the gate and stepped into the lane.

A well-dressed lady garbed all in black had been walking toward the junction, but at the sound of the gate swinging, she halted and whirled, then seeing them, she came striding back.

Their party halted, and Constable Price murmured, "Mrs. Foswell, the minister's wife."

"Good afternoon," Mrs. Foswell called as soon as she was within speaking range. "I'm Mrs. Foswell, and Viola Huntingdon was a dear friend. I've just come from the cottage. I thought to call on poor Madeline and ensure she has all she needs, but she appears to be out. That said, I had also hoped to come across you." She paused, then asked, "You are the investigators sent to find Viola's murderer?" She immediately answered herself, "Of course you are." She nodded to Price. "William."

The young constable knew his role and promptly introduced Stokes, who then did the honors for Barnaby and Penelope.

Mrs. Foswell looked suitably impressed as she exchanged nods. "I'm sure Viola would feel relieved to know her sad death will be investigated by such senior people. Now"—she stood straighter, raising her chin to a commanding angle—"I want to render whatever help I can. This is a small village, and that such an incident could occur within our community is quite shocking. It simply cannot be tolerated."

Penelope felt Stokes's elbow nudge into her side. "Thank you, Mrs. Foswell." Penelope could already see some of what the minister's wife and Viola Huntingdon had had in common. "Would that everyone was as forthcoming when we seek to investigate a crime. In this instance, at this point, it would be most helpful if you could share your view of the deceased. We've been given to understand that Miss Huntingdon wasn't universally appreciated."

MARRIAGE AND MURDER   63

Mrs. Foswell sighed. "No, indeed. That's quite true, although it was purely because Viola not just saw but commented on people's shortcomings. She saw that as her role—to help people face their faults and therefore fix them. She wasn't one to let what she saw as bad or inadequate behavior slide by unremarked. She had quite high standards, both for herself and for those about her." Mrs. Foswell's expression grew resigned. "Sadly, Viola wasn't the most tactful person in her interactions with others."

Penelope thought those comments neatly summarized all they'd heard of Viola's behavior. Tact had definitely been something she'd lacked. Penelope ventured, "We've heard that you were Viola's closest friend. Madeline has told us of the gentleman Viola had written to her about, the one who had recently come into her life. Did Viola mention anything of that man to you?"

Mrs. Foswell's expression grew faintly hurt. "No. She never mentioned such a person at all." She drew breath, paused, then said, "Frankly, I was surprised to hear of this mystery man. I've seen the letter Madeline received, and while I hesitate to suggest such a thing, I have to wonder if, perhaps, the man wasn't a figment of Viola's imagination. Something to make herself sound more interesting to her sister, who I believe Viola was just a touch jealous of, and then she further embellished the fiction to make herself seem even more dramatic." Mrs. Foswell looked meaningfully at Penelope. "If you know what I mean."

"Yes, I see." Penelope considered Mrs. Foswell's suggestion for all of three seconds, but the man seen striding across the fields had been real, and whoever strangled Viola had certainly not been imaginary. "On another point," Penelope went on, "we've heard of Viola's aquamarine bracelet. Do you recall seeing it?"

"Of course." Mrs. Foswell proceeded to give a decent description that matched what Madeline had told them. "Viola wore the piece whenever she went anywhere beyond the cottage."

"Did you see the matching necklace Viola told her sister her admirer had given her?" Penelope asked.

Mrs. Foswell's features pinched, hurt once again surfacing. "No. I never saw any necklace, just the bracelet."

Penelope smiled at the older woman. "Thank you for your frankness, Mrs. Foswell. You've given us quite a few points to ponder."

"Yes, well." Mrs. Foswell appeared somewhat mollified. "If there's anything else I or David—Reverend Foswell—can help with, please do call on us."

Stokes assured her they would do so, and they parted with good wishes all around.

Stokes commended Constable Price for his assistance that day and dispatched him to stand guard at Lavender Cottage, then with Barnaby and Penelope, turned toward their carriage, still waiting in the lane.

As they walked, Penelope mused, "In actual fact, in one afternoon of investigating, we've learned quite a lot."

"But how it all fits," Barnaby said, reaching for the carriage door, "and who the man who strangled Viola Huntingdon is remains very much up in the air."

"I vote," Stokes said, "that we get ourselves to the comfort of the King John Inn, then after a good dinner to replenish our reserves, we put our heads together and see what we can make of what we've learned."

Madeline stood on the front porch of Glossup Hall and stared at the impressively solid dark-green-painted door.

Lord Glossup's residence was significantly larger than she'd imagined, a sprawling Elizabethan mansion with two wide wings stretching away on either side of a central block topped with a tower. The redbrick façade faced south and boasted three stories topped by a lead roof edged with a crenelated balustrade beyond which a plethora of tall chimneys with ornate pots reached skyward. The last red rays of the setting sun reflected off the mullioned windows as Madeline glanced back, across the circular forecourt to the mouth of the tree-lined drive she'd taken after following Ashmore's High Street southward.

The sun was sinking toward the horizon, and it was getting quite dark. She should have waited until tomorrow, but the need to get her apology to his lordship done and off her chest had compelled her, and she'd set out for the Hall without any real thought for how long it would take to reach the place.

She didn't think anyone had noticed her arrival. She could leave and return tomorrow, and no one would be the wiser.

But that would mean another night of amorphous guilt weighing on her soul.

She turned back to the door, drew in a deep breath, and lips firming, grasped the bell chain and tugged.

She fidgeted and waited, then the door was opened by a kindly-looking butler.

He smiled at her as if finding unknown ladies on the doorstep was nothing new. "Good afternoon, ma'am. Can I help you?"

Madeline raised her chin a notch and announced, "My name is Miss Huntingdon, and I would like to speak with Lord Glossup." After a second, she added, "If that's possible."

The butler bowed. "I will inquire of his lordship, but please, Miss Huntingdon, do come inside."

Madeline stepped across the threshold, expecting a dark and gloomy interior. Instead, the high-ceilinged front hall was well-lit by windows in the tower above, giving the space a surprisingly airy quality.

"Your coat and bonnet, miss?"

"Oh yes." Madeline unbuttoned and shrugged out of her fashionable redingote and unpinned and handed the butler her bonnet.

He took both and set them on the coatrack, then led her to an open door that gave onto a comfortable and—given its size—remarkably cozy drawing room. "If you will take a seat, ma'am, I will let his lordship know you've called."

With an acquiescent dip of her head, Madeline moved into the room and heard the door quietly shut behind her. Curious, she looked around. Her first impression was one of quiet gentility, the sort that sees no need to prove itself to anyone. The room was long and furnished with well-padded armchairs and sofas. She walked to the far end, where a large hearth topped by a massive stone mantelpiece played host to a good-sized fire. A sofa set perpendicular to the flames seemed the most appropriate perch, and she sank onto the satin-covered cushion and arranged her skirts, then clasped her hands in her lap and prepared to wait for however long his lordship decreed with some semblance of patience.

Almost a penance. She glanced at the large ormolu clock squatting at the center of the mantelpiece and saw the time was nearing five-thirty.

The click of the doorlatch had her looking toward the door, expecting to see the butler returning.

Instead, Henry, Lord Glossup, stepped tentatively into the room, his gaze fixing on her rather trepidatiously.

Oh! He doesn't know if I'm here to rail at him or…

Madeline rose and blurted, "Thank you for seeing me, especially at this odd hour. I simply had to come and apologize for my unconscionable, ill-considered, and utterly wrongheaded outburst on Sunday. I shouldn't have listened to those silly rumors, and I'm most dreadfully sorry for any wounds I might have unthinkingly caused."

She immediately felt better for having got the words out. They hadn't been any part of her stuffy rehearsed apology, but she felt the uncensored words had expressed her feelings more accurately.

His lordship's relief was evident in his expression. The tight lines relaxed, and as he came forward with greater confidence, with a firm stride and upright posture, Madeline got the distinct impression of a kindly man, but not a weak one—the quiet sort that people often referred to as the backbone of the counties.

He halted two yards away and half bowed. "Miss Huntingdon. In the circumstances, I'm delighted to welcome you to Glossup Hall." He smiled as he straightened, and the gesture warmed his brown eyes. "Perhaps we might start afresh."

She eyed him, then said, "I need to know that you accept my apology. I very much needed to make it, and my only excuse for my deplorable words was that I was laboring under considerable and entirely unexpected grief, and to be truthful, I was so very angry at whoever had so cruelly taken Viola from this world that I allowed those emotions to temporarily overcome my better judgment. I pray you'll forgive—"

He waved his hand as if sweeping the air between them clear. "I quite understand, and your apology is gratefully accepted. And while I admit I found the incident regrettable, I sincerely hope we can put it behind us. In that vein"—he waved her to the sofa—"please allow me to offer you some refreshment. If you walked all this way from the village, you can surely do with a small glass of sherry."

The latter was a question, and sinking onto the satin sofa, Madeline discovered she was, indeed, parched. "Thank you. That would be most welcome."

As she watched him walk to the tantalus against one wall, she realized that while she'd rehearsed her apology, she hadn't thought of what would come after.

He returned with two glasses of golden liquid and handed one to her. She took it and wondered why she didn't find the situation impossibly awkward; she would have predicted she would.

As his lordship moved to claim the armchair opposite, she sipped the unsurprisingly excellent amontillado and hoped its rich smoothness was a portent for how the rest of her visit would go.

After settling in the armchair, he fixed his gaze on her and said, "You must remember that I, of all people, fully comprehend the…shall we say confusion that strikes one when someone close is shockingly murdered. One doesn't see it coming—not at all—and so is entirely unprepared for all the conflicting and often violent and irrational emotions that arise. Such as"—his lips quirked wryly—"that our nearest-and-dearest victim should have known better and somehow avoided their fate."

Madeline lowered her glass and stared at him. All she could manage was a whispered "Yes."

"And the next thought," he went on, "that grows to an obsession is whether there was anything one might have done, or done differently, that would have changed the outcome."

"Exactly," Madeline breathed. He was patently sincere, and clearly, he was speaking from his own experience. And he'd put his finger squarely on the thoughts that had initially crowded her mind.

Henry sipped and studied his unexpected guest and was aware of an impulse—almost a compulsion—to prolong her visit. "I understand you live in London, yet I'm sure I've glimpsed you here, at the church and around the village, on several occasions before."

She nodded. "I visit—visited—Viola several times each year." She paused, then admitted, "It seems so strange that she won't be here next time I come down."

"You'll keep the cottage?" Henry almost blushed and hurried to say, "Forgive me if I've presumed, but I assume there are no other close relatives, and you will inherit?"

"Yes, that's correct. And honestly, I'm rather torn." She paused, sipped, then continued, "Although in recent years—well, the past five—I've made my home in London, my roots are, if not in this village, then in this area."

"You were born and raised here?"

She nodded. "In Salisbury."

Madeline didn't quite know how it happened, but prompted by gentle and unassuming questions, she found herself telling his lordship about her early life in Salisbury growing up as the daughter of the minister of St. Edmund's Church. "Our mother died when I was quite young, and despite

Papa's best efforts, my upbringing was rather constrained by circumstance. But Papa always encouraged us to think and live in the wider world, which I took to heart more than Viola. She was content with living quietly, while I wanted to experience at least a little more of life. That's why, after Papa died, she came here while I went to London."

His lordship was regarding her without the slightest judgment and an expression that stated he was interested in learning more about her, the person.

She found that look more intoxicating than his sherry.

Consequently, when he rather boldly observed, "I own to being surprised no gentleman managed to persuade you to be his bride," she laughed and answered, "Several attempted it, but a lucky escape from a fortune hunter when I was quite young and still in Salisbury rather colored my view of gentlemen and taught me to be duly careful and discerning over those who came calling."

She paused, then added, "Indeed, that lucky escape was in part the reason why, when Papa's death left me able to make a choice, rather than seeking to marry, I opted to go to London and set about making a life of my own, one that didn't rely on any man for its meaning."

"That was forward-thinking of you." Unexpected approval rang in his lordship's tone.

To her surprise, Madeline found herself confessing, "I sometimes think I should feel grateful to that long-ago fortune hunter. He knew I would eventually be wealthy through inheritance and that I was besotted with him, but he found my independent ways too challenging and so rejected me. At least he was honest enough to do that rather than condemn us both to an unhappy union. Strange to say, I ran into him recently for the first time in seventeen years, and I…well, felt absolutely nothing for him. He was just someone I knew from long ago. I hadn't realized my youthful emotions had been so shallow."

His lordship nodded. "I had much the same revelation when my late wife died. We'd married young, and back then, I thought she was the love of my life. But once she died, I realized that while I felt inexpressibly sorry for her, I didn't feel devastated. She hadn't touched my heart in the way or to the depth that I'd thought she had, and so her death didn't matter to me in the fundamental, life-shattering way I had assumed it would."

Regarding him, Madeline smiled gently, understandingly. "It seems we've both learned that, when young, we think we know our hearts, but we really don't."

"Indeed." He sipped, then lowering the glass, asked, "Tell me of your life in London. Where in the capital do you live?"

Madeline readily sketched the bare bones of her life. Quite why she took the chance, she couldn't have said, but she concluded with the information, "I discovered that, like Papa, I had a propensity for investing. Almost a calling. I went looking for those who might help me, and being a female, that list wasn't long, but I found that some of the best firms have no barriers over whom they are willing to work with, and over the years, I've done rather well."

His lordship chuckled. "I have several female acquaintances who I will readily admit know more about investing and running major businesses than I do." He paused, then said, "If you meet the Adairs, as I'm sure you will, given they are assisting Inspector Stokes with this present case, I predict you and Penelope will get along famously. She and her friends are very much of the same independent ilk as you appear to be."

Madeline was fascinated. "I have met Mrs. Adair, although our exchange was confined to matters relating to Viola's murder. Nevertheless, Mrs. Adair and, indeed, her presence did strike me as being rather unusual."

His lordship laughed. "Unusual is the least of it."

She tipped her head. "Do you know the Adairs well?"

"Quite well, and although I admit that I appealed to them for assistance with resolving this case, their involvement is actually at the behest of the commissioner of Scotland Yard."

"They mentioned as much, and I have to say that's quite intriguing." The clock on the mantelpiece chimed discreetly, and Madeline was surprised to realize she'd been chatting to his lordship for half an hour. She didn't know what it was about him that she found so relaxing or so inviting of her confidences. "Good heavens! I've taken up quite enough of your time." She leaned across and set down her empty glass on the side table.

He rose as she did. "It'll be dark outside. I realize I won't be able to persuade you to stay for dinner, but I really must insist on driving you to the rectory."

She had to admit, "I've moved back to Lavender Cottage."

"Even more reason, then. That's even farther, and after all, we have a murderer somewhere near."

She hadn't thought of that, but now he'd mentioned it…and he looked utterly determined to prevail. Graciously, she inclined her head. "Very well, your lordship. You may drive me home."

He beamed. "Excellent! And please, call me Henry."

As he went to tug the bellpull, Madeline realized she was smiling. Smiling and much more settled inside than she had been since she'd arrived in the village.

CHAPTER 5

*I*n their private parlor at the King John Inn, Barnaby settled beside Penelope on the old-fashioned settle angled before the fireplace and looked questioningly at Stokes as his old friend sank into the armchair opposite.

Stokes sighed contentedly. "This inn seems to have only improved since I was last here. That dinner was excellent."

"It was," Penelope agreed. "I feel quite energized, mentally speaking." She glanced at Barnaby, then at Stokes. "Should we begin by going over all the facts we've gleaned?"

"I believe," Barnaby suggested, "that it would help to construct a time line of events, such as we know them."

"Agreed," Stokes said. "Let's start with when this 'secret admirer, H,' came into our victim's life. When was that?"

Penelope duly supplied, "According to her sister, it had to have been sometime in August, after Madeline returned to London. It was later in August when Viola started mentioning H in her letters to Madeline."

"Let's say mid-August as the time H first made contact," Barnaby said. "It's mid-October now, so we're looking at the passage of less than two months."

Stokes had pulled out his notebook and was flipping through the pages. "A fast worker, then, this H."

"Well," Penelope reminded them, "Viola described him as amazingly charming."

"So since mid-August," Barnaby said, "H has been visiting Viola at the cottage."

"That seems likely." Penelope frowned and glanced at Stokes, then looked at Barnaby. "But where did they first meet? It can't have been anywhere obvious in the village, much less at the cottage door."

Eyes narrowing in thought, Stokes ventured, "Salisbury, perhaps. It's the only other place Viola visited regularly, and sometimes, she was there alone."

Barnaby nodded. "Shopping or whatever else she went there to do. Given she was a Salisbury native, her area of interaction could have been quite wide."

"I would say that we should ask Mrs. Foswell," Penelope said, "but she was quite put out that she knew nothing of this H, and I think she would have leapt to tell us if, when she was visiting Salisbury with Viola, she'd ever met any man who might be him."

Stokes grimaced. "I agree. This H has been very careful not to be seen by others."

"Except at a distance." Barnaby looked at Penelope. "I assume we're working on the supposition that the gentleman seen by several villagers walking over the fields toward the cottage is, indeed, Viola's 'secret admirer, H.'"

Penelope admitted, "In general, I don't like making such assumptions, yet in this case, given he was seen approaching only at times when Viola would have been alone, I think it's reasonable to make the connection."

Stokes shifted, getting more comfortable. "That he's taken such pains to avoid all others certainly paints this H in an exceedingly suspicious light."

"True," Barnaby said. "But let's return to our time line. Beyond the mention of H in Viola's letters and the sightings of him across the fields, we have no incidents of note until this past Wednesday, when Jim Swinson drove Viola into Salisbury, and while she was there, it seemed a great deal changed."

Penelope nodded. "She sent a letter to her sister on Wednesday morning, and at that point, according to Viola, all in her life was rosy."

"We shouldn't forget that Madeline thought Viola was expecting H to propose," Stokes said.

"So," Penelope said, "Viola was likely expecting to see H quite soon, meaning the next time she would be alone, which was Thursday afternoon."

"But something she learned in Salisbury shattered her expectations." Barnaby looked at Stokes. "You could say that the scales wrought by charm had been ripped away."

Stokes was nodding. "We need to learn where she went in Salisbury—who she met with, what she heard, and what she then knew."

"That's not going to be easy," Barnaby observed. "Salisbury is a large and busy town, and as she was a native born and bred, her acquaintance could be extensive."

Penelope grimaced. "And she was away—out of sight of Jim Swinson—for at least an hour and a half."

"Let's leave the question of what happened in Salisbury for now," Stokes said, "and continue with our time line." He looked at Barnaby and Penelope. "We're up to the point of her leaving Salisbury. What happened next?"

Penelope obliged. "Jim Swinson said she was upset from that point on, as if she grew angrier and angrier but was doing her best to hide it."

"Indeed," Barnaby said. "And when she reached home, with a personality such as hers, she very likely spent the evening and night stewing over whatever she'd learned."

"Then the next morning"—Penelope took up the tale—"she wrote the urgent letter to Madeline and gave it to Mrs. Gilroy to post when she left at noon for her half day off."

A moment of silence fell, then Stokes said, "I think we have to assume that Viola was expecting H to call that afternoon."

"In her shoes," Penelope said, "I would have sent a note and put him off, at least until I'd had time to consult with Madeline and she was present to act as support, and that Viola didn't do so suggests that she had no way of contacting H."

Barnaby nodded. "She didn't know where he lives."

"That realization alone must have been disconcerting." Stokes scribbled the point in his notebook. "Clearly, H was running some sort of swindle—everything points to that."

"Hmm." Penelope looked thoughtful. "What if her expectations of a proposal were correct, and he was planning to marry her for her money?" She frowned. "But why, then, if he was indeed wooing her, be so secretive?"

"I suspect," Barnaby cynically said, "that when we learn who he is, we'll have the answer to that."

"Apropos of his identity," Penelope said, "there's that line in Viola's letter that suggests that Madeline will recognize the man's name and will understand why Viola shouldn't have trusted him." She looked at Barnaby and arched a brow. "Possibly someone from their shared past?"

Stokes huffed. "Likely someone they knew by reputation from their years in Salisbury."

"Madeline seemed to have no idea who the man might be," Barnaby said.

"No point speculating at this stage," Stokes said. "Let's get back to facts. Where were we?" He consulted his notebook. "All right. So on Thursday at noon, Mrs. Gilroy leaves Viola at the cottage and takes the letter to the post. We don't have any information about Viola's movements from that point until she was found dead the next morning by Mrs. Gilroy when she returned to the cottage."

Barnaby said, "We suspect that H called at the cottage on Thursday afternoon, but did he?"

Penelope put in, "We do know that she was dead by four-thirty, when Henry called, and if we accept the evidence of the clock, which seems reasonable, then she died at three-thirty-three or thereabouts." She looked at Stokes. "Did Morgan or O'Donnell check Henry's alibi?"

Stokes nodded. "They did, and he was, indeed, here for lunch and left about three, as he said. And Morgan borrowed a horse and rode down to the farm Henry said he'd called at after leaving here, and the farmer was clear that Henry was there and left about four, again as Henry told us."

"So Henry's clear on firm evidence." Penelope was pleased. "He couldn't have been anywhere near Lavender Cottage at three-thirty-three."

"And," Barnaby said, "I think we can cross Arthur Penrose and therefore Jim Swinson off our list of potential suspects as well."

"I daresay Iris Perkins and Gladys Hooper can alibi Ida Penrose as well as each other." Penelope looked at Stokes. "Who do we have left?"

"Aside from H?" Stokes consulted his notes. "We need to interview Mrs. Gilroy—she was, after all, the last person to see Viola alive—and her son, who apparently had a long-running disagreement with Viola. And at this point, we need to allow for someone we've yet to get wind of."

"We do know that the house was ransacked," Barnaby pointed out. "Whether by the murderer or someone else, we can't yet say, but the fact that only the bracelet and the necklace that H gave Viola are missing and other potentially more valuable jewelry was left behind strongly suggests that the ransacking, at least, was done by H."

"Indeed," Penelope agreed. "But while he's obviously the prime suspect for the ransacking and stealing, we can't yet be certain that he was the one who strangled Viola. He might have arrived after the murderer had fled, and H realized the pieces would implicate him and retrieved them."

Stokes grunted. "The simplest solution is usually correct. For my money, the most likely option is that H, realizing that Viola had seen through his scheme and wasn't about to fall like a ripe plum into his hand, lost his temper and strangled her, then ransacked the house and removed the telltale jewelry."

"That raises two points," Barnaby said. "First, why strangle her rather than simply shrug and walk away? And as for the jewelry, if he didn't kill her, why bother with that?"

They fell silent for a moment, then Penelope answered, "Because he did kill her—although yes, I agree, I can't quite see why—but having killed her, he then realized that the jewelry is, as Stokes described it, telltale. He must have commissioned some jeweler to copy the bracelet and make the necklace to match, and therefore, the jeweler will be able to identify him."

Stokes was nodding. "Our prime suspect is this secret admirer, H. Taking the jewelry—just those two pieces and not the other valuables—only makes sense if he was the one who murdered Viola."

Barnaby pulled an undecided face. "Or he found Viola dead and feared the jewelry would implicate him."

Stokes wrinkled his nose. "Spoilsport." Then he sighed. "That said, you're right. H might not be our murderer, but I still contend he is our prime suspect."

"Whoever he is," Penelope said.

"By all accounts," Stokes said, "he's a gentleman—"

"Or can pass for one," Barnaby put in.

Stokes inclined his head. "Seen from a distance, he's tallish, lean, dark-haired. In fact, he could be Henry, although we know it isn't him."

Barnaby and Penelope nodded.

After a moment, Stokes went on, "If I was H, I would be long gone, but regardless, we have to make every effort to identify him. The only concern I have with us chasing him down is if, in doing so, we overlook a murderer nearer to hand. And no, I don't know who that might be, yet nevertheless, we need to bear that possibility in mind."

"So," Barnaby asked, "what's our next step?"

Penelope promptly stated, "We need to learn where Viola went in Salisbury on Wednesday. Who she visited and what she learned that so upset her. Was it that knowledge that led to her death?" She paused, then, frowning, went on, "Because of what she wrote in her Thursday letter to Madeline about H, we've assumed that what she learned in Salisbury—the reason she was so upset and, later, angry—was wholly to do with him, but what if it wasn't?" She looked at Barnaby, then at Stokes. "What if everything to do with H is purely coincidental and nothing more than a distraction that's getting in the way of us seeing the murderer more clearly?"

Stokes snorted. "That's precisely what I'm worried about. I therefore suggest that, before we divert our attention to what Viola did in Salisbury, our next step should be to interview the remaining potential suspects and any likely sources of information in the village and find out as much as we can about Viola, enough, at least, to know if there's someone of potential significance of whom we've yet to hear."

Barnaby said, "We have the Gilroys, mother and son, and it might be useful to speak with Reverend Foswell. Especially in country villages, men of God often have more insight into their parishioners' states of mind than one might think."

Stokes made a note. "He might be able to steer us toward someone we've thus far missed."

"And once we've checked with all those in the village"—Penelope brightened—"we can head to Salisbury."

Barnaby and Stokes both smiled at her fondly.

Stokes said, "You really think the answer lies there, don't you?"

"I'm sure," Penelope declared, "that whatever caused Viola such emotional turmoil is more or less the root cause of her murder. As far as we know, that was the only major upheaval in her relatively humdrum life, and what's more, it occurred immediately prior to her murder."

Barnaby studied his wife. "Do you think that whatever she learned meant she had to be silenced before she told anyone else?"

Penelope's dark eyes widened. "I hadn't followed the thought to that conclusion, but it is one possible implication, isn't it?" After two seconds of considering the prospect, she looked at Stokes. "Perhaps Constable

Price should remain guarding Madeline Huntingdon until we have this murderer by the heels."

Stokes's expression hardened. "That's an excellent idea."

The following morning, they left Sergeant O'Donnell and Connor, the Adairs' groom, to hold the fort at the inn, while Constable Morgan went with them, riding on the carriage's box seat beside the coachman, Phelps.

As the coach rumbled along the country lanes, Stokes observed, "It's a pity there's no village pub in Ashmore to which we can send Morgan for information. His talents are wasted in a place like this."

The baby-faced Morgan was well known for teasing all sorts of useful information from serving girls and patrons alike. Barnaby smiled in agreement, and Penelope said, "Morgan, and Connor, too, will be of more use to us in Salisbury. I suspect we'll have quite a bit of searching to do to determine where Viola went last Wednesday."

Stokes grimaced. "I can't say I'm looking forward to that. We'll be casting about, searching for the proverbial needle in a haystack."

They rattled around a corner, and as the carriage righted, Penelope glanced out of the window beside her. The northernmost cottages of Ashmore rolled past, then the carriage slowed and turned again, and the pond and green were beside them. Seconds later, Phelps drew the carriage to a halt beside the hedge of Lavender Cottage.

Stokes opened the door and stepped out, but Barnaby and Penelope remained seated. They were only stopping to collect Constable Price, so he could assist them in their interviews with the Gilroys, and leave Morgan in his place so that Madeline Huntingdon continued to be suitably guarded.

As Stokes approached the gate and Morgan jumped down from the box seat, Constable Price, neat and precise in his uniform with his cap under his arm, came briskly down the path from the front door. Smiling with eagerness, he halted before the gate and saluted Stokes.

His lips not quite straight, Stokes acknowledged Price with a nod.

Price lowered his hand. "All quiet here, Inspector. No dramas, and nothing to report."

"Good." Stokes started to turn toward Morgan, but Price drew out a folded sheet and offered it.

"Miss Madeline asked me to give this to you, sir. It's a sketch of the bracelet that's gone missing."

"Ah. Thank you." Stokes took the sheet and unfolded it. After a cursory glance, he stepped back to the carriage and, through the open door, handed the sheet to Penelope.

She took it and immediately fell to studying the drawing, with Barnaby looking over her shoulder.

Meanwhile, Stokes returned to Morgan and Price. "We need to interview the Gilroys, and for that, Price, we need you with us." Stokes nodded to Morgan. "Constable Morgan will relieve you here."

Stokes paused, then addressing both constables, went on, "We've realized it's possible Viola Huntingdon was murdered because of something she learned during her visit to Salisbury last Wednesday. If so, then the murderer might assume she could have written of the matter to her sister, and therefore, he needs to silence Madeline Huntingdon as well. Consequently, until we have our murderer by the heels, we'll be maintaining a round-the-clock guard on Miss Huntingdon."

Price straightened. "Yes, sir." His expression had sobered, as had Morgan's.

Focusing on Morgan, Stokes added, "Don't leave Miss Huntingdon unattended and out of your sight for any reason whatsoever. We'll be back to fetch you after we've finished our interviews with the locals."

Morgan saluted. "Yes, guv."

Penelope folded the sketch and tucked it into her reticule as Stokes returned to the carriage with Price, and Morgan walked up the path and ducked through the cottage's front door.

Stokes paused beside the open carriage door, glanced at Price, and tipped his head toward the box seat. "Climb up and direct Phelps to the Gilroy cottage. I assume it's nearby?"

Eagerly making for the box seat, Price replied, "Yes, sir. It's back past the pond and along the High Street, then around the next corner in Halfpenny Lane."

Stokes nodded and rejoined Penelope and Barnaby in the carriage. As soon as the door was shut, Phelps expertly turned the carriage, making a neat job of it despite the narrowness of the lane. Then they were off, rolling past the pond and around to the south on High Street. They passed the church and the rectory, then the carriage turned left again, this time into a very narrow, more rutted lane.

Luckily, the Gilroys' cottage was, as Price had said, just around the corner.

Stokes got down first, followed by Barnaby, who turned and gave Penelope his hand. She gripped it and climbed down into the lane. After shaking out her skirts, she looked ahead and found a modest and rather ancient-looking cottage before them.

As they walked toward the simple wooden gate, she took in all she could see. Despite its age, the cottage appeared as well cared for as it could be, with whitewashed walls and paintwork in good condition, and the thatch, if not recent, looked sound.

They filed through the gate, and Penelope surveyed the garden beds that filled the areas on both sides of the narrow gravel path that led to the front door. While uninspiring in their autumnal state, the neatly laid-out beds had hosted rows of vegetables. Most varieties had gone to seed, but there were still turnips and spinach to be had.

Stokes had waved Price to precede them, and he led them to a low front door.

As Penelope and Barnaby joined Stokes before the stoop, Price knocked solidly on the wooden panel, then stepped back and to the side.

It was a quiet country backwater, and while they waited, Penelope heard the distinctive *thwack* of an axe sinking into wood. Then footsteps approached on the other side of the door, and it opened to reveal a woman of middle age with worn-down features in a thin, angular face framed by faded blonde curls.

The expression in the woman's washed-out-blue eyes was all anxiety combined with nervousness.

Smiling reassuringly, Penelope stepped forward. "Good morning, Mrs. Gilroy. I believe you know Constable Price." She waved in the young constable's direction, hoping the sight of his familiar cheery face would ease the woman's nerves. "And this"—Penelope indicated Stokes —"is Inspector Stokes, sent down by Scotland Yard to investigate Miss Huntingdon's murder. My husband and I"—a brief wave included Barnaby—"often assist Inspector Stokes in cases such as this."

To Penelope's eyes, Mrs. Gilroy appeared to be the country version of the typical charwoman. She was tall for a woman, but thin with it. She was neatly dressed in well-worn but scrupulously clean clothes, over which a clean bib apron had been tied. Her hands bore testimony to her occupation, being large and strong-looking but with reddened skin and slightly swollen knuckles.

Having taken that in during her introduction, Penelope capped her words with "We would just like to ask you a few questions about Miss Huntingdon—Miss Viola, that is." Penelope summoned a sympathetic expression. "Finding her body must have been quite a shock."

Mrs. Gilroy blinked, then responded, "Oh, horrible, it was." She glanced at the men, then looked back at Penelope, and her nervousness receded a fraction more. "You'd best come inside, then."

Rather awkwardly, Mrs. Gilroy stepped back, and Penelope walked into the small cottage's tiny parlor. Following her, Barnaby and Stokes had to duck to avoid the lintel.

"This way, then." Mrs. Gilroy squeezed past the men and led the way to two armchairs angled before the fireplace. The house's parlor comprised the front section of a single room that stretched the length of the cottage. A small deal table with three straight-backed wooden chairs filled the central third, while the kitchen with its range, counters, and sink took up the final third of the space.

Judging by the bowls and dish on the counter, Mrs. Gilroy had been assembling a pie.

She ignored her endeavors and hurried to fetch the wooden chairs.

Price immediately went to help, and Stokes took from Mrs. Gilroy the chair she had lifted. "Please," he said, "use one of the armchairs and leave these to us."

Penelope sank into one armchair and beckoned Mrs. Gilroy to take its mate.

She did so with some reluctance, even if the knitting bag beside that chair suggested it was her usual place.

After turning two of the wooden chairs to face the armchairs, Barnaby and Stokes sat. As before, Constable Price elected to stand by the front door.

Sensing that a direct, matter-of-fact approach would get the best results, Penelope explained, "We're trying to get some idea of Miss Viola herself. Can you tell us how you found her to work for?"

With her hands lightly grasping her apron, Mrs. Gilroy took a moment before offering, "Well, she wasn't an easy mistress, but she was fair. I'll say that for her. She was very particular over how everything had to be done and fussy over her food, but once you found out what she wanted and gave her that, she was happy. To begin with, years ago when I first started with her, she'd watch over me shoulder all the time, trying to find fault, but these days, she left me to get on with things without any real fuss."

"I see. Now," Penelope continued, "we understand that on the Friday morning past, you went to the cottage as usual. Did you notice anything amiss when you entered the house?"

Clearly remembering, Mrs. Gilroy frowned. "Not at first, but thinking back on it, I'm fairly sure the back door wasn't locked." She glanced at Stokes. "Miss Viola usually locked the kitchen door at night on account of the rear garden abutting onto the woods and the fields beyond, and really, anyone could walk in if they'd a mind to it. She was careful like that. On Friday last, I had me key, of course, and I put it in the lock as usual and turned it, but the lock was already undone." She looked at Penelope. "I didn't think anything of it at first. I thought she must have forgotten to lock up the evening before or perhaps gone out for something earlier that morning."

Penelope nodded, and Stokes asked, "When you entered the cottage, where did you expect Miss Viola to be?"

"I thought she'd be up in her bedroom as usual." Mrs. Gilroy's nervousness had ebbed entirely, and she answered freely. "She'd normally be getting herself up and ready for the day, and she'd come down when I called that I had breakfast on the table."

Stokes nodded and made a note in his book.

"When you first stepped into the kitchen," Barnaby asked, "did anything strike you as out of place?"

Mrs. Gilroy frowned. "The flour bin wasn't properly closed, and a couple of cupboard doors weren't quite shut, either." She looked at Penelope. "That wasn't how I left things, but Thursday—the day before—was one of my half days off, so I thought Miss Viola must have been looking for something…" Mrs. Gilroy pulled a face. "Only she was always so finicky about everything being neat and in its right place, I was a bit surprised she'd left the doors and bin that way." She shrugged. "But I just shut them and got on with my work."

"Was there anything else you noticed?" Stokes asked.

"I do remember thinking it was awfully quiet—I didn't hear any stirrings from upstairs—but I thought Miss Viola must have decided to have a lie-in for once, so I just went on with my usual chores… Oh, that's right." She looked at Stokes. "There were no Thursday-evening dishes waiting on the drainer for me to put away. I thought that was odd, but decided she must have done the putting away herself. She sometimes did but not often."

Stokes nodded. "Right. So you started the porridge."

Mrs. Gilroy nodded, and her hands clutched her apron more tightly. "And once I had it on, I went to tidy the front parlor..."

Every vestige of color drained from her face as she stared unseeing across the room, then her breath hitched, and she looked down and said, "That's when I found her."

Gently, Penelope asked, "What did you do?"

Still looking at the floor, Mrs. Gilroy replied, "Well, I screeched a bit, but there was no one to hear. So I took the pot off the stove, then rushed around to the Penroses and told them what I'd found, and Jim ran to fetch William there." She tipped her head toward Price. "He hadn't yet left his ma's cottage, so he came and saw and sent one of the lads from the farm riding to Salisbury with the news. I couldn't do anything for poor Miss Viola, so after William arrived, I came away home."

Stokes glanced up from his notebook. "You didn't return to the cottage at any point?"

Mrs. Gilroy shook her head. "Truth be told, it'd take something to get me over the threshold again."

Stokes nodded.

"One last question," Barnaby said. "Do you have any idea who the gentleman Miss Viola referred to as 'my secret admirer, H' in her letters to her sister might be?"

Mrs. Gilroy looked taken aback. "I heard the whispers after church, but I thought they were just silly rumors. I'd no idea Miss Viola had a secret admirer." She paused, then added, "Not that I would have expected her to tell me. Miss Viola wasn't one to share anything personal with staff. She only spoke to us about our work. Me and Jim, we were there to do our jobs, and that was the extent of it. We weren't friends, and she wasn't one of those ladies who likes to chatter. She never encouraged anything of the sort."

Barnaby inclined his head. "Thank you. We had gathered that about her."

Penelope nodded. Jim Swinson had said much the same.

Mrs. Gilroy grimaced. "It might've helped her if she'd been more chatty."

Struck by a sudden thought, Penelope asked, "Did you see her when she got back from Salisbury? On the Wednesday afternoon?"

Mrs. Gilroy shook her head. "No. I left for home before she and Jim got back."

"When you saw her on Thursday morning," Penelope continued, "did she seem out of sorts? Upset or…?"

Mrs. Gilroy frowned. "Not upset in the sense of weeping. She wasn't sad. But she was tense and…well, sort of fragile, I thought. Bothered and het up about something, although she never let on about what. But when she gave me that letter for her sister to post, I did sense that she'd reached some sort of decision. She seemed more sure of herself, more confident and settled on her path. Like she knew what she was going to do."

When Mrs. Gilroy fell silent and looked at Penelope, who then looked at Stokes, Stokes tucked away his notebook and said, "Thank you, Mrs. Gilroy. You've been most helpful. Now, I believe you have a son, Billy. Is he at home?"

The instant escalation of Mrs. Gilroy's anxiety was painfully obvious. Her expression trepidatious, she popped to her feet as Penelope, Barnaby, and Stokes rose. Her hands clasped tightly at her waist, she blurted, "What do you want with Billy?"

In a reassuring tone, Stokes replied, "Just routine questions. We're speaking with everyone who's come into contact with Miss Viola over recent weeks."

To circumvent unnecessary argument, Penelope asked, "Is that Billy chopping wood outside?"

Mrs. Gilroy looked at Penelope, her expression that of a rabbit who'd just recognized a fox.

Penelope smiled brightly. "We'll just go out and have a quick word." She moved toward the kitchen. "No need to escort us. Constable Price can show us the way and introduce us to Billy. Your pie is still waiting, and we've taken up enough of your morning."

Hiding a smile at his wife's managing ways—always so effective—Barnaby followed her through the kitchen and out of the cottage's rear door. Constable Price leapt into action and took the lead, while Stokes dallied to reassure Mrs. Gilroy that her presence was not required.

Price led them along a grassy path between more vegetable beds.

Billy Gilroy was chopping wood at the far end of the narrow lot. He was a lean, rather slight young man, but from the ease with which he wielded the axe, he had muscles enough. Of average height, he had untidy dark-brown hair, and his pale features were a sharper—less worn—version of his mother's.

He saw them coming and stepped back from the block, resting the axe head on the ground beside him.

Price nodded to Billy as they halted a yard away. "Billy. The inspector here just wants to ask you a few questions."

Stokes joined them and introduced himself as well as Barnaby and Penelope, giving Barnaby a chance to study Billy. The lad was nervous and on his guard. His eyes darted to take in Barnaby and Penelope, then he returned his gaze to Stokes and nervously licked his lips. "How can I help ye?"

Stokes hauled out his notebook. "We're investigating the murder of Miss Viola Huntingdon. We've heard that you and she weren't all that friendly."

"Friendly?" Billy sneered. "She weren't friendly with anyone here, well, except perhaps Mrs. Foswell. But other than that, she..." He stopped, then ended with "Well, she wasn't what you'd call a nice lady."

"Why do you say that?" Penelope's words rang with genuine curiosity.

Billy was wary, but eventually, when they all waited for him to answer, he offered, "She always took against me. I never knew why. It was almost as if me just breathing or walking along was enough to set her off. She'd bail me up and rail at me—she'd stop me right in the street and have a go at me."

"Over what?" Barnaby asked in mildly curious vein.

Billy shrugged, but when they waited again, rather sullenly, he replied, "She'd taken it into her head that I was getting into the wrong company. That's what she called me mates—the wrong company. What would she know? Anyway, she said that because I don't have a steady job and live with Ma and rely on her to keep me fed, that I was a burden on Ma's shoulders. She—Miss Viola—was always railing at me to get a job and become a man and all that sort of tripe."

"Well," Penelope said, "it's not entirely tripe, is it? How old are you?"

Grudgingly, Billy offered, "Nineteen."

His tone rather harder, Barnaby observed, "Old enough to look for work, then, especially given all the farms around about."

Billy continued to look sullen but had the sense to bite his tongue.

Stokes had been consulting his notebook. "On Thursday afternoon, did you see anyone heading to Lavender Cottage?"

"Nah," Billy readily replied. "I was nowhere near there." Then he ducked his head and shifted on his feet. "I was in the woods over Tollard

Royal way, gathering conkers with me mates. We can get a good price for them in Salisbury."

"When did you get back?" Stokes asked.

"After sunset, it was. Ma was waiting on me for dinner." Billy nodded toward the cottage. "Must've been six when I got through the door."

Barnaby was watching Billy closely. "Your route from the woods to here—you must have passed not far from Lavender Cottage."

"Not so close," Billy promptly countered. "I cut across the fields, didn't I? I didn't go by the lanes."

Stokes looked at Barnaby and Penelope, then, to Billy, said, "That's all for now, although we might have more questions for you later."

Billy shrugged and tightened his grip on the axe. "I'll be here. Nowhere else to go."

They turned and walked away. As they neared the cottage, they heard the axe bite into wood again.

When they reached the lane, all of them were frowning, even Constable Price.

Stokes halted by the carriage and arched a brow at Barnaby and Penelope.

Penelope humphed. "Well, wherever Billy was on Thursday afternoon, it wasn't with his mates gathering conkers in the woods. That was an outright lie."

"I agree." Barnaby glanced past the cottage to the rear of the lot. "There's something he's hiding—something about Thursday afternoon—yet I have difficulty believing he strangled Viola."

Stokes nodded. "True, but he knows something he doesn't want us to know. That's the impression I got."

"But," Penelope said, "is it something to do with this case? Or something else entirely?"

"That, indeed, is the question." Stokes glanced along the lane and frowned. "What's this?"

A uniformed constable they hadn't previously met was huffing and puffing as he jogged toward them. The man reached them and pulled up, then attempted a general salute. "Inspector Stokes?"

Stokes nodded curtly. "Out with it, man."

The constable obliged. "Superintending Constable Mallard sent me to tell you that yesterday afternoon, a bloke tried to sell Miss Huntingdon's stolen bracelet and necklace to one of the jewelers in Salisbury."

Eagerly, Stokes asked, "And was this bloke apprehended?"

The constable's face fell. "No, sir. He ran off as soon as he realized the jeweler knew who the bracelet belonged to. Turned out it was the same jeweler who made the bracelet long ago, and he knew it was Miss Huntingdon's. The jeweler kept the bracelet and necklace and came in this morning to report that the jewels must have been stolen."

Stokes looked at Barnaby and Penelope. To Penelope, he said, "It looks like you'll get your wish sooner rather than later." He glanced up at Phelps, listening interestedly from the box seat. "It seems we're off to Salisbury."

CHAPTER 6

Fifteen minutes later, Madeline walked around the village pond and on down High Street. The church was her destination, and several yards behind her trailed the obedient and unintrusive Constable Price.

Madeline found herself a touch amused by the protective concern the constabulary were displaying toward her fair self, but in the circumstances, with her sister's murderer not yet apprehended, she wasn't fool enough to dismiss any action the investigators deemed necessary.

The Adairs and Stokes had drawn up in their carriage just as she'd been about to set out for the church. She'd spent the earlier hours of the morning sorting and packing Viola's clothes to be given away. There were few of her sister's things she wished to keep, and the realization of how different their lives had become had weighed on her spirit.

That was why she was heading for the church, hoping to find some measure of peace. The investigators had informed her that someone had attempted to sell Viola's missing bracelet and necklace, and they were on their way to pursue the trail in the hope it would lead them to the murderer. They'd swapped constables, taking up the chatty Morgan and leaving the quieter Price to watch over her. As Mrs. Adair had put it, just in case.

Madeline was happy enough to go along with the notion. At that moment, being left totally alone didn't appeal, which was why, while Henry had been driving her home the previous evening and he'd asked—

carefully, even warily—if she might fancy a drive to Shaftesbury to chase away the cobwebs and perhaps have a quiet lunch in a nice little place he knew, she'd accepted with gratitude. She needed to get away from Viola and death and Ashmore for just a little while.

She'd arranged to meet Henry outside the rectory at half past eleven. It was not quite eleven now, so she had plenty of time to seek solace in the church before rendezvousing with him. She'd informed Constable Price of her plans, which he'd accepted readily, merely saying that once she drove off, he would return to the cottage and await her return. His attitude had confirmed Henry's standing among the wider community. Thinking back, she rather suspected that those who had earlier whispered about him being the murderer hadn't been all that serious and had been merely indulging in speculation for titillation's sake.

On reaching the church's lychgate, she went through and climbed the gently rising path to the open church door and walked inside.

Constable Price followed as far as the door. He scanned the empty church and waited until she sat in a pew halfway down the nave before ducking back outside and tactfully leaving her to her contemplation.

Madeline let the silence wrap around her. She wasn't a particularly religious person, but she was the daughter of a minister, and the church had been a constant in her life as it had been in Viola's. She felt closer to Viola, and indeed, her father, when seated in God's house.

She'd been there for perhaps ten minutes, relishing the peace and feeling her soul grow more and more refreshed, when the side door that led to the graveyard opened. She didn't look around at first, but on hearing footsteps approaching, expecting to see Reverend Foswell, she turned with welcome in her eyes—only to discover it was Monty who was walking toward her, a typically charming smile curving his lips.

Really, she thought, faintly irritated, he hadn't changed one iota. That smile was the same smile that, years ago, had captivated her. Now, however, rather than any flutter inside, she had to battle to keep her cynical amusement from showing. The assumption that any female would welcome his presence at any time clearly remained embedded in his brain, along with an expectation that Madeline would again fall for him as her much-younger and far-less-experienced self once had.

Apparently, he was blind to the fact that she'd changed.

True to his customary ways, he gracefully stepped into and sat in the pew in front of her. Placing one arm along the pew's raised back, he swiveled to smile even more winningly at her. "My dearest Madeline, while I understand that your sister's death affects you deeply, and I do sincerely honor you for that, it doesn't do to sink too deeply into grief. That being so, here I am, eager and willing to divert your thoughts." He affected an expression of genuine interest. "I own to being highly curious about what you've been up to since last we met."

Since you threw me over because I was too independently minded for you?

The words were on the tip of Madeline's tongue, but—minister's daughter sitting in a church—she swallowed them unuttered.

She also told herself she couldn't laugh in his face. Instead, after due consideration, she revealed, "After Papa died, I moved to London. I have a house there and amuse myself well enough." Building an investment fund, but she wasn't fool enough to tell him—a self-confessed fortune hunter—that.

"London, heh?" Monty looked mildly impressed. "Do you own the house? That's quite an investment. Whereabouts is it in town?"

"Near the university." She strove to keep her tone even. "I have lodgers."

"Ah." He nodded as if understanding had dawned. "A lodging house."

She didn't correct him. At a stretch, her Bedford Place house could possibly be described as such. "But enough of me. I confess I'm interested in learning of your exploits over the same period. America?" Better she kept him focused on himself, and that had never proved difficult. He had always been his favorite topic.

Sure enough, he brightened and said, "Yes, indeed." Sadly, he followed that with "But I'm quite puzzled that you've never married."

Several responses leapt to her tongue—such as that her earlier association with him had taught her the unwisdom of entrusting her future to a man—but after considering the best way to bring this discussion to an end, she shrugged and said, "Frankly, I never saw the need. With the inheritance Papa left me, I have enough to get by. But"—she studied him and made an educated guess—"you haven't fronted the altar, either, have you?"

And given his long-ago-stated intention, that was surprising.

He sighed feelingly. "No. I never found the right lady for me." The smile he bestowed on her was a too-sweet blend of self-deprecation and fellow feeling. He trapped her gaze and declared, "I should never have let you go."

She managed not to snort or point out that she hadn't been the one to break things off. "Tell me what you got up to in America. In the north-east, I think you said."

"Generally speaking." He waved expansively. "That said, I spent most of my time in New York. That's where all the major business takes place. And"—he shifted to face her directly—"if I do say so myself, I feel I left my mark."

Cynically, she wondered in what way. "What sort of business were you engaged in?" As far as she knew, he had no particular skills.

"It was a bit of this and that. I was really more a finance man, helping to fund various enterprises. It was very lucrative."

"Indeed? As that's the case, I own myself surprised that you've returned to England."

He raised his gaze to take in the church's beamed ceiling. "Believe it or not, I developed a hankering for the auld country. For this land of green pastures and golden fields—the land of my forebears. Until I was over there, I didn't feel the tug, but once I'd accumulated enough wealth not to have to think of money again, I realized I didn't want to spend the rest of my life over there. So I came back." He lowered his gaze and smiled at her. "Just in time, it seems, to meet you again."

Madeline had no intention of encouraging him to pursue any ongoing acquaintance with her. She felt a distinct need to cut this interview short. She glanced at her lapel watch and, with a certain relief, discovered she could honestly state, "I have an appointment in a few minutes. You'll have to excuse me." Thank goodness she'd accepted Henry's invitation.

She looked at Monty in time to see annoyance flash across his face and remembered that, in the past, he had always been the one to define the length of their meetings. Thinking back, she couldn't recall ever walking out on him before.

Endeavoring to hide the smile that realization brought to her lips, she rose, and when he rose, too, she inclined her head. "Good day, Monty." She stepped into the aisle and started walking back to the door.

Naturally, he fell in beside her. After a moment, he ventured, "I sincerely hope, Madeline, that once this sad time has passed, we can… well, not exactly resume where we left off but at least renew our friendship."

A touch repressively, she replied, "I'm really not sure what I will do regarding Lavender Cottage, so I can't say how much longer I'll remain in the area."

She reached the doorway and stepped out into the weak sunshine and spotted Constable Price waiting in the shade of a large tree. His surprise at seeing Monty showed in his sudden tensing, and Madeline realized that as the constable had been watching the main door, he hadn't seen Monty enter the church.

She smiled and fractionally inclined her head, letting Price know Monty was no threat. She turned to Monty and realized he'd been looking down and hadn't seen Price under the tree. She held out her hand. "Goodbye, Monty."

He caught her fingers and bowed over her hand. Straightening, he smiled with a full measure of charm. "For now, dearest Madeline, farewell."

She retrieved her hand and, feeling a smidgen relieved that Price was within hailing distance, stepped past Monty and set off, walking steadily down the drive.

She'd just passed beneath the lychgate when Henry drew his curricle to a halt in the lane. She felt her face come alight and her heart lift. Suddenly, the day seemed much sunnier.

Henry saw her and smiled. "There you are. Right on time."

He leaned across and offered her his hand, and she took it and climbed into the open carriage. She sat beside him and found she was looking forward to the day.

"Now." Henry raised his reins and gave his chestnuts the office. "Let's get some air to blow away the dismals and simply enjoy our day."

Madeline laughed and clutched her bonnet as they started off. Leaning back as the curricle rattled along High Street, she discovered a smile had taken up permanent residence on her face. Sitting beside Henry, she could, indeed, relax and, as he had put it, simply enjoy the day.

From within the deep shade of an old oak by the church wall, William Price watched the gentleman who had—to William's considerable surprise—walked out of the church with Miss Madeline. While Miss Madeline's behavior had made it clear that she didn't view the man as a villain, William wasn't so sure.

The gentleman—at least, he appeared to be a gentleman—was lean of build and dark-haired. Just like their mystery man, but unfortunately also like several other men, including Lord Glossup, who had just driven off with Miss Madeline. But more to the point, William couldn't place the man, and he knew most of those who lived in and around the village.

If he wasn't a villager, what was he doing there?

Clearly, he knew Miss Madeline, which was curious to say the least. But what made William remain still and silent, his gaze trained on the man, whoever he might be, was the change in the man's expression as he'd watched Miss Madeline walk down the path. At first, he'd seemed merely put out, a bit sulky that she'd walked away, but then Miss Madeline had met his lordship and driven away with him, and the man's eyes had narrowed to slits, and his jaw had clenched.

Now, with the rattle of the curricle's wheels fading into the distance, William saw the man mutter something, then he spun on his heel and strode away, heading toward the path behind the church that led to Manor Farm.

William watched the man go until he vanished behind the trees at the rear of the churchyard. Finally stretching, then setting off toward the cottage, William thought again of all he'd observed and made a mental note to mention the strange gentleman to the inspector.

Stokes strode into the Salisbury police station with Barnaby and Penelope on his heels. During the journey from the village, they'd speculated about what the news of the necklace and bracelet might mean but had too few facts to make any predictions.

Mallard was waiting by the desk and straightened when he saw them. He reached across and picked up a gold bracelet and necklace and held them as an offering in his large hands.

Penelope noted his altered attitude. The Superintending Constable appeared as eager as they to push ahead with this case and seemed keen to acquit himself well as he declared, "These are the items the jeweler identified as belonging to the victim."

Stokes nodded to Mallard and accepted the jewelry. Stokes shook out the bracelet, studied it for an instant, then passed it to Penelope.

She lifted the gold links and held the piece up to the light.

Then she frowned and brought the bracelet closer to her spectacles and peered at the stones.

Before she could exclaim, Mallard said, "A local jeweler name of Swithin—an older man, decent solid sort, never any trouble—brought these in this morning. He said a young man came into his shop latish yesterday and tried to sell him the pieces. Swithin recognized both as belonging to Miss Huntingdon and pretended an interest while surreptitiously trying to send his assistant to fetch us, but the young man noticed the silly beggar leave, got the wind up, and legged it. Swithin had no hope of catching him. But the thing is, Swithin said Miss Huntingdon—the victim—came to see him last Wednesday. Seemed the catch on the bracelet had come loose, and as Swithin himself had made the piece as a gift for the victim's mother long ago, Miss Huntingdon brought the bracelet to him and asked to have it fixed. She was wearing the necklace at the time and happily showed it off to Swithin. According to him, she was very proud of that necklace, up until he told her the bad news."

Penelope, along with Barnaby and Stokes, had grown riveted by the tale.

"Bad news?" Stokes asked before she or Barnaby could.

Portentously, Mallard nodded. "Turns out the jewels in both bracelet and necklace are paste. But Swithin swears that the last time he saw the bracelet, the stones were very much the real thing. That was a couple of years back when Miss Huntingdon brought the piece in for cleaning. I didn't know you cleaned jewelry, but apparently, you do."

"Most definitely," Penelope declared. "And aquamarines are tricky to clean."

"Where is Swithin?" Stokes asked, his gaze going to the area deeper inside the station.

"I had to let him get back to his shop," Mallard said. "He insisted he couldn't leave his assistant alone the whole day. But he said he'd be there for you to speak with. Mind you, he didn't seem to know anything about Miss Huntingdon being murdered, and I didn't tell him."

Stokes nodded in approval. "Where is Swithin's shop?"

"Go to the opposite corner of the marketplace," Mallard said, "then on a few steps along Silver Street. Swithin's Jewelers. You can't miss it."

Stokes thanked him, and with nods all around, they left the building.

Morgan had waited outside with Phelps and the carriage. Penelope walked straight to the carriage door, which Connor held for her. She climbed up, and after giving Phelps directions, Barnaby and Stokes joined her.

She and they waited with suppressed impatience while Phelps guided the carriage back around the marketplace. They passed the market cross and turned onto Silver Street. Penelope peered out of the window, squinting ahead. "There it is—Swithin's Jewelers."

The carriage drew smoothly into the curb, and Stokes opened the door and got down. Barnaby and Penelope followed. They paused on the pavement to take stock of the establishment.

Swithin's Jewelers showed the world a well-kept storefront, with two large bow windows on either side of a white-painted door. The glass in the windows was spotless and the surrounds swept scrupulously clean. Blue-velvet-covered trays displayed earrings, rings, bracelets, necklaces, and all manner of jewelry, artfully arranged to make the best of the light that struck through the leaded glass panes.

The door was half glazed, and a bell above it tinkled when Stokes turned the brass knob and led them inside.

The shop had counters running along the side and rear walls, beneath some of which were glass-fronted cases, and more such cases displaying everything from clocks to jeweled combs filled the walls behind the counters. Completing the rather spacious layout, in the center of the shop sat a delicate gate-legged table with three matching chairs, one behind and two in front. The table's highly polished surface supported two small brass-mounted mirrors on stands, the arrangement inviting customers to sit and examine and try on selected pieces.

Prosperous gentility all but hung in the air.

As with Barnaby beside her, Penelope followed Stokes deeper into the shop, she tipped her head toward Barnaby and murmured, "This wouldn't be out of place in Hatton Garden."

"Hmm." Then he murmured back, "Perhaps not Hatton Garden—not enough diamonds—but maybe the lower reaches of Ludgate Hill."

Penelope glanced around, then whispered, "At least there are no customers here at the moment."

She followed Stokes to where, behind the rear counter, an older man stood with the practiced smile of an experienced shopkeeper on his face. He wore a tweed suit that somehow complemented his bountiful whiskers, and the creases in his face marked him as a cheerful sort. But his gaze was as acutely assessing as any shopkeeper's, and as he took in Stokes's rather grim visage, the man's welcoming smile faded into a more tentative look, but then he saw Penelope and Barnaby, and that look grew distinctly confused.

Stokes halted before the counter and, understanding the man's uncertainty, explained, "I'm Inspector Stokes of Scotland Yard, and these are

Mr. and Mrs. Adair, who are acting as consultants on this case. Mr. Swithin, I presume? I believe Superintending Constable Mallard warned you to expect us."

"Oh yes. Well, he told me an inspector would call." Swithin looked vaguely alarmed. "I must say, I hadn't expected Scotland Yard to investigate such a relatively minor incident. I'm not even sure Miss Huntingdon yet knows that her jewelry has been stolen."

Stokes gravely said, "I'm sorry to have to inform you, Swithin, that Miss Viola Huntingdon was murdered in her home last Thursday afternoon."

Swithin paled and clutched the counter. "Oh, good God! Dear me!" He drew in a steadying breath, then went on, "The poor lady! Murdered, you say?"

When Stokes nodded, Swithin continued, "What a dreadful thing." He frowned, then focused on Stokes and earnestly said, "I do hope it wasn't anything to do with the jewels being, well, effectively stolen?" His frown deepened. "Possibly twice. The stones first and then the pieces themselves."

"As to that, we can't yet say," Stokes replied, "but we're grateful to you for bringing the bracelet and necklace to us and reporting the attempt to sell them to you. We understand that Miss Huntingdon brought the bracelet and necklace to you last Wednesday."

Swithin nodded. "She brought the bracelet, and she was wearing the necklace, which had been made to match. Not by me, I should add. The catch on the bracelet had come loose, and as I had crafted the piece and she and her family were longtime customers of mine, she brought it to me to fix. Which I did. However, I couldn't help but see that the stones, which had been quite a fine set of aquamarines, had been replaced with paste. I debated whether to mention it, but I knew she was reasonably well-off, so I very gently inquired, and she was quite taken aback. She immediately had me examine the necklace, and I had to tell her that those stones, too, were paste. Quite good imitations, mind—they would have fooled most people—but they were fake, nonetheless."

"How did she take the news?" Penelope asked.

Swithin looked uncomfortable. "I fear I had given her a terrible shock. It was plain that she hadn't known of the substitution, which didn't surprise me."

Barnaby asked, "Did she mention who she suspected of replacing the stones?"

Swithin shook his head. "But I could tell from her expression and the way she pokered up that she knew who it must have been, and the realization quite floored her. Indeed, I venture to say she was devastated, but of course, a lady like her, she drew it all in, put on her best face, glossed over the moment, and soldiered on. Her sort always do."

Stokes had been jotting notes in his ever-present book. He looked up and said, "Let's move on to the man who brought the jewelry to you yesterday. Describe him if you would."

Swithin pursed his lips and narrowed his eyes as if studying an image in his mind. "A trifle above average height. Youngish—perhaps twenty or so, twenty-five at the outside. I must confess that I'm not adept at guessing young people's ages these days. He had dark hair—dark brown and straightish—and a rather shifty expression. Blue eyes, I think—oh, and he had rough hands. Workman's hands with callused and leathery palms."

Stokes exchanged a glance with Barnaby and Penelope, then in a murmured aside, said, "That description fits two of our suspects—BG and JS."

Barnaby grimaced. "Regardless of whether they murdered our victim or not, either of them might have gone to the house and gained entry after she was dead."

"They had an entire evening and night in which to do so." Penelope arched her brows. "Perhaps it was they who searched the house and found the jewelry and took it away."

"But they left the other, more valuable pieces, remember?" Stokes said. "That doesn't fit with a straightforward robbery, before or after the murder."

Stokes refocused on Swithin and raised his voice. "We believe we know who you might mean—one of two possible suspects. Would you be willing to come with us to Ashmore, the village where Miss Huntingdon lived, and identify the man for us?"

Barnaby added, "We'll take you down in our carriage and return you here the same way afterward."

Penelope added her voice and a smile. "It shouldn't take too long. An hour or so there and the same time back."

"The identification itself won't take much time at all," Stokes said. "You just have to look and point to the man who came here."

Swithin looked torn. After an indecisive moment, he said, "Miss Viola and her family—well, I did know them for a very long time. I suppose I could ask my assistant to watch the shop." He stared at Stokes. "Will I have to confront the villain?"

Stokes smiled reassuringly. "No, not at all. You can remain in the carriage and just point him out to us. All we need is your confirmation of which of the two suspects it was."

"And my confirmation will help catch Miss Huntingdon's murderer?" Swithin asked.

"We believe so," Penelope replied. "At the very least, it will advance us significantly toward that goal."

"Well, then." Swithin raised his chin and squared his shoulders. "I can hardly refuse, can I?" Then he shook his head. "Poor dear lady. If you'll wait just a moment, I'll inform my assistant and fetch my coat."

Five minutes later, with Swithin's assistant installed behind the shop's counter, they all climbed into the coach and set off for Ashmore village at as quick a trot as Phelps would risk.

Barnaby glanced out of the carriage as they rattled into Ashmore from the north. Phelps had made good time, and it was barely four o'clock as they approached the triangular junction at the heart of the village. The pond lay just ahead.

They'd discussed how to approach their two suspects, and Stokes planned to take Swithin to see Jim Swinson first, reasoning that Jim would be the easier to locate, given he would most likely be assisting Arthur Penrose in his orchard.

Phelps slowed the carriage to make the turn onto Green Lane and thus to Penrose and Lavender Cottages.

Seated beside Barnaby, Penelope was looking out at the green and the pond. Suddenly, she sat straighter, her gaze locked on the vista. "There's a group of young men by the pond, and I think one of our suspects is there."

Barnaby rose and rapped on the ceiling. "Phelps, pull up."

Immediately, the carriage slowed, then rocked to a halt.

Swithin was sitting opposite Penelope. She caught the jeweler's gaze. "Mr. Swithin, if you could take a look outside, can you see the young men by the pond?"

Swithin peered out, then nodded. "I see them, yes."

Barnaby looked over Penelope's head and glimpsed a group of

lounging lads. Presumably, Billy Gilroy was among them, but from that angle, Barnaby couldn't make him out.

Somewhat portentously, her gaze locked on Swithin, Penelope asked, "Is the young man who brought the bracelet and necklace to your shop among that group?"

Methodically, Swithin studied the lads, then he stiffened, raised a hand, and pointed. "That's him! The one on the far right."

Stokes had risen and was staring out over Swithin's hat. "You're certain?"

"As certain as I am that I'm sitting here," Swithin staunchly replied. He pointed again, more emphatically. "That's definitely the young man who brought me Miss Huntingdon's bracelet and necklace."

Stokes dropped a hand on the jeweler's shoulder. "Thank you. That's all we need you to do. Please remain here, out of sight, while we speak with the lad."

Stokes turned, opened the door, and descended to the lane on the side of the carriage screened from the green. Barnaby followed, and as Penelope put a hand on his shoulder and negotiated the steep steps, Morgan dropped down from his perch above.

"You heard?" Stokes asked Morgan.

The constable nodded. "I'll circle around." He stepped past Barnaby and Penelope and, sinking his hands into his pockets and adopting an innocent-looking slouch, strode off along the lane toward the junction.

Stokes watched him go, then arched a brow at Barnaby and Penelope. "Right, then. Let's go and have a word with Billy Gilroy."

Stokes led the way around the carriage and onto the green, making directly for the group beside the pond. Barnaby and Penelope followed a yard behind, waiting to see what would happen.

Billy Gilroy saw them coming. For an instant, he dithered, then he turned and fled, making for High Street, only to have Morgan intercept him with a flying tackle and knock him to the ground.

The pair rolled once, then Morgan popped to his feet and hauled Billy up by his collar.

Stokes slowed his approach and murmured to Barnaby and Penelope, "I've always suspected that Morgan misses the more physical side of policing."

Barnaby grinned, as did Penelope.

By the time the three of them reached the pair, Morgan had Billy firmly by the collars of both shirt and jacket, and the lad appeared rather limp and subdued.

Indeed, the face he showed them was filled with fear. Before Stokes could get out a word, Billy blurted, "I didn't kill her!"

Stokes halted a yard away and considered their captive. "Didn't you?"

Although Stokes's intonation was distinctly skeptical, studying Billy, Barnaby was inclined to believe the lad.

From beside Barnaby, Penelope said, "But you can see how it looks, can't you? Miss Viola is strangled, the house ransacked, and two pieces of jewelry go missing, and then you show up in Salisbury and try to sell those particular two pieces to a jeweler."

Billy was shaking his head vehemently. "I didn't strangle her! I never even went to the house—never been inside it in all my life." His panic was evident, and the desperation in his tone lent credence to his statements.

Calmly, Barnaby asked, "Then how did you come by the necklace and bracelet?"

Billy's gaze locked on Barnaby's face. "I took them from where she put them. She left them where anyone could've found and taken them." He shot a glance at Stokes. "No law to say I can't take things others have left lying about, is there?"

Penelope frowned. "She, meaning Miss Viola?"

Plainly encouraged that they were listening, Billy nodded fervently. "She obviously didn't want them anymore, and then she was dead, and I had them, and there didn't seem any reason I shouldn't see what I could get for them."

Stokes was frowning, too. "Tell us exactly how you came to have Miss Huntingdon's jewelry."

Almost eagerly, Billy explained, "Early that afternoon—the day she was killed—I was heading home from Manor Farm. I'd been helping with the baling there, and we stopped a little after noon. I was walking home to get a bite, and the path runs along the back wall of the graveyard, on the other side of the trees, and I was on that stretch when I saw her—Miss Viola—come out of the church. She wandered into the graveyard sort of uncertain, looking this way and that. She didn't see me because of the trees, and I thought she was acting strange, so I stopped and watched her. She went one way, then the other, then finally, she went to a very old grave with an urn on top of the gravestone. She crouched down and pulled something from her bag and stuffed it into the urn. Then she looked around sharpish like, as if checking no one had seen, then she stood up and walked quickly away, back around the church and down to the lane. Seemed she was off to her cottage."

During Billy's account, Stokes had pulled out his book and started taking notes. "So you're saying Miss Viola put her favorite jewelry into an urn in the graveyard." Skepticism weighted the words.

But Billy nodded earnestly. "She did. I can show you where, then you'll believe me." Billy made to head toward the church, having forgotten that Morgan still had hold of his collars.

Morgan pulled Billy up and held him.

"You have to let me show you," Billy all but wailed.

His expression impassive, Stokes glanced at Barnaby and Penelope, then nodded to Morgan. "Let him go." To Billy, Stokes said, "Try to run, and we'll have you in manacles. Be sensible and just lead the way and show us what you think will convince us you didn't kill Miss Viola."

Billy nodded eagerly and turned and walked quickly toward the church, with Morgan keeping pace at Billy's heels.

Barnaby, Penelope, and Stokes followed the pair off the green and onto High Street, then Billy turned under the lychgate and climbed the path to the church door. He went past the door and around the far end of the church, beyond which lay the graveyard.

Billy started along the central path. His steps quickening, he glanced back at them. "It's just along here."

The grave he led them to lay more or less at the center of the graveyard and wasn't just old but ancient. On the cracked gravestone, in the shadow cast by the weathered and worn headstone, sat an equally ancient urn. Billy leaned over and peered inside it, then straightened, stepped back, and pointed into the urn. "I left the handkerchief she'd wrapped about the jewelry. It's still in there."

Penelope stepped forward and looked into the urn, then reached inside and pulled out a fine lawn square. She held it up and examined it, then turned to Barnaby and Stokes and pointed to an embroidered monogram in one corner. "VH," Penelope confirmed. "I think we can accept that this is, indeed, one of Viola's handkerchiefs."

Footsteps approaching on the gravel path had them turning to see a gentleman walking toward them. Judging by his clerical collar, the man had to be Reverend Foswell.

As he neared, he smiled genially. "Good day to you all. I'm Reverend Foswell, minister of this church."

Stokes responded with the usual introductions, and Foswell nodded benignly.

He half bowed to Barnaby and Penelope. "Mr. and Mrs. Adair." Foswell's glance included Stokes when he asked, "Have you made any progress, Inspector?"

With the handkerchief still dangling from her fingertips, Penelope responded, "Progress, yes. Billy here has just told us that Viola Huntingdon visited the church a little after noon on the day she was murdered."

Foswell nodded. "Indeed, she did. I saw her praying in the church but didn't intrude. I was in the vestry when she left." He waved toward the church. "The window looks out this way, and I saw her wander around, then come to this grave. She crouched, which put her out of my sight, and I thought she must have been studying the inscription, which as you can see is quite worn away to the extent that we can't tell who is buried there. But after a moment, Viola rose and left, and I confess I didn't think any more about it." He looked from Stokes to Barnaby and Penelope. "I really didn't think the matter relevant to her death. If I had, I would have come to you earlier and reported it." He looked inquiringly at Stokes. "Is her visit here important?"

Penelope nodded at Billy. "Your sighting of Miss Huntingdon and the confirmation that she was here is certainly of importance to Billy and to our understanding of the case."

Barnaby looked at Billy. "So where were you on Thursday afternoon?"

Billy colored and looked sheepish, but this time, replied truthfully, "In the woods, like I said, but I was hiding the jewelry in a hollow tree only I know about, not with me mates gathering conkers."

Stokes sighed and turned to Foswell. "We intended to call on you earlier in case you had any insights into Miss Huntingdon's state of mind. Perhaps we could go into the church and speak of that now. Meanwhile" —Stokes returned his gaze to Billy—"you've had a lucky escape. You're correct in thinking that, as the jewelry was left in a public place, you committed no crime in taking it. However, I think you'll discover that, in this case, the village community will be rather less forgiving than the law. I advise you to go home and, henceforth, keep your nose clean and do what you can to help your mother and make her proud of you. You'll get much farther in life that way, rather than trying to find shortcuts that involve no hard work. Everything in life worth having is something that has to be worked for. That's just the way life is. Remember that, and you'll get along much better."

"Hear, hear," Reverend Foswell said. "I couldn't agree more."

Stokes tipped his head, indicating the path around the church, and said to Billy, "Off you go. And remember what I said."

Wide-eyed and relieved, Billy ducked his head to them all, then took off, striding rapidly back around the church.

Stokes returned his attention to Foswell. "Now, Reverend Foswell, if you have a few minutes to spare…"

"Yes, indeed." Foswell turned toward the church. "Come inside, and we can talk."

As he and Stokes led the way along the path, Foswell somewhat diffidently said, "Might I ask, Inspector, what Billy has been up to? Whatever it is, it's bound to come out, and people will gossip, I'm afraid, and he's not always viewed in the best of lights as it is. If I know what the facts are, I might be able to guide reactions into a more appropriate vein."

Stokes dipped his head in agreement and proceeded to outline what they now believed had occurred with Viola's jewelry.

They entered the empty church and settled in the two rearmost pews.

Foswell was frowning. "In some ways, that does sound like Viola—like something she might do if she wanted to hide something. But why is a mystery." He looked at Barnaby and Penelope, seated in the pew in front and swiveled to face Foswell and Stokes. "Why," Foswell asked, patently puzzled, "would she hide her jewelry?"

"More specifically," Penelope said, "why did she hide those particular pieces just hours before she was killed?"

None of them had any insights to offer. They spoke with Foswell for several minutes, going over all he knew of Viola and her time in the village, but there was nothing in what he had to impart that shed light on the issues before them.

Eventually, Foswell concluded, "While I'm aware of the strained relations between the Penroses and Viola and of the general view of Viola, which wasn't entirely flattering and, I'm saddened to say, in some respects, was well-deserved, I know of no reason that might have prompted anyone in the village to murder her."

Stokes thanked the minister for his time and his assistance with Billy, then Barnaby, Penelope, and Stokes left the church and, joined by Morgan, who had remained outside, returned to where Phelps waited with the carriage just beyond the lychgate.

Barnaby handed Penelope up and followed, and the three of them joined Swithin, who had remained in the carriage throughout.

Naturally, he had questions, and as reward for his assistance, Stokes filled him in on all that had transpired, explaining at the last that, as Viola had left her jewelry for anyone to find, no actionable crime had been committed by Billy in taking the items and attempting to sell them.

"Oh." Swithin looked puzzled. "How sad. And odd." He looked at Barnaby and Penelope. "She was very fond of both those pieces, you know. And even after I told her the stones were fake, while I can understand her throwing away the necklace, I'm rather surprised she would have discarded her mother's bracelet."

Barnaby glanced at Penelope and saw that the point was a puzzle to her, too.

After exchanging a look with Stokes, Barnaby turned the conversation to more general countryside observations until they reached the King John Inn.

There, after sincerely thanking Swithin for his help one last time, Barnaby, Penelope, Stokes, and Morgan alighted from the carriage, allowing Phelps and Connor to return Swithin to his home in Salisbury.

The four of them stood and watched the carriage disappear down the lane, then, each wrapped in thought, they turned and went into the inn.

CHAPTER 7

*W*ith Barnaby and Stokes, Penelope had only just entered their private parlor, tossed off her bonnet and coat, and sat, when the door opened, and Henry and Madeline peeked in.

On seeing them, Henry smiled. "There you are. We were waiting in the snug in the hope you might have made some progress that you would be willing to share."

Stokes waved them in. "By all means, come and join us."

Penelope smiled warmly. "Indeed. I believe we could do with your insight, Madeline. And yours, too, Henry."

The five of them settled in the various chairs about the fireplace, with Barnaby and Penelope once again on the old settle.

Stokes opened the discussion with "We seem to have taken a significant step forward today." He related what they'd learned from Swithin regarding Viola's visit to his shop on the Wednesday afternoon, which had resulted in him informing Viola that the stones in her bracelet were now fake.

"Oh dear!" Madeline looked horrified. "She would have been…" She broke off, then continued, "Horrified at first, then devastated, then angry."

Penelope thought, then nodded. "That seems to have been the case."

Stokes drew the necklace and bracelet from his pocket and handed both to Madeline. "Are these your sister's?"

Madeline took the pieces and examined both. "This is definitely

Viola's bracelet. I hadn't seen the necklace before, but as Swithin said, it's clearly been made to match the bracelet, so I assume this is, in fact, the necklace Viola wrote to me about." Madeline looked up. "The one her secret admirer, H, had given her."

Stokes nodded. "Well, the reason Swithin got on to us was that Billy Gilroy had the bracelet and necklace and tried to sell them to Swithin."

"Billy?" Henry looked shocked. "I know he's a bit of a difficult lad, but surely, he wasn't the one who ransacked the cottage."

"No," Stokes said, "he wasn't." He went on to describe what they'd learned of Viola's movements in the hours preceding her death and how she'd hidden the two pieces of jewelry in the urn in the graveyard.

Madeline looked utterly bewildered. "Why hide those pieces in the graveyard?"

"Oh." Penelope searched in her pocket and tugged out the handkerchief they'd found in the urn and handed it to Madeline. "That's Viola's, isn't it?"

Madeline examined the embroidery and nodded. "Yes."

"The bracelet and necklace were wrapped in that," Penelope said. "Billy left the handkerchief in the urn when he took the jewelry."

"I think," Barnaby put in, "that with Reverend Foswell's confirmation, we're correct in thinking it was Viola herself who left the jewelry there."

Madeline shook her head, then looked at Stokes. "I don't want Billy charged with any crime. His mother's life has been hard enough without that."

Stokes smiled. "As it happens, Billy didn't commit any crime. Your sister left those pieces in a public place. Finders keepers more or less applies."

Madeline's expression eased, but then her frown returned. "Why on earth did she hide her favorite pieces of jewelry?"

"Perhaps," Penelope said, "because not only weren't they her favorites anymore, given the stones were paste, but to her, those pieces would have been constant reminders of H's perfidy." She looked around the company. "I suspect we can assume that in arranging for such a perfectly matching necklace to be made, H, whoever he is, borrowed the bracelet from Viola to show the jeweler."

Madeline nodded. "He did. She mentioned loaning the bracelet to him in order to have a matching necklace made." She grimaced. "After the fact, sadly, or I would have warned her against trusting any man she had only recently met with her favorite piece. The stones might only have been aquamarines, but they were very fine specimens."

"Swithin mentioned that," Stokes said.

In her mind, Penelope was turning over all they'd learned, trying to see how the pieces might fit. "Do you think," she said, "that it's possible, having realized it had to have been H who stole her aquamarines and had them substituted with paste, that Viola viewed those two pieces of jewelry as evidence of his crime?" Penelope looked at Madeline. "Was Viola likely to have thought that through?"

Madeline's expression firmed. "Oh yes. There was nothing whatever wrong with Viola's ability to put two and two together." She paused, then added, "And in this case, I believe she would have been correct." She looked at the others. "The jewelry itself is the only proof she had of H's actions."

A moment of silence ensued, then Henry cleared his throat and said, "If, as the villagers are saying, this man we believe must be H came to call on Viola on the afternoons that Mrs. Gilroy had off, then Viola would have expected H to call that Thursday afternoon."

Penelope eagerly added, "And she couldn't put him off because she had no way of contacting him."

Madeline leapt on the point. "After learning what she did from Swithin, she no longer trusted H at all, so she hid the jewelry so even if he insisted on trying to take it away, he couldn't." Eyes alight, she looked around the company. "Viola hid the jewelry so H couldn't take it. That's certainly something Viola would do."

"And," Barnaby added, "that's why she chose that particular grave." He looked at Penelope and Stokes. "That grave is so old that no one knows who's buried there, which means that no one would have turned up to put flowers in that urn." He looked at Madeline and Henry. "Given Viola didn't know Billy was watching her, the urn was a safe place to leave the jewelry."

They all seemed happy with that piece of deduction.

After a moment of savoring, Stokes looked from Madeline to Penelope. "Am I correct in thinking that the jeweler who made the necklace to match the bracelet so perfectly was the person who switched the stones?"

Penelope nodded decisively. "Given how well the fake stones fit and that they were good enough to fool Viola, the jeweler would have had to be the one who made the substitution."

"And that means," Madeline said, "that the jeweler who made the necklace will be able to identify who brought him the bracelet to copy and commissioned the work and, presumably, paid him to switch the stones as well."

"That's another reason why Viola might have hidden the jewelry," Penelope said. "Not only were the pieces the sole proof of *H*'s crime, but they were also the best way to trace the jeweler and, perhaps, get back her aquamarines."

"As matters now stand," Barnaby concluded, "those two pieces of jewelry are our most promising route to identifying Viola's secret admirer, *H*, and potentially convicting him of the greater crime of murder."

Penelope looked at Madeline and Henry. "In this area, where would you go to find a skilled jeweler?" With her head, she indicated the necklace in Madeline's hands. "One capable of work of that quality?"

Henry and Madeline exchanged a glance, then looked at the others and, in unison, said, "Salisbury."

Henry added, "Shaftesbury and Blandford Forum are closer, but neither is large nor boasts any jeweler of that level. Salisbury, however, has several that I know of."

Madeline was nodding. "It would have to be Salisbury, I think. I can't imagine Viola allowing anyone to take the bracelet for long. Not long enough to engage a jeweler in London."

"Right, then." Penelope looked at Barnaby and Stokes. "I believe we have a solid lead to pursue."

Henry glanced at Madeline, then ventured, "Actually, aside from learning of your progress, we came looking for you to let you know that Madeline has discovered an unexpected gentleman loitering about the village."

"Oh?" Stokes reached for his notebook, which he'd laid aside, and looked inquiringly at Madeline. "Who's that?"

Under the combined weight of their interested gazes, Madeline colored faintly. "His name is Montgomery Pincer. He's…well, I suppose you could say he's something of an old flame of mine—more a girlhood fancy, really—from the time we lived in Salisbury many years ago. I met him at the church on Monday morning. He said he'd just returned the day before from America. It sounded as if he's been living there for quite some years. He said he was passing and saw me going into the church, and having just heard about Viola's murder, he stopped to offer his condolences."

The others nodded their understanding and waited as Madeline paused, then, frowning slightly, went on, "The thing is, he joined me in the church this morning as well, and I have no idea why he would still be in the area, simply walking about. When I met him before, on Monday, I thought he was on his way from Southampton to Salisbury. I assumed he was returning to his parents' house there."

Penelope frowned. "You said he was an old flame. Is it possible that he has his eye on you? After all, you are still unmarried and will inherit your sister's estate, and"—she gestured to Madeline's subdued yet expensive gown—"you are plainly sufficiently well off in your own right." Penelope paused, then bluntly asked, "Could he be a fortune hunter?"

Madeline's expression eased, and she laughed. "Oh yes. Monty Pincer is assuredly that. For as long as I've known him, which is virtually from childhood, he's been intent on marrying money. Indeed, that was the cause of the rupture between us all those years ago. So yes, it's likely he's still very much of that mind, and he's already told me he hasn't yet married."

She paused, then sighed. "Given he's tallish, lean, and dark-haired, it did occur to me that he might be Viola's secret admirer, except that his name doesn't begin with *H*, and I can't imagine Viola setting aside my past experience with him."

"Nevertheless," Stokes said, scribbling in his book, "do you know where he's staying?"

Madeline shook her head. "The oddity of him still being around the village only struck me later." She looked at Henry. "While we were having luncheon in Shaftesbury."

"Well," Stokes said, "if you see Monty again, ask him where he's staying. It would be useful to know so he won't confuse matters if we end up having to search the area for our mystery man."

Madeline nodded. "If I do cross his path again, I'll ask, if nothing else, to appease my own curiosity."

Penelope had been thinking. She looked at Madeline. "Returning to our earlier point of finally having a solid lead to pursue regarding identifying H, I believe our next steps will involve interviewing Salisbury's jewelers until we discover who made the necklace and substituted the fake stones for the aquamarines in the bracelet." She arched a brow at Barnaby and Stokes, and when they said nothing to discourage her, she returned her gaze to Madeline. "It would be a great help if you could

accompany us. You're the victim's sister and her heir, and you know
Salisbury and the jewelry in question better than any of us."

Without hesitation, Madeline nodded. "Yes, of course. I'll be happy to
help."

The answer pleased everyone, and they settled to make plans for the
following day, then Madeline and Henry accepted the investigators' invitation and joined them for dinner, during which the company spoke of
other, more relaxing subjects.

The following morning, as arranged, Henry dropped Madeline off at the
inn in time for breakfast. Henry had estate business he needed to attend to
that day, for which he'd been sincerely apologetic, but Madeline had
assured him she quite understood, and Penelope had watched the
exchange with a gleam in her eye and a calculating smile on her lips.

After breakfast, the company set off in the carriage and reached Salisbury in good time. Along the way, they had discussed the most effective
strategy to find the jeweler who had made the necklace and had settled on
a two-pronged approach. Consequently, Phelps drove directly to the
police station, where Barnaby and Stokes parted from the ladies and went
inside to inquire of the local force regarding any likely suspects known to
the police among the jewelry-making community.

Phelps then turned the carriage and drove back to Silver Street and
Swithin's Jewelers.

When the carriage drew up outside that establishment, Penelope and
Madeline were handed to the pavement by Connor and, accompanied by
him and Morgan, who had been delegated to assist as required, proceeded
into the shop.

In the lead, Penelope spied Mr. Swithin behind the rear counter. She
smiled and went forward with Madeline on her heels. Swithin recognized
Penelope and, by the way his eyes widened, he also recognized Madeline.

Penelope halted before the counter and nodded amiably. "Good morning, Mr. Swithin."

Swithin returned her greeting with a half bow.

As he straightened, Penelope gestured to Madeline. "I suspect you'll
recognize Miss Madeline Huntingdon of old."

"Indeed." Swithin bowed to Madeline. "Permit me to offer my sincere condolences on the loss of your dear sister, Miss Huntingdon. I was deeply saddened to learn of her death."

"Thank you, Mr. Swithin." Gravely, Madeline inclined her head. "As it happens, it's in relation to Viola's murder that we are here."

Swithin appeared momentarily flustered. "Oh—I do hope that the information I gave your sister didn't in any way lead to her death."

Madeline shared a glance with Penelope, then returned her gaze to Swithin. "As to that, sir, at this time, it's impossible to say. Until we catch the man who killed her, we cannot be certain of his motives."

Somewhat at a loss, Swithin looked at Penelope.

Quickly, she explained, "The jewelry itself is the reason we've returned to consult with you." She looked at Madeline, who drew the bracelet and necklace from her reticule and carefully laid both on the counter. Penelope went on, "We are seeking to identify the jeweler who fashioned the necklace. We presume he was also the person who substituted the paste imitations for the real aquamarines."

Swithin's professional gaze had locked on the bracelet and necklace. He nodded almost absentmindedly. "That's certainly possible—indeed, it's very likely. Only a skilled jeweler could have done this work, and if he was copying the design and fabricating the necklace, it would be the work of minutes to switch out the bracelet's stones. Assuming, of course, that he was the sort of jeweler who would perform such substitutions at his customer's request."

As if unable to help himself, Swithin pulled a loupe from his pocket, picked up the bracelet, and examined the paste replicas. "I thought so when I saw these before, but truly, these are excellent fakes." He lowered the loupe to tell them, "We often see quite poor substitutions, but these would fool most people."

"What of the work on the necklace itself?" Penelope asked.

Swithin put down the bracelet and picked up the necklace. He raised it to the loupe he'd settled in one eye socket and carefully appraised the links of the necklace. "This," he pronounced, "is also truly excellent work. A very decent copy of my bracelet design. Unfortunately, although not surprisingly, there is no maker's mark, so there's no way to tell who did the work."

He lowered the necklace to the countertop.

Penelope regarded him steadily. "Do you suspect or can you guess whose work it is?"

Swithin looked uncomfortable. "There's no way to be sure, and truly,

I'm not inclined to hazard a guess, as one would have to assume that whoever made the necklace was also guilty of substituting the stones."

Studying Swithin—an upright pillar of the commercial community— Penelope realized that pressing him to make a guess was unlikely to bear fruit. She exchanged a swift look with Madeline and, from Madeline's fleeting grimace, assumed she'd come to the same conclusion.

As agreed, they shifted to their next avenue of attack, and Madeline asked, "How many jewelers are there in Salisbury?"

Swithin was relieved they'd let the matter of who made the necklace go and answered readily, albeit with a wry quirk of his lips. "More than you might think. There are at least ten and possibly more. I only really interact with my major competitor, Carlsbrook, whose shop is farther along Silver Street."

Penelope leaned on the counter. "You must know the local fabricating workshops. You and Carlsbrook must discuss the local industry from time to time. Do you have any suspicions of any workshop that might be involved in underhanded practices such as substituting paste for stones?"

Swithin shifted and looked even more uncomfortable, but under the unrelenting pressure of intent gazes from two pairs of eyes, he eventually conceded, "Well, it's really not something we like to speak of, but between us, Carlsbrook and I have heard of at least three jewelers—two relatively recent to the town and one longtime bane on our existence— who might, from time to time, dabble in questionable commissions."

"And these gentlemen are?" Penelope inquired.

Swithin eyed her determined expression and sighed. "Conrad, Kimble, and the old-timer is Jacobs. Their workshops are farther out, not in town. All three have stalls at the market."

Madeline smiled and collected the necklace and bracelet. "Thank you, Mr. Swithin."

Penelope inclined her head graciously. "You have, indeed, been a very real help."

Swithin looked doubtful, but replied, "I'm happy to have been so." He came out from behind the counter to escort them to the door.

Penelope and Madeline followed Connor and Morgan out of the shop. As they stepped onto the pavement and the door closed with a jingle behind them, Penelope smiled. It seemed to her that Swithin was equally happy to have weathered their inquisition and to see them leave his shop.

After dispatching Penelope and Madeline to discover what Swithin could tell them of the jeweler who had fashioned the necklace, Barnaby and Stokes entered the police station in search of information on shady jewelers. While making their plans, Stokes had stated, "The local force always has some idea about dodgy operators on their patch."

They approached the young constable on the desk, and he greeted them with the news that the medical examiner was ready to release Viola Huntingdon's body to her family for burial.

"I'll let Miss Huntingdon—the sister—know," Stokes said. "Meanwhile, we're here to speak with Superintending Constable Mallard."

The constable went to check with Mallard, then returned and showed them to his office.

They entered to find Mallard behind his desk, and as they claimed the chairs before it, he directed an inquiring and rather hopeful look their way. "Any advance?" he asked. "Did Swithin identify the man involved?"

"He did," Stokes confirmed. "But it seems all is not as it appeared at first glance." Briefly, he explained what they'd learned from Billy Gilroy. "And as that was verified by Reverend Foswell, we're treating Viola hiding the jewelry as fact."

Mallard was frowning. "But why on earth would she do such a thing?"

Barnaby outlined their current hypothesis. "Her sister believed Viola was quite capable of such reasoning, and it does fit with her being furious about being deceived and wanting to ensure H got his comeuppance, which is entirely understandable."

"Hmm, yes. I see." Mallard shrewdly eyed Stokes. "Are you after tracing the jeweler, then?"

Stokes grinned. "That's why we're here—to pick your brains as to dodgy jewelers in Salisbury."

Barnaby put in, "They have to be skilled to have copied the bracelet so well."

Mallard sucked his teeth, his gaze growing distant as he trawled his memory. Eventually, he admitted, "There are all sorts of jewelers in this town. There are two well-established firms—Swithin's and Carlsbrook's. I've never heard a whisper about either. Straight as a die with reputations to protect, so I doubt it would be either of them. Next, there are four smaller outfits with shops in the streets around the square, but all of those are trying to make their mark, and getting taken up for shady doings isn't going to help them with that." Mallard straightened. "I'd say your best bet will be one of the five who have stalls at the market. Each have work-shops outside town—out in the villages—and they're the ones we keep our eyes on as the most likely outlets for stolen items." He grimaced and looked at Stokes. "Hard to catch them, though. They see us coming and spirit away anything incriminating long before we can get close enough to nab them."

Stokes nodded understandingly. "Markets are always difficult. So"—he glanced at Barnaby—"we have five possibilities."

Leaning forward on his forearms, Mallard said, "I honestly can't see it being anyone else, so the stallholders you want are Hatchard, Jacobs, Kimble, Millbank, and Conrad."

Stokes jotted down the names, and Barnaby asked, "When's the next market day?"

"Tomorrow." Mallard leaned back. "All five should be in the square by eight in the morning. All five stalls are scattered along the central row."

Stokes had been consulting his notebook. "While we're here"—he looked at Mallard—"and I ask purely to be thorough, have you had any reports or concerns regarding a Jim Swinson or William—Billy—Gilroy, both of Ashmore village?"

Mallard thought, then shook his head. "Can't say either name rings any bells, and I don't know as we've ever had any reason to suspect anyone from that tiny place of anything. But I'll check."

"Thank you," Stokes said.

"What about a Pincer?" Barnaby asked. "Montgomery—Monty—Pincer, apparently a Salisbury native believed to have spent the past several years out of the country, but now recently returned."

Mallard frowned. "Pincer? How far back was it that he was living here?"

Barnaby calculated, then grimaced. "Possibly as many as ten or even fifteen years ago."

"Ah. That explains why the name doesn't register," Mallard said. "I moved up here from Southampton five years ago. But I'll ask around. There are some old hands still about who might remember if we've ever had cause to look sideways at this Pincer."

Barnaby inclined his head. "Thank you. It might be nothing or not connected with the case, but he seems to have turned up at a curious time. That might just be coincidence, but…"

"Coincidences are suspicious," Mallard darkly opined.

Barnaby grinned. "Indeed."

Stokes tucked away his notebook and nodded to Mallard. "Thank you for the help. We might see which of the local jewelers we can cross off our list today, and we'll be back tomorrow to investigate the stallholders at the market."

Mallard pushed away from the desk as Stokes and Barnaby rose. "If you need any help taking anyone up," Mallard said, "we'll be happy to assist."

With nods and smiles all around, Barnaby and Stokes left Mallard to his day and headed out to the front desk. There, Stokes requested a list of the names and addresses of the four minor jewelers in the town. The young constable was happy to help and even sketched a crude map of the center of the town, showing the relevant locations.

Thus armed, Barnaby and Stokes walked out of the police station. They halted on the pavement and looked toward the market square, presently empty of stalls. "Now," Barnaby said, "to find the ladies and combine our information with whatever they've learned."

⁓

Barnaby and Stokes walked down Endless Street and reached the square to see Morgan striding their way.

The experienced constable had been escorting Penelope and Madeline on their quest. He grinned and halted and, when they joined him, saluted and said, "The ladies decided we needed to eat next, so they're waiting in the ladies' snug of the Haunch of Venison." He waved across the empty square. "Miss Huntingdon said it was the best place for us all to have some lunch."

Stokes smiled. "And who are we to argue?" He waved at Morgan. "Lead on."

Morgan grinned, spun on his heel, and strode back the way he'd come.

The Haunch of Venison was situated opposite the market cross, which stood in the corner of the square where Silver and Minster Streets met. The inn was a very old half-timbered building, but obviously well kept, and judging by the crowd of patrons, it was the favored place for the gentry to dine in Salisbury. Even though it wasn't market day, the rooms hosted a goodly throng and were buzzing with talk.

Morgan paused in the doorway to the snug set aside for female patrons and pointed to where Penelope and Madeline were seated at a table for four beside one of the front windows.

Stokes nodded, then glanced at the taproom opposite. "Get yourself something to eat and take some food out to Phelps and Connor." They'd spotted the pair with the carriage, which was drawn up on the other side of the street.

Morgan saluted and happily took himself off, leaving Barnaby and Stokes to join the ladies.

With smiles of greeting, Barnaby and Stokes drew out the empty chairs.

Before Penelope could commence the inquisition plainly hovering on her tongue, as Stokes sat, he looked at Madeline. "Before I forget, the medical examiner sent word that Viola's body has been released for burial." He settled and gently asked, "Have you thought of what you want to do?"

Madeline's expression blanked, then she lightly grimaced. "I'll need to have a word with the local undertaker. I expect he'll be the same man who handled my father's burial."

Penelope shared a quick glance with Barnaby, then said, "We'll come with you if you like. Perhaps we should attend to that immediately after lunch and get it out of the way?"

"Thank you," Madeline said. "I think that might be best." She paused, then sighed. "I'll also need to speak with the minister of St. Edmund's. Viola would have wanted to be buried near our parents."

His tone kind, Barnaby prompted, "You'll also need to inform whichever solicitor administered your father's will."

Madeline nodded. "The firm is here in Salisbury. I'll think about the service overnight, then return tomorrow and call at the church and make the necessary arrangements and notify the solicitor as well."

The others nodded supportively.

The serving girl arrived to take their orders, and after the girl bustled off, Penelope informed Barnaby and Stokes, "Initially, Swithin wouldn't hazard a guess as to who had made the necklace, but eventually, he unbent enough to give us the names of three jewelers who might be involved in less-than-reputable practices and whom he believed capable of such work."

"Did he, indeed?" Stokes reached for his notebook. "What were the names?"

"Kimble, Conrad, and Jacobs," Penelope supplied.

Stokes looked up from his notes. "Those are three of the five names Mallard gave us. Apparently, all five have workshops outside the town and trade through stalls in the market."

"And," Barnaby said, "market day is tomorrow."

Penelope grimaced. "I forgot to ask what day the market ran, but"— she waved at the window and the view of the empty square—"obviously, it's not today."

"We'll have to come back tomorrow," Barnaby said, "and speak with those five."

Madeline offered, "Swithin said Kimble and Conrad were relative newcomers to the town, but that Jacobs was..." She glanced at Penelope. "How did Swithin put it? A long-standing bane on their existence?"

Penelope nodded. "By 'their,' he meant the existence of him and the other well-respected jeweler in town, Carlsbrook." She paused, then said, "I think we can put Swithin and Carlsbrook at the bottom of our list of suspects. Reputation is everything for jewelers, and Swithin and it seems likely Carlsbrook, too, would be well aware of that. I doubt either would risk their standing by having anything to do with fake stones."

"Mallard said much the same," Barnaby said. "However, there are four more minor jewelers here in town that, for completeness's sake if nothing else, we should investigate, at least to the extent of being able to cross them off our list."

"As the five who deal through the market have workshops out of town," Stokes said, "there's no sense in trying for them today."

Their drinks arrived, ferried out by a smiling serving girl, and another girl brought out their meals.

They settled to eat and drink in comfortable silence, which Penelope eventually broke with questions for Madeline about Salisbury and the surrounding countryside.

Only after they'd pushed aside their empty plates did they return to the task at hand.

"We could split up," Penelope suggested. "That would be quicker."

Stokes and Barnaby had been studying the list the young constable had provided.

"Possibly," Barnaby conceded, sitting back. "But if we do strike any glimmer of a lead, we'll need Stokes there to exercise his authority, and any delay might give the workshop in question time to hide any evidence."

Stokes nodded. "An excellent point." He looked at Penelope and

Madeline. "And we'll also need both of you to use your sharp eyes and your knowledge of jewelry to ask the right questions." He shook his head. "Splitting up won't work."

Reluctantly, Penelope conceded their points. "All right. So we stay together and visit the four shops." She paused, eyeing Stokes, then ventured, "Actually, Stokes, it might be best if you remain in the carriage, out of sight, while the three of us go in and learn what we can. You do seem to set off alarms even before you speak."

Stokes grimaced but couldn't deny that. After his long years in the force, a certain aura hung about him like a cloak and all too often was readily detected by wrongdoers. "Well, we can try that and see how it goes. If you get any sense of something shady going on and need my authoritative presence, you can send Madeline out to fetch me."

Everyone was agreeable.

Penelope looked at Barnaby. "Where are these minor jewelers located?"

Stokes produced the map the constable had sketched, and with Madeline's knowledge of Salisbury's streets, they traced the quickest route that would take them first to the undertakers, then to all four shops.

With that done, they rose. Barnaby paid the bill while Stokes fetched Morgan, and they left the Haunch of Venison, crossed the street, and climbed into the carriage.

They settled, and Barnaby consulted the map, then called to Phelps, "Gibsons' Undertakers on Canal Street, Phelps. Canal Street should be just ahead on the left."

A second later, Phelps set the horses in motion, and they rattled off along the street.

After Madeline, supported by Barnaby and Penelope, called at the undertakers and made the necessary arrangements, they returned to the carriage and continued along Canal Street to the first of the jewelers on their list. When the carriage halted outside a smallish shop on the north side of the street, Penelope faced the others and said, "I've been thinking. Perhaps if Barnaby, Madeline, and I enter as a group, and Madeline and I ask the jeweler about the necklace design—without letting him get a close look at the stones—and if, as we suspect he will, he doesn't claim the piece as his, Madeline and I can look further at his wares, and under cover of that, Barnaby can quietly ask the owner about substituting paste replicas. Just a very general leading query. From the owner's reaction, we'll at least get some idea of whether he's willing to entertain doing such work."

Barnaby, Madeline, and Stokes shared glances, then all agreed there was nothing to be lost by attempting such a charade.

Subsequently, Penelope pushed open the door to Findlayson's Jewelry Shop with Madeline at her heels with, as a last touch, Madeline wearing the necklace.

With Barnaby bringing up the rear, the ladies made for the nearest glass-topped counter and pored over the pieces displayed beneath the glass. The salesman came up on the other side of the counter. Smiling, he said, "Good afternoon. I'm Mr. Findlayson, owner of this shop. Are you looking for anything specific, mesdames?"

Penelope and Madeline exchanged a glance, then Penelope leaned forward and confided, "Actually, we're interested in finding pieces of a similar design to this necklace." She indicated the links draped about Madeline's throat. Madeline stepped back a pace as if to better show off the piece, ensuring the stones were sufficiently far away from the jeweler that he was unlikely to detect that they were fake. Penelope went on, "The necklace belongs to a friend of ours. It was a gift, so she doesn't know who made it. We've borrowed it for the day, hoping to locate the jeweler who created it." She opened her eyes wide. "Was it you or one of your workers?"

When Findlayson looked torn, Madeline added, "We're interested in commissioning several pieces."

Findlayson faintly grimaced. "I'm afraid that's not my work, but"—with a sweep of his hand, he indicated the other display cases in the shop—"if you care to look through my wares, it's possible something might catch your eye."

Penelope and Madeline looked duly disappointed, but consented to look over the man's offerings, which, indeed, were very different in design and, to some extent, even in execution. The work on the necklace was quite fine, while Findlayson's pieces were heavier.

Barnaby had been trailing the ladies, doing his best to look suitably bored. When, eventually, the pair stopped and appeared to be debating the merits of a cuff, Barnaby halted a little way away and endeavored to catch Findlayson's eye.

Seeing that the ladies were absorbed, Findlayson responded to Barnaby's unvoiced summons and backtracked until he stood opposite Barnaby. "Can I help you, sir?"

"I've heard," Barnaby murmured with a glance in Penelope's direction, "that the latest paste imitations are really very good, easily passing for the real thing. I wondered whether you or anyone you might know sometimes fabricated pieces with paste instead of stones to bring the overall cost down."

Findlayson straightened, his expression turning first to one of horror and then to personal affront. "Really, sir," he spluttered, "I…I don't know what to say. I would never consent to doing such a thing—never! And I'm shocked you would think I would even consider it."

The growing ire in the jeweler's gaze had Barnaby quickly backing down. "Just an innocent inquiry." Barnaby held his hands wide. "I had no intention of casting aspersions—not at all."

Penelope and Madeline—who had, of course, been listening avidly—pretended to have just noticed the discussion. Penelope came bustling across. "What's that?"

"Nothing, nothing, my dear." Hurriedly, Barnaby turned her toward the door. "But I think it's time we left."

"Indeed!" Poker-straight and glaring from behind the counter, Findlayson added, "And I would take it kindly, sir, if you did not return!"

Barnaby bundled Penelope and Madeline from the shop and followed on their heels. The three piled back into the carriage, with Barnaby pausing on the pavement only long enough to tell Phelps, "Go! On to the next one."

After clambering into the carriage and closing the door, Barnaby collapsed on the seat beside Penelope, who was grinning widely.

"That was interesting," she observed, merriment dancing in her eyes.

Madeline, too, was smiling. "Poor Findlayson. Instead of a sale, he ended up being insulted."

Barnaby humphed and looked at Stokes, who was regarding him questioningly. "Suffice it to say," Barnaby informed him, "that Findlayson is not our crooked jeweler."

Of course, Stokes demanded the full story, and Penelope and Madeline readily provided it, while Barnaby pretended to be greatly put out.

By the time Stokes stopped laughing, they'd reached Melrose Jewelers on Rollestone Street, and it was time for them to enact their charade again.

They did so with similar results and traveled on to Gisborne Jewelers on Bedwin Street and finally to the Crowe Jewelry Emporium on Castle Street.

At each establishment, their increasingly polished performance elicited the same shocked and scandalized response.

After they'd clambered back into the carriage and informed Stokes he could cross Crowe off the list as well, Barnaby sat back and remarked, "I suspect I've wrecked my reputation as a gentleman among Salisbury's minor jewelers."

Smiling, Penelope patted his knee consolingly. "Never mind. It's all been in a very good cause. Having eliminated those four as possibilities, as well as Swithin and Carlsbrook, we can now confidently focus on our five jewelers at the market. One of them will most likely prove to be the jeweler we seek."

Stokes had spent his minutes waiting in the carriage reviewing the facts they presently knew. As the carriage rolled out of Salisbury and took the road to Coombe Bisset with Tollard Royal some way beyond, he suggested, "Let's use the time to the inn to go over the case."

When the others looked willing, he went on, "From all we've gathered to this point, the only person with a known motive for ransacking the cottage was Viola's secret admirer, H. Everything we've learned points to him calling on her on Thursday afternoon. By the evidence of the clock, she was killed at three-thirty-three or thereabouts. Virtually everyone in the village with the remotest reason to wish Viola harm has an alibi for that time. H is the only one unaccounted for. We therefore assume he's Viola's killer—for exactly what reason, we can't know, but possibly because she threatened to expose him in some way—and after strangling her, H searched for the items of jewelry that effectively linked him to her, but because Viola had hidden the pieces in the churchyard, H didn't find them."

Penelope was nodding. "Presumably, he gave up and fled the scene and, most likely, was gone when Henry called at the cottage at about four-thirty."

Stokes nodded. "So H is our man, and thanks to Viola, we have one clear avenue through which to pursue him."

Her expression now starkly grim, Madeline said, "We need to use the clue she left us to hunt H down."

Barnaby shifted, rearranging his long legs. "I agree that the most direct route to identifying H is to find the jeweler he commissioned to make the necklace and, presumably, substitute paste for the aquamarines in the bracelet."

"It's not as if," Penelope added, "we're following a lead that's years old. We know the jeweler received the commission less than two months ago. He can't have forgotten such a special order or who asked for the work in such a short time."

"Indeed." Stokes sat back. "So I take it we're in accord that, tomorrow, we'll return to Salisbury as early as we can and investigate our five prime candidates for the role of dodgy jeweler."

The others smiled and agreed, and thereafter, as they bowled on into the countryside, a comfortable silence descended.

Idly, Barnaby stared out at the passing landscape, at the hedges and trees lining the road, with the gentle hills rolling across the distant horizon. Within the group, there was a palpable air of being on the hunt and that despite the negatives of the day, they were progressing step by steady step. He judged that they all felt a great deal more confident that they would soon learn H's identity, and then, with any luck, they would have their murderer.

Dusk was closing in when Phelps finally turned the horses in to the yard of the King John Inn.

Penelope stirred and, through the gathering dimness, looked at Madeline. "It'll be dark soon. You must allow Phelps to drive you back to the cottage."

Madeline might have demurred, but both Barnaby and Stokes added their voices to Penelope's, and Madeline subsided into the comfort of the carriage with good grace.

Barnaby followed Stokes down the carriage steps, then handed Penelope to the ground.

With Stokes, they turned to watch as Connor shut the carriage door, then climbed back up to sit beside Phelps.

Phelps nodded to them, then jiggled the reins and steered the horses into a turn, then drove back out of the inn yard and turned the carriage toward Ashmore.

"Well," Stokes said, stretching his arms over his head, "I don't know about you, but I'm looking forward to another excellent dinner and an undisturbed night in a comfortable bed."

Penelope laughed. "No babies to rouse you in the dead of night?"

Lowering his arms, Stokes nodded. "Exactly."

Barnaby laughed and, trading stories of their experiences with their various offspring, they headed into the inn.

Leaning back against the leather seat, Madeline swayed gently as the well-sprung carriage bowled along. Without the others to provide distraction, her mind inevitably turned to her task for that evening, namely drawing together the elements of the burial service her older sister would have wanted for herself.

Unsurprisingly, she and Viola had never discussed the matter, so the best Madeline could do was to recall the points Viola had insisted on in the service they'd arranged for their father five years ago.

Her mind slid into the past, to the sense of loss she'd experienced then, and the echo of the same emotion—different degree, perhaps, yet with the same harrowing, hollowing quality—that swirled within her now.

Viola had been sufficiently older that, logically, it had always been likely that Madeline would, at some point in her life, have to organize Viola's funeral.

But not yet!

As she thought of the reality facing her, Madeline still felt buffeted by the unexpectedness and the associated shock.

With a mental effort, she forced her mind into the slightly detached state necessary to consider which hymns and prayers Viola would have wanted. Given their years spent so closely entwined with the church, Madeline knew the possibilities by heart and could also cite the scriptures her sister would have preferred to have read.

She decided on the content, then juggled the order before committing the whole to memory. She would discuss her proposed service with the minister tomorrow in what would be the last assistance she would ever render her sister.

That, and seeing justice done and Viola's murderer caught.

Those words resonated in Madeline's mind as the carriage slowed to turn south, then a short way on, turned west, onto the last stretch of lane toward Ashmore.

With nothing else to occupy her thoughts, Madeline found the silence weighing on her increasingly heavily, increasingly oppressively.

On impulse, she rose and tapped on the panel in the carriage's ceiling.

It promptly opened, and Connor asked, "Yes, miss?"

"Please pull up just ahead." She dropped back to the seat and looked through the window. "At that stile coming up on the left."

The carriage slowed, then rocked to a halt.

Before Madeline could open the door, Connor dropped down and opened it for her. "Is there a problem, miss?" he asked.

She summoned a smile. "No, no. I just need some air." She took the hand he offered and climbed down to the lane. She glanced up at the driver, who was looking down with some concern, and smiled reassuringly. "Nice as this carriage is, I feel I've spent too many hours today cooped up inside it."

As both men relaxed, she tipped her head southward, over the fields. "The path beyond the stile leads to the woods at the rear of Lavender Cottage. It's not far at all to walk from here, and as I said, I need the fresh air."

Madeline had agreed to put up with a guard until the murderer was caught, but she couldn't imagine that embarking on a short, spontaneous walk over open fields to the rear garden of the cottage would expose her to any great danger, and William Price would be waiting at the cottage.

Luckily for her, neither Phelps nor Connor had been present when the matter of guarding her had been discussed, and both responded to her words with smiles of understanding.

"Right you are, then, miss," Phelps said. "If you're sure you're happy to walk the last little way?"

She nodded decisively. "I am sure, yes. Thank you for bringing me this far."

"Our pleasure, miss." Connor saluted her, then said, "Here, let me give you a hand over the stile."

She readily accepted his help, then stood on the other side of the stile and waved the carriage away.

Then she drew in a deep, deep breath, filling her lungs with the sweet scent of scythed hay, and felt the peace that until then had eluded her throughout that day wrap around her.

With a gentle smile, she set off along the path toward the line of trees that screened the rear of Lavender Cottage.

CHAPTER 8

Feeling increasingly easier in her mind and significantly more refreshed, Madeline walked steadily toward the trees. Born in the country yet now living in London, she relished the clear country air whenever she could get it. Her earlier resolution—her commitment to see justice for Viola—still rang in her mind and fueled her determination. As she paced along the old right-of-way, she revisited the investigation and the advances they'd made that day. All in all, matters were progressing as well as she could hope for, and she was truly grateful to God for sending three such experienced and competent investigators to prosecute Viola's case.

That thought brought to mind Barnaby's advice that she needed to notify the family solicitor. The Salisbury firm of Farnham and Sons had handled the family's wills and also the purchase of Lavender Cottage. She underlined her mental note to remember to call at Mr. Farnham's office tomorrow, after she'd met with the minister at St. Edmund's Church.

Reviewing what she and the solicitor would need to discuss led to the question of what she was going to do after Viola's funeral. Would she keep the cottage? She considered the possibility but couldn't see much point in doing so. The cottage had been Viola's dream, not hers. Her life—well-ordered, comfortable, and secure—awaited her in London…yet if she was brutally truthful, now, with the transitory nature of life so dramatically demonstrated, she had to wonder if that life in London, satisfying though it had been to this point, would continue to be enough for her.

In the long run, would that life fulfill her?

Perhaps it was time to think anew about what her life in the years ahead should be.

She continued pacing but a little slower as she pondered such conundrums.

She was approaching the line of trees that were the outliers of the strip of woodland that ran along the cottage's rear boundary when movement ahead drew her eye, and she saw Monty walking along the edge of the wood toward her.

From the smile that lit his face when he realized she'd seen him, he was obviously intending to intercept her.

Madeline stifled a sigh. She truly wished that he wasn't there—that she didn't have to deal with him. Yesterday, while she and Henry had been in Shaftesbury, she'd accepted an invitation to dine with him at Glossup Hall. Although she was in mourning and there was always the question of propriety, Henry had pointed out that they would be surrounded by his staff and that a quiet dinner would give her an opportunity to tell him what they'd discovered that day.

Given how supportive he'd been, she'd decided she owed him the update and that her reputation would survive a quiet dinner.

Henry had said he would call at the cottage in his curricle at five-fifteen, and knowing him as she now did, she didn't doubt that he would be on time. As Monty drew nearer, she couldn't help but contrast Henry's solid reliability, his constancy and steadfast nature, with the fecklessness and _un_reliability of the man before her.

Regardless, she could all but hear her father say that was no excuse to be rude and summarily dismiss Monty, so she found a polite smile, halted at the edge of the wood, and extended her hand.

With his customary grace, Monty grasped her fingers and bowed over them. As he straightened and she retrieved her hand, which he only reluctantly released, he said, "I saw you in the field and thought I should at least act as your escort through the wood. There is a murderer on the loose, after all."

Madeline merely inclined her head and, with a wave, invited him to join her as she walked on, following the narrow path that led through the wood and into the cottage's rear garden. They'd been later than she'd hoped leaving Salisbury, and while she would have liked to tidy her hair and brush off her gown before Henry called, she accepted that was now unlikely, not least because Monty would do his best to delay her with incidental conversation.

Sure enough, his next words were "Have you been out of the village today?"

She nodded. "I went to Salisbury to assist the investigators."

"Oh? In what way?"

She was about to explain when Stokes's request flashed into her mind. "Actually, the inspector in charge of the case wanted to know where you lived, and I realized I don't know." She glanced at Monty, but his expression was his usual charming yet unrevealing mask. "You haven't mentioned it. So the inspector asked me to ask you the next time I met you."

A frown appeared in Monty's eyes, darkening his face. "Why does he need to know?"

"Well, they are investigating a murder, and you are a gentleman who lives in the area and, clearly, is in the vicinity of the cottage." She waved ahead to where the walls of the cottage were now visible through the trees. "Mostly, it's for the inspector's records in case they end up searching the area thoroughly." She paused and waited.

When Monty seemed to be debating giving her an answer, she started to wonder why.

He glanced at her, his gaze sweeping her face. No doubt seeing her increasing puzzlement, he smiled rather wanly and offered, "I have a house outside Bowerchalke. Just a bolt hole, really. Now, I wanted to ask" —he paused for a second—"about your sister's funeral. I would like to attend, if only to support you in that sad hour."

Madeline knew a deflection when she heard one, but calmly replied, "It will, I hope, be held at St. Edmund's in Salisbury. I need to meet with the minister to settle on a date and time."

Somewhat to her relief, they'd reached the edge of the wood, and Monty halted. "I'll leave you here." He nodded ahead. "It appears you have guards aplenty."

Madeline looked and saw William Price and Jim Swinson working in the cottage's vegetable garden. She smiled and, over her shoulder, directed a polite nod Monty's way. "Goodbye, then."

She stepped out of the wood into the open edge of the garden. As she headed for the path that led to the kitchen door, William and Jim saw her and waved.

She waved back, feeling distinctly lighter. She returned her gaze to the house, and the clatter of wheels in the lane drew her attention past the corner of the cottage, and she saw Henry drive up in his curricle.

To her amazement, her heart leapt—for the first time in her life, she actually felt it do so, actually understood what the phrase meant.

Her smile widening, she increased her pace and deviated around the cottage to reach the front gate and the lane beyond.

Henry saw her coming, and his smile was one of welcome and expectant delight.

She couldn't help but beam back.

She opened the gate and let it swing shut behind her as she walked to the curricle's side.

Henry leaned across and gave her his hand to help her up to the seat beside him.

She settled, and he expertly turned the curricle and set the chestnut pacing back around the pond and on along High Street, out of the village toward Glossup Hall.

As the trees bordering the lane enclosed them in shadows, Henry rather hesitantly admitted, "Both my staff and I are looking forward to this dinner. I confess I haven't entertained in…quite a while."

Madeline glanced at his face and understood. "Since Kitty died at that house party?" During the previous day, he'd told her all about that terrible time.

He nodded. "Yes, and so you are in great charity with the staff. They've been starved of the chance to show off their paces for the past five years."

She laughed, then smiling, said, "Well, I'm looking forward to sampling their efforts." She waved ahead. "Drive on."

He grinned, the expression easing the all-too-serious lines of his face, then he flicked the reins and sent the chestnut into a more rapid trot.

In the dark hours of the night, William Price was deep in dreams, stretched out on the pallet he'd laid at the top of the stairs in front of Madeline Huntingdon's bedroom door, when someone large tripped over him.

William woke to curses. "What?" Groggy, he tried to get to his feet, but the thick blanket had tangled around his legs.

And not just his legs but someone else's, too!

The intruder got free first and aimed a kick at William, which he had to roll to the side to avoid, only to have the intruder seize the moment, leap over William, and thunder down the stairs.

Flinging the blanket aside, jaw set, William launched himself into the chase.

The intruder raced through the cottage's kitchen to the rear door, wrenched it open, and without a single glance back, fled through the kitchen garden.

William followed, but as he went out of the door, he heard Madeline's footsteps hurrying down the stairs.

He was her guard. He was there to protect her, and that had to be his first priority.

And obviously, someone was, indeed, out to harm her, so William couldn't risk leaving her alone, not for any reason.

What if he lost his quarry? What if his quarry hit him on the head, left him for dead, and came back for her?

On the garden path, William slowed, then halted, and breathing heavily, watched the unknown man—the intruder had definitely been a man—vanish into the dense shadows of the wood.

Madeline came rushing up. Clutching a thick wrap she'd wound around her nightgown-clad shoulders, she halted beside William. "What happened?" She followed his gaze. "Did someone break in?" She turned to study him, concern in her face. "Are you all right?"

William smiled wryly. "Just my pride bruised, is all."

She made a scoffing sound. "I can't see why it should be. You stopped him getting to me, after all."

William shrugged and answered her first question. "He—whoever he is—tried to sneak up to your room and tripped over me." He slanted her a boyish grin. "Lucky I didn't listen to you and sleep in the box room downstairs."

Soberly, Madeline nodded. "Indeed. Thank you for being so stubborn in the execution of your duties."

Their breaths were fogging in the cold air. She took William's arm and turned him toward the cottage. "Come inside, and I'll make you some hot cocoa. I don't want to be responsible for you catching your death."

They returned to the cottage and the kitchen. Madeline prodded the fire in the stove until it was blazing, then put on some milk to warm. Although she hadn't done such mundane chores for some time, she hadn't forgotten how.

With the milk heating, she turned to William, who at her insistence, was seated at the little table. "How did he get in?"

William pondered that, then shook his head. "I didn't hear anything —no window breaking or being forced." His puzzled frown deepened. "And we both checked the doors and windows, too, before we went up."

He pushed to his feet and padded to the kitchen door. Madeline joined him, bringing one of the lamps she'd lit. In the light the lamp cast, they studied the lock on the door.

After a thorough inspection, William stated, "There's no sign of it being tampered with."

"No," Madeline agreed. "And yet, it was unlocked."

William nodded. "Even though we both checked that it was locked before we went upstairs." He met her gaze. "How?"

Grimly, Madeline replied, "He had a key." She sighed. "Viola must have given her secret admirer, H, a key."

William grimaced and hesitantly offered, "Or did Billy Gilroy borrow his mother's key?"

Madeline pulled a face, then hurried to lift the milk from the stove. She busied herself making hot cocoa for them both, then glanced at William, who had returned to the chair by the table. "What did you see of the intruder?"

He grimaced. "It was so dark, I could barely make anything out. And once he'd leapt over me and started down the stairs, he never looked back —never gave me any chance to see his face."

Madeline set down both mugs of cocoa and slid into another chair. "What about outside? It was dark, but there was some moonlight."

William sipped and nodded. "He—he was definitely a male—was tallish, leanish build, and, I would say, dark-haired."

Madeline sighed. "So it could be Billy or, to my mind more likely, Viola's secret admirer, H."

William sipped again, then added, "If Jim Swinson had managed to get a key, it could have been him, although I don't think it was."

"Or," Madeline said, cradling her mug between her hands, "it could have been someone else entirely."

～

Early the next morning, Madeline and William got themselves ready to go to the inn in Tollard Royal and report the excitement of the night to Stokes and the Adairs.

Madeline hadn't slept well after the intrusion and was grateful that Henry had offered to take her and William in his curricle to join the others at the inn.

Madeline made porridge, and she and William sat at the table, drizzled honey over their bowls, and ate.

After several silent minutes, Madeline said, "The more I think about the incident last night, the more it seems it was as the inspector feared— that H, whoever he is, believes that Viola had, or might have, revealed something about him in her letters. Something that I might use to identify him."

William nodded. "It does seem that way. I can't imagine why Billy Gilroy or Jim Swinson or anyone else would want to try to creep up on you."

Madeline tipped her head his way. "True. It always seems to come back to Viola's secret admirer." She paused, then added, "I do wish she'd told me his name."

They were tidying the kitchen when the rattle of wheels in the lane heralded Henry's arrival.

The relief Madeline felt on seeing his face was, she told herself, out of all proportion to the situation, yet she couldn't pretend she didn't feel safer, more secure, with Henry there, by her side.

Of course, he took one look at her face and instantly asked, "What's wrong?" He glanced at William's uncharacteristically solemn expression. "Has something happened?"

She and William exchanged a glance, then, between them, proceeded to describe the nighttime incident.

Predictably, Henry was shocked. "Good Lord! He actually came inside?"

"And up the stairs." William beckoned Henry to the kitchen door and showed him the undamaged lock. "We're sure he came in this way, because we're certain we locked the door before we went to bed, and it was open—unlocked—when he left."

"He had to have had a key," Madeline said, "which reduces the suspect list to Billy Gilroy and our mysterious H, and there seems no reason that Billy would seek to harm me."

Slowly, his gaze on her, Henry nodded. "I agree it's not Billy. As matters stand, he has no reason whatsoever to attack you, and living in the village, he has to know that William has been staying here, standing guard."

The sincere concern in his eyes warmed Madeline from the inside out.

Then, his expression firming, he met her gaze. "As soon as you're both ready, I suggest we depart for the inn. Stokes and the Adairs need to hear about this sooner rather than later."

With that, they all concurred, and a bare ten minutes later, Henry helped Madeline up to his curricle's seat and checked that William was safely perched on the rear board, then Henry picked up the reins and set his chestnut trotting rapidly for Tollard Royal.

When Madeline, Henry, and William reached the King John Inn, they went straight to the door to the private parlor, knocked perfunctorily, and entered to find Penelope, Barnaby, and Stokes sipping tea and coffee, with the remains of their breakfasts already cleared away.

Penelope took one look at the newcomers' faces and immediately asked, "What's happened?"

Beside and opposite her, Barnaby and Stokes had also come alert, lowering their coffee cups to better study the visitors.

Henry steered Madeline to a chair and held it for her, then sat in the chair alongside.

Constable Price took up his customary stance by the door.

Madeline glanced at Henry, then looked at Penelope. "Last night, an intruder came into the cottage. He crept up the stairs, but luckily, William"—she threw a grateful glance at the young constable—"had insisted on sleeping on a pallet in the corridor outside my room, and in the dark, the intruder tripped over him."

Stokes transferred his gaze to Price. "I take it he got away?"

"Yes, sir." The young man looked a trifle crestfallen. "I got tangled in the blankets, and by the time I'd got free, he'd leapt over me and down the stairs, and he raced out of the back door."

"William very bravely gave chase," Madeline put in, "but gave up the pursuit to stay with me, for which I was exceedingly grateful."

Stokes nodded to Madeline and looked at Price. "Good decision, Constable. Your brief was to protect Miss Huntingdon, and you made the right choice."

Price looked a lot happier.

"Now," Stokes said, "did you get a look at this intruder? Any hint as to his identity?"

"Not really, sir," Price replied. "The moon was out, but nowhere near full, so the light was weak. All I could see was that he was tallish, leanish, and had dark hair, which fits most of our suspects."

When Penelope arched her brows at Madeline, she responded, "I didn't see the man at all. I only heard the ruckus."

"Obviously," Barnaby said, "he must have moved quickly and confidently, so not an older man."

"Not Arthur Penrose, certainly," Penelope concurred. "But the description could fit Billy, Jim, and most likely of all, *H*."

Henry said, "We can't imagine why, as matters stand, either Jim or Billy would have attempted such a thing. Living in the village, both would know Price is staying at the cottage."

"Excellent point," Stokes acknowledged.

Penelope capped that with "And that brings us back, once again, to *H*."

"There's also the fact the intruder must have had a key," Henry said. "We all checked, and the lock hasn't been tampered with, and Madeline and William both confirmed that the rear door was locked before they retired."

Madeline nodded. "Sadly, I can imagine that Viola might have given her secret admirer a key to the cottage. She did tend to believe in her own invincibility, and having lived a rather sheltered life, she didn't always perceive dangers that, to others, are obvious."

Penelope grimaced. "Such as handing her bracelet over to a man she'd only known for a few weeks."

"Exactly," Madeline concurred.

"However"—Penelope tipped her head in thought—"we shouldn't lose sight of the point that if it was H who broke into the cottage, presumably to attack Madeline, then whatever Viola had learned about him is critically important to him."

"And," Barnaby added, "that makes him dangerous. Potentially very dangerous."

Stokes was nodding as he tucked away his notebook. "Given we have no idea who H is, we also have no real sense of how far he might go to silence—as he thinks—Madeline."

Madeline snorted. "Which is truly ridiculous given I know nothing."

"Even so," Henry gravely said.

"We need to learn who H is," Penelope stated with renewed determination.

"And take him into custody before he has a chance to act again," Stokes said.

In magisterial tones, Henry stated, "That he's acted in this way dramatically increases the need to apprehend him."

Everyone nodded in fervent agreement.

Barnaby eased his chair back from the table. "The night's events add impetus to our plans for today."

Penelope nodded. "Canvassing the jewelers at the market remains our surest route to identifying H, indirect though it might be."

"After last night," Henry pressed, "we need to act with all speed."

"And thank goodness," Madeline said, "today is market day."

"We need to take H into custody as soon as we possibly can." Stokes rose and made for the door. "Let me summon the troops, and we can make a more detailed plan." He opened the door and left, before closing the door behind him.

Studying Henry and Madeline, Barnaby remarked, "The one reassuring aspect of the incident last night is that it proves H is still in the area. For whatever reason, he hasn't decamped."

"And," Penelope said, "that's yet another reason for us to do our utmost to find him today."

Stokes returned, leading O'Donnell, Morgan, Phelps, and Connor. As Stokes shut the door behind Connor, he explained, "In a case like this, the more heads the better, and it will help if all of us know the details of our plan and our goal."

Barnaby nodded and waited while the newcomers joined Price in taking up stances against the wall on either side of the door, then for their benefit, Barnaby briefly explained about the bracelet and necklace and the substitution of paste for the bracelet's original set of aquamarines, all presumably at the behest of the mysterious *H*, who was their prime suspect in Viola Huntingdon's murder. "By locating the jeweler who did the work, we hope to learn H's identity. The town's five potentially shady jewelers are expected to be at their stalls in the market today. Mallard named them as Hatchard, Jacobs, Kimble, Millbank, and Conrad. All five have stalls in the market's central row."

Penelope added, "According to Swithin, one of the town's premier jewelers, the three more likely to be our target—meaning the jeweler who executed the commission for H and made the necklace and switched the bracelet's aquamarines for paste—are Conrad, Kimble, and Jacobs."

Morgan raised a hand and, when everyone looked his way and Stokes arched a brow, asked, "How do you propose to approach each jeweler?"

O'Donnell added, "Being in uniform, Morgan and I will need to play least in sight." The sergeant's shrewd gaze came to rest on Stokes. "And begging your pardon, sir, but you should as well. We're all too identifiable as police."

Stokes grimaced, then looked at Penelope and Madeline. "Perhaps you two and Barnaby should play the same charade you used with the four minor jewelers yesterday."

Penelope described to the others how she and Madeline had pretended to be looking for a piece similar to the necklace in design—thus checking whether the jeweler's work was of the right ilk—with Barnaby following and surreptitiously inquiring about replacing stones with paste.

While Penelope spoke, Madeline drew the necklace and bracelet from her reticule and laid both pieces out on the table so all could see them.

Morgan and O'Donnell stepped forward to examine the jewelry. After a moment, Morgan shook his head and looked at Stokes. "I don't think that charade will work, sir. Dodgy jewelers are always on their guard and wary and careful over who they deal with."

O'Donnell nodded. "They wouldn't stay in business long if they weren't."

Morgan transferred his gaze to Penelope. "That's why I think that, after clapping eyes on you, ma'am, and Miss Huntingdon, no market jeweler who dabbles in illicit commissions is going to believe a gentleman like Mr. Adair is going to attempt to give you or Miss Huntingdon a piece with paste instead of stones."

Penelope stared at Morgan, then grimaced and conceded, "In that, I fear you might well be right."

"I was thinking," Morgan went on, glancing back at the trio still hugging the wall, "that Connor would be much more believable if he asked about aquamarines. Not paste." Morgan looked at Stokes and Barnaby. "The real ones. The jeweler who switched the stones out mostly likely still has them, waiting for the right customer to sell them on."

Looking distinctly eager, Connor came forward to look at the jewelry.

Penelope studied him critically. Her groom-cum-guard was dressed in entirely ordinary clothes, neat and plainly good quality. More, he'd proved over the years that he could speak well, in a gentlemanly fashion, if required.

Connor looked up and said, "Even better—and perhaps more believable—I could say my master is looking for a good set of aquamarines." He nodded at the bracelet. "I could describe the general size of the stones and see if the jeweler bites."

O'Donnell added, "If this dodgy jeweler replaced the stones only a month or so ago, then the odds are that he still has them, but is starting to feel keen to offload them. They must represent a certain amount of cash to him, and he'll want to make the trade."

A short and lively discussion ensued, the upshot being that all agreed going after the real aquamarines might well be their best means of identifying which jeweler was the one involved.

Penelope stated, "Aquamarines are not a popular choice these days, so I agree it's very likely the jeweler who made the substitution still has the real stones."

"And," Stokes said, "if a jeweler does produce a set of real aquamarines, we can step in and check the stones against the bracelet. If the stones fit, he'll be our man."

Everyone was enthusiastic about the ploy.

"If I might suggest," Barnaby said, "it would smooth our way if Penelope and Madeline, attended by me and Henry, go past the stalls first. The ladies can cast their eyes over each jeweler's wares"—he looked at Penelope and Madeline—"as if you're considering buying, and so determine whether any of the jewelers has the right style and skill to have fabricated the necklace. From all we've heard, it's quite fine and rather distinctive work."

Penelope pounced on the idea. "That's an excellent notion. That way, Connor won't need to approach all five jewelers in his search for real aquamarines."

Stokes looked at Connor. "Can you tell real stones from paste?"

Connor blinked, clearly surprised to have been asked, then replied, "I've been working for the Adairs for four years. I know how real jewels sparkle and gleam. Paste doesn't do that."

Barnaby chuckled. "Regardless, once Connor gets offered real stones —and they will be real if the jeweler scents a good deal—then we can close in and confirm before we ask the jeweler in question how he came by the stones."

"That should be interesting," Stokes observed, clearly looking forward to the moment. He looked around the gathering. "Right, then. Any further questions, or are we ready to depart for Salisbury market?"

The answer didn't need to be articulated, as all those seated rose, and determination showed in every face.

In short order, they quit the parlor, left the inn, and piled into and onto the coach and also into Henry's curricle, and with renewed purpose and resurgent hope, set off for Salisbury.

～

Penelope surveyed Salisbury's marketplace. They'd clearly arrived at the time when attendance at the weekly market was at its height, which would suit their purpose excellently well.

On Barnaby's arm, with Madeline and Henry beside them, Penelope kept her eyes peeled as they made their way through the bustling throng of marketgoers toward the central aisle. Inconspicuous in his everyman's attire, Connor trailed a few yards behind, while Stokes, O'Donnell, Morgan, and Constable Price were farther away, loitering by a lamppost on the edge of the square as if idly watching events from a distance in case any pickpockets or the like attempted to ply their trade.

On reaching the mouth of the central aisle, the couples paused and surveyed the brightly hued stalls lining the way on both sides. "Let's walk all the way down once," Barnaby said, "more or less in the middle, as if merely looking around. We can take note of the jewelers' stalls and get some idea of each jeweler's work without attracting their attention."

Penelope nodded. "At the other end, we can turn back and approach the ones we think most likely."

Henry and Madeline agreed, and together, the four of them moved into the crowded walkway. Salisbury was a prosperous town, and there were plenty of gentry and well-to-do citizens ambling about the stalls, providing camouflage of sorts. The noise that blanketed the area was considerable, made up of myriad conversations, most conducted at volume, combined with the raucous cries of vendors hawking their wares.

With Barnaby, Penelope wended this way and that, moving slowly down the aisle. Henry and Madeline kept pace, but the couples were often separated by other marketgoers moving in the opposite direction.

The first jeweler's stall they came to bore a sign along the front of the table identifying it as belonging to Kimble Jewelers. Penelope and, a few minutes later, Madeline cast their eyes over Kimble's offerings. After both moved on, their gazes met, and as one, they shook their heads. Kimble's designs were much heavier, sturdy, and mannish. He wasn't their target.

They continued down the aisle, and by the time they reached the far end and turned to look back along the twin lines of stalls, Penelope felt confident in stating, "For my money, Jacobs is our best bet."

Madeline agreed. "His work was the finest, the most like the necklace."

Henry humphed. "Even I could see that he might have made it."

"And"—Barnaby looked at Penelope—"correct me if I err, but Jacobs was one of the three jewelers Swithin named as potentially shady."

Penelope nodded. "He was the one Swithin labeled a longtime bane on his and Carlsbrook's existence."

Connor had ambled up and was standing close enough to hear. "Was that the middle stall, the one with the middle-aged man with curly dark hair?"

"That's the one." Penelope determinedly looped her arm more firmly in Barnaby's and glanced at Madeline and Henry. "Shall we?"

Together, the couples moved into the still-considerable throng. Once again, Connor followed a few paces behind. They didn't hurry, still ambling as if they had no specific destination in mind, but once they reached Jacobs's stall, Penelope stepped out of the flow of traffic and fronted the counter-like table, and Madeline joined her.

With easy smiles for the stallholder—a pale average-sized man with large, light-brown eyes and a thick mop of black curls crammed beneath a plaid cap—they examined his wares, exclaiming over the delicacy of the work. The jeweler responded to their praise with a certain amount of charm, and Penelope confirmed that he made pieces on commission.

With apparent reluctance, the ladies moved on, rejoining Barnaby and Henry. The couples continued strolling, but stopped two stalls farther along and, reasonably screened by the passersby, turned to witness what came next.

Doing an excellent job of projecting the image of a put-upon servant taxed with a boring task, Connor walked up to Jacobs's stall and explained to the man—who they all assumed was Jacobs himself—about Connor's master's need of good-quality aquamarines. Straining their ears, they heard Connor improvise, "They're for a pretty little gift for his ladylove."

Barnaby made a mental note to pay Connor a bonus. That was exactly the sort of information a shady jeweler would find reassuring.

Even from a distance, the four observers could clearly see Jacobs debating whether or not to take their bait.

Then Jacobs smiled at Connor, said something that made Connor come to attention, and reached beneath the table. Jacobs looked down, drew out a key from his waistcoat pocket, and unlocked what appeared to be a metal lockbox. After opening the box, he rummaged inside, then drew out a small velvet pouch.

Barnaby looked toward where Stokes and the others were—albeit unobtrusively—watching them like hawks. After checking that Jacobs's attention was elsewhere, Barnaby raised his hand and signaled to Stokes and his men. Once he was sure they were on their way, Barnaby returned his gaze to the action at Jacobs's stall.

Penelope had kept her eyes fixed on Jacobs, and Barnaby followed her gaze to the black-velvet-covered tray Jacobs set on the table. Then he opened the pouch, tipped and shook it, and a handful of good-sized pale-blue stones slid out onto the tray.

Conner leant forward and studied the stones, using one finger to move them on the tray.

Edging forward with Penelope, Barnaby heard Jacobs explain, "These only recently came into my possession. On commission, they are, so they won't be going for a song, but when it comes to aquamarines, these are exceptionally fine specimens. I doubt your master will find better, not loose as these are."

Having completed his examination, Conner smiled and, straightening, nodded, apparently to Jacobs, but in reality, that was their agreed signal indicating that Connor believed the stones were real and also of the right size to be the ones taken from the bracelet.

With a swift glance, Barnaby confirmed Stokes and his men were almost upon them, then with Penelope all but tugging him on, he strode forward, swiftly closing the distance to Jacobs's stall.

Henry and Madeline moved with them, and in less than a minute, with Connor stepping to the side and keeping his gaze trained on Jacobs, Barnaby, Penelope, Madeline, and Henry fronted the stall, forming a wall between Jacobs and all other marketgoers.

Jacobs startled, and alarm entered his eyes. He stared as Penelope swooped in and took possession of the tray with the jewels. With Madeline, who had the bracelet in her hand, Penelope compared the sizes of the genuine aquamarines Jacobs had spread on the tray with the fake stones that had been put into the bracelet.

On catching sight of the bracelet, Jacobs stiffened, then started to slowly rise.

Penelope looked up and confidently stated, "These are the stones that were originally in the bracelet."

Jacobs sprang to his feet. In panic, he turned to flee through the stall behind his and into the next row, only to come face-to-face with Morgan, backed by Price. The constables had anticipated Jacobs's reaction and had circled around to block his escape.

Stokes arrived, clapped Barnaby on the shoulder, and moved past and around Jacobs's table to confront the jeweler. "Jacobs, you're under arrest for the substitution and consequent theft of these aquamarines."

Watching Madeline carefully put the aquamarines back into the pouch and drop the bracelet in as well, Jacobs sighed. "I should have known better than to have any dealings with that charlatan."

"Oh?" Stokes said. "And which charlatan is that?"

Jacobs looked at him and frowned. "And who might you be?"

Stokes smiled wolfishly. "Inspector Stokes of Scotland Yard."

Puzzled, Jacobs frowned harder. "Since when does Scotland Yard concern itself with lowly substituted stones?" He glanced at the others gathered about, then returned his gaze to Stokes. After a second of swift thinking, Jacobs asked, "Might it possibly be to my advantage to tell you everything I know about how I got those stones?"

Stokes studied him, then inclined his head. "Possibly. But I suggest we repair to Endless Street and surroundings more conducive to this conversation."

Barnaby glanced around and saw that, unsurprisingly, they were attracting a good deal of attention.

Jacobs saw the same. Lips setting, he bent and pulled out his lockbox. "Just let me lock my goods away, and we can go."

They all waited while Jacobs secured his wares, then hoisted the box in his arms. Flanked by Morgan and Price, Jacobs followed Stokes and O'Donnell out of the market, with Barnaby, Penelope, Madeline, Henry, and Connor trailing close behind.

They emerged from the market square and crossed Blue Boar Row, then turned up Endless Street.

A little way along, they came upon their carriage with Phelps waiting patiently on the box. Barnaby paused and turned to Connor, who'd been following at their heels. Barnaby smiled. "That was excellent work back there."

Penelope and Madeline added their praises, and Connor brightened at their compliments. They left Connor to resume his normal duties beside Phelps—and no doubt, to regale the coachman with the latest exciting happenings—and continued along the street.

As they drew level with the police station, Madeline suddenly halted and, from the pocket of her jacket, drew out a small watch and checked the time. "Damn," she muttered.

Barnaby and Penelope had paused and waited, as had Henry. When they all looked inquiringly her way, Madeline explained, "That took longer than I'd expected. I need to see the minister at St. Edmund's Church to discuss Viola's funeral, and while he'll be at the church for the next hour or so, after that, he'll be out on his visits." She looked to where Stokes and his men were ushering Jacobs through the door and sighed. "As much as I want to learn who H is, I can't put off seeing the minister."

Penelope closed her hand over one of Madeline's. "Go and see the minister. Whatever Jacobs tells us, if at all possible, we'll wait for you before taking our next step."

"I'll go with you," Henry said. "Best not to go about alone."

"Indeed." Barnaby nodded approvingly. "We'll almost certainly still be here when you finish with the minister. Join us then."

With some relief, Madeline nodded and took the arm Henry offered, and the couples parted, with Madeline and Henry continuing along Endless Street toward Bedwin Street and the church, while Barnaby and Penelope turned and followed Stokes and his men into the police station.

CHAPTER 9

With Penelope, Barnaby entered the police station to see Mallard walking into the foyer to join Stokes, O'Donnell, Morgan, and Price, who were gathered about Jacobs. The jeweler had taken on a distinctly hangdog look, and if anything, that expression deepened at Mallard's approach.

While bending an unrelentingly severe look on Jacobs, Mallard said to Stokes, "I was just about to head out to look for you. I've got some information on that other gent you asked about, but it can wait until you've heard what Jacobs here can offer. We've had our eye on him for quite some years, but never had a chance to put a finger on him." Mallard looked more cheerful. "Perhaps our luck has turned, and today is the day."

Jacobs's expression grew increasingly despondent.

They waited while Mallard arranged for Jacobs to be officially signed into police custody, then followed Mallard and the hapless Jacobs down the stairs to the basement and into an interrogation room.

The room was small and, with their rather large party crowding in, grew distinctly cramped. Being below ground, the stone-walled chamber was decidedly chilly. A bare room, it boasted a simple narrow table over which a single lamp hung, and four hard wooden chairs were the only seating.

Mallard directed Jacobs to the chair at one end of the table and waved Penelope, Barnaby, and Stokes to the three other chairs. Mallard himself retreated to stand against one wall, joining O'Donnell, Morgan, and Price, and with those others, settled to observe.

Jacobs had, by now, realized that Barnaby and Penelope were filling roles he didn't understand.

Seeing his confusion, Stokes explained their presence as consultants to Scotland Yard, a piece of information that did nothing to ease Jacobs's mounting concern. He stared at Stokes. "This can't be about the aquamarines. Scotland Yard, let alone high-society consultants, don't come knocking about such things."

Rather than reply, Stokes drew out the pouch he'd retrieved from Madeline and laid out the bracelet and placed the aquamarines beside it, matching the various stones with the fakes currently in their settings.

As a simple, straightforward demonstration that the aquamarines were, indeed, the stones taken from the bracelet, the move was quietly effective.

After studying the bracelet and stones, Stokes looked at Jacobs. "Do you know the name of the lady to whom this bracelet belonged?" When Jacobs stared at the evidence and kept his lips shut, Stokes asked the obvious next question. "Did she instruct you to replace the stones with paste and sell the stones, as you admitted, on commission?"

Jacobs raised his gaze and looked at Stokes, but still said nothing.

Barnaby sighed as if bored. He flicked a finger at the bracelet and stones. "We can all see that the stones are a perfect match, and if need be, it will be easy to get another jeweler to confirm that." To Jacobs, he said, "There is no chance that you will avoid the charge of stealing the aquamarines."

Stokes had been studying Jacobs. "Would it help if I explained that the lady to whom this bracelet belongs—a Miss Viola Huntingdon—was recently murdered, strangled to death in her own parlor, and the man who brought you the bracelet, your untrustworthy charlatan, is our prime suspect?"

As Stokes's revelation had unfolded, Jacobs's eyes had grown wider and wider as all resistance vanished. "Murdered? Good Lord!"

"Indeed." Stokes nodded. "Fencing a bit of this and that is one thing. Being an accessory to murder is something else again."

Helpfully, Penelope added, "That's a hanging offence."

Thoroughly rattled, Jacobs looked from one to the other. "I don't know anything about any murder. What do you want from me?"

Stokes promptly replied, "The name of the man who brought you the bracelet, asked you to copy it as a necklace and, at the same time, replace the aquamarines in the bracelet with paste. A clear and accurate description of him would also help your cause."

Jacobs wet his lips. "I can do the description well enough. A gentleman, or so you'd take him to be, the way he carries himself, walks, the way he's always dressed. He's middling tall, a trifle taller than me but younger. Leaner. Athletic-looking. Handsome, too, with dark-brown hair, straightish and neatly cut, and blue eyes. He's charming when he wants to be and a peevish, irritating beggar when he doesn't, which is most of the time. He's come to me on and off over the years—over the past decade and more—with similar requests to copy some piece and switch out stones for paste." Jacobs shrugged. "I saw no reason not to do the work for him. For all I knew, he could have been a gentleman gradually replacing the stones in his wife's jewelry to cover up his gambling debts and using the pretext of getting some new, matching piece made to engineer the opportunity to switch the stones." Jacobs looked at Stokes, then glanced at Mallard. "Not my place to question, is it?"

Her tone flat, Penelope said, "So in your eyes, you were performing a helpful service."

Jacobs wasn't sure how to react to that. Warily, he murmured, "Yes."

"So," Barnaby said, reclaiming Jacobs's attention, "who was this gentleman with the continual need for fake stones?"

Stokes helpfully prompted, "You can start with his name."

Jacobs grimaced. "Farmer. He always said he was Mr. Farmer."

When everyone else in the room stared in varying degrees of disbelief at Jacobs, he hung his head and admitted, "I know, I know. I never did think it was his real name, but that's the one he always gave me, and I had no reason to go hunting for his real identity."

Silence reigned as they all digested that—and that their great hope of learning the mysterious H's name had vaporized before their very eyes.

Eventually, Stokes sighed and said, "You're a shopkeeper—a jeweler. And you've interacted with this man many times over the years. You have to know more about him, so try harder with your description."

"For instance," Penelope said, "was he English? Did he have any particular accent?"

"Oh, he's English through and through," Jacobs said, "and as for accent, I'd say he was a local, born and bred. His roots have to lie close to Salisbury."

"Anything distinctive about his dress?" Barnaby asked. "Did he wear a signet ring or carry a cane?"

"No ring, no cane." Jacobs paused and was clearly consulting his memories. "In fact, I never saw any jewelry on him at all. No pin. Nothing. And he rarely wears a hat. As for his clothes, they were unquestionably a touch above average. Well-cut and tailored. From them alone, you would have said he was a gentleman, and he spoke like one, too." Jacobs paused, then tipped his head toward Barnaby. "But he wasn't as upper-class as you."

To Penelope's surprise, Jacobs transferred his gaze—now shrewd and calculating—to Stokes and added, "Or you, for that matter."

More than anything else, that convinced her that Jacobs was telling them all he knew, and that his observations were acute and, most importantly, accurate. Very few would correctly detect Stokes's background. A thought occurred, and she leaned forward, her gaze fixed on Jacobs's face. "Do you have any reason to think that Mr. Farmer, whoever he is, isn't actually a gentleman?"

Jacobs held her gaze for several seconds, then replied, "Not exactly that he isn't a gentleman. His hands are those of a gentleman—never did a day's hard labor, that one. But I always got the impression that he was…well, dancing on the edge, so to speak. Meaning the edge of the gentry. He was one of them, but he walked right on the edge of being a gentleman. He was never anything but polite to me, but he was always just a bit too arrogant with it."

Stokes snorted. "There's polite, and then there's asking you to replace real stones with fakes."

"How did that work, incidentally?" Penelope asked. "With the aquamarines, you said you were selling them on commission. For him? If so, do you have some arrangement with him to pass on the proceeds?"

Perhaps Jacobs could arrange a meeting.

But Jacobs shook his head. "He always knew the approximate price of the stones he had me replace, and we'd agree on a total that I could reasonably expect to make on their eventual sale, then from that, I deducted my price for making the new matching piece plus my fee, then I'd pay him the rest up front."

"So," Stokes said, "he's been in the habit of bringing you jewelry and essentially trading it for cash for years?"

Jacobs shifted on the chair. "I wouldn't have put it quite like that, but…yes, that's more or less how we dealt."

"How often did you do work for him?" Barnaby asked.

Jacobs shrugged. "He appears every four or five months with a new piece. All very different in style, but the same deal—replace the stones, make a matching piece, and give him the difference in cash."

Barnaby exchanged a look with Penelope and Stokes, but there was nothing else they could think of to ask.

From his position by the wall, Mallard asked, "Do you have any idea where this Mr. Farmer lives?"

Jacobs started to shake his head, then stopped, and after a moment's thought, offered, "Somewhere local, meaning somewhere around Salisbury. I've glimpsed him a few times over the years, walking in the streets."

No one had any more questions. They pushed back from the table and rose.

Stokes glanced at Mallard and tipped his head toward Jacobs. "I take it you'll be happy to arrange accommodation for Jacobs here?"

Mallard grinned like a shark. "It will be Salisbury City Police's pleasure, Inspector."

Jacobs deflated and slumped in the chair.

With Penelope and Stokes, Barnaby quit the interrogation room, leaving Mallard, O'Donnell, Morgan, and Price to escort Jacobs to a cell.

The three of them climbed the stairs, then gathered at one side of the foyer, exchanging glum and dispirited looks.

"We've hit a dead end, I fear," Stokes rumbled.

"Of course the damned man used an alias!" Penelope looked disgusted.

"The interesting thing," Barnaby observed, "is that he's used the same alias for years. Possibly for more than a decade."

Stokes growled, "This joker needs to be caught. There's no telling how many other women he's charmed out of their jewelry."

Neither Penelope nor Barnaby disagreed. They stood and thought and searched for ways forward.

Eventually, Penelope sighed. "It feels as if we took a giant leap forward, but we didn't land where we thought we would."

Barnaby felt equally dejected, and Stokes's expression said he felt the same.

And from Mallard's, O'Donnell's, Morgan's, and Price's faces as they slogged up the stairs and joined them, they felt just as flat.

Then Stokes turned to Mallard. "What was that information you had for us?"

"Oh yes." Mallard perked up. "It's about that cove, Pincer. I caught up with a few of the old-timers, and they remembered him. The whole family, really. Seems the Pincers were an old town family, gentry, and originally, well regarded and respected, but as the years rolled by, they fell on hard times, and the word is that the current Pincer is a layabout and a wastrel, a profligate who sweet-talks his way through life."

Penelope looked intrigued. "Go on."

Mallard obliged. "They said he was the sort who was forever hunting his fortune via some likely lass—he's charming to the back teeth, apparently—but wise parents see through his blarney and steer their daughters well clear, and he never struck success by that route."

"That fits with Madeline's view of him," Penelope said.

Mallard tugged at one earlobe. "The one strange thing is that your husband here said Pincer has been out of the country over the past years and only just got back, but the old-timers—and more than just one—say they've seen him here and about, just as always. They're certain he's been here all along, not away someplace else."

"I see." Stokes exchanged a look with Barnaby, then asked, "Where does Pincer live?"

"I was told," Mallard said, "that the old Pincers had a big house in town, but they sold up and moved out to a cottage in Bowerchalke. Tiny little village, that is, and the oldies say that now the senior Pincers have passed on, the cottage is a run-down wreck of a place, Pincer the younger never being one to spend money on repairs."

Eyes narrowing, Penelope said, "During the drive here, Madeline told us that she unexpectedly ran across Pincer last evening near her cottage, and Stokes had asked her to inquire where he lived, so she did, and he told her he was living in a house outside Bowerchalke. Note, house and outside the village."

Mallard shook his head. "The old-timers are very sure Pincer's home is a ramshackle, falling-down hovel of a place at the heart of the village."

Barnaby added, "Pincer didn't exactly lie to Madeline—he led her to think something other than the truth. But even more telling, he's been here, in and around Salisbury, the whole time."

Stokes looked grim. "He hasn't spent the past decade overseas, and even more interestingly, he fits the description of Viola's secret admirer, *H*."

Penelope looked distinctly troubled. "After his history with Madeline —and it sounds as if she had a lucky escape—surely Pincer wouldn't have set his sights on Viola. More to the point, Madeline said Viola knew about the association between Madeline and Pincer and why it ended, so Viola must have known better than to get involved with him."

"Although his name doesn't begin with *H*," Barnaby said, "it's possible that if he's also Jacobs's Mr. Farmer, using aliases comes naturally to him." He paused, then straightened. "We need to speak with Madeline. There are too many inconsistencies in Pincer's stories—the several it seems he's told."

Stokes had been consulting his notebook. He snapped it shut and turned toward the door. "We also shouldn't forget that based on physical description, Jacobs's Mr. Farmer could easily be Monty Pincer, who might also be masquerading as our mysterious *H*. The descriptions are all the same."

Barnaby and Penelope led the way to the door. Stokes strode at their heels, and Mallard fell in beside him.

Mallard glanced at Stokes. "You think Pincer's the murderer?"

"Other than the name," Stokes replied, "and with a man who commonly uses aliases, who knows what weight we should attach to that, there's a case to be made that he is our man." Pushing through the door behind Penelope and Barnaby, Stokes stated, "We need to speak with Madeline. Then we should find and interview Monty Pincer."

Mallard hurried to keep up. "Laying hands on Pincer might not be straightforward, but where's Miss Huntingdon?"

Penelope and Barnaby had already turned right along Endless Street. Over her shoulder, Penelope said, "Madeline went to St. Edmund's Church to organize her sister's funeral."

Madeline came out of the church door, paused just outside, and closing her eyes, turned her face up to the weak sunshine.

In the wake of arranging for her sister's funeral, she felt in need of warmth, of a reminder of life.

And then there was what the deacon—an older man who had known both sisters for many years—had told her.

Apparently, Viola had visited St. Edmund's on Wednesday afternoon, the afternoon before she died.

The deacon hadn't spoken to Viola, and Madeline couldn't fathom what purpose had brought her sister there. Not on that day.

Frowning slightly, she opened her eyes and looked around and spotted Henry sitting on a gravestone and watching her. His expression was stern and rather somber.

Puzzled, for when she'd left him, he'd been quite relaxed and at ease, Madeline walked across the grass and halted before him. "What is it?"

Wordlessly, he rose and pointed to the grave opposite the one on which he'd been sitting.

Madeline turned, then bent to read the name inscribed on the headstone. "Harold Montgomery Pincer." She checked the dates, then straightened. "That must be old Mr. Pincer, Monty's father."

"Indeed. Now look at that one." Henry pointed to a grave two plots on.

Madeline walked across, crouched, and peered to read the headstone. It was older, more worn, and more difficult to make out. Then the words came into focus.

She sucked in a breath, rose, and stared at the grave as understanding dawned. "Montgomery Harold Pincer," she slowly enunciated, "who must have been Monty's grandfather."

Henry had come to stand beside her. "And what are the odds that Monty's full name is Montgomery Harold Pincer, like his grandfather?"

"If the family made a habit of alternating the names..." Eyes widening, Madeline turned to Henry. "I never knew his middle name."

Henry held her gaze. "Do you think that, if he decided to approach your sister, he might have taken to using his middle name? Perhaps to distance himself from his previous association with you and emphasize that he was now a different man, a reformed character rather than a scoundrel she needed to keep at a distance."

"To underscore that the past was finished and done with..." Madeline's features firmed. "Oh yes. That's exactly the sort of thing Monty would do. He was always remarkably effective in glossing over anything he didn't want you to focus on."

Henry nodded. "So he told your sister he was a changed man and now went by the name Harold."

Madeline was nodding more and more definitely. "I can even hear Monty saying that—and what's more, I can imagine Viola accepting whatever tale he told and giving him the benefit of the doubt. She'd been raised in the church, so to speak, and giving people a second chance, turning the cheek as it were, was an ingrained part of her nature."

Suddenly sure and remembering what she'd so recently learned, Madeline gripped Henry's arm. "And there's more!" In a rush, she told him of what the deacon had just told her. "He saw Viola come out of that park across the street." With her head, she indicated the plot filled with green lawn and old trees. "The deacon thought it rather odd, because from the way she behaved, he believed she'd been hiding behind some trees while watching two men talking, and one of the men matches the description we've had from so many others of our mysterious H—which also describes Monty."

"Did the deacon see if she followed the men?"

"She didn't. He said they left, and once they had, she came in here"— Madeline waved at the church—"and sat quietly for some time. The deacon said that she appeared shaken, even devastated, but also distracted, as if she had several things on her mind all competing for her attention. He would have spoken with her and offered comfort and support, but he had a meeting with parishioners about a baptism, and when he came out of the office, Viola had gone."

Madeline turned to Henry. "Everything fits. It was Monty who was Viola's secret admirer, and she overheard something in the park that made the scales fall from her eyes, and she'd also just learned that he'd stolen her aquamarines. She finally saw him as the snake he truly is."

Madeline paused, assembling the scenario in her mind. "Viola would have seen all that, and she would have grown angry. She would have taxed him with his perfidy when he next called on her—on Thursday afternoon. When he realized she was furious and intended to expose him and have him taken up—and she did intend that, because she'd hidden the bracelet and necklace, her proof of his crimes—he killed her."

"And then," Henry said, captured by her urgency, "he ransacked the cottage, looking for the jewelry so it couldn't be used to track him down."

Madeline gripped Henry's arm tighter. "We have to go and tell the others."

Grim faced, Henry nodded. "My thoughts exactly. The sooner they hear of this, the better."

He gave her his arm, and she took it, and together, they walked quickly down the path that led around the church to the lychgate.

In the park across the street from St. Edmund's, Monty Pincer had spent the past ten minutes trying to convince Seamus O'Reilly's principal henchman, Johnson, that very soon, Monty would be able to make a down payment on the large amount of money he owed O'Reilly.

O'Reilly was the major moneylender in the district and had been for years. Because O'Reilly, largely acting through Johnson, operated strictly within the confines of the law, the authorities turned a blind eye to O'Reilly's "business" dealings.

Monty hadn't wanted this meeting and, on one level, resented being forced to report to Johnson so frequently—essentially at the man's beck and call—but he didn't dare not turn up and then discover O'Reilly had foreclosed on the cottage in Bowerchalke, the only asset Monty possessed.

At least he'd been able to choose the venue for these over-frequent meetings. His family had once owned the house that bordered the park on the east, and Monty had spent many a childhood afternoon playing beneath these very trees. Being in the park evoked memories of happier, carefree days, before Monty had grown up and life had turned against him.

Now, he sat on a bench, screened by thick bushes from the street, and worked to convince Johnson to give him just a little more time. Sadly, charm had never swayed Johnson, which left Monty scrambling to cobble together a believable argument. "As I keep saying, the younger sister is the better bet for me, and she's significantly wealthier, too."

He strove for the right blend of confidence and outright assurance as he went on, "I even went to London to make sure of her wealth and discovered she's a dark horse, indeed. I chatted up her maid, and it seems Madeline has not just the house in Bedford Place—which is much grander than she'd led me to believe—but she also has significant wealth tied up in investments managed by one of the premier firms in England."

After meeting Madeline in the church on Wednesday, he'd attended another of these meetings with Johnson, and the man's building impatience had spurred Monty into taking the train to London to confirm Madeline's wealth. What he'd learned had sent his heart soaring, and when he'd returned on Thursday afternoon and ridden toward Lavender Cottage and spotted Madeline walking across the fields, he'd seized the chance to strengthen his hold on her.

Not that it had worked. And then she'd driven off with Lord Glossup!

The image of Madeline laughing at something his lordship had said rose in Monty's mind and taunted him. Battling a frown, he thrust the vision aside and refocused on Johnson. Thinking of what he'd just revealed, and that Johnson might find it hard to swallow, plastering a quietly delighted smile on his lips, Monty shook his head and said, "I wouldn't have believed it of a female, but I know her father was heavily involved in investing, so I expect she learned the knack from him."

It was hard persuading Johnson of his chances of success when Monty himself was prey to a niggling inner fear that he wouldn't be able to secure Madeline's affections. His act of desperation in the wee hours of Friday morning had only sunk his hopes further—and what a close call that had been!

Summoning every ounce of sincerity he possessed, Monty pressed, "I tell you, it's only a matter of time. Soon, she'll be eating out of the palm of my hand, and the result will be well worth the wait for you and O'Reilly."

Johnson was a large, heavyset man, not gentry, but he'd spent years with O'Reilly, who was, and some of the man's polish had rubbed off on Johnson. He was always neatly and conservatively dressed and, despite his size, could readily pass unnoticed in a crowd. He had a large head and oval face and wore a brimmed hat, the rim of which shaded a pair of smallish but shrewd brown eyes. Johnson's gaze was sharp, as was his mind, and he rarely missed anything said or seen.

Now, Johnson turned to look at Monty with an expression of deep skepticism wreathing his face. "Let me get this straight," Johnson rumbled. "Wednesday last week, you told me you were off to pop the question to this rich spinster that you've been courting over the past months and that any day, you'd be able to make a sizeable down payment. Then on Saturday, you tell me it's all off, because the spinster's younger sister has turned up, and she's even more wealthy, and so now, you'd ditched the older one and were focusing on the younger one, and because the younger one had always held a torch for you, it would all go smoothly. Then *this* Wednesday—two days ago—you told me all was on track with the younger one, and any minute now, I'd hear wedding bells. But *now*, you tell me you need yet more time to come up with even a small contribution."

Monty struggled not to react to the menace rippling beneath Johnson's even tones. He never raised his voice, yet just that tone sent visceral fear racing through Monty's veins. He fought to preserve a calm, confident expression. "That's right. I haven't yet got the cash, but plainly, I'm good for it. Obviously, I can't simply waltz up and ask the younger sister to marry me. I have to manage the transfer of my affections in a believable way. The last thing I need to do is make the younger sister suspicious, but I swear, she's well and truly on my hook. After all, she's nearly my age and still unwed. What does that say to you? And there's no one else lining up to claim her hand, even though she's a ripe plum just waiting to be plucked."

"And squeezed, heh?" Johnson's cynicism rang loud and clear. He studied Monty, then shook his head. "It never ceases to amaze me that spinster ladies don't see right through men like you."

Monty smiled. "It's part of my charm."

Johnson snorted. "No doubt." He paused, clearly weighing the situation, then he huffed. "All right. I'll give you until Sunday. Meet me here then, same time. And you'd better have some good news and something to put against your account."

Hugely relieved, Monty assured him, "I will."

Johnson clearly remained unconvinced. "Just remember, don't try to scarper. Like I've said before, there's no way you can outrun O'Reilly's reach."

The words sent a chill through Monty, and he vowed, "I have no intention of going anywhere. Fate, fickle female, has finally deigned to smile on me again, and for me, the fruit is lying on the ground here, not anywhere else."

Johnson nodded his large head. "Just remember that." He heaved his bulk from the bench and stood.

Monty followed suit, and side by side, they walked toward the park's gate.

As they reached the gate, which was heavily shaded by the park's trees, Johnson's gaze locked on the church's lychgate, directly across the road.

Monty noticed and looked that way and saw what Johnson was watching so intently.

The pair of them paused just inside the park as the lychgate opened, and Madeline stepped through. Whoever held the gate for her was obscured from view by the roof of the lychgate.

"Here." Johnson tipped his head toward Madeline. "Isn't that the lady you're thinking to wed now? The younger sister?"

Monty's blood chilled at the evidence that Johnson had been checking up on him enough to recognize his mark. "Yes," he replied, wondering what to do even as, instinctively, he donned his most charming smile.

Then his heart leapt and started to pound as the man who'd held the gate for Madeline followed her onto the street. Madeline didn't wait for Lord Glossup to offer his arm but looped her arm in his, and together, they walked rapidly toward the center of town, then his lordship gestured, and they crossed the road and continued walking together away from the park.

Monty stood frozen just inside the park gate. Madeline and his lordship were walking so close…just like a couple.

Johnson was regarding Monty through narrowed eyes. "That didn't look to me as if she was waiting to be swept off her feet. I thought you told me there was no competition for her hand, so are you going to tell me that's her brother?"

Fleetingly, Monty met Johnson's gaze. Fear rose up and choked him, then he hauled in a breath, and desperation welled and hardened his features. "No—she doesn't have a brother. But he's no one special." Monty didn't have a choice. "Here." He stepped out of the gate. "I'll show you."

Driven, determined, and desperate, he strode rapidly after Madeline.

With Madeline on his arm, Henry walked quickly along Bedwin Street, making for the intersection with Endless Street and the police station closer to the square.

Madeline kept pace, equally eager to take their news to Stokes and the Adairs.

Then firm footsteps coming up behind them had them exchanging a glance and slowing.

The man following reached them and impudently seized Madeline's free hand. "Madeline, my dear! What a delightful surprise to find you here."

Henry and Madeline halted. For an instant, Henry stared, astonished, at the tall, lean, dark-haired gentleman bowing over Madeline's hand, then he realized who the man must be.

From the startled expression on Madeline's face and the way she instinctively edged closer to Henry, she was equally stunned. This was the man she believed had killed her sister. Henry sensed the battle she was waging not to let that show in her face as Pincer—it had to be him—straightened.

"I was just up the road"—Pincer waved vaguely in the direction from which they'd come—"and saw you walking along. Naturally, I came to offer my escort."

Pincer directed a challenging look of dismissal at Henry.

To buy Madeline time to come to grips with the outlandish situation, Henry pretended to have misinterpreted Pincer's glare and, reaching across Madeline, held out his hand. "Good afternoon. I'm Lord Glossup. Friend of Madeline's family. And I believe you're Montgomery Pincer. Madeline has mentioned you."

The approach threw Pincer off his stride, and ingrained manners had him grasping Henry's hand.

They shook hands, and Henry could almost see Pincer's brain working through Henry's words and concluding that he might not pose any real threat to Pincer's plans after all.

The hardness in Pincer's face dissolved into charming cordiality, then Henry saw him direct a swift glance across the street. Following it, Henry saw a large man ambling slowly along and patently observing them.

Henry's intervention had allowed Madeline time to gather her wits. She smiled at Monty. "Dear Monty, I didn't expect to come across you here, either." She waved ahead. "We were just heading for Endless Street."

Henry, bless him, realized her intention and stated, "I have an appointment with my solicitor in his offices along there."

As well as the police station, Endless Street played host to several of the larger legal chambers.

"Perhaps," Henry went on, looking from Madeline to Pincer, "you might accompany us, Pincer, and keep Miss Huntingdon company while I'm closeted with my man."

"I would be delighted." Monty's expression matched his words. He was beaming as he waved them onward. "Shall we?"

Madeline made no attempt to draw her arm from the safe harbor of Henry's but was forced to allow Monty to wind her other arm in his. She held back her emotions and managed a wan smile for him, then as a trio, they walked on along the pavement.

She tried not to focus on the thought that the man who had strangled Viola to death was walking by her side, his arm anchoring hers. The important thing, she told herself, was to get Monty as close to the police station as possible. With any luck, they would see a constable coming to or leaving the building and be able to enlist his aid in seizing Monty.

Of course, Monty used the moments as they walked along to chatter and, beneath the mundanity of his comments, ask apparently artless yet prying questions. Henry proved adept at batting those away without revealing anything, and Madeline did her best to contribute and keep Monty's attention diverted from where they were leading him.

Several times, she noticed that he glanced over his shoulder, and once, turning her head, she caught a glimpse of a large man walking along the pavement across the street. The man was hanging back but keeping pace as if he was watching to see what would happen. Madeline found that curious, but she didn't have time to dwell on the point. As they approached Endless Street, a group of people came marching around the corner.

Madeline was hugely relieved to see Penelope, Barnaby, and Stokes among the group, along with Price and several of Stokes's men.

Henry, too, recognized the others and lengthened his stride, just as the oncoming group registered the three of them approaching and did the same.

Pincer had been looking over his shoulder again and was momentarily unbalanced by the sudden surge as he was propelled forward by Henry and Madeline. "Here, I say!" He stumbled, hurrying to get his feet moving faster. "Why the sudden rush?"

Then he looked ahead and saw the answer.

Pincer halted—simply planted his feet and stopped.

Before Henry and Madeline could yank him forward again, Pincer seized Madeline's arm with both hands and hauled her roughly back, away from Henry. "No," Pincer said, horrified desperation in his face. Then he started backpedaling, pulling Madeline, now stumbling herself, with him. "Stop!" With his gaze locked on the approaching police, he yelled, "Stay back!"

Led by Stokes, the group slowed, uncertain.

Henry heard their footsteps slow, then halt, but all his brain could focus on was that Pincer was hurting Madeline, twisting her arm and making her wince.

For quite the first time in his life, Henry saw red. "Oh, for heaven's sake!"

He stepped around Madeline and plowed his fist into Pincer's face.

"Ah!" Pincer squawked and reeled back, releasing Madeline to clutch his nose.

Henry drew Madeline to him and, wrapping his arms protectively around her, backed away.

Then Morgan, O'Donnell, and Price rushed in and seized Monty Pincer.

Madeline saw the constables grappling with Monty, and she slumped against Henry's chest, where she felt safe and utterly secure. When, a moment later, the constables stepped back, revealing Monty with his hands secured behind his back and his nose streaming red, her mood lifted considerably.

Penelope bustled up with Barnaby. "Are you all right?"

Madeline nodded but made no move to leave the circle of Henry's strong arms. "We were hoping to lead Monty to the police station, but this worked even better."

Stokes and Mallard came up. Mallard was studying the man who'd been following Madeline, Henry, and Pincer along the opposite pavement. Large, heavyset, tending portly, and dressed in the manner of a quietly prosperous businessman, the man had halted and was openly watching the constables lead Pincer away.

Henry nodded toward the unknown man. "Pincer kept glancing in his direction."

"Several times," Madeline added.

"Did he?" Mallard glanced at Stokes. "That's Johnson, O'Reilly's man in town."

"O'Reilly being?" Stokes asked.

"The biggest moneylender in these parts." Mallard looked at the man across the street. "Let me have a word with Johnson and see if there's anything he's willing to share with us." Mallard tipped his head to where the constables were chivvying Pincer along. "In the circumstances."

Stokes nodded. "Good idea. We'll wait here."

They stood and watched as Mallard lumbered over to the opposite pavement and, after nodding to the man, whose expression had settled into one of quiet satisfaction, Mallard halted and simply said, "Johnson. Obviously, you know Pincer. I take it he's one of your master's clients."

The group across the street could just hear Johnson's rumbling reply. "Ex-client, I'm thinking."

Mallard said, "I don't suppose you'd like to tell us what you know of Pincer's recent doings."

His gaze on Pincer as he was marched around the corner into Endless Street on his way to the police station, Johnson clearly debated, then said, "In this case, I can't see any reason why I shouldn't." He transferred his gaze to Mallard's face. "You know the boss doesn't hold with our clients doing anything that might land them on the wrong side of the law. This might serve as a warning to others, heh?"

"I'm all for keeping people on the straight and narrow," Mallard said. "And who knows? Helping with this case might even get O'Reilly a little credit with the local bench."

Johnson nodded. "Seems a decent outcome. I'll take it."

Mallard tipped his head toward Endless Street. "Come on, then. The inspector from Scotland Yard will want to hear it from your lips, direct."

"Scotland Yard?" Johnson's gaze landed on the group opposite and instantly singled out Stokes. Far from being reluctant, Johnson's face lit with curiosity. "Seems Pincer's gone up in the world. I've never spoken to a Scotland Yard inspector before." Johnson smiled faintly as, with Mallard, he set off to cross the street. As they neared the others, he added, "Never had reason to before."

Mallard snorted and waved the others on. They obediently turned and, increasingly eager to learn whatever details Johnson might divulge, strode off for Endless Street with Mallard and Johnson bringing up the rear.

CHAPTER 10

They were within sight of the police station when Madeline
checked her watch and halted. "Oh, heavens!"

Henry, Penelope, and Barnaby halted as well, while Stokes, Mallard,
and Johnson skirted the group and went on.

"What is it?" Henry asked.

Madeline looked at him and sighed. "I so wanted to hear what Monty
has to say, but I must, absolutely must, call on the family solicitor, Mr.
Farnham, and advise him of Viola's death."

Penelope and Barnaby nodded encouragingly. "You really should,"
Barnaby said. "It's never helpful to let such matters slide."

"No, indeed," Penelope said. "There's been nothing in the news sheets
to alert your solicitor, has there?"

Henry snorted. "Ashmore is a tiny village and not that easy to reach.
A lady dying in a cottage out there isn't of much interest to Salisbury's
residents, much less to the reporters, who would have to find some way to
get out there and ask their questions."

"And for such parochialism, I'm sincerely grateful," Madeline stated,
"but it does mean that I need to visit Mr. Farnham's office and tell him
Viola is gone."

"Definitely," Barnaby concurred. "Is his office far?"

Madeline waved to the west. "It's just around the corner in Castle
Street. I shouldn't be long."

"Well," Penelope said, "I'm sure Stokes and Mallard will want to

interview Johnson first." She glanced at Barnaby. "We certainly do."
Returning her gaze to Madeline, Penelope concluded, "So if your visit to
the solicitor doesn't take long, you'll most likely be back before we start
interrogating Pincer."

"That would be ideal," Madeline said.

"I'll go with you," Henry said. "If we're merely going to Castle
Street, we should definitely be back in time." He glanced at Barnaby. "As
the magistrate for the area in which the murder was committed, I would
like to be present when the accused is interrogated."

Barnaby grinned. "If necessary, I'll use that to delay proceedings." He
nodded westward. "Go, and we'll hold the fort and wait on your return."

Relieved, Madeline took Henry's arm again, and they turned and
walked away.

Barnaby offered Penelope his arm, and they continued to the police
station.

On entering the foyer, they discovered Stokes and Mallard conferring.
The pair reached some decision, and Stokes directed Morgan and Price to
escort the defeated-looking Pincer down to the cells.

Stokes beckoned O'Donnell to attend him where he stood with
Mallard. As Barnaby and Penelope walked up, the sergeant presented
himself, and his voice lowered, Stokes instructed, "Once you have Pincer
settled in a cell, go and ask Jacobs to take a look at all the prisoners down
there—there are six others, apparently—and see if Jacobs recognizes
anyone as his Mr. Farmer."

O'Donnell grinned and saluted. "Yes, guv." He turned and strode off
after the others, who had disappeared down the stairs to the basement.

Stokes turned to Penelope and Barnaby. "No Madeline or Henry?"

Barnaby explained the pair's necessary errand. "With any luck, they'll
be back before we're ready to talk to Pincer."

Stokes nodded. "Right, then. Let's see what we can learn from Mr.
Johnson. Quite aside from filling in the time until Henry and Madeline
return, the more facts we have with which to confront Pincer, the
better."

With that, they all agreed. Mallard had arranged for them to speak
with Johnson in an interview room on the ground floor. "Much less off-
putting than the interrogation room downstairs. At least for the general
public."

He led them to a good-sized room with windows looking out on an
inner courtyard. Johnson was already seated at the rectangular table,

about halfway down one long side. The investigators filed in and chose seats while Mallard performed the introductions.

Penelope and Barnaby's presence caused Johnson's eyebrows to fleetingly rise, but he merely nodded respectfully to them and returned his gaze to Stokes and Mallard. Penelope and Barnaby chose seats beside each other, across the table from Johnson and a little farther up the room, leaving the places directly opposite the man to Stokes and Mallard.

Penelope sat, clasped her hands on the table, and angled herself so that she could observe Johnson and also Stokes and Mallard.

After the policemen had settled, Stokes nodded to Mallard, inviting him to take the lead.

Mallard clasped his large hands, leaned forward on his forearms, and fixed his gaze on Johnson.

O'Reilly's man seemed entirely relaxed, quite at ease and even a little amused.

"Just a pleasant conversation here," Mallard stated, and Johnson inclined his head. "So," Mallard continued, "what can you tell us about Monty Pincer?"

Johnson considered his answer, then offered, "I can tell you that he's not a man anyone in their right mind would ever place an ounce of trust in."

Mallard nodded. "How did he come to be of interest to your master?"

Johnson shrugged. "The usual way. Debts. Pincer's been running up debts here, there, and everywhere more or less for all of his life. He often plays the game of taking from Peter to pay Paul. That's how he came to O'Reilly's attention. He looked into Pincer's assets and discovered that, lo and behold, the run-down hovel Pincer calls home has a nice parcel of land attached—land Pincer currently agists for next to nothing. He's no farmer and has no idea of the worth of what he owns." Johnson smiled like a shark. "The boss looked and saw pretty hills, a spring-fed brook, and nice pastures and decided he wouldn't mind having a piece of land like that out Bowerchalke way. Sleepy little spot with no nosy neighbors. So he told me to offer Pincer a consolidation loan."

"Meaning," Stokes clarified, "a loan to pay off all his other loans, leaving your boss—O'Reilly—as Pincer's sole creditor."

Johnson nodded with a touch of respect. "You understand it, then. The way the boss likes to run things is to let them—the punters, like Pincer—run for a while, all the time getting deeper into debt, as they do, so that when the time eventually comes and we call in the loan, there's no option for them but to hand over whatever they've used as collateral as payment. In Pincer's case, that's the deed to his cottage and land in Bowerchalke."

"Let me guess," Barnaby said. "You feel that Pincer has now run far enough, and you're ready to foreclose, as it were."

Johnson grinned. "Right you are, sir." He looked at Stokes and Mallard. "Especially as it seems that Pincer is going to be spending some time as a guest of Her Majesty."

"As to that," Mallard said, "what do you know of Pincer's recent activities? We're particularly interested in his pursuit of a lady named Viola Huntingdon."

Johnson frowned. "If I've got this right, then the lady Pincer bailed up today was this Viola's younger sister?"

"That's right," Stokes said and waited.

Johnson sat back. "Well, all I can tell you is what Pincer told me, and if you've got any handle on the man at all, you'll know to take anything that comes out of his mouth with a very large dose of salt."

"We know," Penelope said. "So what did he tell you?"

Johnson was about to oblige, but then hesitated. After a moment, he looked at Mallard. "Here. If I tell you what I know—what the blighter told me—I won't have to appear before any beak, will I?"

It was Stokes who replied, "Unless you have some information that only you know that proves pertinent to our case against Pincer, then it's highly unlikely you'll be called on to make an appearance."

Johnson pondered that qualified response, then huffed. "I figure putting that nincompoop behind bars will be doing the boss—and all of society—a service. So…" He raised his head and ran his gaze over their faces. "Over recent weeks, Pincer's been feeding me a line about courting some wealthy spinster in some village. Pincer never told me her name, but I looked into it quiet-like, and the village was Ashmore, and the lady lived at Lavender Cottage, and her name was Viola Huntingdon. From what I learned, it seemed like Pincer's estimation of her worth was more or less on the mark. So I waited to see what would happen. While the boss was hoping Pincer would run fully aground and hand over the deed to the place in Bowerchalke, if Pincer was to pay his debts and all interest in full, well…" Johnson raised his heavy shoulders in a shrug. "That would do, too. Chances are he'd run himself aground again later. His sort always do.

"So I waited, but as Pincer was running close to the time when we'd likely roll him up, I made sure he knew to report to me a few times every week to tell me how matters were progressing." Johnson met Stokes's gaze. "With men like Pincer, it doesn't pay to let up the pressure."

"I see," Stokes said. "So from what Pincer told you, you understood that he was attempting to lure Viola Huntingdon into marriage."

Johnson nodded. "And when we met last Wednesday, he more or less told me that he was about to pop the question to this Viola. He was certain—absolutely bleedin' confident—that she would agree. He said he'd already broached the subject, and she was eager as could be. He was scheduled to meet with me Saturday—last Saturday—and bring a down payment, but instead, he fronted up with this tale that his pursuit of Viola was off because her younger sister had returned to the village, and she— the younger one—was even more wealthy, so he was now focusing on her, and he expected all to go smoothly because, apparently, this younger sister had always had a soft spot for him."

Johnson huffed. "I probably should have told him enough was enough and foreclosed then and there. But it was such a strange story, and I was curious as to what the silly beggar was up to, so I told him I'd give him another few days—a week tops—and arranged to meet with him Wednesday."

"That was the Wednesday just past?" Stokes clarified. "Two days ago?"

Johnson nodded. "After he left—this was on the Saturday—I sent a man down to Ashmore to see what he could learn on the quiet, and he came back and reported that the reason Pincer's pursuit of Viola Hunt-ingdon had come to naught was that the lady had turned up dead. That was why the sister had returned, but Pincer hadn't told me any of that." Johnson sniffed. "Still hasn't."

"And did he turn up on Wednesday?" Stokes asked.

"Yes," Johnson said, "but just with more weaselly words about how everything was on track and that soon, I'd hear wedding bells. As you might imagine, by then, I was running out of patience, so I told him to report back today. Which he did, but he was still spinning the same tale, just with new shiny bits. He told me he'd gone to London and checked, and the younger sister was a lot wealthier than even he'd imagined, and that he would soon ask her to marry him but that he'd had to go slower than he'd hoped, yet he was certain the wait would be worth it."

Johnson paused, then added, "I almost asked him whether the sister, who must be in mourning, would marry him anytime soon—just to see if he would tell me anything about the older sister dying—but in the end, I held my tongue. I could see Pincer was on his last throw of the dice, and his scheme falling in a heap would suit the boss, so I didn't say anything more. Just kept the pressure on and let him run."

Johnson smiled rather smugly. "And that's when we came out of the park and saw the younger sister—my man had given me a good description—with Lord Glossup. He's a magistrate in the area, so of course I know him by sight."

Mallard muttered, "Of course you do."

Johnson shrugged. "The man I sent to the village had said he thought there was something brewing between his lordship and the sister, and there the pair were, acting like a couple, and Pincer had just told me she was his. I pointed out to Pincer that it appeared he had some serious competition. Of course, the silly beggar had no choice but to try to make it look like all was as he'd said."

"Ah," Penelope said. "That was why he was holding on to her in that ridiculous manner."

"Seemed he wanted to make the point to me, and also to the sister and his lordship, too, how he—Pincer—expected things to be." Looking at Penelope, Johnson helpfully offered, "Men like Pincer are like that. They think they can make it clear how they want and insist things should be, then smile and charm everyone into falling into line. Deluded, they are, but that's how they behave."

Penelope was impressed by the insight.

Stokes stirred, drawing Johnson's attention. "Would it surprise you to know that we believe it was Pincer who strangled Viola Huntingdon to death?"

Johnson's expression immediately turned impassive. After a moment, he sat back in the chair, his gaze steady on Stokes's face. After a full minute and more, slowly, Johnson nodded. "Aye, that would surprise me."

Penelope, Stokes, and Mallard frowned.

"Why?" Penelope was the first to ask. She went on, "Viola had just discovered that Pincer had arranged to have the aquamarines in her favorite bracelet swapped for paste. We believe she confronted him with that crime, perhaps threatening to have him taken up by the police, and he panicked and strangled her."

Johnson pressed his lips together and plainly cogitated, then shook his head. "All I can say is you've got that wrong. Men like Pincer, they always believe they can talk their way out of damned near anything, any situation. And the younger sister hadn't come back yet, had she? So at that point, Miss Viola Huntingdon was Pincer's only available ticket out of his very deep hole." More definitely, Johnson shook his large head again. "Quite aside from that he'd never have the spine for it—his sort just don't—I can't see him killing the lady he saw as his golden goose. Not when killing her would leave him with nothing. Killing her wouldn't advance his cause, not in any way."

Penelope, Barnaby, Stokes, and Mallard fell silent, their expressions telegraphing the effective upending of their until-then certainty as to Pincer's guilt.

After a moment of studying their faces, Johnson shrugged. "Just my take on it, but in my experience, wastrels like Pincer, when desperate, might do something stupid, but they are cowards at heart and weak with it, and I've never in all my years known any to resort to violence. In extremis, if the option is there, men like Pincer run."

Silence engulfed the room.

Eventually, Stokes looked at Mallard, then Stokes turned to Johnson. "Thank you for your frankness. You've been a very real help."

Johnson flashed them all a smile almost as shark-like as Stokes's. "Pleased to have been of assistance and earned some points with the local plod."

Stokes returned the smile with a degree of respect, then, sobering, looked at Mallard. "I believe we have all we need from Johnson. It's time we spoke with Pincer himself."

Mallard, Barnaby, and Penelope nodded and showered thanks on Johnson, which he accepted with some grace.

At Mallard's wave, Johnson led the way out and into the foyer, then with a last nod to them all, he continued out of the building's main door.

Barnaby halted in the foyer with Penelope, Stokes, and Mallard. He looked at the others, and it was patently clear they were juggling and shuffling facts and insights and felt, as he did, rather at sea, no longer as certain as they had been as to who had killed Viola Huntingdon.

Eventually, Mallard broke the weighty silence. "Johnson has known Pincer longer than anyone we know, and through being O'Reilly's lieutenant for more than a decade, Johnson understands Pincer's sort, likely better than anyone."

Penelope looked torn. "Monty being Viola's murderer seemed to fit so well, but…" She raised her hands, palms up. "I can't help but agree with Johnson's reading of Monty's character. When confronted, cowards rarely act decisively."

Stokes grimaced. "And by the medical examiner's account, this murder was a very deliberate and decisive act."

Barnaby added, "Johnson was correct in saying that Monty had staked everything on getting Viola to marry him. His existence as he knew it was riding on him achieving that goal, and he had no other option at that point in time." He paused, then added, "If Viola had confronted him over the aquamarines, he would have talked—excused, persuaded, cajoled. Even if she hadn't accepted his explanation, he would have left and come back later. He wouldn't have murdered her." He glanced at the others. "Murdering her wouldn't have suited Monty's purposes, not in any way."

Mallard grunted. "Even I'm finding it harder and harder to see him killing her."

Footsteps sounded on the basement stairs, and they turned and watched as O'Donnell came up from the cells. He saw them, smiled, and walked across to join them.

O'Donnell nodded to them all, then halted and reported to Stokes, "We put Pincer in the end cell, then got Jacobs out of his and asked him to take a gander at all the other prisoners and tell us if there was anyone he recognized. There were seven other prisoners in total, including Pincer, and some of the others had similar coloring and roughly similar builds to Pincer. Jacobs was happy enough to do what we wanted, and he went around the cells, looking in through the peepholes."

"And?" Stokes prompted.

O'Donnell grinned. "Jacobs got to Pincer's cell, and we could tell from Jacobs's face alone that he knew the bloke. Jacobs called, 'Farmer!' and Pincer looked up, and his face, too, said he definitely recognized Jacobs."

Stokes nodded. "Right, then." He looked at Mallard. "So at least we've got Pincer on the charge of having the aquamarines replaced with paste."

Mallard bobbed his head. "We can hold him on that while we sort out this business of the murder."

"Good! You're still here."

They turned to see the medical examiner, Carter, come hurrying down the stairs.

All business, Carter bowled up to the group, nodded to all, then stated, "Something's been bothering me about this case—specifically about the evidence at the scene—and this morning, I woke up, and the clouds had parted, and finally, I could see the issue clearly."

Greatly interested, they all closed around Carter, and Stokes prompted, "What issue?"

Earnestly, Carter explained, "It was the clock—or rather, where it had supposedly fallen in relation to where the body lay." He glanced around the circle of faces. "I have a very good visual memory, essential in this line of work, and the position of the clock—the broken clock—kept nagging at me. I just couldn't quite see how or why it broke and ended up where it was found, on the hearth nearer the kitchen rather than on the same side of the hearth before which the body fell."

Penelope, clearly intrigued and trying to visualize the point herself, observed, "From what we've heard, if we were standing in the parlor and facing the fireplace, the body lay in a crumpled heap in front of the left side of the hearth, and the clock was lying on the hearth, toward the end on the right." She looked at Carter. "Is that correct?"

"Yes." Carter looked at Mallard. "You saw the scene, too."

Frowning slightly, Mallard nodded. "The victim lying on her back in a heap as if the murderer had simply let go once she'd breathed her last, and she'd crumpled to the ground where she'd been standing."

"Exactly so!" Carter looked at them all eagerly. "Now, put yourself in the victim's shoes and think of how you would move in response to someone calling at the cottage. If the person came to the front door and the victim admitted them and led them into the parlor, she would almost certainly have positioned herself to the right of the fireplace and turned to face her visitor. That's the usual way, putting the rest of the house at the victim's—the houseowner's—back, as it were. In such a situation, going to the left isn't something you would naturally do."

Barnaby was resurveying the scene in his mind. "But she was found to the left of the hearth, with the small table pushed aside..." He focused on Carter and found the man looking at him encouragingly. "The murderer came in through the rear door and walked through the kitchen and dining nook to the parlor, most likely following the victim."

"Yes!" Carter all but bounced on his toes. "That's the first thing. The murderer came from that direction. You can see it, can't you?" He glanced at the others. "The murderer knocked on the rear door, Miss Huntingdon let them in and led them through the kitchen and dining area into the parlor, then she turned to face them, and there she is, more or less standing on the spot where she died."

Stokes rumbled, "That supports our current thinking. We believe the murderer approached through the rear garden."

Carter nodded eagerly. "Our murderer certainly did, but that's not the crucial point. We now have our victim standing to the left of the hearth and the murderer to the right. They aren't that close to the fireplace—I believe the fire was alight at the time—but are positioned two feet or so in front of the edge of the hearth. The initial placement of the small table that was later pushed aside more or less fixes that distance. "Now"— Carter paused to catch his breath—"there were two ornaments on the mantelpiece."

Penelope supplied, "A vase with flowers in it was on the left, and presumably, the carriage clock stood on the right."

Carter beamed at her. "Absolutely right, dear lady. The carriage clock normally stood on the far right of the mantelpiece. If one looks closely, you can see the mark on the mantelpiece's surface. The clock had stood in exactly the same position for quite some years."

Mallard was frowning. "So the clock was on the right and fell and broke…"

Carter pounced. "How?" He glanced around the circle of their now-frowning faces. "Think of it—see it in your mind. The murderer was standing on the right. He must have lunged toward the victim, across the hearth and in front of it, and then his hands are locked about the victim's throat. There's little evidence of either victim or murderer moving much —just enough to push the small table aside and ruck up the rug, indicating that, if anything, they moved away from the fireplace."

"Away from the mantelpiece and the clock standing on it," Penelope murmured.

Everyone was imagining the scene, then Stokes focused on Carter. "Spit it out, Carter. What, exactly, are you trying to tell us?"

His expression turning sober, Carter stated, "I'm saying that for the life of me, I cannot see how the clock could have been accidentally broken during the act of the murder itself. The murderer couldn't have accidentally knocked it down. His back was to it. And the victim was too far away, with the murderer between her and the clock. Moreover, in looking back over my notes, there were no slivers of glass or indications of breakage where the clock was found. The only slivers of glass I did find were on the edge of the hearthstone and the floor below that edge." He sighed. "My initial assumption was that the clock got knocked off the mantelpiece during the struggle, only there was no violent struggle or fight, and the mantelpiece is wide as well, so examining the issue in the light of what I now know, it couldn't have happened that way. Moreover, if somehow the clock did get knocked off the mantelpiece and struck the edge of the hearth where I believe it was damaged, the clock would have fallen on the floor there, not where it was found."

Barnaby stated the clear conclusion. "You no longer believe the clock got accidentally knocked off the mantelpiece and fell and broke."

"No." His expression determined, Carter went on, "I now believe that, after strangling the victim, the murderer noticed the clock and saw the opportunity. They deliberately reset the clock for three-thirty-three, then struck it on the edge of the hearth to break it and left it on the hearth for us to find."

Stokes was jotting in his notebook. "That's very cold-blooded calculation."

"It certainly is." Carter looked around the circle. "But more, my conclusion suggests that the murder took place significantly earlier in my estimated window for time of death. I would now say that the murder most likely occurred between one o'clock and three o'clock, and if anything, I would tend toward the earlier end of that period."

"Your current conclusion also means," Penelope said, "that the murderer most likely has an alibi—a cast-iron alibi—for three-thirty-three."

Carter half bowed to her. "So I would suppose." He glanced around at the others. "The murderer entered the cottage through the rear door and most likely left the same way between the hours of one and three o'clock, and whoever they are, they will have an unimpeachable alibi for three-thirty-three."

Penelope glanced at Stokes and saw him furiously scribbling.

Then Stokes looked at Carter and nodded. "Thank you. That's excellent work."

Carter beamed. "My pleasure, Inspector." He nodded all around. "I'll leave you now—I have another body to see to."

The others added their thanks, and with a bounce in his step, Carter headed back up the stairs.

Stokes resumed his jotting, but they'd barely caught their breath when the police station's main doors burst open, and Madeline and Henry came rushing in, bringing a small, dapperly dressed gentleman with them.

The man was of portly build and garbed in a dark conservative suit paired with a tapestry waistcoat in muted hues. He had curly graying hair peeking out from beneath the brim of a pale-gray hat, wore highly polished boots, and carried a silver-headed cane. His mien seemed serious if a trifle flustered by the rush, but his most outstanding feature was a pair of mobile bushy eyebrows that danced above a pair of shrewd blue-gray eyes.

As they pulled up before the others, Madeline, Henry, and the gentleman were all out of breath, and the three sported similar expressions of shock and earnestness.

"Thank God," Henry announced, "that you haven't started with Pincer yet." He indicated the gentleman. "This is Mr. Farnham, the Huntingdon family solicitor, and he has information you need to hear."

Madeline stepped in to perform the introductions, confirming Farnham's standing and making him known to Stokes, who introduced Penelope and Barnaby. Plainly curious, Farnham shook their hands. Unsurprisingly, he was already acquainted with Mallard and exchanged a reserved nod with the policeman.

Then Farnham looked around the open foyer. "Now, I do have matters of note to convey to you…"

Mallard took the hint. "Perhaps your revelations might be better made in the interview room."

Farnham nodded. "My thoughts exactly, Mallard. Thank you."

After speaking to the constable behind the desk, Mallard led the group to the interview room off the corridor beyond.

As with alacrity they moved to claim chairs about the table, Penelope saw her own burning curiosity reflected in the faces of Barnaby, Stokes, and Mallard.

Henry looked concerned and very serious as he held Madeline's chair for her, then he sat beside her, with Farnham taking the chair on Madeline's other side.

Everyone settled and fixed eager gazes on the dapper solicitor.

Having set his hat on the table, Farnham cast a swift, shrewd look around those gathered and, without waiting for further invitation, commenced, "First, let me state that until half an hour ago, when Miss Madeline Huntingdon informed me of her sister's murder, I was not aware that Miss Viola Huntingdon had passed, much less that she'd been killed. You may be sure that if I had known, I would have come forward earlier. However, as we are here now, let me give you what information I possess regarding Viola's recent interactions with me and my office. She —Viola—came to see me several months ago and instructed me to look into the specifics of the boundary between Lavender Cottage and the neighboring property owned by a Mr. Arthur Penrose."

Penelope stiffened and exchanged a fleeting, wondering glance with Barnaby before returning her attention to Farnham.

"My clerk," Farnham went on, "is a very thorough man, and he pulled out every map and sale notice concerning both properties. We worked our way through the lot and came to the conclusion that Viola was correct in her assertion that at some point in the past, the boundary had been illegally shifted, removing a considerable slice of land from the Lavender Cottage plot and claiming it for Penrose Cottage."

Farnham leaned forward slightly to glance at Henry. "There is a question of long-established use of the land, but in terms of formal title to the acres in question, that indisputably lies with Lavender Cottage."

Farnham sat back and resumed speaking to everyone. "I informed Miss Viola of that circumstance about three weeks ago, and she instructed me to commence legal proceedings to formally reclaim the land. To do that, I needed to draft several documents, and she made an appointment to return to my office and sign the papers on the afternoon of Wednesday last week. As I understand it, that was the day before she was murdered."

Stokes looked up from his notes. "And she kept the appointment?"

"She did," Farnham replied, "but for quite the first time in all the years I've known her, she was late."

"How late?" Barnaby asked.

"About twenty minutes or so," Farnham said. "It didn't really matter, as I'd kept the hour free in case she wanted to talk further about the case. But when she came in, she was in quite a taking over a completely different matter."

Barnaby bit his tongue and hoped no one else prompted the solicitor.

No one did, and Farnham obligingly continued, "It seemed she'd just learned that a gentleman she had thought herself on the verge of accepting a marriage proposal from was only interested in her wealth. An hour earlier, she'd apparently had Swithin—of Swithin's Jewelers here in town, a sound man—tell her that the stones in her aquamarine bracelet, a keepsake of her mother's given to her by her late father, were now fake, as were the stones in the matching necklace this man—Montgomery Pincer, who Viola referred to as Harold—had given her as a gift. Pincer had borrowed the bracelet to facilitate the making of the matching necklace, and at all other times, the bracelet had remained in Viola's possession. The conclusion that Pincer was responsible for the substitution was inescapable. Naturally, Viola was devastated to learn of such a betrayal of her trust, but on leaving Swithin's shop and starting up the street toward my chambers, she saw Pincer with another man in the market square. Although I don't believe that, at that point, Viola was sure as to what she hoped to achieve, she followed the pair when they left the square. They went to a small park opposite St. Edmund's, and she hid behind the trees and bushes near the bench on which they sat and eavesdropped on their conversation, only to discover that they were discussing her! That was when she heard from the despicable rogue's own lips that he was only interested in her for her money. By the time the men left and she came on to my chambers, she was…well, not quite incandescent with fury but close to it."

Farnham faintly winced at the memory. "She showed me the bracelet and the necklace and insisted that she wished Pincer to be taken up by the police"—Farnham tipped his head toward Mallard—"and charged with theft." Farnham sighed. "My duty always lies with my client, so in all good conscience, I advised her against taking such a step."

He glanced around the circle of faces. "I'd known Viola since she was a girl, and I knew she would hate—absolutely hate—having her naivety displayed for all the locals to see and wonder at and gossip over. I pointed that out, and as I expected, the prospect gave her pause. When she asked for my advice on how to deal with Pincer, I agreed that she should break off the connection immediately and, as she was so upset about the missing aquamarines, that she should suggest that if he gave her back the stones, in exchange, she would give him the necklace, that being the only physical evidence that would allow the theft to be traced to him. I stressed that she should not frame the offer as a threat but approach the matter as a negotiation. I strongly advised her not to threaten him outright, as he probably knew her well enough to know, as I did, that she would never pursue the matter publicly."

Farnham sighed. "She'd calmed down by then but wasn't yet certain as to what she would do about Pincer. She agreed to consider my arguments and said she would write to Madeline and seek her counsel as well. As I knew Madeline, I encouraged that. I did offer to keep the jewelry for her, on the grounds Pincer might be tempted to protect himself by stealing the pieces away, but she insisted she would keep the items safe."

That's why she hid the jewelry in the urn, Penelope thought.

"After that," Farnham continued, "we moved on to the matter that had brought her to my chambers that day, namely, the documents regarding the boundary dispute."

Stokes looked up from his notebook. "Did she take any away with her?"

"She did," Farnham replied. "There were several documents for filing with the court that she signed and I retained." He glanced at Madeline. "I will acquaint Miss Huntingdon with those at another time, but on Wednesday"—Farnham returned his gaze to Stokes—"Viola took with her two letters for delivery to the relevant parties. I did offer to have them delivered by my servers, but with Ashmore being so out of the way, that would take time and also be an added expense, and Viola was adamant she could deliver the letters very easily herself."

Penelope leaned forward. "To whom were the letters addressed?"

"As you might expect," Farnham said, "one was to Mr. Arthur Penrose, informing him of the pending legal action. The other letter was a courtesy notification to the local magistrate for the district." Farnham nodded at Henry. "Namely, Lord Glossup."

Stokes shot a glance at Henry. "Did Viola ever give you this letter?"

Henry shook his head. "However, thinking back, on that Thursday morning before Humphrey relieved himself against her hedge, Viola was walking toward me in a rather determined fashion, and she had some paper in her hand. But then she saw Humphrey in action, and she screeched and started shouting." He looked at Madeline. "That might have been the letter." Then Henry frowned and looked across the table at Barnaby, Penelope, and Stokes. "I wonder what became of it."

Grimly, Stokes added, "And the letter to Arthur Penrose."

Everyone looked at each other, only to find their expressions reflecting the uncertainty, questions, and conjectures writhing in all their brains.

After a moment, Stokes looked at Farnham. "Thank you for your assistance, sir. You've given us much to digest."

Farnham grimaced and picked up his hat. "Would that I could be of more help." His chair scraped on the floor as he rose and bowed to the company. "If you have no further need of me, I'll be on my way."

Madeline rose as well, as did Henry, and together, they escorted the solicitor to the door, along the way making whispered arrangements regarding future meetings to discuss the settlement of Viola's estate.

The others waited until Madeline and Henry returned and, with uncertain expressions, sank onto their chairs.

Stokes sighed and told them, "Johnson explained to us that Pincer was set on proposing to Viola as a way to repay his debt owed to Johnson's boss, O'Reilly, but after her death, Pincer transferred his campaign to you." Stokes nodded at Madeline. "However, when informed that Pincer was our prime suspect for Viola's murder, Johnson explained, exceedingly convincingly, why he doubted Monty was our man." Stokes glanced rather sourly around the table. "Johnson's arguments were so sound, he swayed us all."

Mallard grunted unhappily but didn't disagree.

"Then," Stokes went on, "just before you two arrived with Farnham, Carter, the medical examiner, came looking for us. Carter explained that he now believes the carriage clock was deliberately broken by the murderer so that we would believe the murder happened at three-thirty-three. In light of that conclusion, Carter has revised the time of the murder as being between one and three o'clock, more likely earlier than later."

"And of course," Penelope explained, "that means our murderer almost certainly has an unshakeable alibi for three-thirty-three."

"And now," Barnaby concluded, "we've had Farnham with his surprising news, which has shifted all the facts around and added others we didn't know before, with the end result showing us a completely different picture to the one we thought we were looking at mere hours ago."

They all digested that.

Frowning, Henry stated, "Yet as matters stand, we still don't know when Viola died or who strangled her."

Penelope grimaced. "Sadly, critical though those points are and in spite of our previous beliefs, at this juncture, both are entirely up in the air."

Barnaby stirred and sat straighter. He looked around the table. "From this point on, we need to anchor our thinking on solid, verified fact. We've been led astray by accepting some apparent facts too easily and also by assuming some observations mean more than they do."

Nods came from everyone, then Mallard glanced around and asked, "So what now?" He eyed Stokes. "Pincer?"

Stokes considered, then nodded and straightened in his chair. He looked at Barnaby and Penelope. "However, we're going to have to be careful not to lead him. We need to get him to tell us what happened at Lavender Cottage—"

"Without prompting him," Penelope filled in, "to describe or agree with one of our assumptions, which might now be entirely wrong."

They briefly debated the location for Pincer's interview and decided that the interrogation room in the basement, near the cells, would better underscore his new reality.

Mallard hauled his bulk upright. "It might be cramped with all of us in there, but if we bring him up here, he's likely to get the idea that he might yet talk his way out of being charged with anything."

Stokes nodded as, with a scraping of chair legs on the floor, all of them rose. "If he senses hope, he'll seize it and run, and we don't have time to waste bringing him back to earth."

Mallard headed for the door, opened it, and led the way to the foyer, where he and Stokes gave orders to have Pincer taken to the interrogation room, along with extra chairs.

Ten minutes later, Stokes, Barnaby, and Penelope led the way into the interrogation room. The chill in the small chamber hadn't improved, and the stone walls created an odd resonance that made their trooping foot-steps loud and distinctly ominous.

Monty was already seated in the single chair on the other side of the narrow table, facing the door with his hands manacled and his shoulders drooping. He barely glanced at them as they filed in, and Stokes claimed the chair directly opposite, with Penelope and Barnaby on his right, while Mallard, who had lumbered in behind Barnaby, took the chair on Stokes's left.

Henry and Madeline had followed Mallard and moved to sit in two chairs placed against the wall, a few feet behind Penelope and Barnaby. O'Donnell and Morgan stood at attention behind Monty, their presence within arm's reach intentionally intimidating, and Constable Price came in last, closed the door, and took up a position with his back to the wall nearby.

The instant the door shut, Monty raised his head, looked at Stokes, Barnaby, and Penelope, and blurted, "I didn't kill her! You have to believe me. It wasn't me!"

Everyone blinked. Stokes had paused in the act of drawing out his notebook. Smoothly, he continued the action, met Monty's gaze, set the book on the table, and slowly nodded. "All right. But if you want to convince us and any judge and jury of that, you need to tell us exactly what happened last Thursday—the day Viola Huntingdon was murdered —from the moment you arrived at her cottage."

Monty was already nodding like a bobble-headed doll. "When I got there—"

"When exactly was that?" Barnaby asked.

"One-thirty on the dot." Monty went on, "Viola liked me to arrive at that precise time. Her housekeeper left at noon, and Viola liked to have her luncheon and tidy away and have time to…well, I suppose you would say primp. She expected me at one-thirty, so that's when I got there."

"You came across the fields at the rear of the cottage and entered through the kitchen door," Stokes said.

Monty nodded. "That was what I always did." His tone almost eager, he explained, "I didn't really want to be seen by the whole village, and Viola didn't want the gossips to know, either. I think she feared being made fun of, so me coming and going via the fields and the kitchen door suited us both."

"Was the rear door unlocked?" Penelope asked.

"Yes," Monty replied. "It was always unlocked during the day."

"But Viola trusted you," Barnaby said, "and she'd given you a key, hadn't she?"

Monty paused. His gaze darted between Penelope and Barnaby to Madeline, and he patently debated lying, but then, hauling his gaze from Madeline and fixing it on Barnaby, Monty swallowed and nodded. "She gave me a key to the kitchen door a few weeks ago. I'm not sure why. I didn't ask for it."

"But it came in handy, didn't it?" Stokes's tone was cutting. "It was you who used that key to get into the cottage last night." When Monty just stared at him, Stokes grunted. "Just answer yes or no. Thanks to Price, nothing came of it, and at this point, it's no longer important."

Monty thought, then hung his head. "Yes, it was me."

"Why?" Barnaby asked.

Monty shifted on the hard chair. When they all simply waited, he eventually offered, "I was hoping to convince her—Madeline—to marry me."

Mallard growled, "In the age-old way of convincing a woman. You worm!"

No one else said anything, but the weight of condemnation in the atmosphere palpably grew.

Hands gripping tight, Monty seemed to shrink as he whispered, "I was desperate."

Stokes glanced at Penelope, who was looking daggers at Monty, then he glanced back at Madeline and Henry, equally furious, then returned his gaze to Monty. "We'll leave that matter for later. For now, tell us exactly what happened—what you saw, heard, and felt—when you opened the kitchen door last Thursday and stepped into Lavender Cottage."

At first, Monty's expression grew distant, then his features subtly altered as if remembered terror was slowly sinking its talons into him anew.

Viewing the change, Penelope thought that Johnson had been absolutely correct. Monty was an utter coward. He would never have the backbone to kill anyone.

Monty swallowed and, plainly in the grip of his memories, said, "Viola wasn't there to meet me. She usually was, and I was a little surprised. I called out, but she didn't answer. And then I realized how quiet the place was. Unnaturally quiet. Slowly, I walked on toward the dining area. I didn't know what was going on, but then I reached the dining table and looked into the parlor, and I saw her…"

His recoil, his blatantly genuine revulsion at the remembered sight, put paid to any lingering notion that he might have been Viola's killer. Not even the best actor on the London stage could manufacture that depth of horror.

Hoarsely, Monty went on, "She was dead. Obviously dead. She was lying there in a heap, her eyes wide open and staring, her tongue…" Monty closed his eyes and visibly shuddered.

In a matter-of-fact tone, Stokes asked, "Did you check for signs of life?"

Vehemently, Monty shook his head. "I couldn't bring myself to go near her, much less touch her." He swallowed hard and said, "And it was beyond obvious she was dead."

"Did you notice the clock lying on the hearth?" Barnaby asked.

Monty opened his eyes, his gaze growing distant once more, and he nodded. "I saw it, but I didn't touch it."

"Did you see what time the clock showed?" Stokes asked.

Monty shook his head. "I didn't look. What was the point? She was dead." He lifted his manacled hands as if to gesture, then let them fall back. "She was just lying there, dead."

Stokes studied him for an instant, then mildly inquired, "So what did you do?"

Monty exhaled and fixed his gaze on the table between them. "I just stared. I was frozen for I don't know how long. It was…horrible. Then it slowly sank in that if she was dead, I'd lost all hope of paying O'Reilly."

To Penelope, that rang true. She glanced briefly at Henry and Madeline and saw that Henry was holding Madeline's hand, and Madeline was gripping his as if it were a lifeline.

As Penelope returned her attention to Monty, he went on, "It was like a terrible nightmare unfolding in my mind. I suddenly thought, what if you found the jewelry—the bracelet and necklace? You'd realize the stones were paste and check the jewelers, and Jacobs could identify me as the man who had the stones replaced—as he just did." Monty's voice had taken on a fearful edge. "I panicked. And then I looked at her and realized she wasn't wearing either piece. Ever since I gave her the necklace, I never saw her without both. She was delighted with them and always wore them whenever she was with me." He twisted his clasped hands, and the manacles clacked. "I had to get those two pieces back, then there'd be nothing to connect me with Viola. So I searched. I started with her bag, the tapestry one she always carried whenever she went out. She always left it sitting on the hall table, just inside the front door, but someone had been there before me, and the bag was upended and dropped on the floor and the contents strewn everywhere. No necklace or bracelet, but I didn't really think she would have carried her favorite jewelry in her bag. I went upstairs and searched her bedroom. I searched there and everywhere else I could think to look."

His expression stated he was reliving those moments in his mind. "I even searched in the kitchen. I'd heard that sometimes women hid their jewelry there, in the cupboards or the flour bin, but there was nothing there either."

Penelope leaned forward and asked, "After searching in the flour bin, did you go back to the body?"

Monty looked almost shocked at the suggestion. "No. I didn't see any reason to." Then, with obvious candor, he added, "I couldn't make myself go back in there, where she was lying dead, anyway."

Penelope nodded and sat back.

Monty gave her a wary look.

"So what happened next?" Stokes asked.

After a moment of thinking, Monty picked up his tale. "I was getting more and more desperate, and I knew time had to be getting on, so I left. I went out through the kitchen door, through the woods and on through the fields. I was in such a state, imagining this and that and thinking of Viola lying there, that I wasn't as careful as I usually was. I went over the stile and dropped onto the Tollard Royal-Ashmore lane just as the minister was driving past in his gig. He saw me and smiled and saluted with his whip. I had to drum up a smile and wave back. I don't know how well I managed, but he didn't stop, just bowled on, and as soon as he was out of sight, I pelted across the lane and into the field where I'd left my horse and rode home to Bowerchalke."

Stokes flipped back through his notes, read, then said, "You arrived at one-thirty. Judging by the extent of your search and the time you spent before starting it, it must have been two-thirty or thereabouts when you encountered Reverend Foswell."

Monty shrugged. "About that. Perhaps the reverend can tell you when he saw me."

"You can be sure we'll ask," Mallard rumbled.

Monty looked at Mallard, then ran his gaze over the faces of Stokes, Penelope, and Barnaby. "But you believe me, don't you? I didn't kill her. She was already dead when I got there. Without her"—he raised his hands in a defeated gesture—"I wouldn't have had anything. I needed her alive."

Stokes shut his notebook and tucked it into his pocket. "As to whether you'll swing for Viola Huntingdon's murder, I can't yet say, but you will be charged with the theft of her aquamarines, which we recovered from Jacobs. As he's already identified you as the man who commissioned him to swap the stones, and we have witnesses aplenty that the substitution wasn't carried out at Viola's behest, that charge will stick."

Oddly, Monty was nodding, his expression suggesting he was almost eager to face the lesser charge. "And you'll find who killed Viola, won't you? Then you and everyone else will know it wasn't me."

Stokes's expression turned stony. He regarded Monty for a moment, then stated, "We'll definitely be pursuing Viola's murderer, but you may be very sure that the notion of saving you from the hangman's noose won't contribute in even the smallest way to our motives for doing so."

With a look of utter disgust on his face, Stokes rose, as did everyone else. Without another word to Montgomery Pincer, they turned and quit the room and left him to his fate.

In procession, they trooped up the stairs and halted in the foyer.

Stokes sighed. "He's not our murderer. If we say that the murderer broke the clock to give themselves a cast-iron alibi—and by Carter's account, that's the only viable explanation for the broken clock—then Monty has no strong alibi for three-thirty-three."

Grimly, Barnaby stated, "The murderer—the real murderer—does have that invincible alibi for three-thirty-three. The only mistake they made in setting that up is that they didn't allow for Monty arriving at one-thirty and finding Viola already dead."

Penelope wrinkled her nose. "If Monty hadn't turned up, the chances are this case might never have been solved."

Barnaby nodded. "The murderer thought they were being very clever in resetting the clock and breaking it, but in reality—"

"In light of the very short list of suspects," Penelope stated, "through that action, the murderer turned the finger of suspicion directly at themselves."

CHAPTER 11

It was too late to reach the inn at Tollard Royal in time for dinner, so they requested a private room at the Haunch of Venison, and after dispatching Phelps, Connor, O'Donnell, Morgan, and Price to take their ease in the taproom, the investigators gathered around the oval table to satisfy their appetites and, ultimately, decide how best to proceed.

As per Stokes, Penelope, and Barnaby's habit, while they ate, they talked of other things. Mallard, Henry, and Madeline were faintly puzzled by that behavior but followed their lead.

Eventually, their plates were empty, and the liquids in their glasses had sunk to acceptable lows. The serving girls came in and cleared the platters and plates, and Stokes and Barnaby refilled everyone's glasses.

The instant the door shut behind the girls, Stokes leaned back and ran his gaze over the faces about the table, all turned expectantly his way. He faintly grimaced. "All right. Let's rejig our thinking. It might be said that my earlier concern over our pursuit of H distracting us from a murderer nearer to hand has been borne out, except that we needed to learn what Monty found when he arrived at the cottage to understand what happened."

Barnaby inclined his head. "Without Monty's testimony, which in this instance I believe we can credit, we could not know, much less prove, who murdered Viola."

Penelope sighed. "I think we all know who the murderer is. The

Penroses had a much more powerful motive to remove Viola than anyone was aware of, and while, physical capability aside, Arthur Penrose is vouched for by Jim Swinson, Ida Penrose is not."

"She has no alibi for the time of the murder," Barnaby said. "However, she does have an unimpeachable alibi for the time the murderer set on the clock before they broke it."

"What's more," Penelope said, "I believe Ida's afternoon tea with Iris Perkins and Gladys Hooper was a pre-arranged event. Therefore, Ida knew she would have that unbreakable alibi for three-thirty-three."

"And," Barnaby added, "she's tall enough, and she bakes constantly and makes bread, so she has strong countrywoman's hands."

Stokes sighed. "Be that as it may, when it comes to our new prime suspect, we have nowhere near enough information to construct a solid, unchallengeable time line for the murder."

Henry nodded. "Speaking as a magistrate, you don't have sufficient information to charge Ida Penrose. She might be the only person known to fit the criteria you now have for Viola's murderer, but that's not proof she committed the crime."

Stokes and Mallard were nodding.

"That means we need to go back and collect the necessary information." Penelope looked at Stokes. "Due to the distraction of H, we've yet to interview several potentially key witnesses."

When Stokes raised his brows at her, inviting her to continue, she went on, "There are three acknowledged gossips in the village—Mrs. Foswell, Ida Perkins, and Gladys Hooper. Their titles won't have been bestowed without cause. Ergo, it's likely all three know more than we're aware of, given we haven't interviewed two of them at all, and we spoke only briefly with Mrs. Foswell."

Penelope looked around the table. "I suggest that my first task tomorrow should be to interview all three ladies and see what they can tell us. I've learned it's best not to ask specific questions. I'll get more from them by asking general questions about anything they saw or know that might relate to Viola's murder, then listening to everything they say." She paused, then added, "Aside from anything else, I'm curious to learn what Iris and Gladys observed during their afternoon tea with Ida."

Mallard observed, "Very cool, that—murdering your neighbor, then having your other neighbors around for tea and cakes."

Stokes grunted in agreement, then nodded to Penelope. "You take the gossips. Who or what else have we missed?"

Mallard looked at Stokes. "What about the reverend seeing Pincer in the lane? More like tidying up loose ends, but if the reverend can give you a time, that'll confirm Pincer's story, and it's important we can say that's solid. That everything Pincer's told us is the truth."

Stokes inclined his head. "Good point." He pulled out his notebook, flicked to a new page, and started making a list. "What else?"

Barnaby said, "There's the flour down the front of Viola's bodice." He smiled at Penelope. "I know what you're thinking, but we need to ask Mrs. Gilroy what she left Viola for her luncheon that day. Did that flour come from something Viola had just consumed? Or did it come from the murderer?"

Madeline, Henry, and Mallard were confused by this exchange. Seeing that, Penelope explained, "Ida mentioned baking scones that day. That involves flour, and we—Barnaby and I—have often noticed that our cook and her helpers get flour in their cuffs, so even if they've washed their hands, the flour still dusts things they touch."

Madeline nodded. "I've noticed the same thing."

Absorbed in his list, Stokes huffed. "We also have no idea what became of those solicitor's letters." He glanced at the others. "We might assume they're ash by now, but there's always a chance one of the gossips knows something of them."

"Especially," Madeline put in, "if Henry's recollection is correct and when Viola noticed Humphrey watering her hedge, she had the letter for Henry in her hand."

Penelope nodded. "I'll ask."

"Something else we need to focus on," Barnaby said, "is finding witnesses to Viola's movements in the hour between Mrs. Gilroy leaving her at the cottage at noon and the murder. We now know Viola was at the church, in the graveyard, hiding the jewelry, shortly after twelve o'clock. That's been confirmed by Billy Gilroy and Reverend Foswell, so we can count that as fact. But where did Viola go after that? Did any of the villagers speak with her?"

"If she was dead before one-thirty," Mallard mused, "when Pincer found her body in the cottage, her movements between, say, twelve-thirty and one-thirty are critical."

Stokes, who had been studying his list, nodded. "We need to fill in the gap, so tomorrow, here's what we're going to do." He looked at Penelope. "You interview the gossips."

Penelope promptly looked at Madeline. "It might help if Madeline accompanies me." To Madeline, Penelope said, "The villagers know you, and more importantly, you're Viola's sister. If you're with me, they'll be disposed to being helpful."

"And," Madeline said, "very likely, they'll be more accurate, too. You can count on me."

Stokes looked at Barnaby. "While the ladies are conducting their interviews, I suggest you and I see whether Reverend Foswell remembers encountering Pincer in the lane, and then we should check with Jim Swinson. He and Ida witnessed the altercation between Henry and Viola, and if Henry is correct and Viola had the solicitor's letter for him in her hand, Jim might have seen that, too, and might have seen what Viola did with the letter after Henry rode away."

Barnaby nodded. "Good thinking. If Jim saw something, Ida might have, too."

"Exactly." Stokes considered his list, then looked at Madeline. "With your permission, after conducting our interviews, we'll reconvene at Lavender Cottage, put together all we've learned, and see if we have enough facts in hand to make an arrest."

Everyone murmured agreement.

Henry grimaced. "I need to be at the Hall tomorrow morning to meet with my estate manager, but after that, I'll come down to the cottage to see what's transpired."

Distinctly disgruntled, Mallard said, "I'll have to remain here in Salisbury, but I'll tell Price he's to be the representative of the local force."

Stokes inclined his head. "If we need to make an arrest, it would be useful to have a local with us."

Stokes looked around, as did Penelope. Everyone looked ready and willing to proceed with their allotted tasks.

"Right, then." Stokes pushed away from the table. "It's time to head back to the inn for us, to Glossup Hall for Henry, and Lavender Cottage for Madeline and Price."

"Indeed." Penelope rose. "It's important we behave as if we're still no closer to identifying the murderer. The last thing we need is for Ida to decide that her continued good health requires her to go off on a jaunt somewhere."

The others huffed in agreement, then everyone made their way out of the pub and headed for the carriages.

～

The following morning, Penelope, Barnaby, and Stokes, traveling in the Adairs' carriage, arrived in good time at Lavender Cottage. O'Donnell and Morgan rolled up in the police coach soon after, having left the inn a good fifteen minutes ahead of the faster carriage.

As Madeline and Price were ready and waiting to do their parts, the group congregated in the front hall.

After consulting his notebook, Stokes looked at Morgan and Price. "O'Donnell can remain at the cottage while you two go and interview Mrs. Gilroy. We need to know what she left Miss Huntingdon for her lunch on that Thursday. Once you know the answer, report back here."

"Aye, guv," Morgan said, and Price nodded.

Stokes glanced at Barnaby, Penelope, and Madeline. "We may as well go together to the rectory, but I suspect we'll part ways there. Once you've finished your interviews, come back here, and we'll do the same."

All agreed, and Penelope led the way from the cottage. Madeline fell in beside Penelope as she set a brisk course for the rectory, with Barnaby and Stokes pacing behind.

As they neared the rectory gate, Penelope glanced at Madeline, then looked over her shoulder at Barnaby and Stokes. "We have to remember to elicit information spontaneously. They have to offer it without us prompting."

"Indeed," Stokes replied.

Penelope marched up the path to the rectory door and tugged the bell chain. A few moments later, Mrs. Foswell opened the door. Her face lit as she took them in. "Good morning, Mrs. Adair. And Madeline, dear, I'm very glad to see you."

"Thank you, Mrs. Foswell." Madeline glanced at Stokes and Barnaby, waiting behind her. "Inspector Stokes and Mr. Adair were hoping to have a word with Reverend Foswell. Is he in?"

Mrs. Foswell looked past Madeline at Stokes. "Good morning, Inspector. Mr. Adair. My husband's at the church, setting the hymns for tomorrow's services. You should find him in the nave."

"Thank you." Stokes and Barnaby tipped their heads to the reverend's wife and turned and walked on to the church.

Madeline and Penelope remained on the stoop, and when Mrs. Foswell's gaze returned to them, Penelope smiled. "Madeline and I were hoping to have a word with you, Mrs. Foswell. We're trying to gain a clearer view of Viola's movements immediately prior to her death."

"Oh, well." Mrs. Foswell looked pleased. "Do come in, my dears, and sit, and I'll happily tell you what I know."

Once they were comfortably ensconced in armchairs in the neat parlor, Penelope began, "You see, we now know Viola was up at the church shortly after twelve o'clock, and according to your husband, she left and headed back toward her cottage. We need accurate information about where she went once she left the church." Penelope opened her eyes wide. "We hoped you might know of someone who saw her."

Mrs. Foswell beamed. "Why, I did, of course. I was in the front garden, such as it is, pulling up weeds when Viola came down from the church."

"Do you know when that was?" Penelope asked.

Mrs. Foswell paused, then firmly declared, "It must have been almost twelve-thirty." She eyed Penelope, then said, "I'd seen her go up to the church—striding along very determinedly, she was—at a little after twelve. I was in the garden already, but Viola was so…well, intent on something that she didn't see me, and I didn't call out to her. But I was weeding by the gate when she came down, and although she looked rather distracted yet still determined, as if she was thinking furiously about something, I stood up and greeted her."

Penelope tipped her head. "What did you and she say?"

"After we'd exchanged greetings—and I could see she was torn about getting on—I asked if she'd found what she'd been looking for at the church. I assumed she'd been seeking spiritual support, and she agreed that she'd found what she needed."

That had been a hiding place. Penelope looked at Madeline and saw the same thought in her eyes.

"And then," Mrs. Foswell went on, "Viola apologized and said she couldn't dally, as she had an errand to run before she returned to the cottage."

"An errand?" Penelope managed to mute her surprise. "Did she mention anything about what this errand was?"

"No," Mrs. Foswell replied, "although I did find the notion puzzling." She spread her hands. "What errand could she possibly have had in our village, small as it is? And it must have been in the village, as she implied she was expecting a visitor at the cottage, which is why she needed to return there soon." Mrs. Foswell paused, then added, "Viola could see I was curious, both about the errand and the visitor, and she reached over the gate and squeezed my hand and said she'd visit the next day and explain."

Mrs. Foswell's expression grew troubled. "Only, of course, she didn't, because by then, she was dead." She looked at Penelope. "Was it her visitor who killed her?"

Penelope shared a swift glance with Madeline, then said, "We don't believe so, which is why your information has been so helpful. Until speaking with you, we had no idea Viola ran an errand before returning to the cottage."

Mrs. Foswell's expression lightened. "In that case, my dears, I'm very pleased to have helped."

"Now"—Penelope collected Madeline with a glance—"we must get on."

They rose, and as Mrs. Foswell showed them to the door, she said, "I do hope that you take up this murderer soon so that the villagers can get back to their normal lives. It's been rather discombobulating not knowing what to think."

Penelope and Madeline smiled politely and left.

As they walked back onto the lane, Penelope murmured, "If the murderer is who we believe, it will be some time before this village can resume its normal ways."

Madeline nodded, then with Penelope, paused and turned as the sound of footsteps alerted them to Barnaby and Stokes's approach.

The men joined them, and at Stokes's encouraging wave, they walked on a few paces until they were out of sight of the rectory, then halted.

Stokes promptly reported, "Reverend Foswell confirmed that he encountered a man of Pincer's description along the Tollard Royal-Ashmore road at about two-thirty on the afternoon Viola was murdered."

"So that part of Pincer's tale is true," Penelope said.

"And that," Barnaby said, "increases the likelihood that everything he told us was the truth. At the very least, we can be certain that he wasn't anywhere near the cottage at three-thirty-three."

"There was no way," Stokes said, "for the murderer to know that Pincer would call and find the body so soon after the event. They'd assumed no one would, probably not until the next morning when Mrs. Gilroy came in."

Penelope nodded. "The murderer was counting on that so that the time of death would be accepted as three-thirty-three."

"I can't see any reason to disagree with Johnson's assessment of

Pincer," Barnaby stated. "He's no murderer, which means Viola was killed before one-thirty."

Penelope sighed. "There's really only one person who could have done it. Viola spoke with Mrs. Foswell at about twelve-thirty and had returned to the cottage and been killed with the murderer gone by one-thirty."

"And," Madeline put in, "Viola told Mrs. Foswell that she had an errand to run before returning to the cottage."

"Did she, indeed?" Barnaby met Penelope's eyes. "Let's pray that your gossips can shed some light on that."

"I certainly hope so," Penelope replied.

Stokes looked ahead, up the village's main street. "We still need more facts to nail down our case." He glanced at Penelope and Madeline. "While you two consult your remaining gossips, Barnaby and I will circle around and try to find Jim Swinson."

"Oh," Madeline said. "I saw Jim and Arthur earlier. They were at the far corner of the orchard, rebuilding part of the wall. If you walk back to the cottage, then along the boundary wall, you'll find them easily enough."

Stokes and Barnaby thanked her and strode off for the cottage.

Penelope and Madeline walked more slowly up High Street. Approaching the three-way junction, Penelope debated, "Iris Perkins or Gladys Hooper?" She looked questioningly at Madeline. "Whom should we interview first?"

Madeline nodded to the cottages lining Noade Street, just ahead. "The Perkinses' cottage is closer. It's that one, just along Noade Street."

Penelope looked at the cottage to their left. "Well, then. Let's try there first."

Penelope studied the Perkinses' aptly named Ivy Cottage as she and Madeline walked up the neat stone path. The small stone cottage was almost buried in the creeping embrace of a rampant ivy, with tendrils reaching up to the roof and stretching out across the slopes.

On the veranda, Mrs. Perkins was sitting in a rocking chair with her knitting needles flashing.

Iris Perkins was an older woman with a soft, round figure and a face to match. Her expression was warm and welcoming. "Do come up, Madeline dear. And who's this?"

Madeline introduced Penelope, who smiled and nodded to the older woman. "I like the color of your wool." It was a bright, vibrant blue. "My sons are small, and they'd love that color."

Iris chuckled. "My grandchildren love colorful socks—the rascals say the colors help warm up their feet. All nonsense, but the socks are practical, and knitting them gives me something to do to pass the time." Iris waved them to wicker chairs. "Do sit down, ladies." Her gaze shrewd, she observed, "I'm sure you didn't come here to admire my wool."

"No, indeed." Penelope sank onto a chair and fixed her gaze on Iris. "We're seeking information about Viola Huntingdon's movements in the hours before she was murdered."

Madeline said, "We've just learned from Mrs. Foswell that Viola came down from the church, past the rectory, at what must have been almost twelve-thirty. We're not sure where she went after that and wondered if you might have seen her."

Penelope's heart leapt when Iris started nodding.

"I did see her that morning," Iris said. "I was sitting right here." She tipped her head toward the green, and Penelope and Madeline looked in that direction and realized that from her vantage point on the veranda, Iris had an excellent view of the triangular junction where the three lanes that defined Ashmore met, as well as a slice of the pond and green beyond.

Iris went on, "I saw Viola walk up from…well, I assumed she came from her cottage, but as you can tell, I can't see that far around the corner. But I supposed that's where she'd come from, and I saw her walk through the junction and on down High Street, toward the church."

Penelope tipped her head. "Do you remember what time that was?"

"Well," Iris said, "it must have been a little before quarter past twelve. I'd seen Pat Gilroy walk around and down toward her cottage at least five minutes before, and she leaves Lavender Cottage on the dot of twelve, so when Viola walked past, it must have been about ten minutes past the hour." Iris nodded. "She was heading south, I assumed to the church or the rectory."

Penelope bit back a smile. She was always amused by how people remembered things by linking this event to that. "Thank you. That's very clear. Viola did go to the church. She was there for a little while, then she spoke with Mrs. Foswell for a few minutes, no more, then headed back in this direction."

To Penelope's delight, Iris nodded. "That fits, because I saw her coming back this way. She turned toward Green Lane, but then she stopped, right in the middle of the junction where I could see her, and opened her bag. That tapestry bag she always carried. She rummaged in there and pulled out what looked like a letter, but thinking back, it was longer and folded and had some sort of seal on it, more like something official."

Penelope shot a warning look at Madeline. That had to have been one of Farnham's letters. Returning her gaze to Iris, Penelope asked, "What did Viola do next?"

"Well, she grasped that letter in one hand," Iris said, "and she looked ahead down Green Lane and, really determined-like, marched on and out of my sight."

Penelope lectured herself not to try to fill in what might have happened next. Carefully, she confirmed, "So you didn't see where she went with the letter."

Iris grimaced. "I did think to go down to the pond, just to see what was going on. Viola looked so set on doing something with that letter, but Gladys Hooper was coming for a bite, just a small one to tide us over until afternoon tea with Ida. She's one as bakes such mouthwatering things, one doesn't want to go for tea with a full stomach."

Penelope tried not to look disappointed. "I see."

Iris smiled understandingly. "However, if you want to know what Viola did next, you should go and ask Gladys. She'd been to visit her old aunt as lives farther out along Green Lane and was heading back to have lunch with me. So she was walking along Green Lane at that time, coming this way."

Iris paused and studied Penelope and Madeline with shrewd eyes. "I could tell you what Gladys said Viola did next, and what we thought it might mean, but for your purposes, it's probably best you hear that from Gladys herself."

Despite her impatience, Penelope had to agree. She glanced between Madeline and Iris. "Where does Gladys live?"

Madeline pointed up the same lane. "The Hoopers' house is just up Noade Street."

"Aye." Iris nodded. "And at this hour, you should find Gladys there, getting lunch ready for her husband and sons." Iris paused, her gaze on Penelope and Madeline, then said, "You tell Gladys I said she needs to

tell you all she saw—and heard, too—that morning. She's one as sometimes thinks to hold back a bit for later, if you know what I mean."

"Thank you." Penelope's gratitude was entirely genuine.

"Indeed." Madeline smiled and nodded at Iris as she and Penelope
rose. "I'm truly grateful for your sharp eyes."

Iris smiled widely, the action deepening the creases in her soft face.
"Aye, and those same eyes have seen you and his lordship driving about.
Take my advice—you won't do better than to snare that one. No matter
any misguided rumors, he's a good man."

Penelope met Iris's eyes and smiled broadly back.

Madeline, slightly flustered and blushing, nodded, turned, and
escaped from the porch.

After exchanging a last nod with Iris, still smiling broadly, Penelope
followed.

Barnaby and Stokes paced along beside the stone wall that marked the
disputed boundary between Lavender Cottage land and the acres attached
to Penrose Cottage.

They'd cut across to the wall from the front gate of Lavender Cottage,
making their way across clipped lawn and dodging around trees. On
reaching the wall, they'd turned north and trudged along.

Looking over the chest-high wall, Barnaby watched the side of
Penrose Cottage fall behind them, then the plot that housed the Penrose
kitchen garden ran along the other side of the wall.

To their right, the rear garden of Lavender Cottage spread out, mostly
laid to kitchen garden beds as well.

"Hello." Looking ahead, Stokes paused, then walked on. "What's
this?"

They were roughly midway down the kitchen gardens, and the feature
Stokes had spotted was a crumbling stile built against the wall.

They halted before it, and Barnaby pointed to a bare patch of ground
in front of the stile. The earth held the clear imprint of a shoe. "That's not
a man's boot."

Stokes crouched and examined the shape outlined in the softer
ground, then he rose and nodded. "No, it's not. And it's coming from the
Penroses'." He looked over the wall to where, some way away, the rear of

Penrose Cottage could be seen. "Someone recently came over this stile, heading for Lavender Cottage."

Barnaby crouched and examined the lightly grassed areas around the base of the stile, then pointed. "And here's where she went back." He rose and looked around.

"Well," Stokes said, "we now know how she went back and forth between the cottages in a very short space of time."

"And," Barnaby said, waving to the bushes around the immediate area, "without being seen. Other than from the rear of Penrose Cottage, no one"—he swung around, searching—"in the lane, in the orchard, or anywhere else, for that matter, can see this spot. Bushes or trees cut off the sight lines in virtually every direction."

Stokes looked, too, then nodded. "That means there'll be no witnesses, but it's something we needed to know."

After a last look at the stile, they continued on and, eventually, came upon Jim Swinson and Arthur Penrose refitting stones into a crumbled section of the wall and mortaring them into place.

Both men were happy to pause and give their attention to Stokes and Barnaby.

After exchanging greetings, Stokes said, "We were wondering, Mr. Swinson, when you saw Miss Huntingdon on the morning she was killed, when she berated Lord Glossup over his dog's behavior, whether you noticed if she had anything in her hand."

Jim Swinson frowned slightly, clearly thinking back to the moment. Slowly, he nodded. "She was carrying some sort of paper—like a folded packet of some sort. I thought maybe she'd shake it at his lordship, but she didn't."

"Did you see what she did with the paper after his lordship rode off?" Barnaby asked.

Jim instantly replied, "Aye. She glared after his lordship, clutching the paper tight, then she put it—shoved it, more like—into her bag, that tapestry one she always carried when she was out and about."

Barnaby exchanged a glance with Stokes. Now they knew why the killer had upended Viola's bag.

Stokes looked at Jim. "As I recall, Mrs. Penrose was standing beside you at the time. Do you think she would remember that paper, too?"

Jim shrugged. "Don't see why not. She was standing right there, and there's nothing wrong with Mrs. P's eyes."

Stokes inclined his head. "Thank you. That's really all we needed to know."

～

With Madeline beside her, Penelope knocked on the door of Wisteria Cottage. "Although," she murmured to Madeline, "there's not a shred of wisteria about."

Madeline glanced around. "Perhaps they've cut it down for the winter."

"I don't think you cut wisteria down to the ground," Penelope replied.

They heard footsteps approaching on the other side of the door, and Penelope summoned a smile as Gladys Hooper opened it. "Good morning, Mrs. Hooper. I'm Mrs. Adair, and I believe you're acquainted with Miss Huntingdon. We're assisting the police with their investigations, and we were wondering if we might have a word."

Madeline put in, "We've just come from chatting with Iris. We're trying to determine my sister's movements in the hours before she was killed, and Iris suggested that you'd seen where Viola went after she left the church."

Penelope added, "Viola told Mrs. Foswell that she had an errand to run before returning to the cottage. We wondered if you knew where Viola went after she passed out of Iris's sight and walked on along Green Lane."

Gladys's eyes had rounded, and she beamed. "Oh yes, I did see her, and I saw what happened next." She waved Penelope and Madeline inside. "Come in and sit down, and I'll tell you what I know."

Barely able to contain her impatience, Penelope allowed Gladys to usher her and Madeline into a small, untidy parlor.

"Please excuse the mess." Gladys hurried around, picking up scarves and caps. "Boys, you know. Well, males in general. It's a never-ending chore."

Once Gladys had the place reasonably cleared, she installed Penelope in what was clearly the best armchair and waved Madeline to the other armchair, while she perched on a straight-backed chair and looked at them expectantly.

Penelope inwardly sighed. Apparently, Gladys was one of those who preferred to be led. "We already know," Penelope began, "that Iris saw Viola pause at the junction and take a folded paper from her bag.

According to Iris, Viola then marched determinedly on along Green Lane."

When Gladys, eyes wide, merely nodded, Madeline prompted, "We understand that you were walking from your aunt's house to Iris's for a light luncheon. Your aunt's house lies farther out along Green Lane, doesn't it?"

Gladys nodded. "Yes, it's farther out around the bend."

"So where were you," Penelope asked, "when you saw Viola, and what was she doing at that point?"

Gladys fractionally inclined her head as if approving the question. "Well," she replied, "I was just this side of the bend and walking this way, and Viola was marching—and that's the right word, mind you, as she was awfully determined—toward me from the junction."

"Did she see you?" Madeline asked.

"Of course. I'd be hard to miss, just as she was." Gladys added, "I raised my hand, and she waved back. That's when I noticed the paper in her hand—she had it in the hand she raised, and I wondered what it was. Didn't quite look like a letter, not one in an envelope, you see."

"What happened next?" Penelope asked.

"Well," Gladys said, "I was hoping she'd slow and wait and speak with me, but instead, she took a few more steps, and then"—Gladys paused, no doubt to allow anticipation of her next revelation to build—"she turned in through the Penroses' gate."

Eyes gleaming with the fervor of a true village gossip, Gladys looked at Madeline and Penelope. "Well, *that* got my attention, as you might imagine."

"Oh?" Penelope played innocent. "Why was that?"

"Well, Mrs. Adair, all the village knows that Viola and Ida Penrose don't see eye to eye about much, but especially with that business of the orchard boundary…well, that really soured relations between them."

"I see." Penelope nodded. "So you saw Viola go up the Penroses' front path."

"Aye, but I saw much more than that," Gladys said. "I walked faster because I wanted to see what happened. That big old tree in the Penroses' front yard? There's a spot beside the fence that if you stand just there, Ida or whoever is at the front door can't see you."

Penelope had to hand it to Gladys. "So you stopped on that spot."

"O'course I did," Gladys said. "I wanted to see the fireworks, didn't I? Not that there were any, as it happened, but I was in that spot, listening, and I heard Viola say to Ida, 'This is for Arthur.' And Ida replied, 'He's not here. He's out in the fields.' There was a pause, then Viola said, 'Well, I suppose I can leave it with you to give him,' and I peeked around the tree and saw Viola give Ida the paper Viola'd been carrying."

Gladys sat back and faintly grimaced. "I thought there'd be more, but I knew I couldn't stay there and have Viola find me when she came back down the path, so while Ida was looking down at the paper in her hand and Viola was watching her, I scooted on and walked on to the junction. But I stopped there, at the corner, like, and looked back, and I saw Viola come out of the Penroses' gate and walk on to Lavender Cottage."

Penelope clarified, "You saw her go through the Lavender Cottage gate?"

Gladys nodded. "I decided that was that, scene ended, and went on to Iris's for lunch."

Penelope thought, then asked, "Do you have any idea what time you arrived at Iris's cottage?"

"Iris had been expecting me at twelve-thirty," Gladys replied, "and she commented that I was nearly ten minutes late."

"So," Madeline said, "you reached Iris's at just before twelve-forty."

Gladys nodded. "Seems like."

"Later," Penelope said, "when you went to afternoon tea with Ida, did you mention seeing Viola at her door?"

Gladys pulled a face. "Iris and I debated whether or not to mention it, but it seemed like it might be a sore point with Ida, and either way, we could ask Viola herself about it later, which, all in all, seemed the better road. So we didn't say anything about it to Ida."

Thank heaven for small mercies, Penelope thought.

"At what time did you and Iris get to Penrose Cottage?" Madeline asked, and Penelope refocused.

"Three on the dot, just like always," Gladys replied. "That's always been the time for Ida's afternoon teas."

"While you were inside Penrose Cottage, did you happen to see the paper Viola had given Ida?" Penelope asked.

"No," Gladys replied. "And it wasn't for want of looking, and Iris didn't see anything that might be it, either."

Penelope wracked her brains for further questions. "Have you known Ida and Arthur for long? I assume they're longtime residents of the village."

"Yes, they are." Gladys went on, "I've known both since childhood.

Ida always had her eye on Arthur, even when we were just girls. There was no one else for her, ever. It had to be Arthur. Just as well that he went along with it is all I will say. Ida was single-minded and utterly blinkered about getting him to the altar. Mind you, she's been devoted to him ever since, so it's not as if he didn't get a good bargain there. Only thing was they never had any children, but that happens, doesn't it?"

Penelope tipped her head and, as innocently as she was able, asked, "In your opinion, who would you say is the leader, as it were, in that household?"

"Ida, definitely," Gladys stated. "She's the one as handles almost everything except what Arthur loves doing—the growing and pruning and such. It's Ida who sells the fruit and grain and manages the money. But you have to hand it to her, she always makes it seem that it's Arthur who does it all. She'll never hear of anyone talking him down. He's her man, and you could say that he's her everything."

Penelope drew in a slow breath, then nodded to Gladys. "Thank you. You've been a great help."

She and Madeline rose, and Madeline offered her thanks as well, and they headed for the door.

In the doorway, Penelope stopped and looked back at Gladys. "One last question. What did Ida serve for afternoon tea?"

Gladys beamed. "Scones. Freshly baked. She makes the best scones hereabouts."

Penelope smiled and inclined her head. "Thank you."

She led the way off the porch and on down the path.

Madeline caught up and fell in beside her.

As they walked—increasingly briskly—toward Lavender Cottage, Penelope felt her confidence rise. "Now to put together everything we've learned and see whether we have enough to arrest our murderer."

CHAPTER 12

$\mathcal{B}$arnaby, Stokes, and Henry, as well as O'Donnell, Morgan, and Price, were waiting impatiently at Lavender Cottage when Penelope and Madeline arrived.

The group gathered about the small dining table, and before any of the men could voice a question, Penelope fixed her gaze on Barnaby and Stokes and demanded, "What did you learn?"

Stokes met Barnaby's questioning glance and nodded for him to oblige.

After taking a moment to gather his thoughts, for the benefit of Henry and the other men, Barnaby reported, "Reverend Foswell confirms he encountered Monty on the Tollard Royal-Ashmore lane at about two-thirty. Consequently, Monty's story, including him finding Viola dead at one-thirty, appears sound. Next, while walking along the stone wall that forms the boundary between Lavender and Penrose Cottages, Stokes and I came upon an old stile providing a ready route between the two kitchen gardens, and notably, the stile is screened by bushes and trees from general view. In softer ground before the stile, we found imprints of a shoe, not a man's boot, going both ways—to Lavender Cottage and back to Penrose Cottage."

"Ah." Penelope nodded. "I was wondering how she managed to get back and forth so quickly and without being seen by anyone."

Henry added, "I've been out with Morgan and O'Donnell and took measurements of the shoe print. Highly unlikely to be a man's."

Penelope looked eagerly at Barnaby, and he went on, "Stokes and I questioned Jim Swinson about whether he recalled Viola having anything in her hand when she was upbraiding Henry over his dog, and Jim recalled her holding something like a letter. More, after Henry rode off, Jim saw Viola put the letter into her tapestry bag, and given Ida was standing beside Jim at the time, he believes she saw that as well."

"That explains why the bag was searched and who by." Penelope slotted that puzzle piece into the picture of the murder that was forming in her mind.

"Also," Stokes said, glancing at Morgan and Price, who were standing by the wall, "Morgan and Price spoke with Mrs. Gilroy, and she says she left a pork pie for Viola's lunch that day." Stokes looked at Penelope. "Any chance of a dusting of flour off a pork pie?"

Penelope smiled. "None."

"You might get a flake or two of pastry," Madeline said, "but nothing that could be confused with a dusting of flour."

"Ergo," Penelope concluded, "the dusting of flour came from the murderer."

"One more point," Stokes said. "Morgan and Price thought to confirm that in finding the body, Mrs. Gilroy hadn't touched the clock. She didn't, and she didn't see what time it was showing, either. She says she screeched, then pulled the pot off the stove and ran next door via the front gate and the lane. Apparently, she didn't know about the stile and didn't use it."

"So the shoe prints aren't hers," Penelope stated.

"No," Stokes agreed. "But regarding the clock, after Mrs. Gilroy left the cottage, other than Price, no one came into the parlor until Carter, who moved the clock when he examined the scene. Since then, the clock's been sitting on the mantelpiece, untouched and unnoticed by anyone but us."

Price cleared his throat and offered, "I've asked around the village, and no one has been gossiping about the exact time of death, just that it was sometime in the afternoon between Mrs. Gilroy leaving and Miss Viola going up to and returning from the church and his lordship calling at four-thirty. That's all anyone knows. Seems no one's heard about the broken clock or what time the hands showed."

Stokes looked quietly delighted.

"Good work." Barnaby nodded at Price. "A solid bit of thinking. If no other villagers are aware of it, it seems likely that only the murderer knows what time was shown on the broken clock." Barnaby looked at Stokes and returned his smile. "That's one card we can keep up our sleeve —one we definitely won't play."

Stokes inclined his head. "Unless and until the time is right." He shifted his gaze to Penelope and Madeline. "Now you've wrung all our news from us, what did you learn from the gossips?"

Penelope took a moment to order her recollections, then commenced, "First, from Mrs. Foswell's observations, when Viola left the church and headed back through the village, Viola's attitude was one of focused determination. Viola told Mrs. Foswell that she couldn't dally and chat because she had an errand to complete before returning to Lavender Cottage, where she was expecting a visitor."

Stokes looked eager. "Dare I hope this errand was to Penrose Cottage?"

Penelope's lips curved. "Don't leap ahead. We'll get to the errand in due course."

"I take it the visitor was Pincer," Henry said.

"Viola didn't say," Madeline replied, "but as she promised to tell Mrs. Foswell all the next day, I suspect it was. The time certainly fits."

Penelope resumed her report. "After Mrs. Foswell, we spoke with Iris Perkins, and she confirmed seeing Viola go to the church at a little after twelve, then return through the junction at about twelve-thirty." She looked at Stokes and Barnaby. "From Iris's veranda, where she was sitting, she has an unobstructed view of the junction, but she can't see farther along Green Lane." She paused, then went on, "Iris saw Viola enter the junction and turn toward Green Lane, but then she stopped, opened her tapestry bag, and drew out a folded paper. Iris thought it looked like some official document, as she thinks it had a seal."

Henry stated, "A solicitor's letter should have been sealed."

Penelope nodded. "Iris saw Viola clutch the letter in her hand and determinedly march on down Green Lane."

"Iris didn't see anything more, but she told us Gladys Hooper had," Madeline said, "so we went on to the Hoopers' cottage."

"And Gladys was quite ready to tell us all," Penelope said. "Namely, that she had been visiting her old aunt, who lives farther out along Green Lane, and had been returning to share a light luncheon with Iris when she saw Viola marching toward her with a paper in her hand. Viola and Gladys exchanged waves, and then Viola turned in at the gate of Penrose Cottage."

Penelope smiled as, their expressions eager, all the men leaned forward, then Barnaby impatiently waved at her to continue, and she went on, "Gladys is an accomplished gossip, and she scurried to a spot along the fence outside Penrose Cottage where, unseen, she could hear the words exchanged when Viola knocked on the door and Ida opened it." She paused for breath, and the anticipation about the table palpably rose, then she related all that Gladys had overheard and also seen.

"Gladys saw the letter in Ida's hand?" Stokes asked.

Penelope nodded. "And she also saw Viola leave soon after, and she didn't have the letter with her then, or at least Gladys didn't notice it."

"If Ida had taken the letter into her hands, Viola wouldn't have taken it back," Barnaby said. "Not if she could help it."

"And as it was addressed to Arthur," Penelope pointed out, "Ida wouldn't have refused to take it for him. By all accounts, Ida is Arthur's protector. He gets on with doing what he loves while she deals with the world on his behalf."

They pondered that, then Penelope concluded, "Gladys stopped at the corner and looked back and saw Viola come out of the Penroses' gate and go in at Lavender Cottage." Penelope paused, then smiled and added, "And Gladys's last tidbit of information was that Ida served them freshly baked scones for afternoon tea."

When the men blinked at her, Penelope explained, "Scone dough is made with flour."

She sat back and thought things through, then summarized, "That's the entirety of our information. While we still have nothing that conclusively proves, beyond all question, that Ida Penrose strangled Viola to death, all the facts we've assembled inescapably point to that."

Barnaby and Stokes shared a long look, then Stokes softly grunted. "We're going to have to chance our hand and arrest her and hope that on the balance of the evidence, she'll be convicted."

Barnaby turned to Henry. "What do you think?"

Henry had clearly been weighing up their arguments. He grimaced. "It's hard to distance myself from this case…" He glanced at Madeline, then returned his gaze to Stokes. "However, I believe that on the balance of probabilities, you would get a conviction. Aside from all else, the question arises of who else could have done the deed. From Carter's evidence, we know that the murderer was someone Viola knew, making the pool of suspects small, and virtually all except Ida Penrose are accounted for."

"And," Penelope put in, "don't forget the timing. Gladys saw Viola go in through the Lavender Cottage gate at a minute or so before twelve-forty, and by one-thirty, Viola was dead and the murderer gone. It's difficult to construct any scenario whereby, within that fifty-minute period, someone else came into the cottage, killed Viola, and left the property without encountering Monty coming in from the rear or being seen by anyone in the village."

"Indeed," Henry said. "And then there's the matter of the solicitor's letters. They haven't been found, and the only persons with a motive for taking and burning them are Arthur and Ida Penrose."

"And," Penelope went on, "we know it wasn't Arthur because he spent all the afternoon with Jim Swinson in the orchard."

"The very orchard," Barnaby said, "that was the subject of the solicitor's letters." He looked at Stokes, as did everyone else.

Stokes had been staring at the table, listening to all that was said. Now, he raised his gaze and looked around the gathering, then nodded and straightened in his chair. "So we chance our hand and see what happens. I can't see that we've anything left to ferret out, no further information we might acquire to strengthen our case."

Penelope nodded, too. "We're in possession of all the facts we're likely to learn." She met Stokes's gaze and grimaced. "Like you, I imagine those solicitor's letters are cold ash by now."

Stokes humphed. "She wouldn't have kept them. She's made few mistakes thus far." He drew out his timepiece and consulted it, then tucked it away. "It's close to one o'clock. We should wait until after lunchtime to have the best chance of finding her alone." He glanced toward the kitchen, then cocked a brow at Madeline. "Is there anything we could eat while we wait?"

Madeline laughed, then shook her head and rose. She went into the kitchen, peered into the bread bin, then looked at the others. "I think we can manage sandwiches."

Everyone smiled, and O'Donnell, Morgan, and Price leapt to help.

They set out for Penrose Cottage at a few minutes before two o'clock. Stokes, Barnaby, and Penelope led the way, with Henry and Madeline following and O'Donnell, Morgan, and Price bringing up the rear.

Penelope remained behind Stokes as he went out of the Lavender Cottage gate, along the lane, then turned in at the gate of Penrose Cottage.

Over the sandwiches, they'd come up with a possible way to trick Ida into showing her true colors and incriminating herself. That would give them the clearest, neatest, least challengeable outcome. Whether their gambit would work was another matter.

As she trailed Stokes up the severely neat, rigidly straight path, Penelope drew in a settling breath and prepared herself for an interview that she expected to be akin to a mental chess game.

Stokes halted before the door, raised his fist, and knocked, quite loudly.

They waited.

When no footsteps approached and the door remained firmly shut, Stokes glanced at Barnaby and Penelope, then he faced the door and knocked again, rather more peremptorily.

Standing on and about the stoop, they waited again.

When no one came, Henry said, "I'll take a look around the back."

"I'll go, too." O'Donnell set off, shadowing Henry around the side of the house.

A minute later, Henry returned. "They're in the orchard—Ida, Arthur, and Jim."

"Doing what?" Stokes asked.

"Ida is just standing there," Henry reported, "watching while Jim and Arthur work at cutting down a large branch."

Stokes glanced at the others. "Well, so be it. Fitting in a way, I suppose."

He stepped off the stoop, and with Henry rejoining Madeline, their small procession marched around the house. On the way, they collected O'Donnell, who had remained by the rear corner of the house, watching their quarry, and proceeded down the path between the kitchen garden beds to the gate in the orchard's waist-high stone wall.

They could see the Penroses and Jim Swinson deeper in the orchard, gathered beneath an old tree. The sound of sawing had masked any noise the group had made, and the trio had yet to register their approach.

Stokes opened the gate and stepped through, but before Penelope and Barnaby followed, Henry murmured, "It might be more appropriate if Madeline and I remain here. We'll be close enough to see and hear what's said, but at this distance, we won't intrude nor be tempted to contribute."

Stokes nodded. "Good idea. This is going to need careful handling." He looked at Price. "Best you remain with his lordship and Miss Huntingdon." He glanced at O'Donnell and Morgan. "You two, come with us."

O'Donnell and Morgan looked relieved, while Price looked faintly disappointed.

Smiling slightly, Stokes held the gate open and waved Penelope through. Barnaby followed, and with O'Donnell and Morgan trailing a few paces behind, they made their way down the grassy central path.

They were within ten yards when Ida heard them. She half turned, saw them, and frowned. She didn't alter her stance but remained with her arms folded across her chest and an unwelcoming expression on her face. "What do you lot want?"

Jim, who'd been looking at the branch Arthur had started sawing, heard her and glanced across, then Arthur noticed, stopped sawing, and after seeing who had arrived, he lowered his saw and waited.

Stokes halted two yards away, and Barnaby and Penelope flanked him. O'Donnell and Morgan did their best to be inconspicuous as they halted farther back.

Ida shifted to face the investigators. As far as Penelope could detect, no spark of emotion showed in her strong-featured face. Not even curiosity colored her dark eyes.

She didn't repeat her question, which had bordered on a challenge, but waited, her gaze steady on Stokes, Penelope, and Barnaby. Penelope didn't think she was imagining the slowly rising tide of hostility directed toward them. She was quite sure Ida didn't want them there.

Calmly, Stokes nodded to her. "Mrs. Penrose." He shifted his gaze and acknowledged the men. "Mr. Penrose, Mr. Swinson." Then Stokes returned his gaze to Ida and calmly stated, "Ida Penrose, we're here to arrest you for the murder of your neighbor, Viola Huntingdon."

They'd discussed what they wouldn't reveal, but not how they would conduct this interview, and Stokes's unexpected declaration left even Penelope faintly stunned. The effect on the Penroses and Jim Swinson was even more marked. For an instant, all three froze, not breathing or moving in even the smallest way.

In that second, Penelope would have sworn even the light breeze stopped.

Slowly, Ida's eyes narrowed, but she said nothing.

Uncomprehendingly, Arthur looked at her. "Ida? What's this?"

Stunned, Jim Swinson, too, felt moved to prompt, "Mrs. P?"

Both patently expected Ida to laugh and refute the allegation.

After an excruciating wait, a frown slowly formed on her face.

She's working out how to manage this, Penelope thought.

"You don't know what you're talking about," Ida eventually said. "It's nonsensical to think I killed Viola. Why would I?" She raised her head, almost tossing it as she tipped her chin high. "She was a nuisance, nothing more."

"Except," Stokes countered, "that she'd commenced legal proceedings to reclaim the land lost from her property due to an illegal shifting of the boundary"—he glanced toward the stone wall at the side of the orchard—"between your husband's land and hers."

Ida's arms, still crossed, fractionally tightened. "I don't know anything about that. What proceedings?"

"The ones outlined in the solicitor's letter Viola delivered into your hands on Thursday last week, a few hours before she was killed," Stokes replied.

Ida's tone grew a touch belligerent. "I don't know anything about any letter."

One of Stokes's black brows arched. "Don't you? That's odd, because we have a witness who saw Viola come to your door at about twelve-thirty on the day she was killed, and this witness heard Viola ask to speak with Arthur, and when you replied that he was out in the fields, Viola handed you the letter to give to him. The letter was addressed to Arthur as owner of this property. That letter was seen in your hands."

Stokes shifted his gaze to Arthur Penrose. "Mr. Penrose, have you received the letter—a solicitor's letter informing you of the pending legal action over the boundary—that Viola gave your wife to deliver to you?"

Ida's face might, just might, have paled a fraction.

Now worried and anxious as well as confused, Arthur replied, "No." He turned to Ida and, in a pleading tone, prompted, "Ida?"

Ida's shoulders rose in a slight hunch. Without taking her eyes from Stokes, refusing to look at her husband, she shook her head. "It was all just rubbish about taking you to court. You didn't need to see it. I burned it."

"But..." Arthur looked faintly appalled. "It was a legal paper. And addressed to me."

Still without looking his way, Ida shook her head and repeated, "You didn't need to see it. I took care of it."

Barnaby shifted, drawing Ida's gaze. "Did you 'take care' of the letter you took from Viola's tapestry bag, the one informing Lord Glossup of the legal action? Did you burn that, too?"

Ida looked daggers at him, then sullenly repeated, "I don't know what you're talking about."

"Oh, but you do." Stokes reclaimed her attention. "Let's go through what really happened, shall we? After Viola left the letter with you and went home, you opened the letter and read it—of course you did—and you saw red."

Penelope took a half step forward. "You realized how serious the matter was and that Viola stood an excellent chance of taking away a good third of the orchard." Penelope chanced her hand at guessing Ida's principal motive. "A good third of the orchard Arthur doted on, that was his pride and joy. And you weren't going to stand for that, were you? You've always been the one to make sure this place runs smoothly, that Arthur's life runs as perfectly as possible for him, and that he has everything he wants—all that makes him happy. That's been your purpose through all the years of your marriage—to keep Arthur happy."

The look Ida bent on Penelope suggested that Ida thought all Penelope had said hadn't needed to be stated. "Of course I want Arthur to be happy. He's my husband, isn't he? That's what good wives do—make all the problems in married life go away."

Her expression serious and understanding, even commiserating, Penelope nodded. "And that's why you had to take care of this for him. Why you had to stop Viola's action from going ahead in the only way possible."

Ida opened her lips—apparently to agree—but caught herself and stopped, then with a glare for Penelope, Ida slammed her lips shut.

"So," Stokes smoothly continued, "you burned the letter intended for Arthur, and then—"

"You finished the scone dough you were halfway through making," Penelope said, "put the dough in your cool box—which is what one does to get the fluffiest scones—and dusted off your hands and went to deal with Viola."

From Ida's shocked stare, it was plain to all that Penelope's guess was entirely correct.

After shooting Penelope a faintly astonished look, Stokes carried on, "You left your cottage by the kitchen door, went to the stile between the properties, and climbed over it, leaving a shoe print in the soft ground. You went to Lavender Cottage's kitchen door and knocked, and when Viola answered, you said you wanted to talk, and she let you in."

Barnaby took over. "She led you through the kitchen, past the dining table, and into the parlor."

Stokes picked up the tale. "We have no idea what words were exchanged, but when Viola refused to halt the legal action, you stepped toward her, fastened your hands about her throat, and squeezed until she was dead."

"Incidentally," Penelope chimed in, "while doing that, you left a light dusting of flour on Viola's bodice. When one works with flour, as when making scones, flour invariably gets into one's cuffs, and unless one is careful to shake it out, it tends to leave a telltale trail."

The unexpected facts were starting to shake Ida's confidence.

"After Viola breathed her last," Stokes continued, his tone steady and even and laced with a certainty that was absolute, "you let her body fall to the ground. You turned away, but you remembered the letter—the letter very similar to the one she'd given you for Arthur—that you'd seen in Viola's hand that morning, during the altercation you and Jim witnessed between Viola and Lord Glossup."

"You'd seen Viola put that letter into her tapestry bag," Barnaby said, his intervention again jarring Ida, forcing her to shift her gaze, "and you were worried that letter, like the one she'd given to you for Arthur, concerned the legal action over the boundary."

"So you went looking for Viola's tapestry bag"—Stokes's voice took on a definite edge—"and you found it in the hall, upended it, found the letter, and took it with you as you left the cottage by the kitchen door—"

"Passing over the stile," Barnaby said, "and once again leaving an imprint of your shoe in the softer ground there."

"You returned to your own kitchen"—Penelope took up the baton— "and checked that the letter was as you'd feared and fed it into your stove. Then you retrieved your scone dough and baked the scones you would later serve to Iris Perkins and Gladys Hooper when they called as arranged for afternoon tea."

Ida had been blinking, thrown off balance by the frequent shifts in interlocutor. When they fell silent, waiting to see if their rapid-fire description of what she'd done would bring them the hoped-for reward, Ida stared at them, then drew in a slow breath and glanced at Arthur and Jim.

Seeing the horrified questions in their faces, she insisted, "It's all nonsense. Nonsense, I tell you." Her jaw setting, she swung her attention back to the investigators and belligerently asked, "What time was this, then?"

Evenly, Stokes replied, "We know Viola was dead by one-thirty, when her body was discovered by a friend."

This time, Ida's blink was very slow.

That's shaken her, Penelope thought.

She continued to stare at them as her gaze grew puzzled. Then she shook her head. "That can't be right."

"We're certain it is," Stokes countered, and the investigators and their supporting players held their breaths.

Ida's features hardened, and she tipped up her chin. "What about the clock, then?"

Penelope slammed a lid on her jubilation. They needed Ida to go just a bit further.

Stokes suddenly looked uncertain, his confidence draining away. Almost cautiously, he asked, "What about it?"

As if Stokes's waning assurance had fed hers, Ida confidently stated, "I heard it was broken in the struggle and showed three-thirty-three. So that's when Viola was killed, and at that time, I was here with Iris and Gladys, having scones and tea."

Penelope breathed more easily, and she was sure Stokes and Barnaby did the same. As if merely curious, she asked, "Indeed, you were. But how did you hear about the clock?"

Ida's features turned impassive, and she lifted a shoulder. "Heard it from someone."

"Who?" Stokes pressed.

Ida stared at him, her gaze growing openly malevolent, and said nothing.

"You see, Ida," Barnaby said, "we haven't mentioned the time shown on the face of the broken clock to anyone but those involved in the investigation, and none of us have talked of it to anyone in the village."

"And we know for a fact that Viola was dead by one-thirty," Penelope stated. "That is now beyond question."

"But you are, indeed, correct"—Stokes inclined his head to Ida—"that the time shown on the broken clock was three-thirty-three. Exactly that. But the thing is, the only person who could have set the clock to that time, then broken it by smashing it on the hearth as if it had fallen in some struggle, was the murderer. So other than the investigating team, the only one who knows the time shown was three-thirty-three is the murderer." Stokes held Ida's gaze. "You."

"And because we know that Viola was dead by one-thirty, and it was the murderer who set the clock to three-thirty-three, we know that the murderer will have a cast-iron alibi for that time. Why else go to the trouble of setting the clock to three-thirty-three and breaking it?" Penelope smiled at Ida. "The murderer is you, and of course you set the clock to three-thirty-three, a time when you knew, without doubt, that you would have two unimpeachable witnesses to testify that, at that time, you were nowhere near Lavender Cottage but, instead, in your own parlor, pouring tea and passing around scones."

Barnaby flatly stated, "You, Ida Penrose, killed Viola Huntingdon."

Ida stared at them, then her gaze darted sideways to Arthur and Jim. She took in their shocked and horrified expressions. The understanding that she was the murderer was blazoned across their faces, along with burgeoning condemnation.

Her face worked, then her resistance broke, and uncrossing her arms, she railed at her husband, "That stupid woman! She wouldn't let it be!"

"B-But…" Arthur stuttered, clearly not knowing what to say.

Ida rounded on him. "She was going to take us to court, and she'd win, and you'd lose a good third and more of your trees. And you'd've hated that! And we'd have been stretched for coin, too." She glared at Jim. "We'd've had to let you go, so you can stop looking at me like that. I did what I had to." Her expression fierce, she looked at Arthur. "I did it for you."

But Arthur was already shaking his head. "No." His voice was faint. "Why…?"

Ida swung to face the investigators as if she could explain her actions to them and they would understand. "I gave her a chance to back down, but she wouldn't. She said she'd take the land if it was the last thing she did. Well"—Ida shrugged—"telling me that was the last thing she did, so there."

Curious, Penelope asked, "You really don't think you've done anything terribly wrong, do you?"

Ida recrossed her arms and looked at Penelope, then she jutted her chin at Barnaby. "If someone were going to take his land—land he'd slaved over for years and that was his passion—wouldn't you do something to stop them?"

Penelope conceded, "I would do something, certainly, but I assure you that no matter the circumstances, no matter how fraught the situation, I would never stoop to murder."

Ida stared at Penelope, then sniffed contemptuously and looked away.

Stokes glanced at O'Donnell and Morgan and summoned them with a jerk of his head. Returning his gaze to Ida, he formally announced, "Ida Penrose, I'm arresting you for the murder by strangulation of Viola Huntingdon on Thursday, October fifteenth, in Lavender Cottage in Ashmore village. You will be held in Salisbury pending the next assizes."

Ida didn't look at Arthur. Instead, she glared at the experienced sergeant and constable who approached. After forcibly securing her hands in front of her, O'Donnell and Morgan each took one of Ida's arms and, having to push a little to get her moving, steered her onto the orchard path. Penelope, Barnaby, and Stokes stepped aside and watched Ida, her head still arrogantly high, being led away. She made no attempt to look back but marched on between the policemen, through the gate Constable Price held wide, past Henry and Madeline, who had drawn to one side, and on around the house.

Penelope looked at Arthur Penrose. Shattered, disbelieving, and overcome were some of the words that sprang to her mind, but Jim Swinson had his arm around the older man's shoulders, all but holding him up, and when Penelope caught Jim's eye and raised her brows, Jim nodded. "I'll stay with him."

Penelope turned away from the grief progressively etching itself into Arthur's face.

She took the hand Barnaby offered and gripped tight, and together, they followed Stokes out of the orchard.

Henry, Madeline, and Constable Price joined them as they trailed O'Donnell and Morgan and their captive to the lane, where Phelps had the police coach waiting.

Wordlessly, they all stood around the front gate and watched as Morgan and O'Donnell helped Ida to climb inside, then they shut the barred door on her and climbed up to take the reins Phelps relinquished, while Price climbed to the rear bench.

As soon as O'Donnell, Morgan, and Price had settled, Stokes nodded to them. "Straight to Salisbury. Mallard will be waiting to take her in charge. Then join us back at the inn."

The Scotland Yard men saluted, as did Price, then Morgan flicked the reins and set the old coach rolling ponderously out of Ashmore.

A sound like a gasp drew Penelope's attention to the group of villagers who had gathered on the green. Iris Perkins and Gladys Hooper were there, along with men Penelope took to be their husbands, as well as Reverend Foswell and Mrs. Foswell, and the Gilroys, mother and son. There were others, too, presumably from other village cottages. All watched in somber silence as the police coach rolled off, taking away Ida Penrose, someone most there had known for much of their lives.

It was a sober, rather sad moment, and each appeared sunk in their own thoughts; no one wanted to engage in any conversation.

Similarly wordless, Penelope linked her arm in Barnaby's and, with Stokes and Henry and Madeline following, walked toward Lavender Cottage and their carriage with Phelps back on the box and Connor up behind. Henry's curricle was waiting a little farther along the lane.

As she grasped Barnaby's hand and climbed into their carriage, Penelope wondered how many others in the immediate vicinity were, like her, thinking of how many lives had been changed forever by one single, violent act.

They gathered in quiet relief and slowly burgeoning cheer in the private parlor at the King John Inn. After seeing Ida Penrose into her cell in Salisbury, Mallard returned with the Scotland Yard coach and joined the company.

In recognition of their help, Barnaby and Stokes invited O'Donnell, Morgan, Phelps, and Connor, as well as Constable Price, who had returned with Mallard, to join the gathering in the private parlor.

Once all their glasses were charged, Stokes raised his tankard, called for quiet, and thanked those assembled for their assistance in what had proved to be a tricky case, then called for a toast all around to Justice's ultimate triumph.

Cheers duly followed, and everyone drank.

As she lowered her glass, Penelope observed, "And if, as we should, we are to learn from the mistakes we made, then surely, the lesson from this case is to always—*always*—be sure to talk to the gossips first!"

Everyone laughed and drank to that, too.

Mallard, whose attitude to the Scotland Yard contingent had changed significantly from what it had been when he'd first encountered them, was quick to add his thanks to the interlopers on his patch. He raised his glass to them. "Much as it pains me to admit it, we would never have taken up the murderer—the right person for the murder—if it hadn't been for your dogged persistence and insistence in following the logic of things. That's taught me and my men something, and for that, I do thank all of you."

After the Londoners had gracefully smiled and accepted that accolade with another quaff of their drinks, Henry, standing beside Madeline's chair, cleared his throat, and when everyone looked his way, he hoisted his tankard and declared, "I, too, wish to propose a toast of thanks to all those who came to Ashmore village and helped apprehend the murderer most surprisingly lurking in our midst. While there will be shock and sadness among the villagers, I also know, from experience"—he half bowed to Stokes—"that if a murder isn't properly solved, then the inevitable niggling questions remain and, eventually, blossom into distrust and wariness, which ultimately destroys the very village life that all those who live in small communities hold so dear."

He looked around the gathering and raised his glass to them all. "So on behalf of the village of Ashmore, I thank you all for your help in solving the murder of Viola Huntingdon."

"And," Madeline said, her tone firm and strong as she raised her glass and looked around the company, "I, too, would like to add my thanks to all involved. You have ensured that justice is done. Mere hours before you arrived in the village, I swore to Viola I would seek justice for her, and you've helped me achieve that goal, and for that, all of you have my undying thanks."

The others smiled and inclined their heads graciously, then Mallard humphed. "Small villages—you'd think nothing out of the ordinary ever happened there, and in that, you'd be very wrong. Why…"

The Superintending Constable proceeded to entertain them with tales of several outlandish cases that had occurred in the small villages of Wiltshire and Dorset.

Stokes joined in and described a string of peculiar cases that had occurred in the Home Counties, including one involving headless scarecrows. "Being Scotland Yard, we're the ones the local forces turn to for help, although often, we're as much at sea as they are."

"Sometimes more so," O'Donnell put in. "Remember that time in Weybridge?"

Morgan shuddered. "The jewelry from some merchant's house found hidden in a nearby farm's pigsty." He glanced around at the others. "You have no idea how aggressive and attached to their home pigs can be."

O'Donnell was nodding. "Big beggars they were, too."

From there, the conversations and stories meandered into an ever more light-hearted vein.

Penelope finally found an opportunity to question—interrogate—Madeline on her association with Thomas Glendower. Stokes buttonholed Henry about how Henry's parents, whom Stokes had met five years before, were faring.

The police and Phelps and Connor, meanwhile, were talking business, with Mallard questioning Morgan on life at Scotland Yard, while Constable Price eagerly asked O'Donnell, Phelps, and Connor about previous cases on which they'd assisted.

Barnaby sipped his ale and, with a gentle smile curving his lips, watched as everyone—each in their own way yet all very much a company still—put the recent case to rest and turned toward tomorrow.

Eventually, the company broke up, with Phelps and Connor retiring in order to have the carriage ready to depart after breakfast the next day.

O'Donnell and Morgan followed, being the ones who would have to drive the police coach back to London, and Mallard hired a horse from the innkeeper and, with final good wishes all around, left to ride back to Salisbury. Meanwhile, Constable Price bade them all goodnight and headed off across the moonlit fields. Penelope had learned that Price lived with his parents on a farm not far away.

That left her, Barnaby, and Stokes to wave Henry and Madeline off. The five of them walked out of the inn and halted just outside as the inn's ostler brought the horse and light carriage around.

The ostler halted the horse, and as he climbed down, Penelope walked beside Madeline to the curricle, while Barnaby and Stokes chatted with Henry as he took the reins and climbed up to the box seat.

"Sadly," Penelope said, having already discussed the matter with Barnaby, "we won't be able to attend Viola's funeral."

Despite all the discoveries and consequent excitement, Madeline had managed to finalize the arrangements, and Viola's funeral and interment would be held on Monday, two days away.

Madeline climbed up and sat beside Henry, and Penelope smiled up at her. "We've been away for nearly a week, and the boys will start to wonder."

Madeline smiled back. "I quite understand." She leaned down, caught Penelope's hand, and lightly squeezed her fingers. "I'm most sincerely grateful to you and Barnaby for coming to Ashmore and helping." She glanced at the three men. "You two and Stokes, as well. I seriously doubt Viola's murderer would have been caught without your help." Madeline turned back to Penelope and more seriously said, "Very likely Monty would have been hanged for the murder, and no matter how much of a blight on the community he is, that wouldn't have been right."

With that, Penelope had to agree. "You will call when you're back in town?"

"Definitely." Madeline grinned as she straightened. "Aside from all else, I do think we should pursue your idea of setting up a small private society for ladies who like to invest. I'm sure Thomas and Rose, too, would be in favor."

Penelope laughed. "We'll do that, then, when you return to town."

With promises on that score, and one from Henry that he, too, would call on them when he was next in town, the three Londoners stepped back from the carriage, and Henry flourished his whip in a farewell wave and steered the curricle out of the yard and off along the lane.

For several seconds, the three stood silently, savoring the peace of the country night, then Stokes sighed. "I'm for bed." He turned for the inn, and Penelope and Barnaby followed.

After leading the way inside and up the stairs, Stokes halted at the head of the stairs and nodded to Penelope and Barnaby. "I'll see you at breakfast."

They murmured agreement and turned for their room as Stokes strode down the opposite wing.

As they ambled slowly along the corridor, Penelope mused, "I rather suspect that we'll be traveling down to Ashmore again soon enough." She glanced at Barnaby, a smugly satisfied smile on her face. "This time, to stay at Glossup Hall for a wedding."

He arched his brows but saw no reason to disagree.

Looking ahead, Penelope observed, "A wedding will be an excellent way to turn the negativity generated by the murder to positive hope for the future."

"Hmm." Barnaby thought about that. "That's what marriage should signify, isn't it? Hope for the future, not just for the couple involved but for their community."

A slight frown tangling her dark brows, Penelope inclined her head.

"That should be the way of things, yet as this case illustrates, there are instances where a marriage doesn't work that way. First, there was Henry's marriage to Kitty. That ended in infidelity that, ultimately, led to murder. Then Pincer waved marriage like a flag before Viola's face, and she nearly succumbed. Only luck saved her from what would have been a dreadful mistake. But the worst travesty, surely, was Ida's twist on what marriage should mean. She saw her role as doing anything and everything to make Arthur happy. In her eyes, marriage excused and, indeed, gave her license to do whatever she deemed necessary to achieve what she saw as required by her role. She never discussed her decisions with Arthur. She simply acted as she believed she needed to, and in her eyes, she had the right to do so."

They paused in a splash of moonlight before the door to their room, and Penelope looked at Barnaby and sighed. Then she softly smiled. "But seeing the times marriages lead people astray, even into murder, only serves to make me appreciate the benefits of a marriage that works properly all the more."

Barnaby chuckled. "Marriage that works properly. Is that how you see us?"

"Of course!" Her head tilted, Penelope grinned at him.

"I was wondering," he admitted, smiling into her dark eyes, "how to tactfully point out that our marriage seems to go along rather nicely with murder adding spice on the side."

She nodded sagely as he reached around her and opened the room's door. "Ah yes, but the important distinction is 'on the side.'" Moving into the room, she added, "Very firmly outside our personal sphere."

EPILOGUE

DECEMBER 5, 1840. ST. NICHOLAS' CHURCH, ASHMORE, DORSET.

*B*arnaby, Penelope, and Stokes did, indeed, visit Ashmore village again. On a crisp winter morning, they were among the company who gathered to witness the wedding of Henry, Lord Glossup, and Miss Madeline Huntingdon.

"Out of adversity, good things do grow," Penelope whispered to Barnaby as the radiant bride, now on the arm of her new husband, who could not have looked prouder, all but skipped up the aisle.

"New shoots," Barnaby whispered back, "growing up from a field of desolation."

That was certainly the way matters seemed as, smiling as widely as the rest of those there—most if not all of the village congregation as well as a small army of the groom's and bride's London friends—Penelope and Barnaby fell in behind the happy couple and followed them up the aisle.

Given the bride was still in mourning for her late sister, the wedding had been designed as a quiet affair, but the villagers were so glad to put the recent past behind them that they'd thrown themselves wholeheartedly into welcoming their new lady of the manor. The church had been bedecked with seasonal greenery, and the singing of the hymns had been wonderfully enthusiastic. More, Henry and his household had risen to the challenge, and literally everyone there was invited to the big house—meaning Glossup Hall—for the wedding breakfast.

For a time, Penelope chatted with her sister and brother-in-law and the various close friends who were present. Charlie Hastings was there along with his recently acquired wife, Claudia. The pair engaged Stokes and Mallard in a discussion of the improvements being made to the policing of the less-salubrious precincts in London, a project in which the couple had developed a deep interest.

Of course, the village gossips were out in force. Penelope made time to chat with Mrs. Foswell as well as her husband, who had officiated at the ceremony. Iris Perkins introduced Penelope to her husband, and Penelope also spoke with Gladys Hooper and met her husband and three strapping sons.

Unsurprisingly, at least to Penelope, the village had gathered around Arthur Penrose, supporting him through the ordeal of his wife's trial. Ida Penrose had been found guilty and sentenced to death by hanging, but had been moved to London with the sentence still to be carried out, and Arthur and the village had—in Penelope's opinion sensibly—endeavored to move on.

Apparently, Arthur's widowed sister, Martha, had never seen eye to eye with Ida. On being introduced to Penelope by Jim Swinson, Martha confided, "I always suspected Ida was a little strange. She was so…well, *obsessive* over anything to do with Arthur. He's my younger brother, so I was always passing judgment, as one does with younger brothers, and as you can imagine, that never went down well with Ida. In the end, once I married and moved away, I stayed away. But now my James is gone and our boy is in the navy, it seemed sensible to come back to the village and do what I can for Arthur. Thanks to Ida, he's one as now needs taking care of. He doesn't even know how to boil an egg, poor man."

"I expect Jim is a help, too," Penelope pried.

"Oh yes!" Martha nodded. "I don't know what Arthur would do without Jim to remind him of what needs doing in the fields and orchard. Gradually, Arthur's coming back to us, finding his way again, which is what we must hope for."

"Indeed." Pleased to know that positive shoots were blooming there as well, with a smile and a nod, Penelope moved on.

Madeline had told her that she was taking steps to have the boundaries of Penrose Cottage and Lavender Cottage redrawn so that Arthur—and possibly Jim in the future—wouldn't lose a third of the prized orchard to which Arthur had devoted his life. As Madeline had staunchly declared, "And if anyone thinks that's giving Ida what she killed Viola to get, then all I can say is that I don't need that piece of orchard, but Arthur assuredly does. Now more than ever."

Penelope couldn't have agreed more, especially as, courtesy of several reciprocal visits to their London homes during which she and Madeline had further developed their idea of a ladies' investment society, Penelope had gained a much clearer notion of Madeline's wealth. Monty Pincer, now incarcerated and likely to be transported, would be ill if he ever learned just how fat was the pigeon he'd let fly away.

Eventually, Penelope found her way back to Barnaby's side. He was standing with Stokes at the edge of the lawn beside the path leading down to the lane. When she looped her arm in his, Barnaby smiled down at her. "Are you ready to head back to Glossup Hall?"

She ran her gaze over the company. "Yes, I think it's time. Soon enough, everyone else will realize that, as we're all going to the same feast, they can transfer their conversation to more congenial surroundings."

"Indeed," Stokes rumbled. "And here come the bride and groom to lead the way."

Sure enough, emerging through a sudden eruption of rice, Henry and Madeline, holding hands and laughing as they ran, came rushing down the path.

Penelope, Barnaby, and Stokes clapped and cheered as the pair went past, then with the rest of the congregation, streamed down the path and out through the lychgate to where the Glossup Hall coachman, in full livery, had a landau drawn by a pair of glossy blacks waiting.

Henry helped Madeline to climb into the carriage, then quickly followed.

The crowd surged all around, calling out good wishes even though they'd see the happy couple again soon.

The coachman flicked his reins, and the carriage rolled slowly off, passing the Adairs' waiting carriage along the way.

As the congregation bustled off to their various conveyances to travel the few miles along the lane to the Hall, Penelope and Barnaby made for the carriage door Connor was holding open, with Stokes ambling beside them.

As they reached the carriage, Penelope heaved a huge sigh.

When Barnaby, Stokes, and even Connor looked at her questioningly, she beamed and said, "Another happy ending. I do so appreciate it when we manage one of those."

All three men chuckled, and they climbed aboard and headed up the lane to enjoy their latest triumph.

Dear Reader,

In my letter in the previous book, I noted that most frequently, the title of a novel suggests itself as a story take shape as being the obvious description for that particular book. In this instance, that was certainly the case, with this story involving and revolving around several different perspectives on the combination of marriage and murder.

Indeed, the theme of marriage and murder even stretches back to my long-ago title, *The Perfect Lover*, in which you first met Henry Glossup. Over the years (since 2003!) many of you have asked for Henry's story. Finally, it has arrived, and Henry has his day and finds the happiness he's long deserved. I hope you've enjoyed this latest installment in the continuing adventures of Barnaby, Penelope, Stokes, and friends.

As for what's coming next, in *The Murder of Thomas Cardwell* (July 17, 2025), we return to London and Jordan Draper, Roscoe's right-hand man, who on being dispatched by Roscoe to learn what "nefarious activities" another man-of-business wishes to bring to the attention of the authorities, discovers the man dead.

Information and descriptions of earlier volumes in THE CASEBOOK OF BARNABY ADAIR series—*Where the Heart Leads, The Peculiar Case of Lord Finsbury's Diamonds, The Masterful Mr. Montague, The Curious Case of Lady Latimer's Shoes, Loving Rose: The Redemption of Malcolm Sinclair, The Confounding Case of the Carisbrook Emeralds, The Murder at Mandeville Hall, The Meriwell Legacy* and *Dead Beside the Thames*—can be found following.

Barnaby, Penelope, Stokes, Griselda, and their friends and supporters continue to tackle the solving of crimes with undimmed enthusiasm. I hope they and their adventures solving mysteries and exposing villains will continue to entertain you in the future just as much as they do me.

Enjoy!

Stephanie.

. . .

For alerts as new books are released, plus information on upcoming books, exclusive sweepstakes and sneak peeks into upcoming novels, sign up for Stephanie's Private Email Newsletter http://www.stephanielaurens.com/newsletter-signup/

Or if you don't have time to chat and want a quick email alert, sign up and follow me at BookBub https://www.bookbub.com/authors/stephanie-laurens

The ultimate source for detailed information on all Stephanie's published books, including covers, descriptions, and excerpts, is Stephanie's Website www.stephanielaurens.com

You can also follow Stephanie via her Amazon Author Page at http://tinyurl.com/zc3e9mp

Goodreads members can follow Stephanie via her author page https://www.goodreads.com/author/show/9241.Stephanie_Laurens

You can email Stephanie at stephanie@stephanielaurens.com

Or find her on Facebook
https://www.facebook.com/AuthorStephanieLaurens/

COMING NEXT:
THE MURDER OF THOMAS CARDWELL
The Casebook of Barnaby Adair #11
To be released in July, 2025.

Jordan Draper has spent his adult life working for Roscoe, London's gambling king. When Roscoe receives an appeal for advice from upright man-of-business Thomas Cardwell regarding unspecified nefarious activities on which Thomas has unexpectedly stumbled, Roscoe dispatches Jordan to discover what's afoot. Jordan arrives at Thomas's office and discovers Thomas has just been murdered. Soon, Jordan is working alongside Inspector Stokes and Barnaby and Penelope Adair, together with the victim's sister, Ruth, to unravel the perplexing mystery

of why anyone would murder a man as honest and unthreatening as
Thomas Cardwell.

Available for pre-order by March, 2025.

RECENTLY RELEASED:
The ninth volume in
The Casebook of Barnaby Adair mystery-romances
DEAD BESIDE THE THAMES

*#1 NYT-bestselling author Stephanie Laurens returns with a confounding
case that sees her favorite sleuths acting to save a friend wrongly accused
of murder.*
*When a detested viscount is found murdered by the banks of the Thames
and Charlie Hastings becomes the prime suspect, Barnaby and Penelope
Adair join forces with Stokes to discover the real story behind the
unexpected killing.*

Charlie Hastings is astonished to find himself accused of murdering
Viscount Sedbury. Admittedly, Charlie had two heated altercations with
Sedbury in the hours preceding the man's death, but as Charlie is quick to
point out to Stokes – and to Barnaby and Penelope – there are a multitude
of others in the ton who will be delighted to learn of Sedbury's demise.

As Penelope, Barnaby, and Stokes start assembling a suspect list,
Charlie's prediction proves only too accurate. Yet the most puzzling
aspect is who on earth managed to kill Sedbury. The man was a hulking
brute, large, very strong, and known as a vicious brawler. Who managed
to subdue him enough to strangle him?

As the number of suspects steadily increases, the investigators are
forced to ask if, perhaps, one of their suspects hired a killer capable of
taking Sedbury down. With that possibility thrown into the calculations,
narrowing their suspect list becomes a futile exercise.

Their pursuit of the truth leads them to investigate the many shady
avenues of Sedbury's life, much to the consternation of Sedbury's father,
the Marquess of Rattenby. Rattenby does not want Sedbury's distasteful
proclivities exposed for all the world to see, further harming the other
family members who Sedbury has taken great delight in tormenting for
most of his life.

In the end, the resolution of the crime lies in old-fashioned policing coupled with the fresh twists Barnaby and Penelope bring to Scotland Yard's efforts.

And when the truth is finally revealed, it raises questions that strike to the very heart of justice and what, with such a victim and such a murderer, true justice actually means.

A historical novel of 62,500 words interweaving mystery and murder with a touch of romance.

**The eighth volume in
The Casebook of Barnaby Adair mystery-romances
THE MERIWELL LEGACY**

#1 NYT-bestselling author Stephanie Laurens returns with her favorite sleuths to unravel a tangled web of family secrets and expose a murderer.

When Lord Meriwell collapses and dies at his dining table, Barnaby and Penelope Adair are summoned, along with Inspector Basil Stokes, to discover who, how, and most importantly why someone very close to his lordship saw fit to poison him.

When Lord Meriwell dies at his dining table, Nurse Veronica Haskell suspects foul play and notifies his lordship's doctor, eminent Harley Street specialist Dr. David Sanderson. In turn, compelled by a need to protect Veronica who is at Meriwell Hall as David's behest, David calls on his friends Barnaby and Penelope Adair for assistance.

However, as the fateful dinner was the first of a house party being attended by the local MP and his family, the Metropolitan Police commissioners also consider the Adairs' presence desirable, and consequently, Barnaby and Penelope accompany Stokes to Meriwell Hall.

There, they discover a gathering of the Meriwell family intended to impress the visiting Busseltons so that George Busselton, local MP, will agree to a marriage between his daughter and Lord Meriwell's eldest nephew, Stephen. But instead of any pleasant sojourn, the company find themselves confined to the hall and grounds while Stokes, Barnaby, and Penelope set about interviewing everyone and establishing facts, alibis, and the movements of those in the house.

To our investigators' frustration, while determining the means proves straightforward, and opportunity reduces their suspect list, motive remains elusive, and their list of suspects stays stubbornly long.

Then the killer strikes again, but even then, the investigators are left with the same suspects and too many potential reasons for the second death.

What did the killer hope to gain?

More importantly, will he kill again?

At last, the investigators stumble on a promising clue, yet following it requires sending to London for information, and their frustration builds. As the clock ticks and they doggedly forge on, they uncover more and more facts, yet none allows them to identify which of their prime suspects is the murderer.

Will they get the breakthrough they need, one sufficient to exonerate the innocent?

When the answer arrives, they discover that the Meriwell family legacies are more far-reaching than anyone realized, and that the crimes involved and the motivation for the murders is far more heinous than anyone imagined.

A historical novel of 78,000 words interweaving mystery and murder with a touch of romance.

PREVIOUSLY RELEASED IN THE CASEBOOK OF BARNABY ADAIR NOVELS:

Read about Penelope's and Barnaby's romance, plus that of Stokes and Griselda, in
The first volume in
The Casebook of Barnaby Adair mystery-romances
WHERE THE HEART LEADS

Penelope Ashford, Portia Cynster's younger sister, has grown up with every advantage - wealth, position, and beauty. Yet Penelope is anything but a typical ton miss - forceful, willful and blunt to a fault, she has for years devoted her considerable energy and intelligence to directing an institution caring for the forgotten orphans of London's streets.

But now her charges are mysteriously disappearing. Desperate, Penelope turns to the one man she knows who might help her - Barnaby Adair.

Handsome scion of a noble house, Adair has made a name for himself in political and judicial circles. His powers of deduction and observation combined with his pedigree has seen him solve several serious crimes within the ton. Although he makes her irritatingly uncomfortable, Penelope throws caution to the wind and appears on his bachelor doorstep late one night, determined to recruit him to her cause.

Barnaby is intrigued—by her story, and her. Her bold beauty and undeniable brains make a striking contrast to the usual insipid ton misses. And as he's in dire need of an excuse to avoid said insipid misses, he accepts her challenge, never dreaming she and it will consume his every waking hour.

Enlisting the aid of Inspector Basil Stokes of the fledgling Scotland Yard, they infiltrate the streets of London's notorious East End. But as they unravel the mystery of the missing boys, they cross the trail of a criminal embedded in the very organization recently created to protect all Londoners. And that criminal knows of them and their efforts, and is only too ready to threaten all they hold dear, including their new-found knowledge of the intrigues of the human heart.

FURTHER CASES AND THE EVOLUTION OF RELATIONSHIPS CONTINUE IN:

The second volume in
The Casebook of Barnaby Adair mystery-romances
THE PECULIAR CASE OF LORD FINSBURY'S DIAMONDS

#1 New York Times *bestselling author Stephanie Laurens brings you a tale of murder, mystery, passion, and intrigue – and diamonds!*

Penelope Adair, wife and partner of amateur sleuth Barnaby Adair, is so hugely pregnant she cannot even waddle. When Barnaby is summoned to assist Inspector Stokes of Scotland Yard in investigating the violent murder of a gentleman at a house party, Penelope, frustrated that she cannot participate, insists that she and Griselda, Stokes's wife, be duly informed of their husbands' discoveries.

Yet what Barnaby and Stokes uncover only leads to more questions. The murdered gentleman had been thrown out of the house party days before, so why had he come back? And how and why did he come to have the fabulous Finsbury diamond necklace in his pocket, much to Lord Finsbury's consternation. Most peculiar of all, why had the murderer left the necklace, worth a stupendous fortune, on the body?

The conundrums compound as our intrepid investigators attempt to make sense of this baffling case. Meanwhile, the threat of scandal grows ever more tangible for all those attending the house party – and the stakes are highest for Lord Finsbury's daughter and the gentleman who has spent the last decade resurrecting his family fortune so he can aspire to her hand. Working parallel to Barnaby and Stokes, the would-be lovers hunt for a path through the maze of contradictory facts to expose the murderer, disperse the pall of scandal, and claim the love and the shared life they crave.

A pre-Victorian mystery with strong elements of romance. A short novel of 39,000 words.

The third volume in
The Casebook of Barnaby Adair mystery-romances
THE MASTERFUL MR. MONTAGUE

Montague has devoted his life to managing the wealth of London's elite, but at a huge cost: a family of his own. Then the enticing Miss Violet Matcham seeks his help, and in the puzzle she presents him, he finds an intriguing new challenge professionally…and personally.

Violet, devoted lady-companion to the aging Lady Halstead, turns to Montague to reassure her ladyship that her affairs are in order. But the famous Montague is not at all what she'd expected—this man is compelling, decisive, supportive, and strong—everything Violet needs in a champion, a position to which Montague rapidly lays claim.

But then Lady Halstead is murdered and Violet and Montague, aided by Barnaby Adair, Inspector Stokes, Penelope, and Griselda, race to expose a cunning and cold-blooded killer...who stalks closer and closer. Will Montague and Violet learn the shocking truth too late to seize their chance at enduring love?

A pre-Victorian tale of romance and mystery in the classic historical romance style. A novel of 120,000 words.

The fourth volume in
The Casebook of Barnaby Adair mystery-romances
THE CURIOUS CASE OF LADY LATIMER'S SHOES

#1 New York Times *bestselling author Stephanie Laurens brings you a tale of mysterious death, feuding families, star-crossed lovers—and shoes to die for.*

With her husband, amateur-sleuth the Honorable Barnaby Adair, decidedly eccentric fashionable matron Penelope Adair is attending the premier event opening the haut ton's Season when a body is discovered in the gardens. A lady has been struck down with a finial from the terrace balustrade. Her family is present, as are the cream of the haut ton—the shocked hosts turn to Barnaby and Penelope for help.

Barnaby calls in Inspector Basil Stokes and they begin their investigation. Penelope assists by learning all she can about the victim's family, and uncovers a feud between them and the Latimers over the fabulous shoes known as Lady Latimer's shoes, currently exclusive to the Latimers.

The deeper Penelope delves, the more convinced she becomes that the murder is somehow connected to the shoes. She conscripts Griselda, Stokes's wife, and Violet Montague, now Penelope's secretary, and the trio set out to learn all they can about the people involved and most importantly the shoes, a direction vindicated when unexpected witnesses report seeing a lady fleeing the scene—wearing Lady Latimer's shoes.

But nothing is as it seems, and the more Penelope and her friends learn about the shoes, conundrums abound, compounded by a Romeo-and-Juliet romance and escalating social pressure...until at last, the pieces fall into place, and finally understanding what has occurred, the six intrepid investigators race to prevent an even worse tragedy.

A pre-Victorian mystery with strong elements of romance. A novel of 76,000 words.

The fifth volume in
The Casebook of Barnaby Adair mystery-romances
LOVING ROSE: THE REDEMPTION OF MALCOLM SINCLAIR

#1 New York Times bestselling author Stephanie Laurens returns with another thrilling story from the Casebook of Barnaby Adair...

Miraculously spared from death, Malcolm Sinclair erases the notorious man he once was. Reinventing himself as Thomas Glendower, he strives to make amends for his past, yet he never imagines penance might come via a secretive lady he discovers living in his secluded manor.

Rose has a plausible explanation for why she and her children are residing in Thomas's house, but she quickly realizes he's far too intelligent to fool. Revealing the truth is impossibly dangerous, yet day by day, he wins her trust, and then her heart.

But then her enemy closes in, and Rose turns to Thomas as the only man who can protect her and the children. And when she asks for his help, Thomas finally understands his true purpose, and with unwavering commitment, he seeks his redemption in the only way he can—through living the reality of loving Rose.

A pre-Victorian tale of romance and mystery in the classic historical romance style. A novel of 105,000 words.

The sixth volume in
The Casebook of Barnaby Adair mystery-romances
THE CONFOUNDING CASE OF THE CARISBROOK
EMERALDS

#1 New York Times *bestselling author Stephanie Laurens brings you a tale of emerging and also established loves and the many facets of family, interwoven with mystery and murder.*
A young lady accused of theft and the gentleman who elects himself her champion enlist the aid of Stokes, Barnaby, Penelope, and friends in pursuing justice, only to find themselves tangled in a web of inter-family tensions and secrets.

When Miss Cara Di Abaccio is accused of stealing the Carisbrook emeralds by the infamously arrogant Lady Carisbrook and marched out of her guardian's house by Scotland Yard's finest, Hugo Adair, Barnaby Adair's cousin, takes umbrage and descends on Scotland Yard, breathing fire in Cara's defense.

Hugo discovers Inspector Stokes has been assigned to the case, and after surveying the evidence thus far, Stokes calls in his big guns when it comes to dealing with investigations in the ton—namely, the Honorable Barnaby Adair and his wife, Penelope.

Soon convinced of Cara's innocence and—given Hugo's apparent tendre for Cara—the need to clear her name, Penelope and Barnaby join Stokes and his team in pursuing the emeralds and, most importantly, who stole them.

But the deeper our intrepid investigators delve into the Carisbrook household, the more certain they become that all is not as it seems. Lady Carisbrook is a harpy, Franklin Carisbrook is secretive, Julia Carisbrook is overly timid, and Lord Carisbrook, otherwise a genial and honorable gentleman, holds himself distant from his family. More, his lordship attempts to shut down the investigation. And Stokes, Barnaby, and Penelope are convinced the Carisbrooks' staff are not sharing all they know.

Meanwhile, having been appointed Cara's watchdog until the mystery is resolved, Hugo, fascinated by Cara as he's been with no other young lady, seeks to entertain and amuse her...and, increasingly intently, to discover the way to her heart. Consequently, Penelope finds herself juggling the attractions of the investigation against the demands of the Adair family for her to actively encourage the budding romance.

What would her mentors advise? On that, Penelope is crystal clear.

Regardless, aided by Griselda, Violet, and Montague and calling on contacts in business, the underworld, and ton society, Penelope, Barnaby, and Stokes battle to peel back each layer of subterfuge and, step by step, eliminate the innocent and follow the emeralds' trail...

Yet instead of becoming clearer, the veils and shadows shrouding the Carisbrooks only grow murkier...until, abruptly, our investigators find themselves facing an inexplicable death, with a potential murderer whose conviction would shake society to its back teeth.

A historical novel of 78,000 words interweaving mystery, romance, and social intrigue.

The seventh volume in
The Casebook of Barnaby Adair mystery-romances
THE MURDER AT MANDEVILLE HALL

#1 NYT-bestselling author Stephanie Laurens brings you a tale of

unexpected romance that blossoms against the backdrop of dastardly murder.
On discovering the lifeless body of an innocent ingénue, a peer attending a country house party joins forces with the lady-amazon sent to fetch the victim safely home in a race to expose the murderer before Stokes, assisted by Barnaby and Penelope, is forced to allow the guests, murderer included, to decamp.

Well-born rakehell and head of an ancient family, Alaric, Lord Carradale, has finally acknowledged reality and is preparing to find a bride. But loyalty to his childhood friend, Percy Mandeville, necessitates attending Percy's annual house party, held at neighboring Mandeville Hall. Yet despite deploying his legendary languid charm, by the second evening of the week-long event, Alaric is bored and restless.

Escaping from the soirée and the Hall, Alaric decides that as soon as he's free, he'll hie to London and find the mild-mannered, biddable lady he believes will ensure a peaceful life. But the following morning, on walking through the Mandeville Hall shrubbery on his way to join the other guests, he comes upon the corpse of a young lady-guest.

Constance Whittaker accepts that no gentleman will ever offer for her —she's too old, too tall, too buxom, too headstrong…too much in myriad ways. Now acting as her grandfather's agent, she arrives at Mandeville Hall to extricate her young cousin, Glynis, who unwisely accepted an invitation to the reputedly licentious house party.

But Glynis cannot be found.

A search is instituted. Venturing into the shrubbery, Constance discovers an outrageously handsome aristocrat crouched beside Glynis's lifeless form. Unsurprisingly, Constance leaps to the obvious conclusion.

Luckily, once the gentleman explains that he'd only just arrived, commonsense reasserts itself. More, as matters unfold and she and Carradale have to battle to get Glynis's death properly investigated, Constance discovers Alaric to be a worthy ally.

Yet even after Inspector Stokes of Scotland Yard arrives and takes charge of the case, along with his consultants, the Honorable Barnaby Adair and his wife, Penelope, the murderer's identity remains shrouded in mystery, and learning why Glynis was killed—all in the few days before the house party's guests will insist on leaving—tests the resolve of all concerned. Flung into each other's company, fiercely independent though

Constance is, unsusceptible though Alaric is, neither can deny the connection that grows between them.

Then Constance vanishes.

Can Alaric unearth the one fact that will point to the murderer before the villain rips from the world the lady Alaric now craves for his own?

A historical novel of 75,000 words interweaving romance, mystery, and murder.

ABOUT THE AUTHOR

#1 *New York Times* bestselling author Stephanie Laurens began writing romances as an escape from the dry world of professional science. Her hobby quickly became a career when her first novel was accepted for publication, and with entirely becoming alacrity, she gave up writing about facts in favor of writing fiction.

All Laurens's works to date are historical romances, ranging from medieval times to the mid-1800s, and her settings range from Scotland to India. The majority of her works are set in the period of the British Regency. Laurens has published over 80 works of historical romance, including 40 *New York Times* bestsellers. Laurens has sold more than 20 million print, audio, and e-books globally. All her works are continuously available in print and e-book formats in English worldwide, and have been translated into many other languages. An international bestseller, among other accolades, Laurens has received the Romance Writers of America® prestigious RITA® Award for Best Romance Novella 2008 for *The Fall of Rogue Gerrard.*

Laurens's continuing novels featuring the Cynster family are widely regarded as classics of the historical romance genre. Other series include the *Bastion Club Novels,* the *Black Cobra Quartet,* the *Adventurers Quartet,* and the *Casebook of Barnaby Adair Novels.*

For information on all published novels and on upcoming releases and updates on novels yet to come, visit Stephanie's website: www.stephanielaurens.com

To sign up for Stephanie's Email Newsletter (a private list) for heads-up alerts as new books are released, exclusive sneak peeks into upcoming books, and exclusive sweepstakes contests, follow the prompts at http://www.stephanielaurens.com/newsletter-signup/

To follow Stephanie on BookBub, head to her BookBub Author Page: https://www.bookbub.com/authors/stephanie-laurens

Stephanie lives with her husband and a goofy black labradoodle in the hills outside Melbourne, Australia. When she isn't writing, she's reading, and if she isn't reading, she'll be tending her garden.

www.stephanielaurens.com
stephanie@stephanielaurens.com

www.ingramcontent.com/pod-product-compliance
Ingram Content Group UK Ltd.
Pitfield, Milton Keynes, MK11 3LW, UK
UKHW020854090325
455838UK00020B/437